Lainy's Tale

S L ROSEWARNE

Lainy's Tale

Copyright © S L Rosewarne 2023

ISBN 978-1-915962-21-8
First published 2023 by Compass-Publishing UK

Typeset by The Book Refinery Ltd
www.TheBookRefinery.com
Cover artwork by © Tammy Barrett

To Moll, who lives on forever in these pages. And, of course, to Lainy, whose literary journey is only just beginning.

1

Lainy's Tale

'I've got good news, Moll,' said my owner, Suki, stroking my back just the way I liked it. 'Andrew's commissioned more interviews, and I only need do a few more walks for the next book, then that can go off to my editor.' She smiled. 'And I'm really enjoying spending some time with Joe.'

I opened one eye and stretched out in the sunshine on her bed.

'The only thing I'm not sure about is taking on Lainy. She seems a bit of a handful. What do you think?'

I rolled over and nudged her. Of course we should adopt Lainy. I'd been planning it for weeks.

But before I continue, I should introduce myself. I'm Moll, a Jack Russell terrier, though who on earth was Jack Russell? I'm a mature dog now, at 14, but apart from needing longer naps and shorter walks, life hasn't changed much. I am a bit hard of hearing, and my eyesight and teeth aren't what they were, but most importantly, I am still custodian of Suki.

Her husband, Pip, died three years ago just after his 65th birthday when Suki was only 43; she was a lot younger than him, but we hadn't thought he'd leave us on our own so quickly. Of course, neither had he.

Just before he departed, he made me promise to look after her, make sure she was happy. So, for the past three years, that's what I'd tried to do, to the best of my abilities. I found her another partner (several times), though that didn't quite go according to plan, but to my relief, life now seemed to be entering a smoother stage. No more rollercoaster relationships, just steady work and good friends. Much more restful.

I jumped onto the chair by the window where Pip used to sit and stared out at the village of Flushing opposite, trying to see it with his eyes. Falmouth Docks was spread out before us. The little passenger ferries trundled over to St Mawes and Flushing like toy boats on a silver sea. In the far distance, I knew roughly where St Anthony's lighthouse was, but only because we'd had a picnic on the beach below. All this beauty before me, which I'd not only explored on all four paws, but Suki had written about it in her walks books. I was famous!

Trouble was, I'd had a health scare recently, which had made me think about the future. I couldn't walk far enough to help Suki with her books any more. Which was where Lainy came in.

We'd met 4 year old Romanian rescue Lainy a few months back; she'd had a rough start in life and several homes hadn't worked out, so she was up for adoption once more. She was troubled, yes, but I sensed a fine intelligence, a quick wit and an eagerness to learn. She was also extremely affectionate and lively, so I was sure she would be able to keep up with Suki even on the longest of walks.

So, it was time to think ahead. We needed to adopt someone I could train up to look after Suki when I was no longer here; take over my mission to make sure she was happy. Someone who would also be her long range walking companion and be a good addition to our household.

Everything seemed to be going according to (my) plan, until Suki had a phone call from her elderly neighbour, Bill, asking for help. Of course Suki said yes. She does this, Suki, drops everything to help people which is all well and good, but it meant my plans to get Lainy were put on hold. Today was the first time she'd even mentioned Lainy since helping Bill. It was definitely time for action.

When we went out for our morning walk, I left various messages on our community noticeboard; a wall next to the postbox by the corner shop. One of them was for my boyfriend

Titch, who I knew would tell Tess. Tess was in charge of Lainy's adoption and I suspected she was getting as frustrated as I was.

Sure enough, the next day, Tess came round, but without Titch, to my disappointment. Still, this was business, and Titch was many things but not a business dog.

'What's up, Suki? Are you OK?' Tess was a few years older than Suki and had a deep, kind voice and long fair hair that she usually wore in a ponytail. Today she wore a big sweatshirt with writing on and she smelt of kindness and understanding and endless treats; cheese, cold sausages and gravy bones.

'I'm fine,' said Suki, though she obviously wasn't; you could tell by her choice of earrings. Today's were like tiny curled up shells, and stress rose from her in a stream of acrid vapours. Even her dark curls were flattened. 'Just a bit busy that's all. I'm really sorry about having to postpone Lainy, but my neighbour's poorly, and so's his cat, and he hasn't got anyone to do his shopping, and I've got a deadline for work, and Andrew rang to see if I could finish another piece of research by early next week and...'

'Whoah!' Tess said. 'I'm exhausted just listening to you. Why don't I make us both a cuppa?'

Suki nodded and sat down. She never usually let anyone else make a drink in her kitchen, but Tess was different.

I went and sat by Tess, to keep her company. But also because she might give me a treat while Suki wasn't looking. I sat, then lay down at her feet. Put my head on one side. Yes! A tasty biscuit.

Tess made the drinks and returned to the kitchen table. 'Does your neighbour have anyone else who could help him?'

Suki took a slurp of tea and gasped at the heat. 'Yes, his daughter but she's away. She's due back - oh, tomorrow actually.'

'In that case, she can take over,' Tess said firmly. Tess who is *always* helping other people. 'But obviously I want to know if you're still up for having Lainy.'

'Well, yes,' Suki said. 'I mean, no. I'm not sure. I can't think straight.' I could see my carefully laid plans whistling out of the door without further help. I nudged Tess who looked at me and winked, ever so subtly. My whiskers quivered, but in a good way. This meant that Tess Had A Plan. Phew.

'OK,' Tess said, pushing Suki's phone towards her. 'Why don't you ring your neighbour and ask him to make sure his daughter can take over tomorrow. Or the next day, latest.'

Suki bit her lip. 'Oh, I...' She caught Tess's look, took a deep breath and dialled.

'Hello, Bill?' Her voice quavery. 'What?' Burbled coughing and spluttering down the phone, from Bill. 'Oh, that's good news. I'm so pleased.' She smiled. 'No, I'm not upset at all. It's been a pleasure helping you. I'm so glad. Get better soon. Bye!' She rang off, her voice sounding higher and freer. She put her phone on the table and beamed, leaning down to scratch behind my ears, which I loved. 'Bill's daughter's on her way,' she said. 'She rang him earlier and she's coming to stay for a couple of weeks.'

'Splendid!' cried Tess. 'Now, I'm sorry to rush but I've got to be at work soon. How about if you have Lainy for a sleepover, say tomorrow night? That will give you a chance to see how you all get on. If you're sure.'

Suki hesitated a fraction, then nodded. 'That sounds a great idea,' she said. 'I'd love to have her, it's just that everything's been a bit bonkers recently.' Her face relaxed, and stress slipped out of the open window like wisps of smoke.

'I'm so glad,' said Tess. 'In that case, I'll bring Lainy round after work tomorrow. It's probably better if she has her tea here.'

'OK,' said Suki, and I could sense a tentative happiness rising up inside her. It smelt like a spring morning: fresh and edged with primrose promise. 'We'll look forward to that, won't we, Moll?'

I barked and got up, even though my back legs were a bit stiff with arthritis. I was so relieved that my plans were going ahead, I even managed a little twirl. I would make sure everything would be fine for when Lainy arrived.

The following evening, Tess brought Lainy over, all whirling tail, flattened ears and foreign barks. She couldn't help coming from Romania, but she was difficult to understand. I greeted her slowly, to calm her down; we sniffed bums and approached each other at a polite ninety degree angle. Gradually she quietened and her ears flicked forwards: a good sign in this instance.

Tess departed, in a rush as ever, and Suki sank onto her haunches, at Lainy's level. 'Hello, Lainy,' she said, unclipping her lead. She took Lainy's bed, bowls and food, and prepared Lainy's dinner. Her tail whirred in excitement, so Suki sensibly put our bowls down at opposite ends of the kitchen while we ate.

I've always been a fast eater, but Lainy was something else. I suppose living on the streets doesn't teach you good bowl manners, but even I was astonished at how quickly her food went. I took her outside in the back yard for a wee, then brought her back inside.

'Now is quiet time,' I said, lying down on my bed as Suki laid Lainy's bed, not far from mine in the living room. 'We relax.'

'Why?' she barked.

'We digest our food better if we rest after a meal,' I explained. New dogs need to be taught house rules. 'Now, come and lie beside me while I tell you what's what.' I ran through the basics of what she needed to know, and then stopped. 'Have you got that?' I wasn't sure how good her English barking was.

She nodded, slowly. 'I think, yes,' she said in that funny accent of hers. She lay down with her nose on her paws. To an ordinary human she might have looked relaxed but I could tell that every muscle was strained, ready for flight. Poor girl, to be living in that state of constant anxiety.

'All right, girls?' said Suki. 'I'm going to ring Joe then we can watch that new drama on telly. OK?'

I lay down, ready to listen to Joe. Suki usually put the loudspeaker on her phone and I liked Joe's voice, deep and soothing like treacle.

He had come into our life a few months ago because he wanted to buy a signed copy of one of Suki's walks books for his mum. They started emailing - a lot - and then meeting. In contrast to the last man in Suki's life, Joe seemed kind and dependable. Mind you, I'd thought that before and it hadn't ended well.

But I could tell they cared for each other, and I had hopes of that friendship growing deeper. They chatted on the phone several times a week, as well as meeting for walks, which was a good start. And maybe it was better if they just stayed friends. Less upset. We'd had enough of that with the last one.

'Hi, Joe,' Suki said. 'Yes, Lainy's here. Tess brought her round not long ago.' She laughed. 'Both she and Moll are lying in their beds and we're going to watch that new drama on Netflix. How was your day?'

I drifted off after that, because she went into the kitchen while they were talking about a difficult job he was doing, but I looked forward to seeing him again. He was a good friend to Suki, which meant he was a good friend to me. And could be to Lainy, too.

'Where did you live before you came here?' I said to Lainy. I could hear her mind was whirring round too fast. I remembered what Tess had told us, but I wanted to hear it from Lainy herself.

'You want know?' Her voice was unsteady and clipped.

'Of course.'

Lainy was quiet for a bit, stretching her long, racehorse legs. At first I thought she didn't want to talk, and then I thought, perhaps she didn't know where to begin.

'Start when you were little,' I nudged. She was four now, and I knew a lot had happened in those first years.

'I was born in city,' Lainy said. 'We live in street, my mother and my two brother and two sister. I not remember my dad: he went when we were very young.'

She said it very matter of factly, but I felt for her. Imagine, no father. 'What was it like, living on the streets?'

'Very different how you live,' she said, 'but we free. No one own us. We have no home. We not talk humans, and we fight for food.'

Her stilted English reminded me how different our origins were. I thought of my Suki, of regular mealtimes, of our warm bed, of lying next to her, always knowing where she was. Well, almost always.

'We scrap and we fight,' Lainy said. 'We always wary: and all the time, we listen.'

'What for?'

'For enemy. The Rapitori.' She shuddered, and I could see fear chasing down her spine. 'It mean captor. The men capture dogs and take to shelters.'

'Wasn't that better than living on the streets?' I asked. 'Didn't you get fed and looked after?'

Lainy gave a Romanian shrug which indicated that I'd said something stupid. 'They call them Public Shelter, but really they *kill* shelters.'

I gasped, and my whiskers shook.

'And we know that if you go to shelter, you not come out. Alive,' she added.

I shivered. 'So what happened to you?'

'I am separate from my family,' Lainy said, trembling. 'Gangs of men come to different part of city and take many dogs. They use big net and clubs.' Her voice shook. 'They smell so bad, these men, of black anger. Usually we have warning that they come, but this time no warning, and all my family capture.' Her ears lay flat, and I could smell her horror, like black dust.

'How did you manage on your own?' I could imagine little Lainy, all alone, trotting through the streets, starving. Poor wee puppy.

'I meet another mother few street away,' she said. 'She look after me. Sort of,' she added, and those two words said everything that she couldn't.

Just as I was thinking that perhaps we should halt this harrowing tale, Suki appeared, holding her phone. She was still talking to Joe: I could tell by her voice which went warm and summery when she spoke to him.

'I'm just taking them some treats,' she said to him as she handed us one of my favourite toys; a rubber thing stuffed with biscuits and yogurt, then frozen. Lainy looked at hers, puzzled, and looked at me, then Suki, who laughed. 'I don't think Lainy's ever seen one of these before,' she said. 'Show her, Moll.'

So I did. You held the rubber thing in between your front paws, and it was cold because it had been in the cold box, but you licked and licked it and it tasted of winter and ice cream and it was very soothing which was perfect timing as Lainy really needed calming after those horrible memories.

Lainy copied me, and I could hear Suki smiling. 'Ah, they both look very content,' she said. A click. 'I'm sending you a picture, Joe. And how about a walk later in the week? I'd like you to meet Lainy. She's going to be part of the family soon, I hope.'

'That would be great. How about Wednesday before work?' Joe said, his rumbling voice soothing down the phone. 'Eight thirty by the beach?'

'Perfect,' she said. 'See you then.'

'Let me know how they get on overnight, and what you decide,' Joe said. 'I don't start till nine tomorrow so I'll be around first thing.'

'Thanks, Joe,' she said, with a smile in her voice. 'I will.'

She put down her phone and, having checked we were OK, turned on the television. Gentle classical music came forth and I sighed with relief as I licked. I hadn't meant to upset Lainy by asking about her background, but it might help us to understand her if we knew where she'd come from and what had happened to make her how she was.

When Lainy finished, she washed herself thoroughly and lay looking at me with an unblinking stare I found a bit unnerving. It's generally considered bad manners in the canine community to stare, but perhaps they weren't taught this in Romania.

Lainy seemed unfazed. 'I go on?'

I hesitated. 'If you're sure it's not too much.'

Lainy snorted in a Romanian fashion. 'Memories gone,' she said scornfully, though I'd seen how affected she'd been earlier. 'Now I here. With you. Safe.'

I was impressed. She was a brave girl, but I could smell the fear that lingered on her breath, that clung to her fur. 'Please go on,' I said gently.

'I stay on street,' she continued. 'But one day I eat bad meat from bin. I am sick, very weak, and then they get me; the Rapitori.' Her bark shook, but she went on. 'Big net come over my head and they throw me and other dogs in van and it is dark and smell so bad and we are all so frighten for we know how bad these men are.'

'What happened?' I could hardly speak.

'They take us to shelter.' She stopped and was silent for so long I was worried. 'It very bad,' she said finally. 'All dogs together in cages. Old dogs, young ones, sick ones, healthy ones, dogs having puppies, dogs dying.' Again that shrug. 'All together. Little food, little water, dogs go mad and eat each other. It smell of shit and fear. The people that work there hate us and they hit and kill us for no reason. It is bad, bad place.'

I closed my eyes, but I could still see the images ballooning inside Lainy's head. I could almost hear the sound of those desperate dogs barking for help, the stench of wee and poo and death and illness and puppies crying and the dull thud of dogs being hit. The howls of pain as they were tortured, then killed. 'But you got out?'

Lainy nodded. 'I did. Kind woman come. I no understand her because she speak strange language and I only know Romanian. But she smell clean and good and I must trust her; I have no choice. I must get out. So I go with her, and some other dogs, to place that smell of chemical. They look at my teeth and feel me all over and put needle in me and make me wet and clean, but I have food and water and after a bit I let the kind girl stroke me.'

I thought back to what Tess had said. The woman must have been from the English charity who rescued Lainy and took her to the vet, that was good.

'And then we are put in tiny cages and shoved in van and we travel for very long time. And then they say we arrive in England. We go to home.'

I hardly dared interrupt, I was so gripped. 'You had a family to go to?'

Lainy's tongue peeped out and she began licking, licking; a sure sign of distress. Her ears flattened and her eyes dulled. 'Yes,' she said abruptly. And fear rose off her like a swarm of bees.

That was it, I decided. We'd had enough nightmares for one night. The things that poor girl had gone through. A change of scene was needed, so I got up and nudged Suki with my nose.

'Oh, is it time for walks, Moll?' She looked over at Lainy and frowned. 'Poor girl, she doesn't look very happy, does she? OK, let's go round the block. That might cheer her up a bit.' She got up. 'Come on, girls. Let's go!'

Lainy looked up, still licking, ears flat. 'What happen now?' Her breath came in short bursts. 'We go where?'

I realised she probably thought we were going to take her somewhere strange, or get rid of her. I would have to spell things out better in future.

'Nothing to worry about, Lainy,' I barked gently. 'Every evening we have a last wee then we come back and have biscuits before we settle down for the night. We go together. You'll be fine.'

She looked at me, then at Suki. 'OK.' She still sounded unsure, but Suki gave her a treat as she slipped her lead on.

'All right, Lainy?' Suki stroked her so gently, I could see Lainy relax a fraction.

I led the way, despite my stiff joints, showing Lainy all the important places to sniff, where to leave a message, where we might chase a cat, that sort of thing. As we walked, I noticed her tail come up again, her ears prick forward. I was impressed. She'd gone through so much. And we'd only heard a tiny part of it.

Surely she deserved another chance?

2

The next morning, we took Lainy back to Tess's house and Suki said, 'I'll give you a ring later if that's OK. I just need to make sure I can juggle work with Lainy's needs. You suggested training, and agility, I think?'

Tess nodded. 'Yes, I think she'd have fun and she could get to know other dogs, teach her some life skills, that sort of thing.' I loved Tess's voice: I could have listened to it all day, it was so relaxing.

'OK.' Suki bent down, gave Lainy a stroke. 'See you soon, Lainy-Lou.' She straightened and waved at Lainy as we walked down the road, back home.

When we got inside, she rang Joe, as promised.

'How did it go?' Joe said.

'Really well,' said Suki. 'Lainy slept in the living room and I didn't hear her in the night. I've just taken her back to Tess. Said I'd give her my decision later.'

'And...?'

'Well, from what Tess said, Lainy's going to be hard work. Do I really want that?'

'Hard work in what way?'

'Well, she nips men's feet, that's why she couldn't stay in that home in Truro. She bit the husband's feet, then the son's, and chased their cat. They had to walk around in wellies.'

Joe laughed. 'And they still wanted to home her? She must have a terrific character.'

'She does. She's very affectionate. And gorgeous looking - those big black eyes with eyeliner, and that funny puffy tail.'

Joe paused. 'I suppose the thing is, how busy are you at work?'

'I'm working on the new book, then I've got work for Andrew. I mean, it's manageable, but...'

'But do you have time for Lainy? I mean, you do help a lot of people.'

'Well, I like helping.' Suki sounded rather flustered.

'I know; you did a lot for your neighbour and his cat.'

'Well, yes, but I didn't do that for long.'

Joe laughed, kindly. 'Was that because Tess made you ring up and it turned out that Bill's daughter had arrived?'

'Well...'

'And before that, I seem to remember it was that homeless guy outside Tesco. And before that...'

'I felt bad that they were so much worse off than me,' Suki said. 'I had to do something.'

Joe paused. 'So helping Lainy would be different, because...?'

'Well, I didn't invite the others to live with me.'

'No. But if you stopped helping other people, would you have time for Lainy?'

'Yes. No.' Suki stopped. 'I don't know.' She sighed. 'What happens if she bites my friends?'

'No dog bites for the sake of it. I'm sure Tess will help you find out what Lainy's triggers are, and hopefully forestall any biting. You haven't got any men living with you, so that's a good start.'

Suki sighed. 'But I've got no experience with rescues.'

'But Tess has, and my last dog was a rescue. I'm sure she knows lots of other people with experience of rescue dogs. We'll be able to help.'

'I don't know that I'm the right person for Lainy,' Suki said quietly, her voice shimmering with doubt.

'I think you are.'

'Why?'

'Because you're kind, you're patient, loving and understanding and you want the best for Lainy. Who else could give her more than that?'

There was silence. 'Wow,' said Suki finally, with a touch of awe. 'Did Tess pay you to say all that?'

Joe laughed. 'I mean it, Suki. Lainy really needs someone who can give her what she deserves. And that's you. Or rather, you and Moll.'

Suki was quiet. 'Well,' she said.

'And now I must go, I've got to be in Camborne soon. Let me know when you've made up your mind.'

I felt like cheering. As it was, I snorted with delight. She'd listen to Joe. And also, I realised, he'd told her what he thought of her. That was a big step forward.

'Well, thanks, Joe,' she said, and the way she said it made me tingle. I had a good feeling in my nose about this.

Mind you, I reminded myself, my nose had been wrong on previous occasions.

Later, when Suki finished work, she shut down her computer and turned to face me. 'Walk, Moll?' she said, with a strange smile so I sensed she was hiding something. She reached for her phone, dashed off a quick message and said, 'Ta da!', then put her phone in her back pocket. Was it to do with Lainy?

I jumped off the bed and followed her to the front door where she put on my lead and we headed out of the door. But instead of going to the car, we went the other way, turned the corner and stood in front of Tess's front door. Suki rang the bell and we waited, hearing Titch and Lainy shouting hello from inside.

Then the door opened and Tess stood there, smelling so happy. She flung her arms round Suki and said, 'I'm so glad you're going to have her!' Then Lainy came out and barked and her tail went round and round like a whirlwind, and we were all tripping over each other and it was very joyous and smelt of cheese and treats and all the best things in life.

Suki laughed and we all calmed down and Tess went to get Lainy's bed and food and bowls and said, 'I'll drop them round to yours later. You'll also need her passport and insurance stuff. And I need to discuss the fee for the charity, as well.'

'Of course,' said Suki. 'I thought I'd take Lainy with us for a walk now if that's OK?'

'Good idea,' said Tess, and Lainy hopped around again until I had to yip to calm her down, and Tess clipped her lead on, and we all went back to Suki's car and I showed Lainy how to jump in, and we went for our first walk, all together, knowing that Lainy was going to be part of our family from now on.

3

I was looking forward to hearing the next instalment of Lainy's tale. I mean, it was a horrific story, but I knew it had a happy ending. I don't consider myself to have led a sheltered life; I am a bitch of the world, but compared to Lainy, I felt very pedestrian.

So I waited until we'd had our tea, settled down, and Lainy had a good wash. I was glad to learn that despite her difficult start, hygiene was a priority. When she'd finished, she looked up at me and winked. 'You want I go on?'

I yipped yes. 'Only if you want to.'

'Of course. I here now,' she said. She lay with her nose on her paws, and I waited.

'We come over in big truck,' she said. 'We hear muffle voices, strange smells, and I am last to go and I am so frighted. I not know what happen to me.'

I thought back to when I met Pip and Suki. I was so fortunate compared to these poor dogs. 'I suppose everything smelt strange,' I said.

She nodded. 'They say I with family in Cornwall - this is where we are now, yes?'

I nodded.

'I am give to man and woman and girl and old dog called Wilber. The peoples show their teeth at me but I cannot run free. I not know what they want.'

'Did Wilber not tell you the rules?'

'A bit. He tell me we live in house but I must wee and poo outside. They put this thing round my neck and then put rope on it and drag me outside. But I frighten; I think where do they take me? So I not go. They say they take me for walk. Walk? With this thing round my neck? They crazy. I stand and I say NO, we not walk when you pull me so hard round my neck I no breathe. That very frighten.'

She'd started speaking faster, and the more agitated she became, the more fractured her speech.

'Then all the time, the little girl, she pick me up. She carry me round much of the time and I no like. The woman she say not do that, but girl scream if she have put me down so she take no notice.'

'That's terrible,' I said. 'We have strict rules here. No one is allowed to pick me up. I have Suki trained.'

'I try tell girl no; I bark and growl, but she no listen, and after long time, I so tired and so frighted, I nip at her. Just little so she understand. Like with my brothers.'

'Quite right,' I said. 'We have to train them. Just what I do.'

'But they no like.' Lainy sounded so confused and tired, I really felt for her. 'When I little, we bite and fight and always chewing and jumping and playing. That how we learn. Here it is all different and I no understand.'

'No, it is difficult,' I said, dimly remembering when I was a pup, though I'd never had Lainy's problems.

'When I nip the girl to tell her no, she scream, then the mother she shout and drag the girl away, and the man come and he hit me hard on nose so I bite him back, and he hit me again, and all the time is shouting, shouting. It smell so bad, of fear and angry.'

I was silent, imagining the scene. How could humans behave so irresponsibly?

'Every day they drag me outside and yank at my neck so I no breathe and I very sore and scared. Where we go and who are all these peoples outside? I already learn to be fear of humans. No trust. Now I know this even more.' She sighed and stared at me. 'When I go out, I want chase cars, cats, peoples running. Fun things.'

'Well, of course,' I said. 'That's what walks are for.'

'But there when I chase car, the man he hit me on my flank. I growl but he do it again, so I nip him on leg, as warning. But he shout, and woman shout and I am shut in cage outside and no food and no water and the smell is fear.' She shook herself, and I could see the whites of her eyes. 'I never been alone before.'

'I should think not,' I said. 'You were a pup.'

'On streets I with my family or other dogs. Even in shelter I am with other dogs. I very scare and I not know what I do wrong.'

I could hardly speak at this injustice. 'You poor girl. But what about Wilber? Didn't he help?'

Lainy licked her lips, fast. 'He say I must follow rules. And I ask what are rules and he say I should know by now.' She paused. 'Everything so strange. I used to running all day, free. Now I do nothing all day and I have too much energy. What I do with? I no allow to run or escape and when we go outside they yank me all time so my neck hurt. On streets we pee where we want and here they shout and hit me if I pee in house.'

'I'm so sorry, Lainy.' I edged closer, gave her a lick.

She shook herself again; a de-stress shake that was also part thank you. 'When I do something they no like - this is most of time - they shout at me and I frighten. The man shout when little girl come near me. Then he get close to my face and shout so I panic. I growl to say no and he ignore and I have to nip his nose. He hit me again. All they say is NO, NO, NO. Shouting. I do everything wrong. And the more they shout the more fright I get.'

'That's terrible.' I was so appalled I could barely bark.

She sighed. 'They want us not bark, not pee, not sniff, not jump, not chew and not chase. So they no want us be dogs?'

I bowed my head. She was clever, this girl. 'Humans can be very hard to understand,' I said, 'but not everyone is like these people. They were very bad.'

I'm not sure Lainy heard me, for she continued, 'The little girl she like pat my head so hard I get ache in head. And she stick things up my nose and I no like. She poke my ears and I no like and I have to bite to say NO. Please stop this! But Wilber he say I in trouble now and the man he shout and scream and kick me and shut me in dark shed outside again. No food. No water. It cold and I very scare.

'I wonder what go wrong so quickly. I hungry, but I used to hungry. I frighted but I used to fear. But this different sort frighted. These people hate me but why? What will they do to me?' She looked at me with that direct, unblinking stare. 'I wish I stay in shelter, at least end to it there.'

That comment chilled me. For a dog so young to be thinking... But as I opened my mouth, she continued speaking. I think she'd almost forgotten I was there.

'I not know how long I stay in shed but I very weak and one time I think I at home with mum. We all eat big carcass with my brothers. Then I wake up and my head go round and my legs wobble. When the door open I am too fright to move. I can smell my wee and poo on my fur and I feel so bad. Why live like this?'

I shuddered. Those bloody people. I could kill them.

'The woman she drag me outside and hose me down, and I hate the cold water, and I shiver outside for it freezing while they inside and warm.

When she come back she with a different woman and I think oh no. Who this to do bad things to me? I shiver from fear and very cold, but this woman she smell good. She no come near me but crouch down and she wait. She talk very soothing and she smell kind. She say she is Anna and she talk to me calmly while the mother she cry and complain. Anna ask for towel to dry me but I no let anyone touch me. And the man he come and shout and I can feel Anna angry. Not with me, but with them.

Slowly she hold out hand to me with treat. But she no come near. She wait. I worry. What she do now? I sniff, then back off. Come forward and sniff again. She put more biscuit on floor and I eat I am so hungry. And she smile and her calm voice like clean water flowing down street, and she put more and more biscuit on ground and I eat them all and she ask for bowl of water for me and I drink all that too. And I feel bit better but I think what happen now? She go and leave me with this horrible people?'

'And did she?' I breathed.

Lainy looked up, as if surprised I was still there. 'No,' she said. 'She take me away from horrible peoples to her house.'

I barked with relief. This tale of Lainy's was tortuous. My whiskers had never had such a work out.

'She have other dog and now I realise I no go back to horrible peoples, I am so happy I lick and kiss her all over. I am so happy to be free!'

I was quite overcome by this stage, and a tear or two escaped as I lay there, thinking of the joy that young pup must have felt. I also wanted to find the horrible people and bite them really badly. And leave them in the shed with no food or water, and hose them down with cold water and leave them outside and see how they liked it. 'So you went to live with kind Anna who smelt nice?' I said.

Lainy shook her head. 'No. Her dog is very nervous. So I am worry. Do I have to go back to horrible peoples? Is everyone like that?'

I shut my eyes, briefly. Poor, poor girl. 'But you didn't go back there?'

Lainy looked at me - her thoughts must have been miles away. 'No,' she said faintly.

I could smell the fear radiating off her and I moved closer, nudged her with my nose. I wouldn't normally do this to a strange dog, particularly such a distressed one, but her story really moved me. I was even more determined, now, that we should look after her. That Lainy deserved a special home. Our home. And I knew that Pip - and Suki - would agree.

Tess came round later with Lainy's belongings, and she and Suki sat at the kitchen table and scribbled things on paper and drank tea and then Suki said, 'You mentioned that Lainy had had several homes. What happened to her?'

Tess stroked Lainy gently and I could see how much Lainy trusted her, which was incredible, thinking of what she'd been through. 'She was found on the streets, in Romania, separated from her parents, then taken into a kill shelter. Luckily she was rescued by this charity, and brought over here with some other dogs. But her first home didn't work out, and she was very traumatised when I first met her.'

'Poor girl,' Suki said. 'And yet she's so affectionate and trusting.'

'She is,' said Tess, smiling as Lainy made gooey eyes at her. 'And I can tell she's going to be really happy here.' She produced some paper work. 'Now, this is Lainy's passport, her insurance details...'

And I tuned out, because she didn't mention what had happened to Lainy after she was rescued from the horrible people. I'd have to wait for the next instalment. The important thing was that she was here, now, and we would try and help her redress whatever had gone wrong in the past.

At that point the doorbell rang. Instantly Lainy sprang into action; head jerked up, ears flat, eyes rolling, teeth bared, the hot, raw smell of panic radiating from her.

Suki got up to open the door, looking at Lainy nervously. 'Is she OK?'

Tess called Lainy over to her. 'We don't know what went on in her past, but most rescue dogs don't like sudden movements or loud noises.' Tess quickly put her on her lead, stroking her, produced treats, doing her best to calm Lainy down.

Suki opened the door and there was Petroc, an elderly friend of ours who lived in Flushing. As he came in, I sniffed at him and he bent down to give me a long, satisfying stroke. 'Hello, Moll,' he said, his long coat swishing against me as he bent down. 'Poor Lainy, she is nervous, isn't she?'

I must say, Lainy's reaction had shaken me a little, and I could see it had upset Suki too. She smelt anxious, and her face had gone pale. Most dogs bark at doorbells, or people walking past; that's part of our job, to defend our loved ones, but it was the speed at which Lainy reacted, or overreacted, and the terror pouring off her that was worrying.

'It's OK, Lainy,' I said. 'Petroc is our friend. He's very old and lives in Flushing and we often walk over there and have tea with him. He has lovely biscuits.' But Lainy was still barking and smelt so worked up, she wasn't taking much in.

'Petroc is our friend,' I repeated firmly.

Lainy was still barking at the new intruder, who stood still, waiting for Lainy to calm down. What a sensible man.

Tess ignored Lainy until she stopped, then said, 'Good girl,' softly and threw Lainy a few treats. Gradually Lainy crept nearer to Petroc, ate the treats and sniffed him. Her ears gradually went up, so did her tail and I could smell the fear slowly evaporating. So far so good, but what a noise! We'd have to do something about that.

Lainy bounced around Tess, but gradually she calmed down a little, and Suki joined them both at the kitchen table again.

'Lainy's going to be your priority now,' Tess said gently. 'Are you sure you're ready for that?'

'Well, yes,' said Suki. 'But she's very nervy, isn't she?'

'She is, but I think she will really benefit from a quiet household with just you and Moll,' said Tess.

'As long as you're quite sure I'm the right person to do this.'

'You are, as long as you can keep your other commitments down,' Tess said. She had pockets full of treats and her voice was deep and calming: just what we all needed.

'Yes. I can see how important it is for Lainy.'

Petroc leaned forward. 'So, my dear, if someone asks you for help, what will you say?'

'No,' said Suki. 'No, I will,' she added, almost to herself. She looked at Tess. 'Will she always be so frightened of strangers?'

Tess patted Suki's hand. 'Given her past, it's not surprising she's scared of people she doesn't know. But don't worry. Most rescues behave like this at first. But a guideline is the Rule of Threes. Rescue dogs need three days to decompress, three weeks to learn your routine, and three months to start feeling at home.'

Suki nodded. 'That sounds good advice.' She sounded more certain.

'And you realise, you can't fix Lainy,' Tess continued. 'With your and Moll's help, and with love, patience and understanding she will gain confidence. But she has these triggers - think PTSD - and she will take a long time to get over that.'

'PTSD?' Petroc said. 'I didn't know dogs could suffer from that, though I suppose there's no reason why not.'

'No. I hadn't thought of that either. Poor Lainy.' Suki paused. 'So a doorbell ringing could cause some of her symptoms?'

'Yes, that was a good example,' said Tess. 'We don't know what her triggers are at the moment, but certain things may remind her of her past, just like us. So we need to get to know her better, and find out what those triggers are, then we can help her.' She smiled. 'Just remember, the way to Lainy's heart is through her stomach.'

On cue Lainy tried to snaffle another treat from Tess, and they all laughed.

'And I can help with training and queries,' said Tess.

'Tess wouldn't suggest you did this unless she was absolutely certain you could handle a dog like Lainy,' said Petroc.

'Absolutely not,' said Tess.

At this point, Lainy trotted over and jumped onto Suki's lap. Good timing, girl.

'See?' Tess laughed. 'She'd like to stay!'

Lainy looked up at Suki and licked her chin, so Suki laughed. 'Of course she's staying!'

Lainy gave me one of her unblinking stares, then winked. I gave a muffled bark to hide my laughter. But Lainy had shown her love and belief in us. She had a good sense of humour, which we would all need. I guessed that she would be hard work, but worth it.

But part of me wondered just what we'd let ourselves in for.

4

Suki put Lainy's bed in the bedroom beside hers, while I slept on Suki's bed, by her feet, with one eye on the door, just in case - you never knew what might happen.

The first night passed without incident, apart from when some hedgehogs decided to pay a visit to the back yard. That resulted in a volley of barking, but soon Lainy calmed down and we had a quiet night.

Once we'd breakfasted, I told Lainy, 'Now Suki has her shower, then her breakfast, then she cleans her teeth with a buzzy thing, and once you hear that, you know it's time for our first walk.'

Lainy sat with her head on one side. 'And where we walk?'

'Sometimes on the beach near here, sometimes on the Beacon, which is a big field not far from here.'

Lainy stared at me, taking it all in. 'And Suki, she go to work?'

I noticed her English was much better when she wasn't stressed. 'She usually works from home but sometimes she goes to an office in town. You'll see.'

So Suki put both our leads on, filled up her pockets with treats, and off we went, down the hill past where Sandy lived. 'She's from Romania as well,' I told Lainy, 'but she hasn't got a curly tail like yours. And she's very quiet.'

'You mean I too noisy?' Lainy said with a flash of amusement in her dark eyes.

I hesitated. Despite her humour, I had a feeling she might be upset easily. 'Well, it was quite noisy when Petroc arrived last night,' I said.

Lainy sniffed, her nose working overtime. She smelt like she was about to say something, then changed her mind.

'But I understand it's all very strange,' I said hastily. 'It'll take a while to get the hang of things. Now, here's a great place for smells, then we go down this steep hill, and there's a grassy bit to have a poo.'

We both did our business, then trotted along in the weak sun, enjoying the dew and cool earth, while Suki let us sniff and wee as much as we wanted. It was a pleasant, unhurried walk and gave Lainy a feel of the neighbourhood. All went well until we met a spaniel when Lainy's hackles went up and she lunged forward, barking wildly, pulling Suki with her.

'Lainy, it's all right,' Suki said. I could smell her alarm, but I have to say she dealt with the situation well, and soon Lainy calmed down enough to continue our walk. Even so, distress streamed out of Lainy's nose. Her ears and mouth smelt of a sharp anxiety that was most unpleasant when tinged with fear and the unknown.

'I know it must seem difficult,' I said carefully. 'But most of the dogs round here are perfectly friendly.'

'I not know,' she said, uncertainty still rising off her in clouds. 'I always am ready just in case.'

'I understand,' I said, though I didn't, not really. 'But I've never been hurt by any of the dogs around here.'

Lainy muttered something under her breath that I suspected was a Romanian swear word, but I decided to ignore that and took pleasure in introducing her to Greenbank beach, and the two grassy areas on the way home. She didn't say anything, but I could smell her taking it all in.

Once home again, Suki took off our leads, made sure we both had a few treats and plenty of water, and sat down at her computer.

'This is where she usually works,' I told Lainy. 'So we doze now until lunchtime.'

Lainy looked puzzled. 'Where I doze?'

'You can sleep on your bed, or in your crate,' I said. 'Whichever you choose.'

'I choose?' she said, her eyes lighting up.

'You do,' I said. 'Wherever you'll be more comfortable. And when you're ready, I'd love to hear more of your story.'

Lainy blinked, obviously thinking hard. 'OK,' she said, though I could smell waves of exhaustion coming off her. She looked from her bed to her crate, trotted over to her bed and lay down. I had a feeling I'd have to wait till later for the next instalment.

The morning passed without incident, and I noticed that while Lainy looked relaxed enough, her nose was always twitching, and her ears moved like satellite dishes, round and up and down with great speed. But then Lainy did everything at great speed, I was coming to realise.

After Suki had her lunch, and we both had little snippets of ham from her sandwich, she did some more work and then looked at her watch.

'Come on girls, time to go and meet Joe for a walk,' she said, with a lilt to her voice.

'Who is Joe?' said Lainy, her ears flattening once more.

'She spoke to him on the phone the other night,' I said. 'He's one of Suki's good friends. A nice, kind man. You will like him.' This was partly an order and partly so that she wouldn't worry. Still, I felt I should explain a bit more. 'When Suki's husband died, several years ago, he made me promise to look after her.'

Lainy looked at me searchingly. 'How you do that?'

That was a good question, and one I'd had trouble working out myself. 'I found her a new man, but that didn't quite work out, then another man, but he wasn't right either, so we went back to the first one.' Lainy looked really puzzled. 'A bit like your homes not working out.' But I realised it was nothing like that. 'Though the men were really kind.' She looked utterly confused now. 'Anyway,' I added, realising that I'd made a complete mess of trying to explain things, 'She and Ted split up, but she met Joe and they are very good friends, and his dog died and he doesn't have another one yet, but he is kind and good and he likes Suki very much.'

Lainy was silent for a moment, obviously trying to make sense of my garbled explanation. 'And Suki like him?'

'She does, yes.'

'They happy together?' she said hopefully.

'Yes,' I said, wondering how much Lainy knew about happiness. Not much, I suspected, but she was obviously a romantic at heart. Which I felt was a good thing. 'But at the moment they're happy just being friends.'

Lainy stared at me, but didn't say anything. She had quite a lot to take in, one way and another, so that was OK.

I could sense Suki's rumble of excitement as we drove to Mabe church, a favourite haunt of ours. Would Joe be there already? And yes, there was his battered red van that smelt of rubber, plastic, tubes and all sorts of strange things.

'What he do?' said Lainy as we jumped out of the car and ran over to sniff the van.

'He's a plumber,' I said, though I had no idea what a plumber was.

'Ah yes,' she said. 'He mend toilet and boilers and heating. I know because Anna husband is plumber.'

'Oh,' I said, slightly put out. Though at least I now knew what a plumber did.

Joe was tall and he smelt of kindness, fresh air and digestive biscuits; he always had a stash in his van, I'd discovered, and a flask of tea with him. 'Hello, Moll,' he said, bending down to stroke me and pass over a treat. 'And Lainy. How nice to meet you.'

Lainy's ears went back, her ears flattened and she snapped at his hand. Quickly he withdrew it before she managed to nip his finger.

'Sorry, Joe,' said Suki sounding flustered. 'She's a bit nervous.'

'That's OK.' He threw some treats on the ground. 'Sorry, Lainy. That was a bit too much too soon, eh?' He smiled at Suki. 'No worries, Suki. She's got to get to know people in her own way, in her own time.'

Suki smiled gratefully. 'Thanks, Joe. I don't really know what to expect, but I gather she's afraid of men. She's been known to nip their ankles.'

'Well, I take it as a compliment that she hasn't had a taste of mine yet.' His deep voice was upbeat as he smiled. 'Don't worry. My dog Peanut was a rescue and it took him a while to settle in and get to know people. Everything's new for Lainy and she must feel really confused, poor girl. Now, shall we head up the hill first and then go round the quarry?'

'Good idea.' I could smell Suki's quiet gratitude. And mine; Joe had gone up in my estimation. Again. Suki looked at Joe. 'Is that a new company sweatshirt? What does CHAP mean?'

Joe grinned. 'Grant's girlfriend designed it. CHAP means Cornwall Heating and Plumbing. What do you think?'

Suki smiled back. 'Well, it's obvious that you're a bloke, so I think it's a good idea. Great advertising.'

'Glad you approve,' Joe said, as we walked up the steep muddy path by the side of a big field, while Lainy walked beside us on the lead, ears flattened. The ground was damp and smelt of horse dung.

'I suppose you have to keep her on the lead for now?' Joe asked. Lainy didn't pull, but anyone could see she how tense she was; eyes wide, panting slightly, her nose twitching faster than any other dog's I'd seen.

'Yes. Tess said to keep her on the lead for about a week,' Suki said. 'Because I've walked with her quite a lot already, it shouldn't be too much of a problem, but better be on the safe side. Though if we come to a really quiet place that's enclosed, I might let her off.' She smiled. 'What's this big job you're working on?'

'Some people near Helston have bought an old 14th century farmhouse,' Joe said. 'The garden was overrun with brambles; I don't think anyone's touched it for ages and the house has been empty for years. Ivy was growing in through the windows, that sort of thing.'

'Poor house,' said Suki. 'It seems such a shame to let it deteriorate like that.'

'Yes. The idea is to bring the house back to how it was; to be lived in by a family, not for holiday lets or anything.'

Suki was keeping a close eye on Lainy, I was glad to see, but listening to Joe as well. 'How many bedrooms?'

'Six, four of which will be en suite. They want new central heating, so that means new boiler, pipes and radiators of course, and four new bathrooms plus a washroom downstairs, so there's a lot to do.'

'I bet,' said Suki. 'Any chance I could go over and have a look sometime?'

Joe nodded. 'There's a public footpath that goes past the farmhouse, near the back of the housing estate on the outskirts of Helston; near the school playground. I was going to suggest we walk there one day after I've finished work.'

'Good idea,' said Suki, as we came to a quiet enclosed space near the quarry with hawthorn bushes growing high around us on all sides. She looked around. 'I might let her off for a minute, see how she is.'

I could sense Joe's uncertainty but he didn't say anything. We all walked along in single file, with Lainy in the middle, all of us slightly on edge. But Lainy trotted along, seemingly content. She sniffed where I indicated, did a few wees in choice places, and we all began to relax.

Further on we came to a clump of rocks where we usually sat and had a drink. Suki had brought treats for us and biscuits for them and Joe produced his flask and poured them tea. We sat in companionable silence, munching, then Lainy and I wandered off to have a sniff close by.

'She seems to be OK, don't you think?' Suki said.

'She's doing amazingly well,' Joe said. 'Well done for taking her in. She deserves a good home and I'm sure she'll be happy with you.'

Suki flushed. 'Thanks, I hope so,' she said. 'I suppose we'd better move on, you've got another job, haven't you?'

'Yes, a last visit in Redruth on the way home,' he said cheerfully. 'Come on, let's go.'

So we walked back the way we'd come, then turned right down a lane leading to a farmhouse. Lainy's ears rotated and her nose swivelled from left to right. I stopped, wondering what she could hear and smell. Horses, a fox, and rabbits. Sweet straw, and hay. Chicken feed. Milk. Cow dung. A horse neighing, dog barking, and the rumble of a nearby van engine.

Suddenly, Lainy was off, tearing down the hill. The speed with which she ran was astonishing, and we all followed her as fast as we could, Suki crying, 'Lainy!', as our frantic feet pounded down the lane.

Joe was the fastest runner, but even he couldn't catch up with her at first. As we reached the brow of the hill, we saw Lainy chasing the van down the lane. Her tail rotated joyously, her ears were pricked, and I could smell the blood pounding round her body. At this point Joe reached her, grabbed her collar, pulling her back from the van.

'For god's sake' cried the van owner. 'Can't you keep that dog under control?'

Suki arrived, red faced. 'I am sorry, she panted. 'She's a rescue and I've only just got her. Are you all right?'

The owner softened a little. 'Yes, love, but keep that dog on a lead,' he said. 'It could cause a bloody accident else.'

'Yes, I'm sorry,' Suki said, hurriedly clipping Lainy's lead on as we stood aside to let the van go past.

As it headed down the lane, I could smell Suki's shock mingled with fear, like curdled milk. 'My god, that was a close shave,' she said, shaking all over. 'Lainy, darling, you mustn't do that, you might have been run over.'

Lainy was still panting happily, eyes shining. She looked properly alive for the first time.

'She can certainly run,' said Joe in awe. 'I don't think I've ever seen a dog move that fast.'

'Yes, but I can't have her chasing cars,' Suki replied. 'He's right, she could have caused an accident.'

'In that case, you'll have to keep her on the lead, certainly round cars.'

'Poor Lainy. It seems awful to have to curtail her freedom like that. I know keeping her safe is the priority, but you can see how much she loved that chase. She's a real hunter, isn't she?'

Joe nodded. 'She certainly is, but you don't want her to be a liability. She needs to use her brain; she's a clever dog.'

'Tess recommended Agility classes,' Suki said. 'They'd teach her to concentrate, and she's so fast, I'm sure she'd love it.'

'Good idea. Scent work is also very good for dogs; helps them focus and it tires them out too. You can see how much Lainy uses her nose; I bet she'd love that.'

'I'll investigate both, thanks for that,' Suki turned to me, having checked Lainy was all right. 'Now, come on girls. Joe has to get back to work, and so do I.'

As we trotted along, I turned to Lainy, as a thought occurred to me. 'Do you just like chasing, Lainy, or do you want to run away?'

Lainy turned to me with her eyes still shining. 'I no run away,' she said scornfully. 'Why I do that? I happy here, with you.'

That was a relief, then.

'I run because I love the chase and I love run fast. Like the wind!'

'OK,' I said. It was true; anyone could see she was built for speed, but how would a hunting dog who loved chasing cars fit into our town life? For the first time, I had severe misgivings.

5

When we got home, we had our tea and settled down while Suki did some work and Lainy said, 'I tell you more, yes?'

'Yes please,' I said. 'You got to the part where you went to stay with Anna but her dog was a bit nervy.'

Lainy settled down, her head on her paws. 'Yes, I stay with Anna but her dog think I am too bouncy and, oh, I chase her cat.'

'That's what cats are for, isn't it?' I said, puzzled, for she sounded ashamed.

'Anna think no. Her cat old and sick but I not know this. Cat he hide outside and Anna very sad and I in trouble.'

'Was she bad to you?' I said, horrified.

'Oh no, but her voice; she sound disappointment,' Lainy said. 'And she very nice so I no like make her upset.'

I nodded. 'So what happened?'

'Anna say I go to new home, where I live with two collies. I think oh no; not like Wilber, and I am so frighted I hide behind Anna. But she talk to me so kind and explain I no need be scared, and we go in her car to place with big big garden near the sea and we meet another woman who smell also kind.

'I smell sickness on her, but she is tall with soft voice, and she drop treats on ground and talk very gentle. I no smell any cruel on this woman and I sniff her hand and I like so I let her stroke me. She smell of biscuit and cheese and that is good. She called Grace, and I think maybe I can trust her.'

'It must have been very strange, being taken to yet another home, with different dogs,' I said, trying to imagine it. Weird smells, unknown dogs, unknown people, unknown everything; and all while Lainy was desperately scared and panicky. I shook myself briskly to try and rid myself of the fear and horror creeping down my spine.

'It is,' Lainy said. 'I very scared. But it better than being with horrible peoples. And this Grace she very kind and the dogs they let me settle. That good. They run and play outside and soon I run and play with them and they teach me lots and soon I not scared.'

'Good,' I said. Such a small word that meant so much.

'And Grace she very kind and slowly I learn to walk with string on my neck. And we go to beach without string and we run along sand and I love because the collies they run so fast and I love running, it like flying and I love jumping too and we do that on the beach and chase seagull.'

Lainy's voice was calmer now, and I could tell how happy she'd been there, with Grace and the other dogs. Contentment seeped out of her like honey. Grace must have been like Tess and Suki; another special person who made dogs feel safe.

'Did you have nightmares?' I asked, thinking she must have had some repercussions from all that horror.

'Yes,' she said, but the way she said it made it clear it was too hard to talk about. 'And panic, but not so much there. I learn to live in house, and go for walks on this string. We have lots to eat and we live on farm far away from other peoples, so it nice and quiet with me, Grace, her husband and the collies. I very happy there and I learn lot and they say I am good dog.'

'I bet you were. I'm very glad you had some happiness,' I said, imagining a smiling Lainy, sleeping contentedly in her basket. 'So what happened?'

Lainy shifted in her bed. 'After some time, Grace start smell bad. She tired a lot and we know something is wrong. One day she cry and cry and tell us she very poorly and she very sorry but we must all go live somewhere else, because she too ill to look after us.'

'But that's terrible.' I could only imagine how poor Lainy felt, having thought she'd found her forever home and then, this...

'We no understand,' said Lainy. 'We shake for we so scared and we not know what happen to Grace. Or us. What is matter? Where we go? What happen?'

'What did happen?' I asked.

'The collies go to her old husband, and Anna she come to fetch me and I so happy to see her. But she say I not live there because her dog and cat worry. But she promise Grace that she find very good home for me.'

'You must have really missed Grace and the dogs,' I said.

'Yes, I miss very much,' Lainy said. 'They all my friend. I never had friend before. And Grace, she best person ever.' She paused. 'Till I meet Tess and Suki, of course.'

I licked my paw to give her time to collect herself for I could see tears filled her huge black eyes, and her whiskers were twitching like crazy.

'So you went somewhere else before you came to us?' I remembered hearing Tess saying something about Lainy being not far away.

'Yes. I go to Ellen and she very kind and she live with big dog call Logan, but she also have cat and I chase cat...'

'Of course,' I said.

'But they not happy when I chase cat, and Ellen she have big husband, very tall, and two son and they both very big too and I scared. They make me think of men in Rapitori, and I very frighted, so I nip their feet.'

I snorted. 'Good girl.'

'And Ellen she very kind and smell nice and she say she like me live there but I can't because cat not happy, and her husband and son not happy because they must walk in big boots all time so I no bite their feet.'

'And that is how we heard about you, from Tess, who took over Lainy's adoption from Anna,' I said, piecing things together. 'I sent a message via Titch. We met you several months ago, though you may not remember.'

Lainy's nose twitched. 'Maybe,' she said, 'but I very sad and I very panic so I not think very good then.' Then her whiskers swivelled. 'No, I do remember, we meet on street. And I think I like you and Suki very much, but I never think I come *live* here.' She lifted her head and her eyes pricked up. 'You mean, you arrange this? That I come here?'

I nodded. 'I did, yes.'

'You are so clever!' cried Lainy. 'How you do that? Oh, I am very thank you. And I try very hard to learn rule and be good and not cause troubles.' She smiled and love shone out of those dark eyes. Once again, I wondered at her ability to trust, after all she'd been through.

'I'm sure you will,' I said, and I knew she meant it. Though after today, I just wasn't sure how this would all work out.

The following week, we met Tess and Titch at a lay-by near Argal. We greeted each other as we always did; noses, bums and whiskers, in that order.

To my surprise, after a few initial yips from Lainy, she was uncharacteristically quiet. Mind you, I had briefed her that Titch was My Special Dog, so I think she was somewhat in awe of him, although she'd stayed with them for a few nights,

Once Titch and I had expressed our love for each other, he turned to Lainy, who was standing by Suki, head on one side, tail at half mast.

'Come and say hello, Lainy,' I instructed. 'You know Titch.' She came over, at a polite 90 degree angle, sniffed his bum and went to stand beside me. Although she'd met Titch briefly, several times, she evidently wasn't used to him. She was quite shy, I realised, and probably unused to greeting strange dogs. It was almost as if she didn't know how.

'Hello again, Lainy,' said Titch, his ears and whiskers perking up. Nothing like a pretty girl to cheer men up; they're so predictable. 'Do you like the home Moll arranged for you?'

She gave a nervous woof. Lost for words, it seemed.

'Good, don't forget, you're safe here. You'll make more friends and you can forget about the past,' Titch said.

It was more of an order than anything else, but Lainy whispered, 'Thank you. Moll look after me very well.'

'Well, of course,' Titch said. His bark was very loud at times, and I could see her ears flinching slightly. 'That's what we do;

we look after each other.' He studied her intently. 'I don't think that's happened to you, has it?'

'No.' Lainy's eyes filled with tears. She seemed incapable of talking much today, bless her.

'Never mind, you've landed on your paws, now. Make sure you look after my Moll and Suki and all will be well.'

Lainy nodded again. 'Promise,' she whispered.

We had to cross the road then, to walk through the woods, and after a while I heard Tess say, 'So what about training for Lainy?'

Suki looked round, saw us and laughed. 'Oh, look, Titch is telling Lainy what the rules are!' She turned back to Tess. 'What do you think? You recommended scent work and you said agility I think? What would most benefit her?'

'I'd suggest weekly scent classes which start at the beginning of next month,' Tess said. 'They're on a Tuesday evening and it's a very small class; only two other dogs, so I think she could cope with that. Then agility starts in the summer, so she should be a bit more settled by then, and I think she'd love agility.'

'That sounds great,' Suki said. 'I don't think she'd like a big class, certainly at the moment. She seems very unsure of other dogs.'

'Exactly. And why don't I come round on a weekly basis for one-to-one sessions so we can assess her as we go along? Make a note of anything that you're not sure about; what disturbs her, what she doesn't like; anything and everything, and that will help build up a picture of how we can best help her.' She paused, as Suki's eyes filled with tears. 'Oh Lordy, what have I said?'

Suki blew her nose. 'Nothing. I'm just so grateful for all this help. I don't know what we've done to deserve it, but I really am so touched.'

Tess gave her a hug. 'You goose. Of course we're here to help. That's what friends do. And you're bound to have a few teething problems with Lainy, but just pick up the phone and we can sort it out. I want Lainy to be happy just as much as you do.'

Suki nodded and wiped her eyes. 'Thanks. She's had such a difficult start in life, and I so hope we can help her to be happy. She really deserves it.'

Titch and I were sniffing a particularly smelly tree trunk and looked at each other, and he winked. I was very glad to see this, as I had great faith in Tess. Yet I was still a little unsure.

'It'll be OK,' said Titch, who obviously sensed what I was thinking. 'You've got me, don't forget.'

I looked up at him and he nuzzled my nose gently. He wasn't a romantic dog, or very tactile, so small gestures like this meant all the more.

'In the meantime,' continued Tess, ponytail swinging, 'I'm doing the Couch to 5k. Do you want to join me?' She laughed at Suki's face.

'You mean running?' Suki said. 'I've never run. Couldn't I walk?'

Tess laughed her rich, warm laugh. 'It's a gentle programme that uses a mix of running and walking to gradually build up your fitness and stamina. In the first week you only run for a minute at a time, and work up from there.'

Suki jumped over a puddle. 'And why are you doing this?'

'Because Paul bet me I couldn't,' she said. 'And you know me, if anyone tells me I can't do something, I have to prove them wrong.'

'In that case, count me in,' said Suki. She looked at Lainy, who was sniffing a pine cone. 'I've just had an idea. Lainy's a brilliant runner, so can we take her with us? It might help her stop chasing cars, do you think?'

'It's worth a go,' said Tess. 'She'll love it, though she'll outstrip us easily. Also, we'd better run somewhere quiet so we don't meet anyone else she can have a go at. We'll have a good incentive to keep up with her!'

I looked over at Lainy, whose ears were up like a cartoon dog I'd seen on television. Her nose was quivering with excitement as she looked at me and winked. 'We go *running*?!' she said.

The following week, Suki and Lainy set off to meet Tess for their first running session. 'It might be better if you stay in the car for the first bit, Moll,' said Suki. 'Apparently we have a brisk five minute walk, then a minute of running, then a minute and a half of walking, and repeat that for twenty minutes.' She groaned as Tess appeared. 'I'll be dead by the time we've done that.'

'And that's when we take Moll and Titch for a nice slow walk,' Tess said, her ponytail swinging jauntily. 'Shall I pop Titch in the car with Moll and they can have a catch up while we do our bit?'

'Good idea,' said Suki. Lainy was bouncing around, tail whirling as she did when excited. 'I'm going to keep her on the lead, certainly to start off with, in case we meet anyone.'

'It's much quieter further on,' said Tess. 'You can probably let her off then. Shall we go?'

'OK,' said Suki, and having transferred Titch to our car, he and I watched them set off along a narrow track which was often used by cyclists, though as it was drizzling, there were no bikes out today.

It was clear Lainy was dying to have a fast run, but she kept at their pace, though it must have been hard. We could only hear the beginning of their conversation.

'How's Lainy been this week?'

'Very good,' said Suki. 'Well, a few near misses. She doesn't like postmen, it seems, so she tried to bite that really nice postie called Fiona. Luckily she always carries biscuits, so when faced with a gravy bone, Lainy decided that was preferable to Fiona's leg.'

'Phew,' laughed Tess. 'Anything else?'

'Lainy will chase anything that moves fast, I've discovered. Cars, cyclists and joggers are top favourites. She's been on the lead so I've managed to stop her, but I'm on red alert the whole time, checking what's in front, what's behind, what might possibly appear from nowhere and set her off.'

Tess nodded. 'It can be like that at first. I know it feels really stressful at the moment, but it's amazing how quickly you get used to it. And once you know what her triggers are, we can work on how to help her overcome them.'

'I hope so,' said Suki. 'I have to say though, apart from her nervousness, she is such an affectionate dog and she has a great sense of humour. I swear she laughs at me every now and then.'

Tess laughed. 'That's incredible, when you think of her journey. From the streets and kill shelters of Romania to a wonderfully loving home with you.'

At this point their voices faded so I couldn't hear any more, but Titch and I watched their efforts at running and walking as they returned. Lainy flew along, feet barely touching the ground. She looked so graceful, and made running look effortless. At first Suki and Tess managed a minute's running without too much exertion; they looked pleased with themselves and laughed. But as they turned round and came back to us, alternating walking and running, I could smell them beginning to tire. They puffed and panted, their faces turning red, their bodies over heated. They smelt of sweat and exhaustion. By the time they returned to us, they could hardly speak, whereas Lainy looked as if she'd had a slow sniff walk.

'We've done it!' Tess gasped, collapsing on the bonnet of her car.

'It wasn't that bad!' Suki cried, though she sounded exhausted.

They carried on gasping, and after a while, when they'd both had some water, Tess looked up and said, 'Are you going to carry on with this?'

Suki grinned and I could smell excitement and joy. 'You bet! I never thought I'd get into running, but you know, I think I could really enjoy this. I mean, I'm crap at it, but I'd really like to get better.' She bent down to stroke Lainy, who was barely panting. 'And this one here is the star of the show. She's amazing, aren't you girl?'

Lainy shook herself vigorously then looked at me and Titch as if for approval. I nodded, as did Titch, and Lainy's eyes sparkled and her face turned into a great big grin. 'I love it!' she said.

At that moment, I knew we'd done the right thing. OK, there would be a few hiccups, but I was sure this girl would be worth it. Thank dog for that.

6

As the weeks went by, Tess and Suki extended their running and walking, and although there was still a lot of huffing and puffing, they smelt very cheerful afterwards. As for Lainy, she loved her new-found freedom and she bonded better with Suki, which I was glad to see.

Titch and I enjoyed these sessions. We could catch up in peace, watch Tess and Suki make fools of themselves, and gradually become proud of their efforts. Lainy was much calmer after she'd been running, and I had an idea of the loving, funny dog she could become once she'd settled in.

Afterwards we often went to a cafe where they had coffee and shared a bit of cake. At first I could tell Lainy found the noises overwhelming: the hiss of the coffee machine behind the counter; the clanking dishes in the kitchen, the rattle of cups and mugs. The scraping of a chair when someone moved; that noise went right through our ears like ripping steel. People calling each other, which reverberated round my head, the far distant noise of a cycle bell, a dog barking, a horse neighing, cars arriving.

Then there were the smells: frying bacon, melted cheese and ham, ripe tomatoes and astringent cucumber. Burnt onions, fried eggs, earthy mushrooms and hot buttered toast. I had a feeling that humans couldn't smell like we did; it was an incredible assault on our noses just smelling the kitchen, let alone anything else.

When the drinks came out, that was another fiesta for our noses; the rich earthy smell of coffee. The tannin waft of tea. The sharp sweetness of lemon drizzle cake packed with citrus, sugar, flour and eggs.

There were so many distractions, it was hard to concentrate on Suki and Tess's conversation at first, but after a snaffled crumb of lemon drizzle, I tuned my ears back in.

'You know, I never thought I'd actually enjoy running,' said Tess as we sat inside the cafe. Her pony tail had slipped while she was running and looked like Lainy's tail when she was frightened; at half mast.

'Me too,' said Suki. She was hardly out of breath now and I was very proud of her. Pip would have been amazed. 'I feel fitter already, and I'm really enjoying it.' She stroked Lainy happily. 'And this one's loving it, aren't you poppet?'

Lainy grinned, just like humans do. 'I enjoy very much.' Her English was really improving. 'I keeping slow for them but they get faster, and I really like!'

Certainly, her coat was glossier, her eyes clearer, and her ears, which always lay flat when out walking, were now upright and alert. Her bushy tail waved like a banner going into battle: this was a different dog to the one who'd arrived a month ago.

'Have you told Joe?'

'I did mention that we were in training,' Suki said. 'We're meeting him tomorrow so I thought we might have a little run then, if he's up for it.'

And so the next day, we met Joe at Mabe church again.

'Hi Joe,' said Suki. They had a hug which smelt of primroses in the sun; full of promise.

'Hi there,' he said. 'Hi Moll and Lainy,' and he produced a bag of treats and gave us a piece of sausage each, which I loved. So did Lainy, by the way she gulped it down.

'You know I said I'd been training for Couch to 5K?' Suki said as we crossed the road and set off up the side of a steep field.

'Yes, that's a great idea. How's it going?'

'We've got to Week Five, would you believe?' She grinned and her pride smelt like warm butter. 'We're still a bit rubbish but we're getting a lot better.'

'What are you doing this week?' Joe stood aside to let Suki climb over a steep stile.

'This week it's a 5 minute walk, then 5 minutes running, 3 minutes walking, 5 minutes running, 3 minutes walking, 5 minutes running and build up to 8 then 20 minutes running with no walking.'

'That's brilliant. Have you done that already?'

'Yes!' Suki said, bouncing up and down on her toes. 'We did it on Tuesday. I'm so pleased, Joe, I never thought I'd be able to do something like this, but I love it!'

He beamed and smelt like he wanted to hug her but refrained. 'That's great news. Well done. Do you want a quick run today?'

Suki grinned. 'I'd love to, but I can't really leave Moll.' She paused. 'I think you said you'd run a bit. Do you want to take Lainy for a short one?'

Joe nodded. 'Yeah, I'd enjoy that. I haven't run for ages, but we could run for five minutes, then back for five minutes; would that be OK?'

'Sure,' Suki said. 'Moll and I will wait here and I might have a run when you get back.'

'OK.' Joe looked down at Lainy, gave her another bit of sausage. 'Shall we go, girl?'

Lainy looked from me to Suki, then at Joe, clearly uncertain what she should do.

''He's safe, Lainy,' I said. 'Don't worry. You run for a few minutes with Joe, then run back. We'll wait here.'

She licked her lips nervously, then looked at Joe, who nodded. 'Shall we go, Lainy?'

With one last backward glance at us, Lainy and Joe set off. I was expecting him to run at a slow trot, like Suki and Tess, but he settled into a steady jog, which increased as he matched Lainy's stride. Lainy looked at him, her ears pricked, and I could smell her delight. She ran faster, then faster still, and Joe kept up, as they grew smaller and smaller until they disappeared round the corner.

'Wow!' Suki said in tones of awe. She turned to me. 'I didn't expect that, Moll did you?' We walked on slowly, listening to two crows fighting in the sky, a lazy bee sampling some late blackberries and a car horn in the far distance. A slow October sun shone on our backs and it was peaceful, thinking of a time when life had just been us. Not that I regretted bringing Lainy into our home, but it was pleasant having some Me time with Suki.

I realised I'd trained her well, for she turned to me and said, 'It's lovely having some time together, isn't it Moll? Sorry it's all been a bit full on since Lainy got here, but it doesn't mean I love you any the less.'

Well, of course I knew that, and as I'd engineered everything, I wasn't unhappy. It was just that Lainy was quite a nervy presence, and while she was learning to relax at home, when we were out she was like an unexploded bomb. You never knew when she might go off.

We continued our slow amble until I heard paw and footsteps pounding towards us. I could hear them well before Suki could; even with my advanced years, my hearing was better than hers, and I looked up as the sound waves travelled along the ground.

Soon Suki could see them and she laughed. 'Oh, look Moll; aren't they doing well?'

A few minutes later they arrived in front of us, both panting and grinning from ear to ear.

'I never realised you could run like *that*,' Suki cried. 'You're brilliant!'

'It's a while since I've had such a good running companion,' Joe replied, gasping slightly. 'She's amazing, isn't she? Look, she's hardly out of breath.'

We looked at Lainy whose eyes shone, her whiskers rotated and her nose twitched with delight. If ever there was a picture of a happy dog, this was it. 'Fantastic,' she told me. 'It freedom!'

I barked in agreement. 'You're born to run, Lainy. Well done.'

She batted her eyelashes with slight embarrassment and gratefully drank a bowl of water, ate a few snacks, while Joe drank a bottle of water and ate a cereal bar.

'When I'm faster, perhaps we could all run together, to get in training?' Suki said. 'I mean, after I've walked Moll of course.'

'I'd love that. I haven't run properly for years but I do enjoy it,' Joe said. 'And it's wonderful to see how much Lainy loves it. She's a real gem of a runner, isn't she?' He stroked my head and gave me a few treats. 'Whereas your talents lie in different directions, Moll.'

'Any time you want a run just let me know,' said Suki as they turned and walked on towards the quarry.

'I certainly will,' Joe said. 'And we don't have to leave Moll behind. She can have a kip in the car and join us later. As befitting her advanced years.'

Life continued and Lainy seemed to settle in well. She was much less jumpy, really seemed part of our family, and all our friends welcomed her too, which was a joy to see. She started to get to know other dogs and was less worried about them, and the regular sessions with Tess seemed to be helping her confidence, too. I began to relax, relieved that Lainy was over the worst, and we could settle down to enjoy life together.

One day Suki was working at her desk in the bedroom, while I snoozed on one of her pillows, and Lainy slept at the foot of the bed: I'd recently given her this promotion and she seemed very content with the honour.

Suki got up, stroked my ears and bent over to give Lainy a kiss on her head. As she did so, a horrible feeling ran down my whiskers.

I'd noticed that Lainy hated anyone getting near her face, but she was so much more relaxed now, surely - but suddenly, quick as anything, Lainy groggily woke, I smelt her fear and panic as she lashed out, instinctively.

Suki jumped back, with a stifled cry, holding her head. Blood poured from her face, as she staggered to the bathroom.

'Oh no, what I done?' Lainy cried. 'It all happen so quick.'

She sounded so distressed that I couldn't tell her off. 'I'll go and make sure Suki's all right,' I said. 'I'm sure you didn't mean it.'

'No!' Lainy cried. 'I so sorry,' and remorse poured off her. 'I dreaming and suddenly I smell someone near me and I think it the Rapitori and I panic and I bite and too late it Suki, I feel so bad, what do I do?'

'Don't worry, Lainy,' I said cursing silently as I trotted down the corridor. So much for relaxing. Suki was in the bathroom, mopping her eye, but I could smell the metallic smell of blood which was spattered all over the basin.

'I'm not sure what to do, Moll,' Suki muttered. She was trembling and I could smell her confusion and fear. 'I think I'll ring Fiona as she's a nurse. Just to be on the safe side.' She grabbed her phone and had a garbled conversation, then said, 'OK, no panic but she said go to the Minor Injuries Department of Falmouth hospital. Lainy caught me above my left eye and it might need stitches.'

She was even paler now, and I barked, for I didn't think she was fit to drive. What happened if she went to sleep behind the wheel?

Suki turned round. 'Now where are the car keys? Where did I put them?' As I barked again she looked at me. 'Actually, I don't think I should drive. But who can I ask for a lift?' She looked at her phone and hit a number, waited while it dialled. 'No reply from Anne.' She tried another number. 'Tess is at work, so that's no good.' She sighed. 'I suppose I could try, but he'll be at work...' She looked at me as if for reassurance. 'OK, I'll try him.' She sat down on a chair with a thud, looking even paler. 'Oh, hi Joe, sorry to bother you, but I've had a bit of an accident and I have to go to the local hospital...'

'What happened?' She'd put it on speaker phone and his voice was crackly.

'I got a bite near my left eye. I think it might need stitches.'

'Right.' I was waiting for him to ask what had happened, but he didn't. Good for him. 'OK, I'm just leaving a job now, I can pick you up in five minutes, OK? Have a cup of tea with sugar; it's good for shock.'

'Thanks so much, Joe, I really appreciate it,' she said in a shaky voice.

'Not a problem. See you in five,' he said, and rang off.

Suki made a hot drink and gulped it down, a little colour returning to her cheeks. Already she smelt less stressed, knowing that Joe was on his way. I wondered if Suki would see Lainy before she went, but she might be too shocked. I headed back down the corridor to the bedroom, where Lainy stood trembling in the doorway.

'I feel so bad,' she whispered. 'This terrible. Is she hurt bad?'

'There's a bit of blood and she has to go to the hospital for stitches, but I'm sure she'll be fine,' I said, mentally crossing my paws. Then a thought struck me. 'Why does this happen, Lainy?'

Her hackles went up and her nose quivered. 'I have flashes,' she groaned. 'I see the Rapitori run towards me and I must bite them. Or the man of the Horrible Peoples. He come toward me with heavy thing and he hit me over head, over and over and I have to bite to tell him to stop. I get flashes like bad dream and the only way I know to stop is to bite fast.' She stopped. 'It no happen since I been here, but sudden I smell someone near my face and I - how you say - panic.'

'I see,' I said. I'd heard Suki talking about this to Tess. It happened to soldiers who'd been fighting in wars, apparently, but not many people knew dogs could have it too. 'That must be really frightening.'

'Is horrible,' she said, her English scattering like broken glass.

'But no one here will ever do that to you, all right?'

Lainy looked up, her dark eyes big pools of terrified black. I could see she was still panicking, so I said, 'What is it?'

Lainy's ears lay flat on her head. 'Will she send me back?' Terror poured off her coat, streaming off her whiskers.

'Don't be silly,' I said. 'She wouldn't do that,' but as I looked back, I saw Suki coming down the hall, clutching her eye. It was still bleeding and I thought, at least, I *hoped* Suki wouldn't do that...

7

After Suki and Joe left, it was very quiet, as if the house was holding its breath. Lainy lay under the bed, too terrified to come out, certain that she'd be moved on yet again. I only hoped that Suki's eye would be all right, and she'd get over this and give Lainy a second chance. I would do everything I could to help that along.

A long while later, the door opened and Suki and Joe came in. I smelt those chemical hospital scents again, but also relief mingled with uncertainty. A sweet and sour smell.

Suki bent down to stroke me as they came in, then turned to Joe. 'Can I offer you a cuppa?' Thankfully she sounded more like herself. 'Cheese on toast?'

'Both would be lovely, thanks,' Joe said. 'I'm starving. But I have to get to another job soon, so it might be easier if I grab a sandwich on the way.'

'If you have five minutes, that's all it'll take,' she said. 'Sit down, please. I'm so grateful.' I had the sense that she was also wary about seeing Lainy and was putting it off.

Looking up at Suki, I saw a patch of what I supposed were stitches above one eye; that must be where Lainy had bitten her. It was beginning to turn different colours, like a rainbow. I had a horrible feeling it might get worse.

Joe disappeared down the corridor to the bathroom; the toilet flushed but instead of returning to the kitchen, I heard him walk down to the bedroom, where I knew poor Lainy was still lying underneath the bed, wrapped in shock and remorse.

I trotted down the hall to try and hear what he was saying. Edging forward, I saw Joe on his knees in the bedroom, making soft noises to Lainy. Gradually she emerged from under the bed and let Joe stroke her. His noises were calming, and already I could sense Lainy's fear seeping out of the door.

'There there, girl,' he crooned, massaging her flank. 'Poor thing, bit of a shock, eh? But don't worry. Suki's been patched up and the nurse said in a week she'll be better. I guess this happened because of what went on in the past, eh? Something horrible?'

Lainy nudged him, and the way she offered herself, with such utter trust, brought tears to my nose.

'Good girl,' he said. 'Now let's have some cheese on toast and a chat to Suki and everything will be OK.' He paused. 'She might be a bit distant for a while, but that's to be expected. Nothing to worry about.'

As he got up, Lainy looked up at him, her head on one side. He looked down and stroked her head. 'It'll be OK, Lainy,' he repeated. 'Coming?'

Hesitantly, she followed him down the corridor, back to the kitchen, where Suki was busy making tea and toast.

'I can't remember if you have sugar in your tea, Joe? And - oh,' she said, seeing Lainy. And she shrank away from her.

'One sugar, please,' said Joe, taking the mug. 'That's great, thanks.' He turned to Lainy and stroked her as I could see she was about to bolt down the corridor. 'I know what's happened is a terrible shock, but I think it's as much of a blow for Lainy as it is for you.'

Suki looked from Joe to Lainy and nodded. Gradually she sank to her knees and gave Lainy a tentative stroke which said so much: I'm stunned, I'm scared and I'm worried you're going to do this again.

Lainy looked up at her and blinked. I'm so sorry, the blink said. It's not really my fault, but I will do whatever I can to make sure it doesn't happen again. Blink. I do love you.

Suki and Lainy looked at each other for the longest time. She stroked Lainy's ears, along her flank, then got up. 'We'll get through this,' she said though her voice was unsteady. 'Now, Joe, cheese on toast it is. I know you've got to get going.'

She pulled the toast out from under the grill, placed two slices on a plate and handed it over. Then she put the rest on her plate and they carried it through to the living room, where they ate in silence, looking out of the window.

I liked that view; we could see over to Flushing, past the docks and up the river. Pip had loved it because there was always something going on, he said.

At night you could hear clanking and banging from the docks. Sometimes a loudspeaker would drift over the water, telling people to go to Level 3 or something. Bright lights shone all night as well as the daytime, and strange smells of foreign fuel drifted across the water. Big cranes and huge cruise ships all moored up there, tug boats and smaller ships, all emitting different noises and smells.

At certain times of the year, when it was dark, fireworks went off, usually in the field opposite. I didn't like them; they were too bright and too noisy, too frightening, and if I thought so, what on earth would Lainy make of them? If she was still here... I made a note on my paw to keep her under the bed while that went on.

In summer I could smell food from barbecues floating over the river from Flushing. Burnt sausages, burgers and fish from the beach. Delicacies from picnics aboard some of the many yachts in the harbour.

Today, because it was winter, a faint drizzle spattered the windows. It was restful, listening to them eat, hearing the rain outside. Glad we were inside, warm and safe. But all along hoping that Lainy's future was safe with us.

'Right, sorry to dash off, but I must go to my next customer,' Joe said. 'That was delicious, thanks so much.'

'It's the least I can do, after the taxi service,' Suki said. 'I'm so grateful, I really am. It was really nice to have some moral support, too.'

'Not at all,' Joe said. 'I'm very glad you rang; you shouldn't have driven yourself in that state.' He looked at her closely.

'You'd better rest for a bit. And let me know how you get on. I'm sure it'll heal really quickly and you won't even know it happened.'

Suki attempted a smile. 'I hope so,' she said. 'But thanks again.'

'My pleasure.' He hesitated by the door. 'See you for a walk later in the week?'

'Sure,' this time Suki's face lit up with pleasure. 'Thanks, Joe. Let me know which day's best for you.'

'I will.' He hesitated and leant towards her, as if he was going to give her a kiss, then changed his mind. Instead he gave her a gentle hug, as if she was fragile. 'Right, I'm off. Bye Moll, 'bye Lainy,' and with a pat for each of us, he headed out of the door.

Suki collected the plates and mugs and took them back to the kitchen, then looked down at us, sitting waiting hopefully for scraps. 'Not today, girls,' she said. But she gave us each a treat instead, then headed back to her desk.

That evening Tess came round without Titch. 'I can't stay long, but I want to hear exactly what happened and see how you are,' she said. Her ponytail had that droopy end-of-the-day look about it, rather like all of us.

Suki's bruise had swelled so much you could hardly see her left eye. 'I look like I've been in the boxing ring,' she said ruefully. 'I had a quick look in the mirror earlier, then thought it better not to look.' She smelt exhausted, like burnt tyres. 'I think I'm still in shock, to be honest. It all happened so quickly and I still can't believe it. I thought Lainy had settled in so well.'

'She has,' said Tess, taking the mug of tea she was offered. 'It's because she's so relaxed that this behaviour is coming out. You see, when dogs are really frightened, they shut down, just like we do. Poor Lainy had to deal with yet another transfer when she left Grace, another foster home, and then coming here. That's a lot of upheaval. It's taken her till now to begin to settle and relax. That's why the symptoms start to show, because she's not so scared any more.'

'I see. But does that mean this could happen again?' Suki was white faced again, and I could smell her anxiety, cold and sour.

'If we learn more of Lainy's triggers, then we can prevent her panics,' Tess's voice was deeper and more tired than usual. 'It's classic PTSD symptoms. In this case, she doesn't like people getting near her face; that's the trigger.'

'Of course. I forgot and let down my guard,' Suki said. 'She's been so relaxed, I thought everything would be OK.'

'It's easily done. I did it with Titch when we first had him. When dogs are startled from sleep they don't think, they just react, even with the person they love and trust the most.' She smiled. 'There's a reason for the saying, Let Sleeping Dogs Lie. We just need to ensure that other people don't get near her face.'

Suki shuddered. 'It makes you wonder what someone did to her in the past.'

'Exactly,' said Tess. 'I've sent you some links to PTSD that you might find useful.'

'Thanks. I'll have a look tomorrow. To be honest, I'm so tired all I want to do is sleep.'

'And that's exactly what you should do. Have an early night.'

'Well, not just yet,' Suki said with a smile. 'Is there anything else I can do to help Lainy?'

'Do you ever play music at home or when you go out? Classic FM or something?'

'Not often,' Suki said. 'Unless I'm rehearsing for choir. I sometimes leave Radio Four on when I go out. I'll try music though - what kind?'

'A lot of shelters play Classic FM because it's usually more soothing,' Tess replied. 'I know some classical music can be stirring, but the stuff they normally play on the radio is calming for most dogs. But you could experiment while you're at home; see what she likes. Some dogs like Fleetwood Mac, some Bob Marley; try anything that isn't too stimulating. And don't play the same stuff all the time or they get used to it.'

'That's interesting. Come to think of it, a friend at choir said their dog has music on all day, but once she recorded some vocal warm ups she was doing with some friends, and her dog started howling. It was very funny!'

Tess gave her deep belly laugh. 'Maybe skip scales, in that case, but see what Lainy's tastes are. Dogs are like us, they all respond to music differently.'

'I'll definitely try that, great idea.' Suki yawned hugely. 'Sorry, I feel a bit bruised and battered and knackered.'

'You probably will for a few days, but sleep when you need to. And if you need any help, just shout. Would you like me to walk the dogs tomorrow?'

Suki shook her head. 'I'm sure I'll be fine.'

'I'm coming over this way anyway so I'll give you a ring and see how you are. Give the dogs plenty of chews and bones and short walks for a few days. It won't hurt them. And we should maybe think about muzzle training for Lainy. Not now though; I'll look out some videos and we can think about it in a few weeks.'

Suki nodded. 'OK.'

Tess hesitated. 'And don't worry if you feel you can't trust Lainy like you used to. You've both had a shock but once you get over this, there's no reason why your relationship shouldn't be even stronger than before.'

Suki nodded. 'Thanks, Tess. That's good to hear.'

Tess gave her a hug. 'Any problems, ring me, OK?'

'Will do, thanks,' she said.

'And now, I'm off. Have something to eat and an early night. Everything will seem much better tomorrow.'

'I will.' I watched as they held each other tight and that lovely Good Friends smell wafted around the room.

Whatever happened, I desperately hoped that Suki would want to keep Lainy. Dealing with her problems looked like it was going to be harder than we'd expected, so I had to find some way of helping Lainy regain Suki's trust, and in return help Lainy regain her confidence. But how?

8

Over the next few days, Suki smelt exhausted all the time, and once we'd had our morning walk, she would go to her desk, as normal, to work, but after a while she would sigh, lie on the bed and sleep.

'What I have done?' Lainy said. 'Her eye not get better.' Despite her distress, her English was improving.

'She's OK,' I said, hoping to dog she was. She hadn't spoken to either of us much since the accident, which wasn't like her.

After a few days, however, she seemed to regain a little energy. She clicked on her computer, and started playing music. Then she stopped playing that tune and listened to another, watching Lainy all the while.

When her phone rang, she sounded pleased. 'Joe, hi! How are you? Thanks so much again for taking me to hospital.'

'No problem. How's your eye today?'

'Well, the bruising's coming out, so it's gone all colours of the kaleidoscope, and it's still rather swollen.'

'You must look spectacular. Poor thing; still, I bet no one's going to pick a fight with you.'

Suki laughed. 'No. I've got to go back tomorrow to have it looked at, so I'll know more then.'

'What time?' He said, quick as a flash.

'Nine fifteen.'

'I'll take you,' he said firmly. 'No quibble, OK?'

'Thanks, Joe,' she said, and I could hear delight and relief intermingling.

'What are you doing?'

'I'm trying out different types of music for Lainy. Apparently reggae and soft rock are the most relaxing music for dogs in shelters. I bet she wasn't played anything in Romania, so I'm experimenting, seeing what she likes best.'

'Great. It certainly worked with Peanut. He loved Bob Marley, but also Elgar to go to sleep to.'

Suki laughed. 'OK, I'll give that a go, too. All recommendations welcomed.'

'How about a walk tomorrow, after the hospital. Would you be up to it?'

'Yes, I'm feeling better today,' Suki said. 'For some reason I've been absolutely poleaxed for the last few days, but I'm getting some energy back.'

'I'm not surprised. You had one hell of a shock. And Lainy? How's she?'

'She's been very quiet, but I read that lavender is good for stress, so I found some oil in the bathroom cupboard and put some on a blanket and she seems to like that.'

'Well done,' Joe said. 'Now, I'd better go, but I'll pick you up tomorrow at ten to nine. We'll walk the dogs afterwards.'

'Thanks, Joe. That would be great.'

So the next morning Joe collected us and bundled us into his van which was dark and smelt of tools and oil and stuff. He'd put two dog beds in the back so we were cosy, and gave us some treats, then drove to the hospital.

'Thanks again, Joe,' Suki said. 'I'm glad they're going to look at it. I don't think it's healing properly. It's all red and swollen.'

Joe glanced at her eye. 'I would have expected it to be a bit better by now. But let's see what they say.'

He dropped her off and once he'd checked we were OK we all waited in the van, listening to the radio.

'What she do now?' Lainy had been very quiet since the accident. She jumped at the slightest noise and was almost back to being the frightened dog that arrived a few months ago. I had to do something to turn all this around, but what?

'She's just going to see a nurse. She won't be long.'

Lainy lay dejectedly with her nose on her paws. Ears flat, she licked her lips a lot, and seemed to have shut down. Eventually she looked up. 'I so very sorry,' she said. 'I ruin everything.'

I nudged her with my nose. 'No you haven't.' I lay closer to her, so she could feel the heat from my body. 'I didn't tell you this before, but I bit a friend of Suki's once.'

Lainy jerked upright. 'You did?'

'I was staying over at a friend's house while Suki was out for the night. She started cooking so I went into the kitchen to help her. She said, "Oh, Moll you are so cuddly," and bent to pick me up. Well, I growled, as I hate being picked up, but she took no notice, so I bit her.'

'And what happen?' Lainy said in awed tones.

I sniggered. 'She cried out. I didn't bite her very hard; just a bit, on her hand. It hurt my teeth, to be honest.'

Lainy was silent but I could smell tension leaking out of her. 'And she bleed?'

'A bit,' I said. 'I think humans bleed more on the face; perhaps I should have done that. But, you see, it's just a bite, Lainy. It's not that important.'

'But I bite Suki. That very bad,' she said.

'It's not that bad,' I insisted, crossing my paws and hoping it wasn't. 'I bet you very soon this will all be forgotten, and we can all go back to being happy again.'

Lainy was silent, then she said, 'I hope,' but she smelt a little brighter.

A while later, Suki reappeared and climbed into the van.

'Well?'

'It's infected,' she said. I could smell suppressed tears, bless her. 'Apparently, I should have had antibiotics when it was stitched up last week, but the nurse said I didn't need any at the time. Turns out he was wrong.'

Joe took a big breath. I could smell his anger but he was trying not to show it. 'So you've got antibiotics now?'

'Yes. Hopefully they'll kick in and it'll start to heal properly in a few days.'

Joe turned the engine on. 'I hope so,' he said. 'Otherwise you're coming straight back.' He looked at her closely. 'Now, I don't think you'd better walk, you look done in, but why don't I walk the dogs while you sit at the cafe with a cup of coffee?'

'No, honestly, I'm fine,' she said, but I could smell exhaustion seeping out of her.

'You're a very bad liar,' said Joe, but I could hear he was smiling. 'My next job isn't till ten thirty, so why don't we go to Devoran where you can have a coffee and I'll walk these two, then I'll join you for a quick cuppa, then take you home.'

Suki opened her mouth to protest, then shut it again. 'Thanks, Joe,' she said, and the quiet way she said it spoke volumes.

I couldn't help feeling this relationship might have legs, as people said. It was one of the few human sayings that made sense.

Although Suki's eye did begin to heal, I realised again how much the whole episode had really upset Lainy. She was incredibly jumpy around strangers, cars and joggers in particular, though at least she talked to me about it.

'I think I settle in here, but now this happen and I frighten,' she said. 'I think, how can I do this? I know you say Suki want keep me, but I have the nightmare and can't stop thinking of bad things and I not feel safe all the time.'

'But you know that you're not going anywhere. You're staying here,' I said.

'I hope,' Lainy said, her whiskers quivering. She was still a picture of stress: ears back, tail down, the whites of her eyes showing.

Then something struck me. 'Suki can't run until her eye heals. Does that make a difference to you?'

Lainy looked up with big, sorrowful dark eyes. 'Very much,' she said. 'I love running, it make me feel free and it so very good.'

'I can understand that,' I said. 'I'd run too if I didn't have arthritis. I'll see what I can do.'

Lainy's whiskers twitched and her ears shot up. 'I like that very much,' she breathed. 'I thank you Moll for all you do for me.'

I felt a ripple of pleasure down my spine. I gave Lainy a gentle nudge with my nose. 'My pleasure,' I said gruffly. I wasn't used to compliments.

Later Tess rang and while she and Suki chatted, I sat, very pointedly, by Suki's running shoes. I heard her laugh. 'Tess, Moll's complaining that I'm not running,' she said.

'Well, I miss my running partner, and I bet Lainy does too,' she said. 'How is your eye? Do you think you might be able to run soon?'

'It's much better,' she said. 'I reckon by next week I'll be OK but I don't want to chance it before then.'

'Of course not. But how about if I take Lainy running this week? I'm really missing it and Titch doesn't really enjoy it. I'd much rather run with someone, if you think Lainy would run with me.'

'I don't see why not,' Suki said. 'She's run with both of us, and she trusts you. It would be good for her, wouldn't it?'

'Absolutely. In that case, I'll take her this afternoon, after work,' Tess said.

And she did. 'Won't be long,' Tess said later, and disappeared with Lainy, who looked brighter than I'd seen her for over a week.

'Well done, Moll,' Suki said. 'That's really going to help Lainy. I should have thought of that before.'

She settled down to work while I had a snooze and before long, Tess arrived back. Instantly I could smell an upheaval.

'Are you all right?' Suki said, as Tess came in, red faced and breathing heavily.

Tess nodded. 'She loved it, though on the way back we met a cockapoo who was a bit boisterous and tried to jump on Lainy. She was a bit freaked out, poor girl. The owner wasn't very helpful.'

Suki bent down to stroke Lainy. 'Poor darling. Is she OK?'

'It gave her a shock more than anything else, I think. The owner had no control over the dog.'

Suki checked Lainy carefully, stroking her all the time. I could see the stress dissipating a little, but poor girl. This was the last thing she needed.

'Any biting?'

Tess shook her head and pulled Lainy's ears gently at the same time as stroking me. 'No, but it would be good to keep Lainy really quiet for the next few days. Give her lots of chews and quiet walks.'

'Poor girl, of course I will.'

'And we'd better start muzzle training. It's always really useful for dogs anyway.'

Suki looked at her. 'You mean you think she might bite again?'

'No reason why she should,' said Tess, rather too carefully. 'But she's upset at the moment and we want to give her the best possible chance. Lower her stress levels and make her happy again, work on building her confidence up. Help her feel safe again.'

'OK,' Suki said. 'Poor girl. We'll certainly have a quiet few days.'

'But I'll take her running every day if I can. I'm getting too unfit and it's really good for me, too. I'll just go somewhere quiet.'

'Thanks, Tess, that's brilliant.'

Lainy looked at me with flattened ears, tail between her legs and stress rising off her coat in a thin vapour. 'I no like those cock poos,' she said, trembling. 'They too bouncy. Too ...how you say... unpredictable.'

I had to suppress a smile; Lainy calling someone else unpredictable?! I said nothing, though. With her, it really was a case of one paw forward, two paws back.

9

For the next few days, we had very peaceful sniffing walks, for which I was grateful. There had been too much drama for all our liking. There was nothing like a long, slow walk in which to smell everything that had been going on: rabbit poo, or even better, fox poo. We could smell messages left by previous dogs that told us if a dog was on heat, or unwell. If they were feeling like sex, or what they'd just eaten. If a dog was happy or sad. Old boots and new boots, and the scent of where they'd walked. Biscuit and sandwich crumbs. Dropped treats. A wealth of information at the sniff of a nostril. All this was very calming for us dogs, which was just what Lainy and I needed.

Joe joined us for another walk around Mabe quarry, and took Lainy for a run which she seemed to enjoy, but even after a fast run, she was still very subdued. As Joe said, 'You're not your usual bouncy self, are you Lainy? Take it easy, girl.'

The following morning we had a phone call from Suki's friend Petroc. We hadn't seen him for a while as he'd been poorly.

'Are you better now, Petroc?'

'I am, my dear, much better thank you. And I'm coming over to Falmouth to do some shopping. Perhaps we could meet?'

'Certainly,' said Suki. I knew she'd missed him while he'd been poorly. 'We're going for a walk down to Greenbank beach as it's low tide.'

'Splendid. I'll meet you down there, if I may?'

'Of course, that would be lovely. We'll see you there in about twenty minutes.'

'Who is he?' Everything seemed to make poor Lainy anxious at the moment.

'He's an elderly friend of ours who lives in Flushing. You met him not long after you arrived here, Lainy. He's kind and clever and has very good crumbs in his kitchen.' I paused. 'He's quite safe.'

She nodded but smelt unconvinced. Everyone was a threat to her, at the moment. However, when we got down to the beach, it was empty, so it was peaceful trotting along the sand, exploring rock pools, chasing the seagulls into the sea, and seemed to calm Lainy. Her sour stress leaked into the salty water, and she started to smell more normal.

Then Petroc arrived, a tall, thin figure smelling a little frail, his long coat flapping in the breeze. Lainy bounded over to meet him, barking like crazy, her extraordinary tail waving like a propeller.

Suki dashed forward to put her on the lead, but Lainy stopped in front of Petroc and looked at him, ears pricked. We all waited.

Petroc looked down and smiled at her, apparently unconcerned. 'Hello, Lainy,' he said, and fumbled in his pockets, threw some treats on the sand. 'I'm very glad to see you again.' He continued to throw treats, which Lainy devoured, then looked up at him and barked, then tore off down the far end of the beach to chase an unruly seagull.

I let out a breath I didn't know I'd been holding and tuned in to the conversation, while still keeping an eye on Lainy who was now running along the shoreline, barking at a swan.

'I'd forgotten how beautiful she is,' said Petroc.

'She is - just very nervous. But how are you? Are you sure you're feeling better? You look a bit thin.'

Petroc smiled. 'I'm fine, my dear. Nothing that a few good meals won't remedy. But tell me what's been going on. I'm a bit behind.'

Suki filled him in while Petroc continued to dole out bits of very tasty Cheddar, and we explored up to the grassy area above the beach which was rich with a variety of scents: pieces of pasty, dropped biscuits, old poo bags, a few cans and a crisp packet.

'Well, life has been eventful,' he said. 'Your eye looks fine, though.'

'It's still a bit bruised,' she said.

'But not for long.' Petroc looked at her. 'I know it's been a terrible shock, but if you think of what Lainy's been through to make her behave like that...'

Suki nodded. 'I know. It doesn't bear thinking about...'

They walked on in companionable silence for a while. Then Suki called to us as it was time to go, put us on our leads and as we walked back towards the High Street, I heard music. Cheerful, jiggy notes that danced in the sunshine. Lainy's ears shot up as she listened, and she stood as still as a tree.

Petroc stopped. 'Do you hear that?'

We all stood still, listening as the music grew faster, and faster still, and made me want to run and chase as if I was a pup. It was exciting and infectious, settling on our coats, running down our legs and into our paws. I'd never heard anything like it.

Lainy's tail began to circle and she twiddled around on the spot, then we looked at each other and she said, 'that is accordion, I know from Romania.'

'Accordion?' I said. 'What's that?'

'It is box,' she explained. 'It make magic sound.'

It certainly did.

'Where's it coming from?' Petroc asked.

'It's probably some student playing music with their windows open,' Suki said.

As we turned up the path into the gardens on the way home, the music grew louder until, at the end of the path, we saw a tall young man standing by one of the wooden benches, holding a box that played music when he squeezed it. I saw what Lainy meant now. It was magic indeed. The sound was sweet and joyful, gentle strains of music floating out from the instrument in his hands.

'That's amazing,' Suki said, in tones of awe.

'What a talent.'

We all stood still, as the music turned quieter now, calmer. I looked at Lainy, who was transfixed. Her eyes were almond shaped, bright and intent. Her tail and ears were up, and the blanket of panic that she'd worn for the last ten days had slipped off, leaving a shiny, vibrant coat.

Suki looked at Petroc as the music came to a halt. 'I'd like to ask him who he is,' she whispered, but at that moment the man started playing faster, and Petroc and Suki tapped their feet and clapped their hands and we scampered around the gardens not knowing quite what to do with ourselves, but like Suki and Petroc, we couldn't stand still.

After a few more minutes the man stopped playing and Suki and Petroc clapped and we barked and the man looked round in a daze.

'I didn't realise there was anyone there,' he said, and he sounded as if he'd had been in another world, and now he'd come back and didn't want to be here. I edged nearer, smelling something bitter, and sadness, and loneliness that clung to him like a wet blanket.

'That was amazing,' Suki said. 'Do you play any gigs? I'd love to come along.'

He smelt bemused; a musty odour. 'I've just started playing at the Chainlocker on Thursday nights,' he said. 'I'm trying to get more gigs.' But the words sounded rough and unused in his mouth.

'Well, I'll definitely come along and bring my friends,' Suki said.

Petroc eyed him closely. 'Where did you learn to play like that?'

'I taught myself the accordion,' he said. 'But I did go to music school, a long time ago.'

'You play beautifully,' Petroc said. 'You have a real talent.'

Suki smiled and held out her hand. 'Hello. I'm Suki and this is Petroc and Moll, and this is Lainy,' as she pointed to us. 'I love your music, and it seems Lainy does too. She looks like a different dog.'

At this, Lainy looked up, eyes bright and smiling, and - I couldn't believe it - she walked up to this man, wagging her tail.

When he looked at her, his sour smell vanished and he crouched down. 'Hello,' he breathed but sensibly let Lainy come to him, and sniff him thoroughly. Her tail remained up, and he rummaged in his pocket for a biscuit which he put on the ground in front of her. Another good move. Lainy gobbled it down, looked up and very slowly he extended the back of his hand. She sniffed it, then looked up at him and I held my breath while he stroked her flank, very slowly.

'She's lovely,' he breathed, and a dimple appeared in one cheek as he smiled at her. 'What's she called?'

'Lainy. She's a rescue, from Romania.'

'Poor girl. She's had some bad times, eh?'

Suki nodded, but I could smell the tears in her eyes as she watched them; the sad man and the damaged dog. It was as if they were communicating through his strokes.

Lainy eyed him warily at first, but relaxed as he stroked her, then trotted back to me with a grin.

'He good at music, yes?'

'He certainly is,' I said. I was watching him closely, and now he was no longer stroking Lainy, he seemed nervous again. 'Well, I must go,' he said, and clutching his accordion to his chest, he hurried off, leaving us staring at his retreating figure. A tall man, slightly stooped, jeans covering his long thin legs, and wearing a short jacket.

'I never asked him his name,' said Suki, disappointment pouring off her like rain.

'He's very nervous, isn't he? Rather like Lainy.' Petroc said.

'Yes,' said Suki. 'Though even more nervous than Lainy by the looks of things. Still, at least we know he plays at the Chainlocker on Thursdays. Would you like to go along one week?'

'I'd love to. Anything to listen to him again.'

'Good. I'll see if Tess and a few others want to come.' She looked down at Lainy and stroked her head. 'I'm glad you made friends with him. And you loved his music, didn't you? I think we'd better do some more research into music therapy.'

Petroc nodded. 'It's excellent for people as well as dogs, I've heard. And who wouldn't want to listen to playing like that? Quite astonishing.'

'Why not come back for coffee, Petroc?'

'I'd love to. Perhaps we can look into this music therapy.'

So when we got home, Suki fiddled around with her phone and suddenly music came out. At first it was very loud; drums and clashing noises, and I could see Lainy licking her lips, the whites of her eyes showing. Suki hurriedly turned that off, but not before Lainy had dived underneath the table. 'OK,' said Suki. 'Let's try something else.'

'How about singing?'

Out of the phone came very high notes, and what a terrible caterwauling that was.

Petroc laughed. 'Maybe not; poor Lainy!'

If Lainy could have put her paws over her ears, she would have done so.

'How about gypsy music?' Suki said.

As the screeching stopped, we breathed a sigh of relief, waiting for the next blast of music. Wild gypsy tunes tore through the flat, weaving up and down the curtains, dancing round the windows, cavorting on the carpets. 'Rather like the young man's music,' said Petroc.

Lainy emerged cautiously from underneath the sofa, one paw at a time, and stood with her head on one side, nose twitching in time to the music. Her whiskers joined in, and Suki jigged round the room, laughing as she saw us. 'Come on, let's dance!'

'I'm afraid my arthritis doesn't like it,' said Petroc, and I had to agree, so we both sat down, feeling a little self conscious, but my whiskers twitched, and Lainy started barking and smiling as she and Suki danced in the living room like mad things. On and on, till Suki grew red faced and panting, and Lainy's teeth broadened into a big grin, and the two of them collapsed on the sofa in a panting heap.

'Bravo!' Petroc cried. 'I think we know which music Lainy likes!'

'We certainly do,' Suki said. 'I think we need something soothing now. Let me see what I can find.'

She got up and fiddled around on her phone. After a few false starts with very loud notes, she pressed another button and there was a totally different sound. I could hear tinkly notes that came from a piano (a friend of Pip's used to play in the pub) and then some breathy sounds which Suki said were a flute. I could feel my muscles growing heavy, my eyelids droopy. Before I nodded off, I looked over at Lainy, who lay with her head raised, ears up like two question marks.

'Is clever, no?' She said. 'The notes, they tumble over each other, then they run alongside like I do with Suki and Joe. Listen, the notes come back, and now it quiet again and we lying down together with Suki. The music tell us we all quiet and safe.'

And my eyes went quite teary when she said that, and I thought, I wish I could tell Suki. If ever there was a case for helping Lainy, this was it.

But perhaps I did Suki an injustice, for she looked at us and said, 'Well, we all knew the effect music has on humans' emotions. But this shows how much it affects dogs too. What an extraordinary morning this has been. I'm so glad you were here to share it with us, Petroc.'

From then on, there was a distinct change which affected us all. It was as if a duvet that had been covering us had slowly lifted off, revealing a clear, warm summer's day.

Suki and Tess started running again, which meant Titch and I got to have some quality time together. I updated him on Lainy and he sighed. 'She's a pretty girl, but she's hard work, isn't she? Don't you wish things were back to how they were, Moll? Nice and quiet, just you and me.'

'I know what you mean,' I replied. 'And she is hard work, but she's worth it, my darling. To see her character begin to emerge. She's beginning to bond with Suki. She's got a great sense of humour, and she's very affectionate.'

'Well, I think you're doing a wonderful job,' Titch said, nuzzling my nose. 'I'm sure once you've got her trained, all will be well. I hate to see you looking stressed, that's all.'

My whiskers twitched. 'I'm fine, darling,' I replied. 'I've got you to discuss things with, haven't I? And Lainy's very receptive. She just can't help it when her past comes back to bite her.'

Titch snorted. 'Rather too literally! As long as you don't regret it, Moll.'

'I'm fulfilling my promise to Pip,' I replied. 'And you know me, I don't go back on my bark.'

'That's one of the many things I love about you,' he replied. And we lay down together, nose to nose, for a little snooze while we waited for the runners to return.

When they did, they were hot and panting, but smiling from ear to ear.

'Oh, it's so good to be running again,' Suki said. She was pink and puffing but happiness steamed off her.

'I don't think your fitness has dropped much at all,' Tess said, slugging back water. 'And your eye looks great now. I reckon the scar will have disappeared completely in a few weeks.'

'I hope so.' They both looked down at Lainy, who was standing between them, grinning inanely.

'And there's one happy dog,' said Tess, giving Lainy a stroke. 'That's lovely to see. She's such a sensitive thing, isn't she? And so loving.' Her ponytail was jaunty today; a good sign.

'She is,' Suki said, panting, her curls askew. 'Just got to get my breath back, and I'll tell you more about this musician.'

'He sounds amazing, and I'd love to come and listen to him.'

'It'd be good to get a few more people. He really is very talented.'

'And Lainy loved it too?'

Suki grinned. 'Yes, the change in Lainy was incredible. One minute she was all rolling eyes and going bonkers, and the next she was transfixed. You could almost see the stress sliding off her.'

'That's fantastic,' said Tess. 'I'm so glad. I'm thinking of using more music relaxation for some of my very stressed dogs. It can help the really wobbly ones sleep and it's good for separation anxiety, too.'

'Lainy could give you a recommendation, couldn't you darling?' said Suki, bending down to pat her. 'So, we'll meet up on Thursday shall we? Petroc and his partner are coming too. I'm quite intrigued by this guy.'

'Why?'

'He's such an undiscovered talent,' Suki said. 'But he's desperately shy. When I started asking him a few questions, he grabbed his accordion and shot off.'

'Perhaps he's only just arrived and is trying to find his feet,' Tess said. 'Or perhaps he has some dark and mysterious past. Whatever it is, I'm sure you'll find out. Meanwhile, I'll see you on Thursday. I look forward to meeting the mysterious musician!'

Thursday came around quickly, but neither Tess nor Joe could go with Suki to the pub, for varying reasons, so she went with Petroc and his partner while Lainy and I waited, listening to the radio.

'What is this music?' Lainy asked. 'Suki say it Classic but what is that?'

My whiskers twitched. I didn't really like to tell her I didn't know, but honesty is usually the best policy. 'I think it's the name of the radio station,' I said. 'I think classical music is the slow stuff that is supposed to be relaxing.'

Lainy snorted. 'It boring, so we go to sleep?'

'I think it's more to calm us down. Stop us being stressed,' I tried to explain. 'Some dogs worry a lot when their owners go out. They don't like being left.'

Lainy tilted her head to one side while she thought. 'Ah yes,' she said. 'When we little we always have dogs around us; our mother, our brother and sister, and for me, all other dogs in street. Then in shelter,' she gave an involuntary shudder, 'there is many dogs. But when we go to new home suddenly we alone for first time. It scary.'

'Exactly,' I said. 'So for dogs in shelters over here, apparently they play this Classic stuff to calm them down.'

'You mean they have kill shelters here?' Lainy's ears shot up in horror.

'No, they're for dogs who are looking for a home, but they don't kill them like in Romania.' I stopped, for in fact I wasn't sure. 'I've met a few dogs who've come from shelters over here and they didn't sound anything like yours.'

'OK,' said Lainy, ears slumping to normal levels. 'In Romania I hear peoples play accordion in cafe nearby my street.'

'Really?' I watched her for signs of distress. 'Were they happy memories?'

'Ah yes, I listen with my mother and my brothers and it very happy.' She smiled and then said, 'the music man, he very sad, no?'

My nose twitched in agreement. 'Yes. He does smell unhappy, and even when his music is joyful, you can still hear the sad undertones, can't you?'

Lainy nodded. 'This man, I think he may have nightmare and panic like me. I think it go when he play accordion, and that why he need to play so bad.'

I sat, looking at her with incredulity. Us dogs are very good at picking up on what's going on with humans, but Lainy's level of empathy was extraordinary. 'Well that's interesting,' I said. 'I suppose we will hear more from Suki when she's spoken to him.'

I got up and passed near Lainy's bed and suddenly, with no warning, she charged at me, with a muffled roar. As soon as it happened, she shrank back and crept to her bed while I stayed rooted to the spot, my whiskers shivering.

Finally, when I'd stopped shaking, I managed to say, 'What was that about?'

'I sorry,' Lainy said in an undertone. I could smell her remorse, dark and bitter.

It was as if it had taken her by surprise, too. As my heart rate returned to normal, I said, struggling to keep calm, 'what brought that on, do you know?'

Lainy lay with her nose on her paws, distress pouring off her. 'I hear music that remind me of the Horrible Peoples, and you come close to my bed, and suddenly - woosh - I am back there, and I must protect myself. It very frighten, but I so very sorry, Moll. I scare you and that not good.' She sighed, and sounded really despairing. 'I try so hard it not happen again, please, I promise.'

There was no doubt she meant what she said, so I tried my best to overcome my shock. 'I understand,' I said. 'But try and make sure it doesn't happen again.' It struck me that this was a stupid thing to say, for I believed her when she said she couldn't control it. 'Maybe, if you feel this coming on, you tell me? Then it's not so scary. I thought you were attacking me.'

71

'Oh no,' she said. 'No, no. I have this trigger, you say? It make me do things like I crazy, and I not crazy.'

'Of course you're not, Lainy,' I said. Even so, I felt I needed a rest. 'Now, why don't we have a snooze and listen to the calm music till Suki gets home?'

I decided to go next door and lie on Suki's bed. Just in case.

10

Suki was bubbling over when she came back, dying to ring Tess and tell her about the gig, so Lainy and I joined her in the living room while she kicked off her shoes and sat on the sofa with one of us on either side.

'I know it's late, but I just had to tell you how it went,' Suki said to Tess, stroking my ears, then Lainy's spine, how we both liked it. We lay and listened, all ears, while smelling Suki's clothes.

Her jumper smelt of pungent beer mingled with the acidity of the wine that she liked to drink. Another smell of dog; she'd met Anne in the pub, who owned Bran, another of our terrier friends. Anne's husband was a good cook and I smelt garlic, beans and tomatoes, mixed with potatoes, cheese, butter, rosemary and salt and pepper. So that was what they'd had for dinner. Having got that out of the way, we could concentrate on the conversation, and find out more about the music man.

'So. How was the musical genius? What does he look like? Age?'

'Oh, he was great,' Suki said. 'He's about six foot, thin, green eyes, rather like a cat, and a dimple when he smiles. Which isn't often. Short dark hair, wears jeans and a denim jacket. I'd guess he's early thirties.'

'Sounds rather cute,' said Tess. 'The music was good, was it?'

'Fantastic. He played some really wild gypsy music, then a few folk numbers and a very sad love ballad, then finished on a really joyous number that got us all up and dancing. Then someone in the audience started singing *Cornwall My Home* so he played that, and asked for some recommendations of Cornish songs, and various people came up, someone with a guitar, and they had a jamming session on stage and it was brilliant. Afterwards, the pub manager asked if Zach would do another session on Sunday afternoons, with the guitar guy, so that's great.'

'Were there many people?'

'It's usually busy on music nights, but it was absolutely rammed by the time they finished,' Suki said. 'No wonder the manager was so pleased.'

'And did you find out anything about the mysterious musician?'

'Not much. Except that he's called Zach Thallon,' Suki said. 'It's strange, but he was like two different people. On stage, while he was playing the accordion, he was this incredible magician, full of energy and music and confidence. Then, as soon as he finished, he sort of fizzled out.'

Lainy and I looked at each other. She was right: music was his salvation.

'Goodness. Did you talk to him?'

'Yes, Petroc and I went up to see him while he was on stage. That was when the manager came up, delighted at his performance, and offered him another gig with the guitar guy. He and Zach were chatting and laughing, but as soon as the guitar man left, Zach looked really out of his depth. It was as if he'd been on a different planet while he was playing, and once he came back down to earth he didn't know what to do with himself.'

Lainy winked at me; she had perfected the art. I was quite jealous, as I could only blink, and it didn't have that nonchalant effect.

'Poor lad,' Tess said.

'It was as if all his confidence had dribbled away and left him with nothing. He looked ever so dejected and vulnerable, poor thing.'

'Oh no,' said Tess. 'You're not going to try and save him, Suki, are you? Please don't. You've got more than enough on your plate with Lainy, dear of her. You really don't have the time or energy to deal with anyone else.'

Quite right, I thought. Well said, Tess.

'No, no, I'm just interested as his music really seemed to calm Lainy. I was thinking he might be a good influence on her, and perhaps they could, you know, help each other. After all, anything that helps Lainy has to be good, doesn't it?'

'If I didn't know you so well, I'd say you were bullshitting me,' came the reply. 'Just be careful, Suki, please. You can't take on any more lame ducks.'

'I promise I'm not taking on anyone,' she said. 'But I would like to find out a bit more about him.' Her voice sounded dreamy. 'I was thinking, my next book could be Walks in the Footsteps of Cornish Musicians, so he'd be perfect to kick that off with.'

'Except that it must be pretty difficult playing the accordion as you go for a long walk, over stiles and through puddles,' said Tess.

Suki laughed. 'OK. I take your point. Look, I promise I won't try and save him. But the journalist in me finds him intriguing. It's a good story, you must admit.'

'Yeah,' said Tess. 'I'm sure you'll find out his story sooner or later.'

The following day, we had a gentle walk with Joe at Mylor Creek. I'd noticed how much more relaxed Suki was with him now. She confided her fears over Lainy; if she was doing a good enough job looking after her. She told him a story about someone she'd interviewed, making him laugh. They were more at ease with each other, which was good to see, but I noticed that while Joe was a good listener, he rarely revealed anything about himself.

Lainy and I trotted ahead, sniffing the foreign territory. 'I like Joe,' she said simply. 'He calm and he no shout or do things quickly.'

'Except for running,' I pointed out.

Lainy gave me one of her enigmatic stares. 'Of course he run fast,' she said, as if I was stupid. 'I think he hurt in past. He very, how you say, wary. He scared get hurt again.'

Now she mentioned it, I could see she was right. 'A bit like Suki.'

'Oh yes. And he very careful who he like. And that is good.'

'Well done, Lainy. You're very observant.'

'I look, you look. We see different,' she said.

'I hadn't thought of that, but yes, we do see different things.'

'And Joe, he peaceful, and he like being on his own,' she continued, warming to her subject. 'He no shove hand in my face. Well, only once and he learn. That good.'

This, I had come to realise, was one of Lainy's pet hates. She backed away and barked, or snapped whenever someone put their hand out to greet her. Why did people do that? It was most uncalled for. How would humans like it if people shoved hands in their faces? They needed someone brave enough, like Lainy, to tell them not to.

'And he like Suki very much,' she added.

'He hasn't said so.'

'No, but you can smell it, no?'

My whiskers twitched. Now she mentioned it, there was that musky smell. It was different to the Ted smell, and much fainter, but it was still there. 'You're right,' I said, and decided to keep a closer nose on them both.

While Lainy and I trotted ahead, Joe and Suki were discussing foraging.

'Do you pick wild garlic?'

Joe nodded. 'Yes, it's great to cook with. And samphire; if the tide was out we could pick some here.'

'I'm not that much of a samphire fan, to be honest,' Suki said. 'It's very salty.'

'You can rinse it.'

'I did, but I'm still not sold on it. What about mushrooms? Do you know which ones to pick? That always worries me.'

'Mushrooms can be tricky,' Joe replied. 'I've never been poisoned yet. But I wouldn't recommend it; it's very easy to pick the wrong ones.'

Suki laughed. 'I know, that's what puts me off. Who taught you to forage?'

'My dad. He knew so much about plants, and my mum's into their medicinal purposes, so I learned a lot from both of them.'

Suki was quiet for a moment, then she said, 'I know you said you were restoring a boat, but what sort is it, and where is it?' she asked.

Joe grinned. 'That's why I suggested we walk here. My boat is along the creek, so I thought I'd show you.'

And the quiet way he said it made me realise how special this place was to him.

We were walking along the foreshore where the tide was out, revealing a muddy expanse of dried out river populated by boats that rested on the bottom like giant ducks. The mud smelt of wet earth, of poo from various birds, of oil from boats and pieces of discarded timber, the odd car tyre and bits of plastic that had washed up the river; very satisfying smells and very different smell to the beach near us, or the grass covered fields.

Then, as we went round the corner, we saw a huge shell of a boat on stilts, rising high out of the mud.

'This is her,' Joe said, reverently.

'Wow.' Suki walked up to the boat, and touched the planks reverently. 'She's gorgeous. How big is she? And what sort of boat?'

'She's thirty foot, made of various types of wood and she's a Falmouth Working Boat.'

'Are they the ones with the big coloured topsails that race in summer?'

'That's it. Though this one has never raced. She was used for taking anglers on fishing trips for many years before I bought her.'

Suki walked round the boat, looking at her from all sides. 'What's she called?'

'White Heather, though she was called Vera beforehand.'

'I thought it was bad luck to change a boat's name.'

'Well, the previous owner did it, so I'm hoping that any bad luck will be his, not mine,' Joe said.

'And why is she on stilts?'

'That's to stop her tipping over when the tide's out,' he said. 'If you have a bilge keel, that has two fins which makes it ideal for beaching in tidal waters like this. This one doesn't so she has to have legs.'

'Why not get one with a bilge keel?'

Joe smiled. 'Good question. That would be ideal here, but I only got this mooring a few months ago, so then I had to build her some legs.'

'That's really interesting,' Suki said. 'I've never thought about what goes on underneath the water.'

'There's no reason why you should, unless you sail a lot, or own a boat,' he said. 'Would you like to come on board?'

'I'd love to. How do we get up there?'

Joe pulled out a ladder that was strapped to the upper side of the boat. 'We climb up this ladder.'

'Right,' Suki said. 'Sorry girls, you'll have to stay here, but we won't be long.'

Lainy and I watched as she climbed up a very steep ladder, propped against the side of the boat. It rose out of the mud and looked impossibly high up, with very narrow rungs.

'What is boat for?' Lainy asked.

'For sailing,' I said, for I had been on several boats. 'On the sea. I've never seen one out of the water, though. They look much bigger than when they're in the sea.'

'You walk on water?' Lainy said, her dark eyes wide in astonishment.

'No, you float on it, and they have big white things called sails that make it go along.'

Lainy looked at me as if I was mad. 'Why people do that?'

I paused, unsure. 'For fun?'

Lainy snorted. Like her winks, her snorts conveyed more than a bark ever could. 'Mad,' she muttered, and went to investigate an old plastic container further along the shore.

I waited, meanwhile, and listened to what Joe and Suki were saying. It seemed to be a lot of boring stuff about boats and wood and stuff, then she said. 'You come here in your free time, then?'

'Yes,' said Joe. 'It's very quiet here. Just me and the birds. There are robins, blackbirds, ducks, a few pigeons from the farm up there. Some herons. And egrets; they're like mini herons but white. Oyster catchers sometimes. Seagulls, of course. My dog loved it here; plenty of exciting smells.'

'It's very peaceful,' she said, and I could sense her listening to the birds nearby. 'Is there still a lot to do to the boat?'

'Yes,' Joe said. 'I won't bore you with the details, but there is a lot. I don't mind, though. It's wonderful seeing how she changes. She needs a lot of attention to detail. Boats need a lot of TLC.'

'Like all of us,' Suki said and I could smell her flush of embarrassment. She and Joe didn't usually talk about things like that. There was a silence, then she said, 'And how long will it take till she's ready to sail?'

'Depends how much time I get to work on her. Probably another year,' Joe said. 'Maybe more.'

I breathed a sigh of relief. I wasn't that keen on sailing; you got wet and you couldn't go for a walk when you wanted, and I thought, what for?

'It must be wonderful having a project like this and seeing it progress.'

'It is,' said Joe, and the simple way he said it made it clear how much this boat meant to him.

'I hope you've taken before and after pictures?' Suki said.

'I certainly have,' he said. 'Though they're all on my phone.' He climbed down the ladder, then held it for Suki.

'I'd love to see them sometime.'

Joe laughed, and it was a deep, rich sound that smelt of joy. 'I'd be delighted to show you, but I warn you they get pretty boring.'

'I'm prepared to be bored.' Suki climbed down the ladder and landed back on the foreshore; I let out a breath that I didn't know I'd been holding. She stood there and looked at him and he looked at her and it was as if time had slowed down, was waiting for something to happen.

'Thank you,' she said. 'For bringing me here. It's very special.'

'It is to me,' Joe said. Then he looked down at his feet before speaking. 'I'm going to a talk at Flushing Sailing Club about restoring wooden boats. I wondered if...'

'If what?'

'If maybe you'd like to come. Though you're probably busy.'

Suki looked at him and I knew she'd say yes, even if it was about making concrete. 'When is it?'

'Tuesday week.'

'I'd love to,' she said. 'What time?'

'7.30. There's a bar, so we could have a drink afterwards, if you like.'

'Perfect,' she said. 'It's a date.' She went hot. 'I mean...'

But Joe smiled, and leaning forward, he tucked a stray curl behind Suki's ear. 'Yes. It is a date.' Then he kissed her, on one cheek. Then on her mouth, and that turned into a longer kiss. And it went on...

Eventually they drew back and she blushed, while they grinned at each other like idiots. People were strange, I thought. Suki wasn't that interested in old boats, I was sure. But Joe was. And sharing interests was, it seemed, important to both of them.

11

Suki had taken music therapy seriously ever since we'd met Music Man, and now we had a variety of music on the go.

When she came back from singing Suki played the songs she'd learnt that session. She pressed a button on her phone and would sing along to the track, with varying results. She had a high, sweet voice, and usually sang in tune, but there were occasions when she was a little off key which hurt our sensitive ears. Mind you, she always checked to see the effect on me and Lainy, and I think she realised when she was flat.

However, Lainy and I had different tastes. 'I like shanty song,' Lainy said one day, her ears pricked up and her mouth in a wide grin. 'Oh yes, I like, they make me happy!'

'They're too noisy for me,' I said, 'all that shouting, particularly in South Australia. No, give me a nice ballad like Cornwall My Home.' I wasn't entirely sure what a Ballad was, but I'd heard Suki use the word and it sounded impressive.

'Ah yes, I like also,' said Lainy. 'Because Cornwall is my home now, yes? Even if I am immigrant.'

I stared at her in astonishment. Where was she picking up these words from?

'But I no come over in boat, and I no claim housing or service from the government,' she continued. 'I not a sponger.'

Government? Sponger? What was she talking about? All of a sudden our roles were reversed and I wasn't sure I liked it. 'Where did you hear about immigrants?' I asked.

'On the television,' she said simply. 'I like some of the musics when they have the advertisements,' though she pronounced it adverTISEments. 'And radio. They have good tunes when they have adverTISEments also, and with the current affairs, they call it? Even when Suki play the Classics music, there is news and I listen, and I think some of these are my peoples.'

My nose twitched and I sat down, humbled by the younger generation. 'Oh,' I said, 'I haven't really concerned myself with that sort of thing.'

'Of course no,' she said. 'You have important mission. Since Pip die, you must look after Suki. Make sure she happy. That life and death, no? You have no time for news!'

And when she spoke, I realised how vital my task had been. Still was... After all, it hadn't been easy, looking after Suki all these years. Not that I minded. If we can't look after our owners, what is the point? But a thought struck me. 'You do know that you need to look after Suki, too?' I said. 'I won't be here forever, you know.'

'Of course!' I wasn't a fan of exclamation marks, but sometimes Lainy spoke with them. 'You do the hard work, Moll,' she said fervently. 'I know this difficult job so I study you all the time so I know what to do. No worry, I learn fast.'

'You do,' I said, 'you're a bright girl. If you could just apply some of that intelligence to your teeth.'

She looked at me with her head on one side. 'Oh, you mean I no bite? This is joke?' She winked. 'You funny, Moll,'

'Well, I hope we don't have any more bites, Lainy. It's not good for my nerves.' She looked so downcast that I felt terrible. 'Though I know you do your best.'

'I very much try my hard,' she said. 'I promise. I no like biting either, and I wish I no have to, but I am getting better, no?' She paused. 'I am so very grateful you have brought me here, and I know this is not plain sailing.' She gave me another of her winks. 'You like my joke?' And she laughed, baring those sharp teeth in a way that made me gulp a little. However, her laughter was so infectious that I soon joined in.

'Glad to see you're enjoying the music, girls,' said Suki as she came into the room.

This set us off even more, because of course it had nothing to do with the music, but we stopped laughing, for neither of us liked the rather bemused look on Suki's face. It was our job, after all, to look after her, and two could do that better than one.

Later in the week, Suki had to go into town so Lainy and I went with her as it was good for Lainy to get used to people and shops and things she hadn't come across before.

'OK girls, I need to go to the library and collect a few things from work, then we can have a coffee at the Pier on the way home. OK?'

Lainy looked at me. 'What is Pier?'

'Oh, you'll like it,' I said. 'It's a cafe on Prince of Wales Pier and they sell coffee and cake. The crumbs are the best I've had in Falmouth, and that's saying something.'

'Really?' Lainy's eyes widened. 'I like this shopping.'

And so we trotted into town. I kept a close eye on Lainy for warning signs: licking lips, whites of the eyes showing, tail down, flattened ears. But although she was nervous, she seemed to deal with it very well. The bonus was that it wasn't too busy and there were always so many new smells to enjoy around town. Dropped bits of pasty, endless messages left by other strange dogs, feet leaving imprints of their owners and their moods. It was a cornucopia of delights. (As Lainy was learning about current affairs, I felt I should continue to extend my literary dictionary. I wasn't sure what cornucopia meant but it sounded like the best treat ever.)

As we came out of the library and walked across the road, Suki said, 'Oh look, there's Zach.' And sure enough, sitting on one of the benches on the Moor was the Music Man, looking droopy. His hair was cut very short, making his face look even thinner.

As we grew nearer, I could smell the sadness that seeped out of him, mixed with something chemically. It smelt bitter and caught in the back of my throat.

'He lonely,' whispered Lainy. 'That very bad smell.'

It was almost as if Suki heard us, for she muttered, 'Poor thing. I wonder if he'd like a coffee.' She approached him very carefully, as she did to Lainy when she first arrived. 'Hello, Zach,' she said quietly, 'We're just going for a coffee and wondered if you would like to join us?'

Zach looked up, and when he saw us, he smiled and his face changed completely. 'Oh. Thank you,' he said, though I could smell how nervous he was.

'He very hungry,' whispered Lainy. 'It no good. You can't think.'

At that moment his stomach gave a huge growl, and Suki laughed and the atmosphere brightened. 'I'm hungry too,' she said. 'So please come with us. My treat.'

'That's very kind.' His face brightened further and a dimple appeared in one cheek.

'I'd like to ask your advice about my dog here, Lainy, who has PTSD. Music seems to really help her, but rather than pay you, perhaps we can have something to eat.'

'Anything to help Lainy.' He beamed at her. 'Thank you very much.'

So we walked over to the cafe where Suki insisted on ordering breakfast for Zach and flapjack for her, then we went and sat outside, for although it was winter, the sunshine was warm and it did us good to feel heat on our coats. Lainy in particular seemed to love the sun. Her whole body relaxed, and all her cares slid off into the warmth.

For now, though, we lay beside Suki and listened to her talking to Zach, or rather, trying to get some information out of him.

As the drinks arrived, Suki said, 'I was born and brought up in St Just. Do you know it? It's an old mining town which used to be very bleak when I was a child but it's much busier nowadays. There's more employment, so the people are happier, and there's a very supportive community.' She waited, but there was no response. 'My brothers couldn't wait to leave Cornwall, but although I worked away for a while, I was keen to get back. I don't like cities; I felt like a fish out of water.'

It was clear Suki needed to work harder to get him to actually speak. Mind you, he was so hungry, perhaps he needed to eat first.

Zach sipped his coffee, crumbled a biscuit and threw the bits onto the ground for Lainy, smiling at her as he did so.

'What about you, where do you come from?'

His dimple disappeared. 'My dad was a surgeon, based in Nottingham.'

'Did you go into medicine too?'

Zach looked down and it was as if a wave of darkness almost knocked him over. He nodded.

Suki must have realised how upset he was, for she said, 'And what brought you to Cornwall?'

At that moment the food arrived, so Suki said, 'Do tuck in while it's hot,' and Zach picked up his knife and fork and attacked the food as if he'd not eaten for a long time.

Lainy and I were sitting up as the smell of his breakfast thankfully overtook his sour, chemical whiff. Creamy scrambled eggs, crispy bacon, spicy sausages, tomatoes, earthy baked beans and richly buttered toast. If we'd been like Labradors, we would have drooled all over the ground. As it was, we gulped and swallowed, hoping for a crumb, but our hope receded with each rapidly devoured mouthful.

All too soon, Zach finished and sat back, looking a bit dazed. 'Very sorry, I was really hungry,' he muttered, and reaching into his pocket he dug out some pills. 'Need my painkillers.' He gulped a few down with the rest of his drink.

'I'm just like that when I'm starving,' Suki said cheerfully. 'My family always ate far too quickly, so I'm used to it.' She gave me and Lainy a treat each. 'So, Zach, what brought you to Falmouth?'

He looked down, then up, and chewed his lower lip. 'I came here on holiday a few times, with a girlfriend, and I...' his voice trailed off and he shrugged, gave a lop sided smile.

'And why not?' Suki said, though I was wondering why he'd come here if he had no job and didn't appear to have any friends either. 'Do you know many people here?'

He looked up. 'A few people,' he said. 'I met them a while ago at music school.'

'Music school! Where did you go?'

He looked down. 'Truro,' he said. 'I stayed in touch with some of the other students, and felt like a change of scene.'

Even I could tell that there was a lot he wasn't saying, but Suki didn't push it. 'And where do you live?'

'Near the docks,' he said. 'I'm looking for somewhere else, though.' Again, this sounded like he was being economical with the truth, but she let it go.

'And you clearly love music,' she said.

'Oh yes,' he said, and his face lit up.

Suki smiled and the atmosphere lifted. 'Well, I was wondering if you might help me with Lainy here,' she said.

He looked down at us, and some of his sour smell disappeared as he smiled and gently rubbed me under my chin which I rather liked. Then he looked at Lainy, who winked at him and he smiled, properly, and his face was transformed. 'She's very nervous, isn't she?' And he dropped a bit of bacon rind on the floor for her.

'Yes, she's a Romanian rescue,' Suki said. 'She had a difficult start in life and it's because of that she's got PTSD.'

The darkness around Zach swirled, and changed shape. I could smell a waft of sweet tasting sympathy as he looked at Lainy. 'Poor girl,' he said softly, and Lainy edged closer. In astonishment we watched as she sat beside Zach and allowed him to scratch her under the chin.

'She's lovely, isn't she?' He made a gooey face at her, dimple and all.

'What do you know about music therapy for dogs?'

Zach carried on stroking Lainy, who appeared to love it. 'I don't, but I do know how effective music is for humans, and there's no reason why dogs should be any different.' I noticed he was much more at ease with dogs than people. 'What happened to her?'

Suki proceeded to tell Zach about Lainy's background. As she spoke, I smelled Zach closely. I could sense another wave of warmth coming from the young man. It smelt sweet, if a little uncertain, and I recognised the signs of empathy. Excellent. Clever Suki.

As she finished, he frowned and looked at us both. Lainy sat beside Zach looking the perfect, innocent dog, incapable of doing any wrong. Just as well he couldn't see her teeth.

'Poor girl,' he said and stroked Lainy all the way along her back.

'I don't know Lainy that well, because she's not been living with me long, but I can tell when she's really stressed and upset,' Suki said. 'The other week, when we met you in the gardens, it was astonishing to see how she reacted to you playing the accordion. One minute she was really terrified, but when she heard your music, it was as if all her worries just melted away.'

'Really?' Zach had relaxed and I could smell his delight, like oozing butter. 'Well, when I'm feeling down, playing a musical instrument or singing can make me feel so much better. It's the best thing ever.' As he spoke, a stream of joy came from him which was sweet to my nose.

This was a long, passionate speech from the Music Man, and we all sat and looked at him.

'I've been doing some research into music therapy,' Suki said. 'It backs up everything you've just said, and apparently music is also very good at helping with anxiety and depression. It can help with nightmares and trying to combat negative thoughts and stuff.'

Zach nodded, thoughtfully.

'And it can help relax tight muscles, and calm fears,' Suki continued. 'It's very good for helping to combat the symptoms of PTSD.'

Zach bit his lip and I could almost see the fear creeping into his head. His eyes looked a bit unfocused too.

Suki glanced at him. 'From what I understand, PTSD is very common,' she said carefully. 'It's a reaction to really stressful, traumatic situations, where the person keeps on reliving certain events.'

Judging by Zach's closed off expression, this could well have happened to him. He crossed one leg over the other and his jeans rode up, revealing a vivid red mess down one leg. It smelt revolting, like burnt flesh.

'Medical staff and the police often get it, but it can happen to anyone,' Suki continued, 'and it can cause nightmares, depression, isolation, that sort of thing. I know someone who wouldn't go out because he was so worried about meeting anyone, and he felt that he couldn't work because he couldn't cope with any responsibility.'

She stopped, but the scared smell continued to pour off Zack. He was silent for so long that I had a feeling all this was for nothing. But just as I smelt Suki's despondency, like sour milk, he fiddled with a teaspoon, and said, very quietly, 'I know what that's like.'

Lainy and I looked at each other and she gave one of her enigmatic winks. Suki opened her mouth, shut it again.

Then Zach said, 'I don't think I'd be here if it wasn't for music.' He spoke so quietly that it was difficult to hear him, but that's what I thought he said. And just as Suki was about to speak, Zach got up, pushing his chair back with a screech. 'Thank you so much for breakfast,' he said, 'I hope to repay you, but I'm afraid I haven't, I mean, I can't afford... I'm so sorry, I really must go.'

He grabbed his jacket and hurried out of the cafe. I hadn't noticed that he hobbled before, though perhaps it was because of his sore leg. All three of us watched him, stunned.

Finally Suki spoke. 'I'm not sure what happened there,' she said, draining her coffee. 'But I'd like to think it wasn't a totally wasted experience.' She stroked both of us thoughtfully. 'I'm sure he was just ... well, he's obviously having a difficult time. Like you, Lainy.' She sighed and looked for her bag. 'Anyway, he's not my responsibility, as I know Tess would say, but you can't help feeling sorry for him.' She looked down and gave us a treat each. 'Can you?'

12

Lain and I talked about Music Man, of course.

'He clever with music but not so happy with his life, no?'

I gave a long stretch, right down my spine, which helped me concentrate. 'Mmm. It seems like he's running away from something.'

'Yes. I think he scared.'

'What of?'

Lainy gave a shrug. 'Who know? But his music very very good. I love his music.'

I was mulling this over the following week when we were walking around the castle with Joe. Suki and Lainy and Joe had started running several times a week, leaving me to have a gentle snooze in the car. Lainy was a welcome addition to our family, but she could be rather intense, so it was pleasant to have a quiet breather now and then.

I lay in my bed in the car, listening to distant voices. Could I hear music? I tilted my head, listening with my good ear. Yes, it sounded very much like the Music Man's accordion. Then I heard Suki's light footsteps, followed by Joe's heavier ones, accompanied by Lainy's light patter. Then the car door opened, and there was Suki, smiling in the doorway.

'Hi, Moll, we were just coming back from our run and saw Zach playing his accordion to a bunch of schoolchildren.' She stood aside for me to jump down, and clipped my lead on. 'Let's have a walk round the castle and see if he's still there, shall we?'

Lainy and I led the way, while I wondered why Music Man was playing at the castle, but the riddle was solved by Joe, looking at a poster tacked to a tree.

'Look. Special children's performance for half term,' he said, pointing to the poster.

'Oh yes,' said Suki, reading it. 'Pendennis Castle is providing a host of amusements for children during half term and on Tuesday it will be Zachary and his accordion, playing tunes that everyone can join in with.' She grinned. 'They loved it, didn't they? Lots of singing and giggling.' She smiled at Joe. 'I'm glad he's getting more work. I wonder how this gig came about.'

'He may not be paid for it,' Joe said as we started walking around the moat, a popular route with dog lovers in Falmouth. I'd been doing it since I was a pup but I still loved it: high quality dog smells and the odd dropped treat. 'Maybe he was doing it to help a friend out.'

'Yes, maybe,' Suki said, 'I was worried when he rushed off the other day. He finished his breakfast and seemed to be OK, but when I told him about Lainy's PTSD he went a bit odd.'

Joe was silent, though I had the feeling it wasn't because he was short on opinions.

'There's obviously something worrying him,' she continued. 'Maybe - oh look, there's Anne and Bran!'

She introduced Anne and Joe, and we played with Bran for a while, but he was young and a bit bouncy for my liking, so I was glad when we continued on our way, and as we came to the final part of our walk, leading past the castle entrance, who should walk out but Zach carrying his accordion.

Lainy and I smelt him immediately; his unsure, sad smell, with slight chemical undertones. His awkwardness made for a potent, choking cocktail that got right up my whiskers. I sensed that he might have run in the opposite direction if he'd been able to, but Suki saw him first.

'Zach, hello!' she said. 'We heard you playing to the children earlier; it sounded great. Did you enjoy it?'

Zach held onto his accordion as if it would save his life. 'I think so,' he said. 'Though I don't know much about children.' He gave an apologetic smile and that dimple winked.

'I know, it's difficult when you're not a parent, isn't it?' She said. 'Oh, by the way, this is my friend, Joe. Joe - Zach.'

Joe seized his hand and shook it firmly. 'Good to meet you, Zach. You certainly know how to play the accordion. It was very impressive.'

Zach flushed; I could smell that hot rush sweeping up his body, hitting his face in an explosion of embarrassment.

'Thanks,' he said gruffly, then turned to Suki. 'I wanted to apologise for the last time we met. You were very generous with breakfast, but I had to...'

We waited, but no reason was forthcoming. Lainy was looking hopefully at his accordion. 'Why he no play?' she said. 'I hear earlier and it make me feel so good.'

'I think he's finished,' I said. Still we waited for him to say something.

'That's OK.' Suki sounded puzzled. 'Have you found somewhere else to live? You said you were looking.'

'I ... possibly,' he said. 'I'm sleeping on a sofa at the moment but someone said there was a room going in a shared house, so I went to see that.' The information came out in a rush, as if he hadn't expected to say anything.

'And was it OK?' Joe said. He was looking at Zach with his usual studied quietness.

Zach turned to Joe as if he'd forgotten he was there. 'Yes,' he said. 'I'm moving in tomorrow.'

'It's not too expensive?' Suki asked. Oh no, I thought. She's doing her lame duck bit again. How can we stop her?

'I can just about afford it if I get another gig or two,' Zach said. 'That's why I did this today. Somebody put me in touch with the woman who does events at the Castle, and she booked me.'

'That's great!' Suki sounded enthusiastic. 'I'm glad things are working out.' She looked down at Lainy who was still looking hopefully at Zach's accordion. 'She loves your playing.'

Zach looked at Lainy, who tilted her head to one side. She winked and I stifled a snigger.

'What sort of music do you like, Lainy?' His voice was deep and soothing when he talked to her.

'She loves gypsy tunes. But she also liked that sad ballad you played.'

Zach looked at Lainy, and a slow smile spread across his face. 'OK, little girl,' he said. He picked up his accordion and there was silence for a moment, while it seemed as if Music Man opened the door to his own private world, and stepped in. He gave a little nod, then his left hand started, independently from his right, and one foot started tapping time as he played a gentle tune like a lullaby. The notes went right down my spine, and Lainy's ears swivelled like two little radars. I saw the pleasure shimmer down her back, and we both settled down to absorb ourselves in the music.

He played with great tenderness. I could imagine playing this to my dear Titch. A sweet way to say I loved him. We hadn't seen him much recently, and I missed him, as I always did. But Tess had said they were coming over later in the week, so that was something to look forward to.

Just as I was about to drift off, the music changed to a cheerful, paw tapping ballad. It woke us up, tingled our senses, and brought joy to our whiskers. Looking at Suki, she was tapping her feet, her whole body vibrating as she smiled till her face lit up. Joe, too, radiated a joyous heat, and then suddenly the music stopped, and no one wanted to break the silence. We'd all stepped into the Magic Music World, and no one wanted to leave it.

Finally Suki spoke. 'Thanks so much,' she said. 'That was really special.' She stroked Lainy and I could smell the pleasure rippling down her spine. 'Aren't we lucky, having our own private gig?'

Zach dipped his head. 'You're welcome,' he said, blushing.

'You're very talented,' Joe said. 'It's a pleasure to listen to you. I hope you get many more gigs. You should be performing at Eden and Hall for Cornwall.'

Zach looked up. 'Oh, I don't think...'

'No, really,' said Suki. 'You need an agent, Zach. Or have you got one?'

He shook his head. 'No, I don't think, I mean... I wouldn't know how to go about that.'

Suki looked at Joe. 'Well, I don't know either, but I'm sure I can find out.' Her eyes were bright at the prospect. 'I'll ask around. Meanwhile, you're playing at the Chainlocker on Thursday, are you?'

He nodded.

'Great. In that case, we'll see you then. Thanks for our private performance, Zach!'

With a certain amount of relief, we headed back to the car. She wasn't about to offer him a bed, or anything. Perhaps she really had tamed her instincts now we had Lainy.

'He's very talented,' Joe said as we reached the cars.

'Isn't he?' She said. 'And you can see how much Lainy enjoyed it.'

We looked at Lainy who was grinning happily, her tongue lolling out, almond shaped eyes gooey with delight.

'I think we all did,' Joe said.

'And yet, when he's not playing, he seems very awkward. Unhappy, don't you think?' Suki said.

I had noticed that Joe didn't like talking about emotions, so I was interested to hear what he'd say. He frowned. 'He seems very unsure of himself,' he said, though judging by the sour smell coming from him, I sensed he thought a lot more than that.

'Yes, he's got very little confidence,' Suki said. 'Strange, when he's such a talented musician.'

Joe said nothing.

'When I told him about Lainy's PTSD, he implied he knew what it was like,' Suki said.

Joe looked searchingly at Suki. 'Just be careful, won't you? Don't take on too much.'

Suki smiled. 'No, I promise I won't.'

They stood looking at each other, and as Joe leaned towards her, I could smell that musky scent, but underneath it all, a current of fear, which seemed strange. He kissed her, very softly, on the mouth, and that kiss seemed to go on for a long time. Then he drew back and said, 'Well, I must be going. See you very soon, Suki. Bye you two.' And he gave us a treat each and jumped into his van.

Suki opened the back of the car so we both hopped in, and waved Joe off. She hummed on the way home, but suddenly stopped, and I wasn't sure why. Surely she should be pleased that Joe had kissed her again? Or was she worried about Music Man? Or both? I had a shifting feeling that things were changing, and I wasn't sure it was for the better.

13

Titch and I lay on our beds - well, he lay in Lainy's - and sniffed each other to see what had been going on since we last met. He smelt of cheese and treats which meant he'd been training with Tess. The cheese smelt good but the treats were a bit synthetic to my sensitive nose. However, underneath was his reassuring, Titch smell that I'd know anywhere. Male strength mixed with his own brand of quirkiness.

'And how is Suki?'

'She's fine,' I said. 'Things are moving on with Joe. But I have a feeling that they're both holding back a bit.' I was keen to talk more about this, but, being a man, Titch didn't seem to find it interesting.

'Good,' he said briskly. 'And Lainy? She seems a bit calmer.'

'She is,' I replied. Discussing Suki would have to wait, then. 'Suki's playing a lot of music at home now and that seems to really soothe Lainy. And of course living with Suki must help.'

Titch nuzzled my muzzle. 'You mean, living with you,' he said, which made me snicker in delight. 'Oh, Moll, I have missed you. I'm deafer these days, and I can't run any more. It's so dispiriting.' He looked at me and my whiskers shimmied. 'But as long as I can smell you nearby, I don't care.'

I licked his nose very carefully. 'I know, growing older's not for the feeble, is it? I think as long as we keep well, that's the main thing. And anyway, my Titch, life over the rainbow bridge is very special, and we'll meet up there, so there's nothing to worry about.' It wasn't like him to worry over stuff like this. 'Is something bothering you?'

Titch scratched behind his ears. 'A few of the dogs in our area have gone over the rainbow bridge recently. One was hit by a car, another ate rat poisoning. You know, it makes you appreciate what a good life we have.'

'It certainly does, and we must make the most of it,' I replied. 'But neither of us are going anywhere soon, so don't fret.' I could tell he had been dwelling on things, and needed distraction. 'Now, I can hear Tess and Suki returning. Are you ready, my darling?'

Titch got out of the bed and performed a leisurely stretch. Back legs first, then front legs, then all down the spine: nothing like it for waking us up. 'I am if you are. Come on, Moll.'

When the door opened, we both jumped down, a little creakily, and trotted along with Tess and Suki, half listening to their chat. Nowadays I had to get nearer to hear what they were saying, so I decided to keep an eye on Lainy, make sure no harm came to her.

Titch laughed when I told him. 'She's the one who's grown up on the streets, Moll. If anything, she can probably teach us a thing or two.'

He was right, of course, though I didn't like admitting I was wrong. 'I know. But lots of things can upset her; cyclists, joggers, though she's much better since she started running with Suki and Tess. Cars, that's another thing. Certain dogs; she doesn't like labradors or spaniels. Or dachshunds, come to think of it.' I paused. 'Oh, and she doesn't like men wearing hoodies or boots. Or loud, sudden noises.'

There was a slight pause. I wasn't sure if Titch had heard. 'Is there anything she *does* like?' he asked.

I snorted with amusement. 'Well, she seems fine with most dogs once she gets to know them. And she's very affectionate once she feels secure.'

'I see. So we have to vet everyone that comes past?'

My whiskers twitched. 'To be on the safe side. It just makes for an easier walk.'

'Stressful, I would say,' muttered Titch. He liked having me to himself, I'd noticed. And it had been a little stressful at first, looking out for all Lainy's red flags, but it was worth it to make life easier.

I scanned the path ahead, noticed a man ahead wearing red shorts, with a very bouncy spaniel charging ahead of him. We'd met them before, though, so I thought Lainy would be all right. Sure enough, Lainy stepped forward, tail wagging hesitantly, then faster, as they approached. The spaniel didn't seem quite sure, so I called to Lainy, 'be careful!' She wasn't very good at reading Cornish dog signals sometimes.

Suki also called Lainy and ran towards her. Suddenly the spaniel bounced on Lainy in much too rough a fashion for anything that could be called play, and Lainy squealed. 'Back off!', but the other dog took no notice, and bounced on her again.

Lainy squealed again, showing her teeth but the man with the red shorts shouted, 'They're only playing, don't worry! Mine's quite friendly.'

'My dog is very nervous, and she's scared. Can you call your dog off, please?' Suki was trying to separate them and managed to dodge the other dog's teeth.

Tess darted forward and grabbed Lainy's collar, moving her out of harm's way, though the man did nothing to help. 'Will you call your dog off, please?' she shouted, but the man whistled ineffectually to his dog, who kept chasing Lainy, trying to nudge her and bounce on her again, while Suki firmly pushed him away.

We all gathered round Lainy, pushing the spaniel away, muttering calming noises to Lainy, while she panted, showing the whites of her eyes, ears flat against her head.

'Poor girl,' I said. 'Some dogs have no manners. Don't worry, Lainy. You're with us. You'll be fine.'

She didn't reply but shook herself vigorously, several times: a good way to get rid of stress. I could smell the fear and anxiety pouring off her, though.

'Come along, Lainy, let's get out of here,' said Suki. 'Poor girl. What an ignorant man, and his dog was no better. Really!'

We turned to watch the man with red shorts and his dog, who jumped up and down like a bouncing ball, and ran off to target another dog. Suki shook her head. 'Some people are so stupid,' she muttered. She kept Lainy on the lead after that, and she seemed to calm down a bit, though I could still smell the jitters seeping down her whiskers that evening even after we had our tea.

Suki was on the phone to Joe, telling him what had happened. 'I heard that stress stays in the body for up to 72 hours, so we'd better keep Lainy quiet for the next few days,' she said. 'She's had a horrible fright, poor girl.'

'Strange, isn't it,' I heard Joe say. 'That she defended herself on the streets when she was a pup, but got so freaked out today. Poor Lainy.'

'I suppose that was before she had such a horrible time with her first owners,' Suki said. 'That must have really knocked her confidence. She's probably having flashbacks now. I'll go and put some soothing music on.'

'Good idea. See you very soon, Suki. Love to the girls.'

As Suki said goodnight to Joe, I looked over at Lainy, lying in her bed. I could still see the stress rising in thin streams from her coat. She'd shut down to protect herself but I could still smell her sadness. It reminded me of someone, but I couldn't think who it was. Then I realised. It was Zach.

Over the next few days, I noticed that outwardly Lainy seemed calm. She lay on her bed as normal, dozing. But to the observant eye, she was nervy and jittery, smelling of fear. Which made me wonder about Zach, and what had happened to him.

I tried to talk to Lainy, but she found it difficult to express her emotions. 'I must quiet,' she said, her ears still flat on her head, tail down. 'I thank you, Moll, but that was not good situation. On street we fight for food or territory but that different. No Romanian dog jump on other dog like that. Very bad manners.'

'I agree,' I said. 'I tell you what, Lainy. How about we get our own back?'

Lainy lifted her head. 'What you mean?'

'I think it's important to teach him a few rules, don't you? After all, that stupid owner isn't going to teach him anything.'

Slowly Lainy's ears rose. 'What we do? You have idea?'

I lay down with my paws on my nose. 'I have a friend who might be able to help us. Let me think on it for a moment.'

Lainy winked at me which I took as a good sign. Already her stress was lifting, I could smell. Now I had to make a plan to restore Lainy's confidence and make her realise how much she meant to us. I also wanted to teach that monkey some manners. Make sure he never jumped on another dog ever again.

A few days later, having sprayed messages on our local community walls, I was satisfied with the feedback, though I didn't want to let Lainy know. She was still anxious, and I thought she might be more worried if she knew what I was planning. Suki, of course, had no idea.

On the days Suki worked at the office in town, we usually went on to walk near the beaches, or the Castle, where there was a large grassy area called the Hornworks, which happened to be where we'd met Red Shorts the first time. News had spread locally, so by the time we were due for our next Castle walk, I was fairly confident that my plan would go ahead successfully.

Sure enough, after work we trotted through town, along by the Docks and up to the Castle. It was a breezy but sunny day, the type when scents were blown far and fast, and the wind was in our favour. As we neared the Hornworks, my nose twitched frantically. I was pretty sure...

We turned the corner, and at the far end of the Hornworks I spotted Red Shorts, though today he wore green ones, if my eyes served me right. No matter, he and the bouncy spaniel were there. Time for Step Two. I glanced at Lainy who had immediately smelt the dog. Her ears flattened against her head and her nose twitched frantically. Panic rose off her in sour smelling waves.

'Don't worry, Lainy,' I said. 'I've got this planned. This is where that little monster gets his comeuppance.'

She looked at me, whiskers shaking. 'You sure?'

'Positive,' I said. 'Think of your mother. She'd say go and fight, wouldn't she?'

'Of course.' Lainy's nose quivered. 'I not usually so scared, but it horrible when he jump on me. Too many bad memories.'

'And the only way to get rid of those memories is to face them,' I said. 'Do you trust me, Lainy?'

A tear slipped out of one dark eye. 'Yes.'

'So. You do what I say. OK?'

'OK.' Lainy glanced at Suki who was busy stuffing poo bags into her coat while talking to a friend. 'So what we do?'

'Follow me.' I trotted off to the edge of the grassy area. Once there, I sat down and barked, something I rarely did. I waited, then barked again.

'What's the matter, Moll?' Suki came running over. 'What's up, darling?' She looked at Lainy. 'What's going on, you two?'

We ignored her, but I gave another bark, then waited as we sniffed around the rubbish bins, always a rich source of smells and food.

A few minutes later, out of the surrounding woods and paths emerged some of our local friends. George, the Great Dane. Donna the greyhound. Charlie the chocolate Lab. Biscuit, the fiery Jack Russell, and several more besides. 'Come with me,' I instructed Lainy and we trotted to the centre of the Hornworks. All the other dogs ran to meet me, and I could hear Suki laughing.

'I don't know what's going on but it looks like a dogs' convention,' she said to her friend.

I turned away; I had to concentrate. Red Shorts and spaniel seemed oblivious but I knew that soon they'd come in this direction, and sure enough, the spaniel saw us and came running over, tail waving like a flag in high wind. I could see him preparing to launch himself at Biscuit who growled, 'Not a chance, buddy!'

'Wait,' I instructed. 'Let him, if you can put up with it.'

'If I must,' he grunted.

Beside me Lainy was trembling, but surrounded by all the other dogs, I could sense she felt safer. 'Be brave, Lainy. It'll be fine,' I hissed. 'We've got you.'

Just then the spaniel ran towards Biscuit. He took off, evidently without a thought in his head, and landed on Biscuit's back. Biscuit growled and fought him off. The spaniel barked joyously at what a good game it was, then George the Great Dane appeared, who gave the spaniel a hefty nudge, which sent him spinning to the ground.

'Don't do that again,' he growled, pulling himself up to his impressive height.

The spaniel picked himself up off the grass. 'No harm intended,' he said, spitting mud from his mouth. 'Just a bit of fun.'

George elbowed him firmly. 'We all know how to have fun. This is NOT FUN,' he breathed quietly.

The spaniel looked up, the first signs of fear crossing his eyes. 'Er, yeah, whatever,' he said, slinking back as if he suddenly wanted to disappear.

Biscuit shook himself hard, and glared at the spaniel. 'Listen, sonny, how would you like it if we all picked on you?'

Fear squirted out of the spaniel's nose. 'I didn't mean anything. It was only a game.'

'A GAME?' I shouted, stepping forward, nudging Lainy to come with me. 'This poor girl has had hell on the streets of Romania, then was treated really badly by some ignorant idiots, and as a result she has terrible nightmares and panic attacks. Then you go and jump on her. What were you *thinking?*'

Lainy stepped forward. I could smell her fear, but it was manageable now. She knew we had her back, and that gave her courage. 'It not FUN,' she spat. 'It very scary.' And her Romanian accent made it sound all the more frightening.

The spaniel's eyes rolled, showing the whites. His whiskers twitched. I nodded to Bertie, who trotted forward and gave the spaniel a nudge. Caught unawares, he staggered and Bertie, a young dog, barked and yapped in delight. 'Fun!' He shouted. 'Isn't this fun?' He then jumped on the dog, exactly as the spaniel had done to Lainy.

The spaniel whimpered and I started to feel sorry for him, but Lainy stepped forward. 'Is enough!' she called, in her clear voice. 'Enough, Bertie!'

Reluctantly Bertie climbed off the spaniel who tried to slink away, but he was surrounded.

'You realise how it feel, to be jump on?' said Lainy. 'It not good, and it not fun.'

The spaniel cowered. 'No. I'm sorry. It was only meant as a game.'

Bertie stuck his head forward. 'When we want games, we ask, and wait till the other dog says yes. Then you can play. If they say no, you go away. Didn't your parents teach you basic manners?'

The spaniel shook his head, ears flapping noisily. 'My owner thinks it's fun,' he said miserably. 'So I thought it was OK.'

'Talking of which,' I said. 'Where is he?'

We all looked over, to see Red Shorts striding towards us, waving one of those sticks to throw balls. He slowed as he neared us, and stopped a few feet away.

'Bingo?' His voice sounded uncertain. 'What's up?'

Bingo hid behind Bertie. I could smell his shame, but maybe, I hoped, that extended to his owner now. I nudged him. 'It isn't your fault your owner's stupid,' I said. 'But you can teach him some manners. You won't do that again, will you?'

Bingo shook his head again. 'No, I certainly won't.'

'And you'll say sorry to Lainy,' the Great Dane said.

Bingo gulped and turned to Lainy. 'I am sorry,' he said, and I could hear how much it hurt him to apologise. 'I'll be more careful in future.'

Lainy nodded. 'OK,' she said. 'You teach your owner, yes?'

He nodded and looked nervously around at the group of dogs gathered round him.

'In that case, you can go,' I said, and we let him slink away, towards Red Shorts.

They both walked off, and as they neared the car park, Bertie shouted, 'Come on!'

All together we ran towards Red Shorts who looked round, did a double take, and shot off towards the safety of his car.

We arrived in a tangled heap on the Hornworks, barking and panting, tails and whiskers entwined.

'What was all that about?' said Suki. 'You lot looked like you were ganging up on that spaniel.' She looked from me to

Lainy, and noted Lainy's shiny eyes, her grinning mouth. 'Well, whatever it was, you look better, so I trust you know what you're doing.' She paused, looking at the other dogs disentangling themselves. 'Come on then, time for tea I think.'

We stood beside the car park, snorting with amusement as Red Shorts hustled Bertie into his car. 'He won't bother anyone again,' muttered George the Great Dane. 'Good work, Moll. We need to teach these young ones some good manners.'

As Lainy and I trotted along beside Suki on the way home, I noticed that Lainy's tail and ears had resumed their normal perkiness.

'Thank you Moll,' she said, sniffing a particularly good bit of grass. 'That remind me of home, on the street. That how we learn, all together.' She sneezed. 'Like family.' And she gave me a huge wink.

14

Life seemed to settle after that. We listened to a lot of music; Lainy was particularly soothed by Elgar's Enigma Variations, and loved a singer called Joan Armatrading, who she said was a real inspiration. At last Lainy's nightmares decreased which meant we all slept better.

Having been to a talk in Flushing with Joe one evening, from which Suki returned smelling warm and happy, a few nights later they went out again, without us!

'You can tell how much she likes Joe,' I said to Lainy one evening, as we snoozed while we waited for her to return.

'Mmmm,' said Lainy. 'How you tell?'

'Yesterday she put on clean jeans when we went to meet him, even though we were going for a muddy walk.'

Lainy nodded, still half asleep.

'And her senses become sharper when she talks to him,' I added. 'I like the way he makes her feel safe and secure.'

'Like Ted?'

'No, not at all like Ted,' I said, realising how true that was. 'We both loved him perhaps too much.'

'How you love someone too much?' Lainy looked up, astonished. 'You mean he was bad person?'

'Not at all,' I said, my whiskers twitching as I thought of Ted. 'He was a very good man, and he loved us so much, but,' I paused, wondering how to explain. 'He had a very sick wife, so he could never be with us properly.' I paused, remembering the power of that intense love, the anguish at parting, so many times. How could love hurt so much? 'Love like that can be dangerous because you put so much in, and can never get enough back.'

There was silence while Lainy looked at me, her huge dark eyes welling up. 'But that so sad,' she said. 'You and Suki deserve the best.'

I shook my ears, quite overcome. 'Thank you, Lainy,' I said, when I'd recovered my bark. I felt croaky all of a sudden. 'But Joe is not like that.'

'He not have sick wife.'

I laughed. 'No, he doesn't have a sick wife, and he's a very different person. I mean, I think he feels things very deeply, but he keeps his feelings to himself.'

Lainy was quiet for a moment. I thought she was asleep, but she said, 'But now Suki know he like her.'

'Because he kissed her?'

Lainy lifted her head. 'Not just that. Because when he speak he choose words very careful. He not use just any word for Suki.'

I nodded; she was right, now I came to think of it.

'And he watch her when she not looking.'

'He does, yes! And his senses flare up when she's around,' I said. There was also that faint musky smell; different to the one she'd had with Ted, but it was definitely growing.

'I wonder if we should hurry things along,' I said. Then I remembered my past efforts that had, sadly, not led to longlasting happiness. We'd had a lot of fun, but a fair amount of heartache too, and we'd all had enough sorrow. 'No, perhaps we'll let nature take its course,' I decided. 'They should work things out themselves.'

Lainy gave me another wink, and settled down for a snooze. I had to admit, for the moment it was pleasant to have some time without any major conflicts or disasters. It gave us all some breathing space.

A few moments later Suki and Joe returned, together. As soon as they came in through the door, I could sense that something had shifted. The musky smell was stronger than it has been so I was interested to see what would happen.

'Coffee?' Suki said. 'Or a glass of wine?'

'Coffee, thanks.'

Suki boiled the kettle, got out two mugs. 'Do you ever drink?'

A faint waft of unease came from Joe, like a wisp of smoke. 'I enjoy a pint sometimes, or a glass of wine, but I'm not bothered about drinking.' The way he said it made me think there was another story here.

'Did you mind me having a glass of wine in the pub?'

'Of course not,' Joe's voice softened. 'Have a glass now if you want, it doesn't bother me.'

Suki looked at him. 'I'm fine. I'll have a tea, I think. Shall we go next door?'

So they came into the living room and chatted and she put on some music and it was soothing listening to their voices, and time ticked by and I was thinking it was time for bed when Joe said, 'Right, I'd better go.'

He stood up, and so did Suki, and I could tell she wanted to say something but wasn't sure how to say it. They stood facing each other, and then Joe stepped forward and gave her a big hug, as if he didn't want to let her go, and then it was as if everything happened in slow motion, and the hug turned into a kiss, which turned into a long kiss, when they seemed to devour each other, but it was slow and unhurried and then it got fast and they drew back, panting, and Suki looked at him and she was shaking and she said, 'Will you stay?'

He looked at her and the sweetest slow smile crept across his face, lighting up every bit from his mouth to his eyes and every nook and cranny in between, and he said, 'wild horses wouldn't stop me,' and I was a bit worried as I couldn't see any wild horses, but she dragged him into the bedroom and for once she shut the door. Lainy and I looked at each other. She winked and said, 'I no think they need our help.'

After that, Joe stayed most weekends but said he must get home on the Sunday. They laughed a lot, and seemed steady and content, which was lovely to smell. We had new walks and picnics; we had evenings all watching a film on TV; giggles while they prepared food together in the kitchen. It was companionable, cosy and made our flat feel like home again.

There was none of the rollercoaster of passion that there had been with Ted; their love was like a steady flame that didn't flicker. Having said that, they did spend a lot of time in the bedroom, from which they emerged pink and rumpled but smelling of joy. It made me so happy, to think that my promise to Pip was finally coming true, and with someone whom I felt we could all really trust.

Lainy was calmer, too, thanks to the music therapy, but also I think because Joe was a very steadying influence. He didn't panic, his responses were always calm and measured. I never heard him tell her he loved her, but it showed in the way he would buy her favourite food, and cook her dinner. Bring her a book that she'd mentioned. Fix a dripping tap or chop some logs. Little things that spoke of love and care. And, of course, in the way he cared for us, always bringing tasty treats and playing with us.

Suki felt safe with him, which was so important. I was so glad they'd finally got together I felt like pinching myself. Was it really true?

The next week, we were walking through town when we heard scuffling and shouting; smelt fear and anger from a gathering of people in the distance. Lainy went into defence mode: ears up, tail up, senses on full alert. Even her fur stood on end.

The rank smell of fear grew as we got nearer, and then we heard shouting. 'My accordion!' a man cried. 'Get off - don't - aaagh!' The voice sounded familiar, and we ran towards him.

'What's going on?' Suki behind us.

As we got nearer, we realised a young man was trying to grab Zach's accordion. Zach was holding onto it for his life, and the two of them grappled with it while the younger one jabbed at Zach.

'Give me that fucking thing,' he cried, trying to wrench it from Zack's grasp.

'No. Get your hands off,' cried Zach, punching the other man in the stomach.

With a cry of exasperation the younger man doubled over, groaning while Zach panted, still clutching his precious accordion. I watched, feeling utterly useless. I was too slow to be of any help, and I was reluctant to encourage Lainy into more trouble.

'Get off him!' cried Suki. 'Stop that!'

'Leave him alone,' cried a few other voices, but no one dared interfere.

The younger man took no notice, so I edged closer, growling. He took no notice but Lainy launched in, straight for the man's legs. I would have done it myself, but my teeth weren't up to it these days. There was a shriek as she evidently bit through his jeans and 'Shit!' he cried, and abruptly let go of Zach. 'Fucking dog!' He aimed a kick at Lainy which missed her flank but caught her nose, and I could smell the adrenaline flooding her system. She was out for revenge. I had a horrible feeling she'd get into real trouble, so I barked, 'NO, Lainy!'

I could sense her anger, hot, strong, and focused on the younger man. Lainy smelt of past hurt, of pain, and loss and grief, wrapped up in her need for revenge. She charged again at the man, but this time he realised what was happening and turned round.

'Get off, you fucking dog,' he cried, and aimed another kick at her which thankfully missed. Lainy bared her teeth, and even I was frightened by the sight of her. She was magnificent and terrifying in her rage. Glorious and strong and indomitable. The sort of dog she deserved to be.

The younger man evidently realised this too, for he started running down the street. Lainy chased him, despite our cries for her to stop, but he dived into a shop and slammed the door behind him, while she stood, barking at the door.

Suki and I ran to Lainy and Suki put on her lead, stroking her, trying to calm her down, though I noticed Suki was trembling too. 'What a brave girl,' she said. 'You are amazing, Lainy. Shame you had to bite him, but what a bastard. Who could do such a thing? Trying to steal Zach's accordion? And kick a dog? It's terrible. What sort of scum...'

'I'll see if he's in the shop, love,' said one of the onlookers, hurrying inside. Brave, I thought. That man was desperate. There were a tense few moments before the onlooker came out again shaking his head. 'He must have escaped through the back door,' he said. 'There's a service lane out the back, he must have gone down there.'

'Thanks for looking,' said Suki, as Zach appeared, clutching his accordion to his chest like a drowning man's lifebelt.

His breath came in short gasps, and I could smell the acidic panic emanating from him, mixed with a stronger chemical scent. I thought he'd speak, but he just stood there, gasping, while Suki looked up at him.

'Are you OK?' she said. 'You don't - oh hang on, he's having a panic attack.' She rummaged in her pocket and pulled out a paper bag that had earlier contained a piece of cake. She shook the crumbs out and said, 'Here, Zach, blow into it.'

He looked at her, wide eyed and panting, just like Lainy did when she was terrified.

'Just do as I say,' Suki insisted. 'Look, I'll take the accordion. Make a balloon shape with the bag, like this, and blow into it.' She shaped the bag and handed it over.

Zach relinquished his precious accordion, took the paper bag and blew.

'And again. Do it several times,' she instructed. 'One, two, three, four...'

Zach blew out, then gasped as the air hit his lungs. He blew out, and in. Out and in. Out and in. I glanced at Lainy, who was trying to mimic his movements. She couldn't breathe into a paper bag, but she was trying to use the same calming techniques, bless her.

Finally Zach stopped, lowered the paper bag and looked at Suki. He was breathing normally again. 'Thank you, that's so much better,' he said. 'How did you know what to do?'

Suki looked down and stroked Lainy as if her life depended on it. 'It's a trick I learned,' she said. 'I had panic attacks years ago and it really helped me.' She tried to smile. 'Except that nowadays it's difficult to find a paper bag.' She handed over the accordion. 'Here you are.'

'Thank you.' Zach took his precious accordion and looked down at Lainy and me, keeping guard over Suki. He smelled calmer, but the chemical smell was still there. 'I have all of you to thank for coming to my rescue,' he said, looking fondly at Lainy. 'She was incredible. She's so fast, isn't she?'

'She certainly is, and extremely brave,' Suki said proudly, continuing to stroke Lainy. Long, thorough strokes that helped flush stress and adrenaline out of her body. 'She's a very special dog. As is Moll, of course. I'm just glad we were passing.' Suki looked around. 'Listen, let's get out of here. Why don't you come back and have a drink and some food? I need to get these two home after all that excitement.'

Zach hesitated, then Lainy gave a quick yip. He looked down at her and gave that lovely smile so a dimple peeked through, and I caught a whiff of understanding. One wounded soldier to another. 'OK, thanks,' he said, and gave Lainy a gentle stroke that she seemed to enjoy. 'That would be good.'

And so our walk was curtailed, but we went round the back of the town, away from the rapidly dispersing people, along the side streets and into Kimberley Park, where we could have a sniff and a breather before arriving home.

Suki and Zach were quiet as we trotted along, lost in their thoughts perhaps, and I wanted to keep an eye on Lainy, as I knew Suki did too. But there was definitely a strong connection between Zach and Lainy, and that was enough to solidify the connection between Zach and Suki.

Lainy was quiet now. Her breathing had returned to normal but I could smell the potent cocktail of hormones still flooding through her. Yet another 72 hours of keeping poor Lainy quiet to let her de-stress.

Zach sat at our kitchen table, a mug of tea in front of him, the accordion close by his side, while Lainy and I watched from our respective beds. The peppery smell of stress and fear clung to his jacket, stuck to his jeans, along with the faint chemical smell that was part of him.

Suki was busy making a huge sandwich with thickly cut fresh bread and slabs of tangy cheddar and sweet and sour pickle. Lainy and I looked at each other, noses quivering.

'There you are,' she said, placing it in front of Zach.

He looked at the food with awe, then tucked in as if he hadn't eaten for a long while. He was certainly skinny enough: his jeans looked several sizes too big, and his wrists poked out from underneath his sleeves like fragile branches. When he crossed his legs, once more I saw the angry marks on his legs, but this time Suki noticed too, for I saw her freeze, and she couldn't seem to look away.

The sandwich disappeared in minutes, then he sat back. I could almost smell the food hitting his system, seeping its way round his blood stream. Colour crept back into his face as he sipped his tea and finally he looked at Suki and smiled.

'Thanks so much,' he said. 'You make a brilliant sarnie.' A dimple appeared in one cheek, and Suki smiled back, relaxing now.

'My pleasure,' she said. 'Another one?'

'No, that was perfect thanks.' He smiled at her. 'You're very good to me.'

Suki shrugged. 'I'm only doing what anyone would do.' She hesitated. 'Do you have friends or family here?'

He looked down at his hands and I noticed scabs and other red marks on them. He twisted his fingers while we waited, the silence growing like a piece of thread that grew longer and more string-like by the moment. Lainy lay not far away from him, her head on her paws. She fixed him with one of her stares, then winked.

He seemed to take comfort and perhaps strength from this, for he said, 'No. I don't have contact with my family any more.'

'Why not?' Suki asked gently.

Zach drained his mug. 'My dad was a surgeon and wanted us all to follow him into medicine. I wanted to be a musician, but Dad didn't think music was a suitable career, so to cut a long story short, I qualified as a medic and eventually I became part of the Medical Emergency Response Team.'

'What does that do?' Suki said.

'We worked in various disaster zones, usually getting badly injured soldiers to hospital as quickly as possible.'

Suki was quiet for a moment. 'That must have been very highly pressured.'

'It was,' he said.

'What drew you to that kind of work?'

He looked down, scratching absently at a scab on his wrist. 'I've always had a low boredom threshold, so being a medic was a great challenge, and working in the ERT meant we had to make really important decisions quickly and I liked the adrenaline of all that, yet we all had to be calm and confident, and sort out problematic situations very quickly.' He shook his head. 'Can't believe I ever did that now.'

Suki leaned forward. 'Go on.'

I could smell exhaustion seeping though him like a winter fog. 'I liked working in a small unit. We became close friends, and we all knew what it was like to operate under that pressure. One small slip and you've lost someone's life. Timing was so important.'

'So what happened?' Suki's voice was almost a whisper.

Another long silence while we waited. Then Zach cleared his throat. 'One day Tom, who was a good friend, led the way into a bombed building to try and get some of our guys out. I was following, but suddenly the warehouse caught fire while Tom was inside. The fire brigade were on their way, but I ran after him, to try and get him out, but the fire took hold so fast...'

I could almost see the poor man and the burning building. Poor Zach...

'I got him out, but he had terrible burns and died on the way to hospital.' Zach's voice was hoarse. 'I've never forgiven myself. I should have been the one to go into that building first. I could have saved his life then.'

We sat there, stunned. The misery and distress in the room was so stifling, I could hardly breathe.

'That's where you got those burns?' Suki said.

He looked up, as if he'd forgotten she was there. 'How did you know?'

'Your trousers rode up. I saw them then,' she said. 'You must have been burned very badly.'

He looked down. 'Five degree burns. I was sent to a burns unit where they treated me, took skin grafts and patched me up as much as they could. But after what happened to Tom, there was no way I could go back to work. Not there.'

'Did you see your family while you were convalescing?'

'Yes. But my father didn't understand why I couldn't face going back. He said I should just carry on, not let something like that stop me. We had a big fallout.'

'You poor thing,' said Suki and I thought, oh no. She's going to want to try and save him now. 'Of course you couldn't go back. Were you able to talk to anyone about what had happened?'

He shook his head. 'No. The rest of the team understood, of course, but they weren't as close as Tom and I were. They carried on working, but I couldn't talk to them about it. And I didn't have any other friends who weren't medics. So I felt ... useless. And in a lot of pain.'

'You've got painkillers?'

He nodded. 'Yes. I need them all the time. The pain is terrible. In fact I need my next lot now. Could I have a glass of water?'

Suki got up and poured him a glass, handed it over. He took the water, felt in his pockets for a pack of pills and took a couple. 'Thanks,' he said.

'And you get panic attacks as part of the PTSD?'

Zach nodded.

'Have you had any help?'

'Music helps,' he said. 'So I taught myself to play the accordion. It's more portable than a piano.' He smiled and his green eyes glinted like a cat's.

'How many siblings do you have?'

'One brother and a sister.'

'Do you see either of them?'

'I don't see Michael much since he moved to France. He runs a vineyard over there. My sister and I were close but she got married and now they live in London and they've got kids so I don't see much of her now.' Regret and loss oozed from his words.

'You must miss her.'

He nodded. 'I do. Very much.'

I could sense Suki wanted to comfort him, to give him a hug, but she held back. 'You haven't mentioned your mum.'

He twisted his long fingers once more. 'She died when I was six. Brain tumour.' He smelt of loss, anger and intense sorrow. A horrible smell, like rusty metal and sour milk mixed together.

'I'm so sorry. You have had a rough time.' Suki was quiet for a moment. 'Do you have any other friends here?'

'A few.' But he sounded unsure, and I had the feeling that he didn't have any.

Again, Suki didn't say anything though I suspected she thought the same thing. 'When did you come to Falmouth?'

'Eight months ago.' His voice sounded flat and defensive. 'That's when I started playing the accordion properly.'

'Really? You're so good.' She took a deep breath. 'Have you got any work other than your gigs?'

He stared at his feet, which were encased in heavy boots that looked thin on the soles from where I lay. Now I looked closer, there was a hole in the tip of one. 'I work in the Kings Head, washing up,' he said. 'And I applied to Tesco but they hadn't got any vacancies. They said to come back next month though.'

Suki's nose twitched, which meant she was thinking hard. 'And where do you live? I've forgotten.'

He shifted, and that peppery awkward smell filled the air. 'A house share, but it's not very...' He looked up. 'I'd like to find somewhere else, but there's so little to rent at the moment and it's difficult when landlords want a month's deposit in advance, and they want proof of residence, that sort of thing.'

'So the houseshare doesn't count?' she said gently.

'Er, no, not really.'

'It's like a squat, you mean?'

'Yes, sort of.' He looked up and gave an apologetic shrug.

'So you'd like to find somewhere else to live?' Her voice, gentle but persistent.

He nodded. 'Yes, but I don't have much money for rent. That's the problem.'

'Have you tried the CAB? Also, a friend of mine works for a housing charity. He might be able to help.' She pulled out her phone and I had a strong sense that she was going to start making lots of phone calls.

I barked, a few sharp yips. Suki looked at me and smiled. 'Quite right, Moll. Now, Zach, I'll write down a few phone numbers for you.' She paused. 'Do you want to charge your phone?'

He flushed pink. 'That's really kind.' He stood up, pulled his phone out of his pocket, handed it over. 'Thank you. I don't want to impose...'

'It's fine. It'll fit this charger,' Suki said briskly. As she stood with her back to him, she said, in a voice that was deceptively casual, 'have you had panic attacks before?' She paused. 'I only ask because I had them in the past, so I know how horrible they are. You get scared in case you have another one, so you stop doing anything that might bring on an attack.'

Zach nodded. 'That's exactly it. I've been thinking I was going mad, and ...'

'Yes, I know,' Suki said gently. 'But I got over them, so you can, too,'

'How?'

'You really do need to talk to a trained counsellor; I'm sure they'd be able to help. Your panics are obviously because of that awful time you had in the fire with your friend.'

'I couldn't talk to a stranger,' he said. 'You're the only person I've ever told what really happened.'

His words sank heavily into the room and lingered like a strong fart. Oh no, I thought. And then Suki and Zach exchanged a look that smelt like matured Cheddar, or sour milk. I wasn't sure that it was a good feeling, for it smelt of past hurt and it was very strong. Too powerful for my liking.

Suki opened her mouth and I had a feeling she was about to offer something else when the doorbell rang. Lainy and I barked loudly, just in case Suki hadn't heard, but also because I could smell who it was; two of my favourite people!

I ran to the door and barked louder, jumping up and down as Suki opened the door. I heard her cry of delight, and Titch and I snickered to each other, nuzzling our muzzles, sniffing our bums and I led the way back to the kitchen. Suki followed, chatting away to Tess as if they hadn't seen each other for months, instead of days. 'Zack's here,' she said, as they walked down the corridor.

'Oh?' Just one word encapsulated so much.

'I'll explain later,' Suki hissed. 'Zach. You remember my friend Tess? And Titch.'

Zach got up hurriedly, knocking over his chair. 'Hello,' he mumbled. 'I was just going...'

'Oh, don't go on my account,' Tess said cheerfully.

'Poor Zach had a run in with some idiot who tried to steal his accordion. Luckily Lainy saved the day.'

'What?' Tess looked at Zach and her pony tail whipped round. 'Do you know the guy who attacked you?'

'I... I don't think so.'

'What happened?'

'I was walking along when I heard yelling behind me, then someone running, then this guy jumped on me from behind and tried to grab my accordion. I shouted at him but he thumped me. Luckily Suki and these two came along and saved me,' he said with that shy dimple.

'The guy was attacking Zach, so Lainy jumped in and bit him on the leg,' said Suki.

'She bit someone?' Tess said.

'Only in self defence,' Suki said, and pride ballooned out of her as she smiled fondly at Lainy. 'That stopped him, though he hit her a few times before running off. Lainy ran after him but he dived into a shop and disappeared. Probably just as well as I think she would have really gone for him.'

Lainy came over, stretched her back, then her front legs, and sat beside Tess, her head on one side.

'Good girl,' Tess said, stroking her velvet ears. 'Did anyone else see what happened?'

'A few people,' Suki said. 'I wasn't sure what to do. I wanted to help, but I didn't fancy getting thumped by this bloke. I nearly rang the police, but I thought they'd take ages to arrive and it'd be too late by then. So I was standing there feeling frightened and useless, while Lainy jumped in and frightened him off.'

'So she chased him down the road and this guy disappeared into a shop?' Tess said. 'I suppose he probably jumped out of a window at the back of the store.' She turned to Zach. 'Are you going to report it?'

'No,' Zach said quickly, then flushed. 'I don't want to involve the police.'

'Zach hasn't got anywhere proper to stay,' Suki explained. 'The police can be a bit funny about that sort of thing. But it's difficult getting accommodation when you don't have much work.'

'Ah. Yes, that is difficult,' Tess said, giving Suki a fixed glare.

'I've just given Zack a few phone numbers,' she said. 'CAB and stuff; they might help.'

'Good,' said Tess, relaxing slightly. 'I wonder if anyone filmed what happened on their phone? Then there'd be some evidence of this guy. The police probably know him anyway.'

'I hope so,' said Suki. 'No one should get away with that sort of behaviour.'

'I must go,' Zach said, standing up. 'Thank you so much, Suki, and glad to see you, Tess.'

'We're coming to your gig on Thursday, so we'll see you then,' Tess said. 'Good luck with the housing problem.'

'Thanks,' he said, and reaching for his accordion, his jacket and phone, he headed down the corridor and we heard the slam of the door as he left the flat.

'Well done for not taking over his life,' Tess said. 'I note that you couldn't help getting involved, but given the circumstances, that's allowable.'

'I couldn't just ignore him, poor man,' Suki said. 'Anyone who can play music like that deserves to be helped. But I was very restrained.'

'Well done,' Tess laughed and gave a huge yawn. 'I must go. I thought I'd call in as we were passing. Walk on Wednesday?'

'Yes, that's perfect,' Suki said, as Tess got up.

Titch and I bade a cheery goodbye; after all, Wednesday was only two days away.

But after they went, my thoughts turned to Lainy. For while she had saved Zach and his accordion, I recalled a conversation I'd overheard shortly after the bite near Suki's eye. Suki had gone for a check up at the hospital and was upset at the doctor's reaction. 'He said that if Lainy bit anyone again, she might have to wear a muzzle. Or even be put down,' she'd said in outraged tones. 'How dare he?'

I wondered if Suki had remembered this. Either way, from now on it wasn't just Suki I had to look after. I had to protect Lainy, too.

15

For the next few days I watched Lainy carefully. She was still quite jittery; once again, stress and anxiety, fear and anger were a dangerous cocktail, but we had quiet walks where we met few people, which helped us be extra vigilant with Lainy.

I was also unsure about this smell coming from Suki when she mentioned Zach. The odour kept changing, but it was so strong it caught in my nostrils, and got stuck on my whiskers. Strong smells meant strong feelings, and we had learned through Ted that strong feelings tended to lead to unhappiness, so I wanted to steer Suki clear of that. Yet Zach was much younger than her. Surely nothing would happen?

I mentioned it to Titch when we had our walk, but he was dismissive. 'Don't be silly, darling. You're worrying about nothing.'

'But the smell...'

He sniffed. 'No, I can't smell anything. You, on the other paw, smell delightful as always, dearest Moll.'

Much though I loved him, he could be very dense at times.

We had a walk with Joe a couple of days later. Suki had already told him what had happened with Zach, but he asked questions and listened carefully as Suki answered. I liked the way he did that, as if he was sniffing the words, then tasting them before replying.

'And Lainy flew at the guy,' Suki continued. 'She was so fast. I suppose she was protecting me. Or maybe Zach.'

Joe was silent.

'I mean, she has met Zach a few times,' Suki continued. 'I do feel for him, having PTSD and no family support. Perhaps Lainy recognised a kindred spirit, and wanted to look after him?'

Joe looked at her and I smelt that he wasn't very happy with that answer. 'Maybe. Or perhaps the situation was similar to one she'd been in before. She might have been frightened and had to fight for her survival. Or maybe she hadn't been *able* to fight, and this time she could.'

'Yes...' I could hear Suki mulling this over.

Joe looked at Lainy, trotting ahead with her ears pricked up. I was sure she was listening. 'If you think of the scary experiences she's had,' he continued, 'she has good reason to have a go at someone who looks, or smells, dodgy. Especially if they're attacking someone she knows.'

'She doesn't like men wearing hoodies, I've noticed,' Suki said. 'Or very big people. Or people wearing black.' She paused. 'Though actually this guy was quite skinny and wearing jeans and a dark jacket.'

'Perhaps it's not so much what they're wearing but what they smell like, or something they do that triggers her,' Joe said.

'Yes, maybe.' She paused. 'I wonder why he tried to steal Zach's accordion? I mean, if you're going to rob someone, you'd go after their money, wouldn't you?'

'Aren't accordions valuable?'

'Zach said he got it from a secondhand shop, so the chances are it's not worth that much.'

'Perhaps the guy had it in for Zach for some other reason. I don't suppose we'll ever know. The main thing is to make sure Lainy's not too disturbed by the incident.'

'Or Zach,' Suki added. 'I'd be upset, wouldn't you?'

Joe looked at her. 'I would, yes.' He seemed to be on the verge of saying something else, but then he said, 'Shall we have a quick run? Just to that far tree over there and back?'

'Yes, of course.' Suki turned to me. 'That OK with you, Moll? You can follow at your own pace, can't you, darling? Or have a little rest.'

I sat down, glad of a few minutes on my own. All this talk about upset wasn't good for my guts. I watched them run ahead, Lainy first and fast: I could smell the exhilaration streaming from her coat, leaving an excited vapour trail. Then Joe, steady behind her, followed by Suki, who caught him up, and passed him.

I smelt her laughter bubbling up, ready to burst out in a happy torrent. 'Last one to the tree's a sissy!'

Joe pushed ahead, but Lainy shot ahead like a bullet. She was so speedy, and elegant to watch, but made me realise how slow I'd become. I lay down for a minute and waited for them to return, hot and panting, laughing and steaming.

'That was brilliant,' said Suki. 'And I don't get nearly as breathless any more.'

'You're so much fitter, it's really noticeable,' said Joe. 'Now, shall we have a quick coffee before we head home?'

'If you've got time.' Suki reached down and stroked my ears gently, the way I liked.

'Yes, my next job isn't till five,' said Joe. 'My turn for coffee, I think.'

They turned and we headed back to where the cars were parked, the others blowing like cattle as they cooled down.

Lainy trotted along beside me, her ears twitching, and I was sure I heard her mutter, 'Bastard.'

I was shocked. 'Lainy! Joe isn't like that, he's...'

'Not Joe,' she hissed. 'The one who try steal accordion. He smell like man at kill shelter. Of chemical. He smell of anger and he kick me so I bite him, and then he kick me again, so I bite him again. I hate him. And other man, at my first home he smell like that, too. He shout and hit me, and lock me outside. I hate him too.'

She sounded so vehement that I was quite shocked, and a little frightened. I'd seen scared Lainy, nervous Lainy, joyous Lainy, and affectionate Lainy, but angry Lainy was quite intimidating.

I was about to reply, when Joe leaned forward and stroked Lainy with a long, slow, massage down her back. She didn't allow many people to do that, but I could see she not only allowed it, but welcomed the feeling. Her tail went up and her nose quivered at his touch.

'Poor girl,' he said quietly. 'You were very brave. And I don't blame you for having a pop at that bloke. No one should steal things, or attack people. Trouble is, we have certain rules here and I don't want you to get into trouble.' He smiled at her. 'Mind you, we need police dogs like Lainy to take charge on the streets. That would certainly cut down on crime!'

He put his arm round Suki and they both laughed, but I could see Lainy's nose twitching, as well as her ears. I only hoped Joe hadn't given her any ideas, and that she wouldn't take matters into her own paws.

That evening I was snoozing after tea, while Suki worked: I could hear the rattle of her keyboard, but she'd left the television on for us in the living room, and Lainy was watching the screen intently. Her head was slightly tilted to one side, and her ears pricked up. I never bothered with the news, but now I tuned in, to see what was so interesting.

'... and now we turn to Minister of State for Crime and Policing,' said the presenter, turning to a man in a suit. 'Good evening, Minister. Crime figures are at an all time high, and still rising. So what can be done about it? There are no policemen on the streets nowadays, and most police stations have shut - is it any wonder that there's so much offending?'

The suit man muttered about the amount of money the government had spent on policing, but didn't say anything about how to get crime rates down. Or had I misheard? No, it appeared not, for the interviewer sounded quite angry.

'As I said, Minister, what can be *done* to get crime rates *down*? If there are no police to help if someone is robbed on the streets, surely the only way people can protect themselves, and others, is to take matters into their own hands?'

'Certainly not,' came the reply. 'We have a police force to deal with criminals. But it's clear that the rising number of immigrants in our communities has had an impact on the level of crime. This is one of the reasons why crime rates have risen recently...'

I stopped listening, because Lainy was staring fixedly at the screen, obviously taking in every word. I had a horrible feeling she was getting some dangerous ideas.

'Lainy, I know you did amazingly well helping Zach with his accordion, but it's not a good idea to do that again, it really isn't.'

She turned to me, dark eyes blazing. 'That stupid man, he say it is fault of immigrants. Well that is me! I am immigrant! And it not my fault! I know maybe there are stupid peoples who do crimes but not me. I need to show there are good immigrants, then people will not look down on us. They will not look at Romanian and think, ah they cause troubles. They steal things.'

She had a point, but I didn't like to encourage her. 'Yes, but ...' how could I change her mind? 'Surely you can set a better example by being good?' It sounded a bit feeble, even to my ears. 'I mean, you don't need to use violence to get a message across. That's sinking to the criminals' levels.'

Lainy's ears went down, then up to half mast. Her head tilted to the other side, and her nose twitched. 'But Joe, he say I very good. He say you need police dog like me to cut down crime on street.'

'It was a joke, Lainy.'

She snorted. 'Not very funny joke.'

'I know what you mean,' I said, trying to mollify her. 'But we don't want you getting into trouble.' I paused, trying desperately to think of something that she would take notice of. And then I remembered a conversation I'd overheard between Suki and Tess. 'Over here, if a dog bites someone, the owner can get into trouble with the police. Sometimes the dog can be taken away. Or even put down.'

'Put down? Where?'

My nose twitched. 'It means... killed.'

'There are kill shelters here?' Lainy looked at me, her eyes black and huge.

'No, but if the police think a dog is dangerous, or if they bite someone, they can ... Do things.'

Fear steamed off Lainy's coat, enveloping her in a white fog. 'I not know that,' she whispered. 'They as bad as Rapitori.'

'Not that bad,' I said, though really I didn't know. 'But if a dog attacks someone, and if the police think the dog is out of control, they can be... put down. Because the dog is dangerous.'

'But dog is not dangerous, it have good reason to attack,' she cried. 'No dog attack for nothing.'

I sighed. 'I know, Lainy, but humans don't necessarily understand that. And our life is run by humans.'

Lainy lay down, her ears flicking back and forth. I could see confusion and outrage swirling around her in a thick, constantly moving mist.

'Please, Lainy,' I said. 'Don't do anything to upset Suki. She's been through so much.'

Lainy looked at me. 'I never do anything to upset Suki!' she protested. 'How you think that?'

'I know you wouldn't deliberately, but if you want to do something, just check with me first, OK?' I said. 'We do things differently here.'

Lainy wrinkled her nose. 'But you believe in justice?'

I stared at her. Where did these words come from? 'Of course,' I said. 'But not violence. I think you're watching too much television.'

'But you make sure that dog learn his lesson last week. We all teach him what is wrong. That could have been violent.'

I felt slightly uneasy. 'I... well, yes. But it *wasn't* violent. That was different.'

'Why?'

'Because we... we decided together.'

'Ah yes, I know. That is democracy!'

I wasn't sure of that word and felt myself on dangerous ground. 'Yes, well, it's all right if we all decide together.'

'OK,' she said. 'So we all decide together?'

I nodded with such relief that my ears flapped. 'Yes. And we decide to keep Suki happy.'

'Of course,' said Lainy. 'We always keep Suki happy.' And she lay down and winked at me.

16

All went quiet after that, thank dog. Lainy still watched the news with avid interest, and muttered at the ineptitude of politicians. Ineptitude was a new word that I'd heard on the radio and liked very much. Even if I didn't know what it meant.

One afternoon, Suki was next door working and had left the radio on Classic FM for us, or rather, Lainy.

'This is boring, tinkly music. Pah! I like heavy rock.' Lainy snorted.

'Heavy rock?' I said. 'What's that?'

'Ah no, it is hard rock.'

'Hard? Heavy? What's the difference?'

'It loud and ... expressive,' she said.

'But you don't like noise that hurts your ears,' I reminded her. 'You said it gives you nightmares.'

Lainy shrugged. 'That different type of music.'

I gave up, and decided to snooze, thinking of tomorrow, when we were due to meet Titch and Tess again. My darling Titch...

Just then Suki's phone rang. She answered it rather abruptly; she didn't like to be disturbed when she was working. She got up, walked out of the bedroom and down the hall. 'Slow down,' she said. 'Hang on, she said what?' Pause. 'OK, where are you? I'll come and get you. Stay right there. Don't move.'

She finished the call and ran into the kitchen, muttering, 'car keys, where did I put them?' She must have found them, for she dashed back into the living room, to say, 'That was Zach. He's in a terrible state. I'd better go and bring him back here, then I'll take him to the CAB, he needs proper help. Stay here, girls. Won't be a minute.'

And she shot out of the door.

Lainy and I exchanged looks. 'I thought she promise not help people,' Lainy said.

'She did. But she can't say no to someone in need. And I think he reminds her of you a bit.'

'Me?' Lainy smelt outraged. 'I nothing like him!'

'No, I mean, he's had a bad time and he needs help.'

'Oh.' Lainy's nose twitched. 'You mean, he come live here?'

'Oh no,' I said, 'at least, I hope not.'

A few minutes later Suki burst through the door, with Zach. His face was white, but his eyes were red; he smelt a terrible mess. The chemical smell was very bad, and sadness and panic streamed from him, in unstoppable tears.

'Come in,' she said, firmly. 'We'll have a drink and something to eat.' She pointed to a chair. 'Sit there.'

Swaying, he sank onto the chair, while Suki filled the kettle and rummaged in the fridge, produced bacon, then bread and eggs. She said nothing to Zach, but turned the volume up on the radio so Classic FM played a little louder. Gradually Zach's tears slowed, he stopped swaying, and Lainy and I lay on the floor near Suki as she fried bacon, then eggs, the smells filling the kitchen so our noses were going into overdrive by the time it was ready.

When she'd made mugs of tea, and put a plateful of bacon and eggs in front of him, he ate, slowly at first, then really fast, like we do. Lainy edged nearer and sat beside him. I don't think he even registered she was there, and at first I thought she wanted some bacon rind (of course), but then I realised she was giving him some quiet understanding. Good for her.

When Zach had finished eating, which didn't take long, he blew his nose and sighed as the colour began to seep back into his face. 'Thank you so much, I needed that,' he said.

Suki looked at him. 'Can you tell me what happened?'

He looked down at his plate. 'It's all such a mess, I don't know where to start.' He closed his eyes, and shook his head, as if he was trying to get rid of something horrible. 'I get flashbacks,' he whispered. 'Going into that building, trying to get Tom out. The noise of the flames, the wall of heat... the sound of him screaming... Yesterday there was a fire on TV. Then last night, I couldn't sleep, and strange voices were shouting at me. Telling me what to do. What not to do. Laughing, mocking me for being stupid. And I can't get rid of them.' He blew his nose again.

'Have you got a cold?'

'Don't know.' He put his head in his hands. 'I don't feel safe, except when I play music, but I can't do that where I live, because the others complain, and I can't go out in the middle of the night, because I'd wake people up, and that's when it's worse. The painkillers used to help, but they don't so much now. And yesterday we were told we've all got to find somewhere else to live and I can't afford proper rent and ...' his voice trailed off and he gasped as his breathing came in shallow bursts.

Suki got up, rummaged in a kitchen drawer for a paper bag and handed it over. 'Blow into that,' she said firmly. 'Come on, blow.'

Dogs can hear a fast heart beat, and his sounded like it was going to jump out of his body. No wonder he was frightened. Gradually, as he blew, his heartbeat returned to normal.

He stopped and looked up at Suki. 'I've really fucked up,' he said, and his voice broke.

'No you haven't. You're just having a hard time.'

At this point, Lainy laid her nose on Zack's lap and looked up at him. He started crying again, silently, but he stroked the top part of her head, which is really soft. He must have stroked a bit hard, because Lainy went pop eyed, but she put up with it, which earned her a lot of treats in my book. And Suki's, judging by the look on her face.

'You haven't fucked up,' she repeated. 'But you do need help. I'll take you to the CAB and they will give you free advice, and there's someone who deals specifically with housing.'

Zach looked up, as if seeing her for the first time. 'Thank you. But there's a huge housing shortage, and so much competition for whatever housing there is, and ...'

'I know,' she said. 'But one step at a time, OK? Can you try and talk to someone about your panic attacks?'

He shook his head. 'I couldn't. No one would believe me.'

'They will,' she insisted. 'I was just like you. I didn't think anyone would listen to me, either. But they did, and it turns out panic attacks are really common.' She waited a moment. 'Also, lots of people suffer from PTSD.' She spoke as if to a young child. 'I know someone who might be able to help.' She paused. 'Wouldn't it be a huge relief not to feel so terrified all the time?'

He nodded.

'Good. But first of all, I will take you to the CAB, who are really kind and helpful, and if we go now, you should be able to see someone without making an appointment, though you may need to wait a while.'

Zach nodded. 'OK.'

'So we'll go shall we?' Suki's voice was calm but firm.

He nodded again.

'And I know someone who works for the Salvation Army, they may be able to help, too,' she smiled. 'Come on.'

Slowly he got up, like a shaky old man rather than a young one. He looked around the kitchen, as if he wasn't sure where he was. Then he looked at Lainy, and me, and gave us a faint smile, dimple and all. 'Thanks so much,' he said, though his voice was so quiet we could hardly hear it.

When we met Tess and Titch the next day, I was even more glad to see them. There was something about Zach I wasn't sure about. 'I can't quite put my paw on it,' I said to Titch.

'He has many problems,' Titch said. 'Isn't that enough to make you unsure?'

'Yes, but ...' then I suddenly realised what my unease was really about. 'Actually, I've just realised, we haven't seen much of Joe recently. He's been coming over to spend weekends with us, but I don't think they've talked for several days.'

Titch looked at me. 'Why is that?'

'I suppose her time's been taken up with Zach.'

'Do you think Joe is jealous?'

I yipped a laugh. 'No! It's not like that.' But come to think of it, Joe did smell strange whenever Zach was mentioned. 'I don't know,' I added. 'Maybe Tess will know.' So we trotted back to where Tess and Suki were walking, talking non-stop as they always did.

'So how did Zach get on with the CAB?' Tess said, skirting a large puddle.

'Zach said he's now on a housing list for several places, but he's also been given a few phone numbers of people who let out a room in their house. That might suit him better, as it's cheaper than normal rent.'

'That's encouraging,' said Tess. 'What about counselling?'

'He's got to sign on with a GP which of course he can't do till he's got somewhere to live. It's this catch 22 situation. But once he's done that there are several charities that can help people with PTSD so that's worth looking into.'

'There's a lot more awareness of mental health, isn't there?' Tess said. 'We were watching a thriller on TV the other night, and the detective had PTSD and panic attacks. A few years ago, no one would ever have put anything like that into a film.'

'No, but that's progress,' Suki said. She was wearing dangly earrings today which was usually a good sign. 'The more people that know about it, the better. We need much more understanding about mental health.'

Tess looked at Suki. 'You said you had panic attacks, a while ago,' she said carefully. 'Was it difficult to acknowledge that you needed help?'

'Very,' said Suki. 'I felt really ashamed of myself. Originally I'd had a panic attack in the car, so after that Pip did nearly all of the driving. I mean, he was doing it to help me, but in a way that made it worse because I was terrified that I'd have another panic attack if I got behind the wheel. I got really paranoid about driving and completely lost my confidence.'

'So what made you realise you had to get help?'

Suki twiddled a curl by her left ear. She often did this when she was thinking. 'I had to drive to visit Pip in hospital, to start with. I mean, it was only half an hour, and I was so worried about Pip, I didn't think about having a panic attack.' She paused. 'After Pip died, I was really freaked out. Terrified. But Pip wasn't there any more, so I had to drive. I heard a piece on the radio about panic attacks, and how they're much easier to deal with if you have counselling, so I saw my GP and she referred me to the counsellor who worked with the surgery.'

Tess threw a stick for Lainy; Titch and I were a bit aged for that sort of thing nowadays. 'Was it a relief to talk to someone about it?'

'Sort of,' Suki said. 'I was worried they'd think I was bonkers, but it turns out panic attacks are very common, and I was given some good coping strategies, which I still use when I need to.'

'But you wouldn't say you had PTSD?'

'No, though of course many people with PTSD do have panic attacks.' She looked at Tess closely. 'What are you thinking?'

'That it's so difficult to get someone to realise they need help,' she said. 'Sometimes that's harder than actually *getting* help, I think. Breaking down all our barriers about being strong and not asking for help, not wanting anyone to know, and all that.'

'Yes, that's exactly it,' said Suki. 'Even though people understand more about mental health now, I still felt it was a weakness. That I was doing something wrong. I was a failure. And I didn't think anyone would be able to help. Whereas nowadays there are several charities that can help with all kinds of problems.'

'Even so,' said Tess. 'It seems weird that it's easier to get help for Lainy's PTSD than it is for Zach.'

'Yes, I hadn't thought of it that way before,' Suki said. 'But I suppose we can help dogs without asking their permission. Also there's much more help around for dogs thanks to skilled animal behaviourists like you.'

'Thanks,' said Tess. 'In a way it's easier to treat dogs like Lainy. For example, quiet sniffing walks are really good for her to decompress, and chewing things is really calming for dogs, but Lainy also needs running to let off steam. Those are all things that are quite easy to do for her. Whereas treating someone like Zach could be much more tricky. It sounds like he's resistant to the idea of getting counselling, even though he obviously needs it.'

'Yes, I think he feels like I did; frightened, embarrassed, ashamed, worried what people might say or think. I've told him that I got help and it made a huge difference, but he has to decide when he's ready.' Suki sighed. 'Anyway, I'm so grateful for all your help with Lainy; it's made a big difference. Now it's time for a run, I think. Shall we pop the pensioners in the car while we have a quick sprint?'

By pensioners, it turns out she meant me and Titch which I thought was a bit rich, but it meant we got to have a little rest and a quiet nose-to-nose chat, which was lovely. We didn't get much Quality Time nowadays as Tess was always so busy with work. So it seemed no time at all before they arrived back, and Tess reached for her phone.

'I've got another client in half an hour so I've got plenty of time to get there.' She started scrolling on her phone; they seemed to spend so much time on those stupid things, when they could be doing important things like eating or walking or sniffing. 'Wow - look - someone's put up a video of Lainy chasing that guy who attacked Zach.'

'Really?' Suki, leaned over to see. 'But that was several days ago.'

'It was posted on Tuesday, but I've only just seen it,' Tess said. There was silence while presumably they watched it. 'Lainy's a real star, isn't she?'

At this, Lainy's ears shot up. 'I am star?'

'It sounds like it,' Titch said.

'I am in sky?'

'It means you've done something special,' I said. 'Someone's taken a video of you.'

We edged closer as Suki stroked Lainy's ears. 'You're famous now, Lainy-Lou! Have a look, girls and boys.'

Tess brought the phone down to our nose level and played the video for us. Sure enough, there was the man trying to grab Zach's accordion, Lainy going to the rescue, then chasing him down the street.

'Very impressive,' said Titch. I could sense a faint tinge of envy. 'Well done, Lainy. Brave girl.'

Lainy's whiskers twitched and her ears rotated. 'Thank you,' she said quietly, evidently unused to praise.

'But look at all these comments,' said Tess. 'Loads of them, and thousands of views. And shares. This is great!' She paused. 'Oh, but then...'

Suki looked at the screen, her voice dropping. 'That's not very fair.'

'What it say?' Lainy said.

Suki stared at Tess, fear radiating off her. 'She's not a dangerous dog. How could they say that?'

'She isn't,' said Tess soothingly, but I could smell anxiety oozing from her. 'Some people don't know what they're talking about.' She carried on reading, and the worry smell grew stronger. 'However, it's provoked a lot of reaction.'

'I don't want anything bad for Lainy.'

'No, and we will make sure that doesn't happen, but we must protect her,' Tess said firmly, her ponytail swinging forcefully. 'I'm thinking of the Dangerous Dogs Act, Suki. God knows how many people have seen this video, and how many more people will see it. She's such a beautiful dog, she's very recognisable. So I think we need to train her to wear a muzzle. In public.'

Suki looked up. 'A muzzle?' she whispered.

Tess nodded. 'I know it sounds harsh, but I'm thinking of Lainy. This video is evidence that she's bitten someone. That doesn't bode well for her.'

'But that's not fair. She was only protecting Zach.'

'I know, but I'm thinking from the police point of view. Because of this, they could say she's a dangerous dog.'

'What?' Suki smelt terrible, like burning rubber. 'But she's not dangerous. Surely the police could see that?'

Tess fiddled with her phone and read out, 'The Dangerous Dogs Act states that "your dog is dangerously out of control if it injures, threatens or frightens someone. Your dog could also be considered dangerous if it attacks another animal, or if the owner of another animal believes they'll be injured if they try to stop an attack by your dog."' Tess gave Suki a hug. 'Sorry, it's not me that makes these laws.'

Suki's voice was muffled, enfolded in Tess's arms. 'So Lainy has to be punished for doing what a police dog would have done?'

'Not punished, it's about protecting her. And you. The thing is, if Lainy had bitten someone and they reported it to the police, that would be a criminal offence. Worst case scenario, she might be taken away from you, and even put down. And you could be sued for god knows how much.'

We were all stunned. What was this barbaric form of law? It was one thing where Lainy came from, but I thought Cornish people loved their dogs? Who were these people in charge of us? My fur stood on end, and Lainy looked bug eyed with confusion. I hoped she hadn't understood all that had been said.

'Bloody hell,' said Suki, leaning against the car. All colour had bled from her face and she smelt very ill indeed.

Tess continued, 'I'm certain Lainy's not a danger to anyone, but now there's evidence that she's bitten someone, the argument could well be that she might do it again.' She gave a rather feeble smile that didn't fool any of us. 'That's why it's important that we protect her. It's not the end of the world, honestly. Loads of dogs wear muzzles and they don't mind. The trick is to get her used to it so she doesn't see it as punishment. Just like we had to wear masks for Covid.' She shrugged. 'I know we didn't like it either but we got used to it, didn't we? It'll be fine. Honestly. There's a really good Blue Cross video which is great for muzzle training. I'll send it to you.'

Suki let out a huge sigh. 'It seems so unfair. I mean, I can see what you mean, but poor Lainy, when she's done nothing wrong.'

'I know.' Tess gave her shoulders another squeeze. 'But as we both know, since when has life ever been fair?'

17

Those words rang in my ears for the rest of the day. Especially when Lainy said, 'And what is muzzle? Why I have to wear? I no understand.'

I was at a loss, so I barked, 'I'm not sure,' because I hadn't actually seen a muzzle so I didn't know what they were talking about. It sounded ugly, and when Suki and Tess talked about it, they smelt like rancid butter. All I knew was that I was fairly sure Lainy wouldn't like it.

But I was also concerned that we hadn't seen Joe, so I was very pleased when he rang Suki later to suggest a walk.

'That would be great,' said Suki. 'We haven't seen you for ages. You been busy?'

'Er, yes,' Joe said. But the way he said it, I sensed something was wrong.

We met the following day, at Argal reservoir. I hoped we would walk over the dam and go to the caravan for coffee. But we walked the other way, round a narrow path that skirted the water. A chill February wind rippled the surface and even the swans smelt cold and fed up.

When Suki mentioned how Zach had rung her in a terrible state, Joe grew very quiet, and again came that fearful, peppery, smell that lingered underneath everything else, growing stronger by the minute. He walked on, as if he was battling something inside his head, while Lainy trotted on ahead.

Finally Joe said, 'So what's this about Lainy wearing a muzzle?'

'Someone took a video and put in on Facebook,' Suki explained.'It showed Lainy biting the guy who tried to steal Zach's accordion, then her chasing him down the street. Nearly everyone thought she was really brave, but a few people said she was dangerous, and what if she bit someone else. Tess knows about all this stuff because of working at the vet, and apparently the Dangerous Dogs Act has been amended so that if you think a dog might attack you, you can report it. And then the dog could be taken away and even, you know...'

I hoped Lainy wasn't listening.

'My god,' Joe smelt shocked. 'I didn't know. My last dog was attacked several times and just think, I could have reported it. I didn't because I was more concerned with making sure he was OK and getting him home.'

'That's just how I felt with Lainy. Who attacked him?'

'Two greyhounds.'

'You must have felt terrible,' Suki said. 'I do whenever things go wrong for Lainy.'

'I was more concerned about Peanut,' he replied.

It was fairly obvious he didn't want to talk about it, but then I remembered he rarely talked about himself.

'But that's terrible for Lainy. Poor girl, as if she didn't have enough to deal with.'

'I know. But as Tess said, a muzzle is the only way to protect her.'

Joe looked at her. 'And you. I'm thinking of your eye.'

Suki bit her lip. 'Well, yes. I hate the idea of Lainy being muzzled, but I don't think we've got a choice. I dread having to train her with it. I'm sure she'll hate it.'

Joe smiled. 'She might be more pragmatic than you think. And it's not as if she's vain, is she? Even with her looks.'

Suki giggled. 'I don't know. You haven't seen her putting her mascara on in the mornings.'

Joe laughed. 'No, but I can imagine it.'

He was quiet as they came to a narrower part of the path, and as they drew nearer, he took her hand. I liked seeing them close like that, holding hands. I hoped he was coming back afterwards, for the night.

'Come to think of it,' he continued thoughtfully, 'a dog down our road wears a muzzle. And look, over there. That greyhound does too. I bet there are lots of reasons why dogs wear them. It might be because they're ill or getting over an illness, or chase cats. Some dogs eat poo and they have to be stopped. So it doesn't mean a dog is dangerous just because they wear a muzzle. In fact, I was always told a dog should be trained to wear one anyway, in case they're injured and have to go to the vet. When they're in pain and frightened, that's when they're most likely to bite.'

'Oh. OK.' Suki's voice was lighter, sounded more reassured.

'And if you can train her to wear one so that she sees it as a game, I'm sure she won't mind at all,' Joe continued.

Suki smiled, her stress smell almost gone. 'Tess sent me a link to a training video which looks really good. You cover the muzzle in peanut butter or something tasty, play games with it, do it up for a few seconds, then take it off and increase the wearing time gradually. You just have to take it step by step, so they're comfortable with it, and never get frightened.'

'I'm sure she'll be absolutely fine,' Joe said. 'She's a tough girl, but she's also sensible, and she'd do anything for you,'

I could smell Suki getting hot with embarrassment. She'd never learnt how to take a compliment.

'Let her take it at her own pace, and she'll soon be trotting round as if she's always worn one.'

'I hope so,' said Suki. 'It all sounds a bit daunting to be honest. But Zach recommended some soothing music for her, so I'm sure that will help.'

The atmosphere changed immediately, and that stinky smell came flooding back.

There was an uncomfortable silence and I could tell Suki wasn't sure what had happened. 'Are you OK?' she said. 'Only, we haven't seen you for a while and I hope nothing's wrong.'

'Oh, no,' said Joe, abruptly. 'Actually, I've been meaning to tell you. I've got a job in Wales. For a few weeks.'

'Wales?' Her voice rose sharply. 'That's... that's a long way. But it's supposed to be lovely. Great walking. So I've heard.' She was talking jerkily, not making much sense. 'I mean, I haven't been, but I... so when are you going?'

'Probably next week,' he said. 'My business partner didn't want the job, so I said I'd go. He can manage without me for a few weeks. Be good to have a break.'

'Of course. Lovely,' Suki said. But I could sense her shock and confusion. 'Well, I hope you have a good time. Sounds great.'

She was fooling no one, at least not me, but at this point Lainy trotted back. 'What is that horrible smell? What is happening with those two?'

'He's going off to Wales,' I said. 'And she's not happy.'

'I not surprise,' Lainy said. 'We will miss him.' And she gave him a little head butt.

Joe looked down and gave a delighted laugh. 'Oh, darling Lainy,' he said, and then saw me and gave me a stroke. 'And darling Moll, too.' He looked up at Suki and gave her a hug. 'I'll miss you all.'

'We'll miss you, too,' said Suki, and I could smell she was trying hard not to cry.

That was the trouble with these two: just when I thought it was going so well, and they were so happy, they took a step backwards.

Over the next few weeks, Tess often came round after work, for a Muzzle Session. Lainy wasn't told about these in advance, so I kept quiet, feeling rather disloyal. However, I could see the advantage in not telling her; she'd only worry, and she was nervous enough, poor girl.

At the first session, Tess accepted a mug of tea and told Suki what they would do. 'I've got peanut butter and pâté to smear over the muzzle, so we'll introduce her to it slowly. Have you seen that video?'

Suki nodded. 'Yes and we've had a go, but I didn't try and do the muzzle up.'

'No, that's right. Take it really slowly. Now, Lainy-Lou, how about a bit of pâté?' Tess covered the muzzle with pâté and Lainy came nearer, stuck her nose in it and licked slowly, then faster. Then she stopped and looked at me. 'This very strange game but I like the pâté,' she said. 'Meat, herbs, bit fatty and salty but nice.'

I shook my head so hard my my ears flapped. I didn't trust myself to say anything. I sat and watched. And waited.

Lainy was horrified when she realised she had to actually put it on.

'I'm sorry, Lainy,' Tess said, stroking her firmly but calmly. We could smell how much she loved Lainy. It oozed out of her, yet at the same time there was no messing with her. 'It's to protect you. And Suki.' Her ponytail was at half mast today. Not surprising.

Lainy turned to me, outraged. 'Protect?' she cried, her dark eyes flashing, ears bolt upright. 'But that what I was doing, stupid peoples! I protect Zach and Suki. And now I must wear this horrible THING? I no understand. WHY?'

Suki was on the verge of tears; I could smell them, hot and wet and miserable. She was unable to speak, but stroked Lainy's back gently, as if that might convey her love and support.

'I know, it probably doesn't make sense,' Tess said, as if she could understand Lainy. 'I'm afraid it's because of people who make laws, and what is acceptable in society.'

I wasn't sure what she meant by that, but Lainy shook herself vigorously to get rid of the angst and stress. 'Stupid law,' she said, but didn't argue any more.

'Clever girl,' said Tess, and that evening she managed to do up the muzzle. For a short time, but it was a start.

Gradually, over the next week, they built up the wearing time inside the house though it pained me to see her, so I looked elsewhere. Until Lainy said, 'It no help me when you not look.' And I realised I was being selfish. After all, it was her that had to wear the thing, not me.

A week later, Lainy reported that they'd met Tess at Swanpool car park where Lainy realised she was expected to wear the muzzle outside; in public.

'I say NO!' She told me later. 'I stand firm in the road and I say NO I NOT walk in this - this THING.' Distress poured off her, like winter rain, cold and relentless.

'So what happened?' I had to ask.

'I not move, but Tess, you know, she very gentle and she talk quiet and she stroke me and she very kind but firm, you know?'

I nodded. 'She does that. She gets her own way, but she makes you think it was your idea.'

'Yes!' Lainy paused to wash her front paws. 'Well, we walk over to beach and there is cafe. On the beach!'

Lainy's experience of eating out was, as far as I knew, limited. She didn't like being near people she didn't know because it could trigger a flashback, and she distrusted strange places for the same reason. 'Oh yes?'

'Yes!' Lainy said. 'We sit outside and Tess feed me ice cream while I wear muzzle. Very odd game.'

'Ice cream?' I said, perhaps more sharply than I'd intended. 'What flavour?'

'Flavour?' Lainy's whiskers twitched. 'I not know, but it cold and sweet and a hint of strawberry, and is best thing I ever eat.'

'Wait till you try vanilla,' I said, somewhat relieved that she hadn't been spoilt too much. 'That is possibly even better than strawberry.'

'Ice cream taste of different things?' Lainy fixed her huge, dark mascara-d eyes on me. 'How they do that?'

Again, I was stumped. 'I'm not entirely sure.' And it struck me that since Lainy arrived, I'd been saying this more and more. Swiftly I changed the topic. 'Were there many people at the cafe?' I asked, for normally this would freak Lainy out.

'Yes, lots of peoples but I eat my ice cream so I no bother,' she said dismissively.

I knew how busy that cafe could get: lots of people wandering by, often with dogs, those queuing up for ice creams and drinks, swimmers, surfers, those with kayaks; a constant stream of people. I was amazed, and suppressed a twitch of my whiskers. I suspected Tess had been rather shrewd. She'd not only got Lainy used to wearing the muzzle while out but also got her used to being around lots of people. Clever Tess.

The following day, we called in to see Petroc. This was part of getting Lainy used to wearing her muzzle in different places so she wasn't so self conscious.

'I think you look rather splendid, Lainy,' Petroc said, giving her a bit of digestive biscuit. 'Gives you an air of gravitas.' He looked over at Suki. 'I'm so sorry about the events leading up to this. But does she have to wear it inside?'

'No,' said Suki. 'Well, not here. We're friends.' And she bent down to take it off.

Lainy gave a relieved shake and went to sit hopefully by Petroc who was making tea.

'So Joe's off to Wales, you said?' Petroc took another digestive biscuit and broke it into pieces, giving us a bit each.

'Yes, everything was going so well, but over the last few weeks we've hardly seen him. We had a walk the other day and we were chatting and it was nice and easy like it usually is, then he went all weird when I mentioned Zach.' She snorted. 'Anyone would think he was jealous.'

'Maybe he is.'

'Surely not. Zach's too young.' Suki accepted a mug of tea but it slopped slightly as she put it down on the table. 'And anyway, I'm not interested in Zach,' Suki cried. 'It's Joe I love.'

Petroc looked at her with his head on one side, like I do when I want something. He waited. Then he said, 'have you told Joe that?'

'No!' Suki smelt alarmed, like burnt toast. 'I might put him off.'

'Why?'

'Well. I know he cares for me, but he's so wary. I don't like to mention the L word. He might take fright and run away.'

'So you haven't told him that you love him, and he's going away.' Petroc sounded calm, and reasonable. 'Maybe there's another reason.'

'Maybe.' She looked up. 'Do you think it might be something to do with Zach?'

'If Joe goes quiet whenever you mention him, there's obviously something he's not happy about. Why don't you ask him?'

Suki looked down, bit her lip. 'I was going to but he rushed off. I do want to ask him before he goes, though.'

'Good idea. Otherwise you'll have to wait till he comes back.' Petroc's smile lessened the blow of this remark.

'I don't want that.' Suki sighed. 'I do hope he's not having second thoughts about us.'

'I doubt it, but whatever it is, he obviously needs time to think things over while he's in Wales.'

18

Joe came round for supper before he left for Wales, and Suki cooked sausage casserole which was one of his favourite meals. After his abrupt behaviour last time we met, I wondered how he would be. But he seemed his normal chatty self with Suki, playing games with us, hiding treats round the room, which we both loved.

All seemed to be fine until Suki mentioned Zach was coming for a walk with us later that week, and that horrible smell came from Joe.

'I really don't think that's a good idea,' he said.

Suki looked up. 'Why ever not?'

Joe looked down at his plate. Only one sausage left... 'It's not safe going for a walk with a stranger. Anything could happen.'

Suki stared at him as if he was mad, 'But this is Zach. He's not a stranger.' Silence, while she looked at him closely. 'Are you jealous?'

' No!' Joe sighed. 'What do you know about him?'

'That he worked for the Emergency Response Team, he fell out with his dad, he's got bad burns, he doesn't have many friends and he has panic attacks and PTSD.'

'If that's true.'

'Why wouldn't it be?' Suki didn't sound cross, just bemused.

'He also takes painkillers.'

'Well, of course, he's in a lot of pain.' Suki stopped. 'How do you know that?'

Joe sipped his coffee, as if he was considering his words even more carefully than normal. 'I have some experience in that sort of thing,' he said.

'What sort of thing? What are you talking about?'

'I think you'll find Zach is addicted to painkillers.'

Suki's mouth opened and shut. 'How do you know?'

'Because I recognise the signs.' He looked at her. 'Of addiction.'

There was a long silence, then Suki said, 'So how come you know the signs?' Silence. 'You know someone who's an addict?'

Joe nodded.

'Who?'

Joe looked up. 'My ex-girlfriend. She's an alcoholic.'

The words rang around the kitchen and Suki's face fell. 'I'm so sorry, Joe. That must have been ... very hard.'

He nodded. 'It was.'

Another silence, while we all tried to make sense of what Joe had said. He hadn't explained anything regarding the circumstances, but brevity was part of Joe's language, it seemed.

'So that's why you don't want me to go for a walk with Zach,' Suki said,

'I'd rather you didn't see him at all, really.'

'Because...?'

'Because it's easy to pour a lot of time, energy and love into trying to fix someone who doesn't want to be fixed.' Pain leaked out of every word and I walked over and sat beside him, in case he needed a cuddle. Sure enough, a hand came down to stroke my head.

'I'm so sorry, Joe,' Suki said. I could tell she was dying to know more, but she didn't push it. It was evident that Joe had suffered very badly through trying to help his ex-girlfriend but I suspected he'd said as much as he could for today. Maybe he'd reveal more another time. 'I understand. I'll scrub the walk idea. I can't promise not to see him, as I bump into him from time to time. But I'll keep contact to a minimum.'

Joe smiled, leaned across the table and kissed her. 'Good,' he said. 'I'm not the jealous type, and I certainly would never try and control you. But I do care about you, and I suspect that getting involved with someone like Zach is only going to end in tears.'

Wise words indeed.

But there was one cold sausage left on his plate. I stared at it hopefully.

After a few more tantrums, Lainy began to accept her muzzle. It was interesting seeing how she adapted but the turning point had definitely been when Tess took her for ice cream, so she got used to wearing Her Nose, as Petroc christened it, outside and wasn't self-conscious. It helped, of course, that Lainy was so food orientated.

'The way to Lainy's heart is definitely through her stomach,' Suki said with a grin one day, and Lainy was certainly getting a lot of very tasty treats whenever she had to wear the muzzle. Bits of chicken, cheese, peanut butter; you name it. I would have been jealous if I hadn't had a little sample myself.

I could tell Suki was still very nervous about the muzzle, and I wanted to give her a shake. After all, if Lainy could adapt, so could she. We met several other dogs who wore them, and it was easy to see the owners who had taken the time to help their dogs get used to them. The converse, of course, were the owners who hadn't bothered.

We met a very angry greyhound who belonged in this category. 'I hate this bloody thing,' he barked, rubbing his nose against the ground in an attempt to dislodge his muzzle.

'Why you have to wear it?' Lainy stood before him, looking gorgeous even with a black muzzle on her snout. She fluttered her eyelashes and I could see the dog bow a little, wishing all the more that he didn't have to wear this disfiguring item.

'I badly wounded a cat,' he said shortly, but with a hint of pride. 'Caused all kind of rumpus, and my owner had to pay the vet bills. You wouldn't believe the fuss; over a bloody cat!'

Lainy was thinking, I could tell; her whiskers were twitching. 'They don't like us to hurt other animals,' she said simply.

'Where I come from, in Romania, people no worry. We must survive.'

The greyhound dipped his head in acknowledgment. 'Dog eat dog, eh?'

'Oh no, we not eat each other!'

She sounded horrified and the greyhound smelt awkward. 'It was a joke,' he barked. 'But a bad one. I apologise.'

'Ah, no need,' she said dismissively, and turned back to me, her tail swishing as we trotted off. 'How ignorant,' she muttered. 'He think we savages?'

But we were glad to find that there were more responsible owners around, too. Another day, we met an owner whose dog was also wearing a muzzle. He was a bit bigger than Lainy and black all over, with a scruffy, curly coat. The owner, a man about the same age as Suki, stopped and said, 'Glad to see another owner taking responsibility for their dog.' He spoke in a very forthright manner, with a deep voice and held out his hand. 'I'm John, and this is Friday.'

Suki shook his hand and said, 'I'm Suki, and this is Moll and this is Lainy. She's the one with the muzzle.'

'Very glad to see it,' he said. 'Friday wears one because he chases cats and will tear them apart if he can, which obviously doesn't go down well with the feline community, or their owners. But he also has a habit of eating seaweed, and any excrement he can find, all of which make him really ill.' He spoke in such a down to earth manner I could see Suki was reassured. 'What about yours?'

'Lainy chased a thief,' Suki said, her voice stronger than I'd heard for a long while. 'Unfortunately someone posted a video on Facebook and a few people were horrified because she bit his leg. My friend, who's an animal behaviourist, said we had to be really careful or Lainy could be taken away, or I could be sued for having a dangerous dog.'

John sighed. 'I'm so sorry, that sounds really bad luck, when she was being so brave.' He bent over to stroke Lainy but she barked loudly: her Back Off bark.

'Sorry,' said Suki, 'it's nothing personal. She's a rescue and she doesn't like strangers. A lot of people put their hands out to stroke her, and she really hates that.'

'I don't blame her,' said John cheerfully. 'I wouldn't like it either. I bet the muzzle puts those people off though. The amount of times I've had strangers coming up to Friday saying that they love dogs, and dogs always love them and they just want to say hello...'

'I know what you mean,' she said. 'It drives me mad. But yes, you're right, it does put people off. And it stops some of those dogs that bounce up and want to steamroller you.'

'I know,' he said with a short laugh. 'And the owner always says, "my dog's very friendly!" Friday hates those dogs. He was attacked a few months ago by a so-called friendly dog and it's taking ages to get his confidence back.'

'Lainy had the same thing,' Suki said. 'Oh, it's so good to meet someone who understands!'

'I think I had more trouble adapting to Friday wearing a muzzle than he did,' John said with a smile. 'I mean, he wasn't very pleased at first, but I was more conscious of it than he was.' He leant forward. 'And then someone said to me, "don't forget, muzzles protect dogs. So tell your dog to wear it with pride and a smile. Own it like a big hat!'

'I like that!'

'And when you see a dog wearing a muzzle, be glad that the owner is looking after their dog and keeping them and other people safe.'

Lainy was sitting beside Suki, ears pricked up, taking in every word. She nodded vigorously, and John laughed.

'Smart cookie, isn't she? Been wearing hers for a while, has she? She looks comfortable in it.'

'No, not long; only a few weeks,' Suki bent down to stroke Lainy. 'She picks things up very quickly though. She's very smart.' I could hear the pride in her voice, and even though it wasn't aimed at me, I felt proud too; after all, it was my decision that Lainy should be part of our family now, and we were responsible for her. And I was glad that we'd met John, for it helped us all look on muzzles more positively now. For who wouldn't want the best for their dogs and to keep them safe?

A week later, Suki went off to interview someone for a Cornish magazine and came back buzzing about Man Down, whoever he was, and that evening she rang Petroc.

'I had the most fascinating interview today,' she said. 'I met this guy called Sam who's had a similar experience to Zach, and, like him, Sam couldn't adjust to coming back home having been working in a really high pressure environment.'

'I can imagine it would be difficult to fit into normal life again.'

'Absolutely. He said he missed the constant adrenaline, and didn't know how to be a father or a husband. He couldn't even load the washing machine. He felt a real failure and started having panic attacks and didn't feel he could talk to anyone so he completely fell apart. Just like Zach. He got so depressed he was seriously considering suicide.'

'Poor man. The sad thing is, there must be many more like him and Zach,' Petroc said. 'So what did he do?'

'Well, he got chatting to a guy in his local, and this man's best friend had killed himself, and he was naturally devastated. He wanted to do something to raise awareness of male suicide, so he and Sam got talking and decided to have an event and see if anyone wanted to come along. The first few meetings were small, but very soon more and more people came along, to talk about their experiences and share their problems.'

'And it's men only?'

'Yes. The initial idea was to prevent male suicide, then lockdown came along and brought about so much depression, anxiety, isolation and loneliness that the groups expanded really quickly.'

Petroc paused. 'Do you think Zach would go along to something like this?'

There was a longer pause. 'I don't know,' Suki said. 'I suspect he may not want to. But I can ask him.'

'I thought you were going to keep contact with Zach to a minimum?'

'I wasn't going to meet him,' said Suki. 'Just ring him.'

Silence, then Petroc said, 'If that's what you want, but I don't think it's up to you or them to persuade him. Zach is not your responsibility. After all, my dear, you've done more than enough already.' He paused. 'You don't want to get so involved that you let others down, do you?'

'You mean Lainy? As if I would!' Suki said hotly.

'I mean Joe,' Petroc said softly.

I was quite glad not to see Zach. I felt sorry for him, but he carried so many problems around with him that it was difficult to breathe when he was around. The air smelt putrid, as if a poisonous gas had seeped into the room.

But as we were walking through town one day, we saw him coming out of a supermarket.

'Suki!' He cried.

She turned and I could smell her hesitation, her promise to Joe. 'Hello,' she said.

'I'm glad to see you,' he said, and he smelt of panic and fear and that horrible chemical smell. 'Have you got time for a coffee?' He smiled and that dimple popped out.

Slowly she smiled back. 'OK, but I can't be long.'

We went to the cafe round the corner and sat outside. Soon, mugs of coffee arrived, then a bacon and egg bap for him. Lainy and I exchanged looks for the smell of burnt, fatty bacon and greasy egg was so tempting. We could have swiped it off the table, but we had better manners than that. We sat close by and stared at him fixedly.

His food disappeared in minutes, then Zach wiped his mouth on the paper napkin and said, 'Sorry. I needed that.'

'Good,' Suki said, sipping her coffee. I could tell she was trying to work out what to say in case he took offence. 'So, how are things? Have you got somewhere else to live?'

'Yes,' he said slowly. 'I've got a bedsit at the top of a house.'

'Oh, that's good. Do you see much of the people who live there?'

'Not really. It's a couple who are at work all day.'

'Do you share a bathroom? Kitchen?'

'I've got my own bathroom, and I have a microwave in my room. I can use the kitchen, but I don't really like to when they're there.' He smiled again, but this time I could smell the effort.

'But you can use it in the daytime? When they're out?'

'Yes.'

'And it's clean?'

He shrugged. 'It's OK. Better than where I was living.'

'What about the bathroom? Does the shower work?'

He shook his head. 'No, and I did leave them a message but nothing's happened.'

'Is there a basin where you can wash?'

'I wash my face,' he said. But the way he said it made me think he hadn't.

'Is there anyone else you could ask about repairing the shower?' Suki said. 'Whoever organised the room for you?'

'Yes, I suppose. I hadn't thought about that.'

Suki bit her lip. 'Well, perhaps you should try them. You need to be able to wash. They probably forgot, that's all.' Silence. 'Do you talk to them at all? In the evenings?'

He shook his head. 'No. They're eating, watching TV. Busy. You know.'

'Did they ask you to join them at all?'

'Not really.'

'It sounds a bit lonely,' Suki said hesitantly.

He shrugged again. 'I'm used to my own company.'

I thought that liking your own company had nothing to do with being lonely. They were entirely different.

'I was thinking about Lainy the other day,' she continued. 'I told you, she has PTSD. Like you?'

He looked over at Lainy and stroked her and that dimple reappeared.'Yes. Does she like the music I suggested?'

'She does and she's making good progress. It's slow but it's bound to be. A lot went wrong in her early years; you can't just flick a switch and eradicate all that, can you?'

He shook his head again, looking at Lainy, and blew his nose.

'I was thinking that I've been really lucky finding Tess who's taught me to understand what Lainy needs, and how best to help her,' she continued. 'And it seems such a shame that there are lots of people, like you, who've had a really difficult time and also need some help. And yet it's more difficult for humans.' She stopped, bit her lip. 'There's a charity that was set up by a man who's had similar experiences to you. A group of guys meet regularly in Falmouth - men only. It's really helped him, and many other people. It might help you too.'

'How?'

'They meet in the evening, and talk about any problems they have.'

He blew his nose again. 'What kind of problems?'

'Depression, anxiety. Loneliness. Worries. Things like that.'

His face clouded over. 'So they sit around and talk about feeling miserable?' He gave a snort.

Suki shifted. 'I don't think it's like that at all. If I'm worried I talk to my friends and that always helps. It's the same thing.'

'But because I haven't got any friends, I should sit in a roomful of strangers and talk to them?'

Suki flushed and I felt really bad for her. 'I didn't mean that...'

'Yes, you did.'

'No! I just mean that sometimes men aren't very good at talking to people if they're worried, or unhappy, and this group has helped lots of other men, and it might help you.'

'No.' Zach got up quickly, his chair scraping so hard against the ground the noise really hurt my ears. 'I might be a mess, but I'm not a charity case.'

'Zach - don't go.' Suki got up, but I could see it was too late.

'I don't need your help,' he said, anger bursting out of him. 'So leave me alone!' And he limped off, knocking into tables and chairs as he went.

Lainy and I exchanged a glance and shuffled closer, put our noses on Suki's lap. 'Oh shit,' she said quietly, thankfully unaware that everyone else was listening. 'I see just what Joe means. I really fucked up there, didn't I?'

19

Any thoughts of Zach were diverted when Suki discovered that her shower was leaking. She rang around various plumbers, but everyone was really busy and despite her pleadings, no one could come and fix it till the following week.

'Damn,' said Suki, speaking to the third person on the phone. 'I'll have to turn the water off all the time, because it's leaking so much.'

'Afraid so,' said a voice. 'If we get a cancellation I'll ring you, but I'm afraid everyone's really busy right now.'

Lainy and I were lying on the bed, as we usually did when Suki was working, and she stared at us. 'I'm wondering whether to ring Joe,' she said. 'I get the feeling that he wants some space, because he's not rung since he's been away. But his business partner might be able to help.'

Lainy winked and Suki laughed. 'I know, but I haven't heard from him for nearly a week and I just want to make sure he's OK.' Her words were faltering, as if they weren't sure which ones would pop out of her mouth.'

'Anyway, I'll... no, I'll text. He might be busy. And then ... well, hopefully he'll reply. Or maybe even ring?' She sat down and started typing a long message. Then she sighed heavily and said, 'No, I can't put all that. Start again.' More typing, then she said, 'OK. It's gone!' And there was a whooshing noise.

We watched the phone, as if it would miraculously bring Joe into the room with us. It was silent. No pings to indicate an incoming message. We waited. Nothing.

Eventually Suki threw the phone on the bed, put a pillow over it, and sat down at her computer. Began typing furiously. After a while, she said, 'Come on. Let's go for a walk round the block. I can't concentrate.'

For the rest of the day she glanced at her phone now and then, but after a while she left it in the kitchen and went to her computer. Tap tap of the keyboard as she wrote, determination rising off her like smoke.

It wasn't until our afternoon walk that we heard that ping from her phone. Lainy's ears shot up. 'It's him,' she breathed.

'How do you know?' I asked.

'I hope,' she added.

Suki scrambled to grab her phone which was in her pocket. 'Oh, it's Tess,' she said with a sigh. She typed a reply, then tucked the phone away again. 'We're having a walk on Friday.'

And so we continued our walk in silence. Suki threw treats for us, like she always did, but she smelt tired and dispirited, like stale bread. She turned her phone off until we got home, where it lay in the kitchen while she gave us our tea.

As we listened to the news on the radio, another ping came in. I looked at Lainy who winked as Suki grabbed her phone. She read the message, and I smelt a burst of fresh air coming from her. 'It's Joe,' she said, her voice rising. 'He's busy working, but he'll ring later.' And she gave a big smile.

'He didn't say what time he'd ring.' Suki broke eggs into a bowl. 'It must be a big job if he's working late.' She added salt and pepper, a sprinkling of mixed herbs. 'I wonder where he's staying?' Taking a fork, she started beating the eggs, but I could see her mind wasn't on food.

Absently she looked round for a frying pan, put it on the stove and added the eggs, stirring gently. 'I really do miss him. I miss sex. And cuddling at night. Having breakfast in bed. I miss our phone calls, our chats. Laughing together. I miss our walks.' Long pause. 'I wonder if he misses me?'

She looked into the pan. 'This isn't cooking. Bloody hell, now the cooker's gone wrong. I... oh, I forgot to turn the gas on!' She looked at us, sitting patiently, waiting in case any stray bits of food happened to drop on the floor. 'Silly me, eh? Well, I think you two deserve something after all that.' She tossed a tiny bit of cheese to Lainy, and a bit of bacon to me. Lainy caught hers mid-air. I let mine fall to the floor where I could see it better. I couldn't always rely on my eyesight these days.

'OK, start again. This time with heat!' She lit the gas on the hob, started stirring just as her phone rang. She lunged at it. 'Damn, damn,' she muttered, swiping the screen. And then the phone stopped ringing. 'DAMN!' She grabbed a tea towel and wiped her hands dry.

I could almost hear her heart rate, beating so fast, could almost see those vessels pumping the blood round her body, giving a good boost of adrenaline. She punched the phone and held it to her ear, waiting. Waiting. And finally, 'Hello! Joe!'

We couldn't hear his end of the conversation. Usually she put the speaker on, but not this time, so we had to imagine him, somewhere far away.

'Yes, sorry to disturb you, but my shower's leaking really badly, and I haven't been able to get hold of anyone to fix it, as they're all too busy, and I didn't have your partner's number or I'd ring him, so I thought I'd just give you a ring and see if...' She paused. 'I mean, I'm sure he's busy as well, but... Oh, OK, that'd be great. Thanks so much.'

Lainy's ears were bolt upright as she tried to listen in, every muscle in her body tuned into the conversation. She turned to me and winked. 'It good they talk,' she whispered.

I nodded and waited, also trying to listen in.

'So how are you getting on? Where are you, exactly?' Muffled speaking. 'No, I don't know Wales. So you're... oh... sounds lovely. Fabulous walking, I bet. Yes, Lainy and Moll would love it.' She laughed. 'Well, I won't keep you.'

Another silence while presumably Joe was talking. 'Oh, that's really kind, Joe, thanks so much. OK, I'll wait to hear from you. Thanks again. Speak later. Bye for now.'

She put down the phone and looked at us. 'Well...' she smiled. 'He's going to ring his partner and see if he'll pop round early tomorrow morning, and fit me in between jobs. He'll ring back to let me know. Joe, I mean. If his partner can't do it, he's got another friend who might be able to help.'

Turning away from us, she turned her attention to the frying pan. 'Oh dear.' She burst out laughing. 'What a mess! Oh well, I'll have scrambled eggs instead.'

She warmed it up, carried the mess to her plate and took it next door, ate it while watching the TV news. 'He sounded a bit ... abrupt, at first,' she said, taking her plate back to the kitchen where she ran water on the dirty dishes, then dried her hands. 'He obviously needs some space. He knows where we are if he wants to get in touch.'

She went next door, back to the TV that she wasn't watching. A somber sounding man was droning on about immigration, and I saw Lainy's ears prick, as she lay listening. Oh no, I thought. Not more of her radical ideas. But Suki's phone rang and she grabbed it, and I could smell the nervous hope as she answered it. 'Hello?' This time she put it on speaker so we could hear.

'My partner can come round in half an hour if that's OK. He'll probably need to come back in the morning, but at least he can figure out what's wrong and then hopefully get you sorted, or at least get a temporary fix until he can get back to do it properly.'

Suki's smile was evident in her voice, even if you couldn't see it. 'That's so kind. I'm really grateful. I have to turn the water off at the moment, because the leak's so bad.'

'That's no good. Listen, his name's Grant and I'll text you his number.'

'Thanks, Joe. I really appreciate it.'

'Not at all. So.' Joe sounded a bit formal. 'How are the dogs?'

'Oh, they're fine,' she said, looking over at us. 'Hoping for a bit of my tea, but no joy.' She cleared her throat. 'Do you have time for walking? I suppose you're working too hard. It's supposed to be very beautiful there,' she was talking rather too quickly.

'I've been trying to walk after work, but the last few days I've had to work late,' he said. 'I hope to have some time soon though. The mountains are stunning, and the rivers, and it's not far from the sea. It's well worth exploring.'

'Sounds like you could do with a four legged companion.'

'Funny you should say that.' Joe sounded back to his normal easy self. 'I think I may have been adopted.'

'What? Who by?'

'A scruffy little fellow with curly black hair. No one seems to know who he belongs to.'

'Has he got a name?'

'He doesn't have a name tag, but I call him Tinker because he keeps trotting in with sticks. I know you've got to be careful with dogs and sticks, but he'll play with one for hours. Then I found one of Peanut's old tennis balls in the van, and he's playing with that now.'

Suki smiled. 'It sounds like you get on well.'

'Well,' Joe paused. 'I swore I'd never have another dog because I didn't want to get too attached, but this little fella's growing on me.'

'What happened with Peanut?'

There was a lengthy pause and I wondered if Suki had said the wrong thing. Joe never volunteered information; was he in the mood for answering questions?

'He got poorly very suddenly,' Joe said, and sorrow leaked from his words. 'He was only 15 but he'd always been so fit. Then one day he started vomiting. I took him to the vet and they did all sorts of tests, but he was still being sick. Then they said he had a blockage in his stomach. They operated, but he died on the operating table.'

The silence that followed was deep and full of anguish. 'I'm so sorry, Joe,' said Suki. 'That must have been terrible. My worst fear is losing Moll - and now Lainy - so I can't imagine how you felt. Still feel,' she added.

Joe cleared his throat. 'So, that's why I wasn't keen on getting another dog,' he said, his voice croaky.

'But Tinker sounds as if he's found you.'

Joe chuckled. 'I think he has. I'll send you a picture.'

'Oh good. I'd love to see him.'

'Well,' Joe hesitated. 'Anyway, I haven't quite finished for the day, so I'd better get on. Let me know if Grant can help, won't you?'

'Yes I will,' Suki said. 'And thanks so much.' As the phone call ended, she stood there, in the middle of the room, holding her phone like a talisman. (I heard that on the radio the other day, and thought when would I ever want to use a word like that? This is the perfect opportunity.)

'Well,' she said to us. 'Perhaps he'll come back with little Tinker.' She paused. 'Sounds like the job's going well. I wonder how long he's going to be away? I should have asked.' She bit her lip. 'He sounded a bit distant at first, which isn't like him. But it's probably because he's busy, and needs time to himself.'

She went back to the kitchen to pour herself a glass of wine, and we could hear humming for the first time in what seemed like ages.

A little while later, Grant turned up. He was a short, wiry fellow with a smiley voice who kept treats in his pockets, so obviously we liked him straight off. Even Lainy took to him, after an initial barking distrust.

'I'll clean the cylinder out and that should do the trick for the moment, but if I were you, I'd order a new shower to be on the safe side,' he said. 'This one's quite old and it'll be much quicker and cheaper to fit a new one.'

'That's really kind,' she said. 'What type would you suggest?'

Grant took some measurements and got his phone out. 'One like this,' he said. Suki's face was a picture of confusion. 'Would you like me to order it, then I can fit it for you?'

'That's really kind,' Suki said. 'If you wouldn't mind, I'd be ever so grateful. And thanks for coming round. It's very good of you to come so late.'

'Happy to help a friend of Joe's,' he said. 'I've heard a lot about you, so I'm glad to meet you at last.'

Suki's face went bright pink. 'Oh,' she said.

Grant gave her a look that I couldn't decipher. He smelt curious, like unripe Camembert, with a hint of laughter. 'Anyway, you've got my number. Let me know how you get on and as soon as the other shower turns up, we can fit it, hopefully next week.'

And off he went. 'Just think, he wouldn't even stay for a cuppa,' said Suki. 'Still, if he's coming back, I can perhaps make him something to eat next time.' She paused. 'I wonder how well he knows Joe, and what Joe's told him about us. That was a very odd look he gave me.' She patted both of us. 'Perhaps we'll find out next week.'

20

'So, now Suki think about Joe *all* the time,' Lainy said the next day after our morning walk.

'Yes,' I said. 'They can realise how much they miss each other.'

'Exactly,' said Lainy with a wink. 'And it stop her thinking about Zach Man. He not good.'

'What do you mean? He can't help how he is. After all,' I added gently, 'you have similar problems.'

Lainy's whiskers twitched. 'I know,' she said. 'But I try very much with my problem, and I listen to how people say. Look,' her eyes gleamed magnificently, 'I even wear that stupid mask on my face. All to protect other peoples when it not even my fault!'

'I know, that's very unfair, and you're right, you have dealt with a lot since you got here,' I said soothingly. 'I think you're very brave,'

Lainy winked. 'Well, I like the music, and the ice cream and the nice treat. It all help very much.'

Sometimes I had the feeling Lainy was quietly laughing at me. This was one of those times. I decided to skate over this. 'But why don't you like Zach?' I pressed.

'Because I know he very hurt but he not even try,' she said. 'Suki she do all this for him but he not do what she say.'

I sat and thought. 'Perhaps he's scared.'

'Of course he scared,' Lainy said. 'That why he take the chemicals.'

'Chemicals? What do you mean?'

'He take the chemicals for his pain. He said, you no hear?'

I wasn't sure I had but my brain was spinning, now Lainy was talking very fast.

'I scared too, but I want be better, so I try do things because I like you and Suki and Tess and I know you want help me, and you give me home and I very grate... grate...'

'Grateful?'

'Grateful,' she repeated. 'It make me very scared to wear the horrible mask and learn to do strange things, but I do this because I trust, and Zach, he not even try.'

She looked up, her eyelashes fluttering. If Titch had been here, he would have fallen at her paws by now. 'Perhaps he doesn't trust us enough?'

Lainy scratched behind one ear. 'Maybe, but that not Suki fault. She try so hard, so he must try more harder.' She looked at me. 'It not easy, having the flashback and the trigger, you know. I have panic too. It not good.'

I was silent. It was difficult to know what to say to that. 'I'm really sorry, Lainy,' I ventured.

'Why you sorry? It not your fault.'

'No, I know.' Lainy's down to earth, intelligent awareness and sensitivity made me think that maybe I missed things about people. I'd always prided myself on being able to understand Suki, but Lainy's understanding was so much wider, and deeper. 'You're very special, Lainy,' I said. 'We're lucky to have you.' And then something occurred to me. 'Can you tell me what it's like when you have a flashback?'

'I tell you before, I think,' she said, 'but every time different. Maybe I see someone who look like the bad mens at the shelter. Or the little girl who never leave me alone. They smell bad. Dangerous. Like dark earth, you know?'

I didn't, but I didn't want to interrupt her. I barked, to carry on.

'This very bad smell make me think of the nasty peoples who no like me, and I very frightened. I shake and I get the panic and I have to run and run, very far from these peoples. But first I bite them,' she added.

'Why?'

'To stop them hurt me again,' she said. 'The bad mens they hit us with bars. The little girl she poke things in my nose and my ears. She pick me up all time so I must stop her. When you say NO over and over, and they ignore, then biting is only way.'

I sat and thought. 'So you think Zach has the same triggers, and flashbacks?'

'Not same, but different.' She looked at me with a flash of a smile in her eyes. 'And he no bite!'

And once again, even though it wasn't really funny, we both laughed, which dispersed the tension and made what she'd said easier to assimilate. After all, we all had our problems. It was a question of how we chose to deal with them, and how that decision affected those around us. Could we help Suki realise this?

We hadn't seen Tess for a while so I was delighted when she rang one afternoon to say she was suddenly free and did we have time for a walk?

I was so pleased to see my Titch again. But after our usual snickering and greetings, I said to him, 'I have to listen to this next bit.'

He was used to this, so he nuzzled my muzzle and said, 'OK, boss,' and we trotted along, behind Tess and Suki.

'So what's new?' Tess said. 'Have you heard from Joe?'

'Yes, you know he's working in Wales. When my shower broke and I couldn't find anyone to mend it, his business partner fixed it for the time being but he's ordered another one and he'll fit that when it arrives. Next week, I hope.'

'Good.' Tess looked around at me and Titch. 'Oh, there they are. So how are things with you two?'

Suki fiddled with a curl over her left ear. 'OK. I think.'

'Are you still together?'

'I think so.'

Tess frowned. 'But you've spoken to him?'

'Yes.' Suki paused. 'He was a bit quiet at first. Abrupt, almost. But that's probably because he's busy.'

'I expect so. He was probably thinking about how to fit a boiler or something. So when's he coming back?'

Suki walked along looking fixedly at the ground. 'I don't know. I didn't ask.' Before Tess could say anything, she added, 'but he's been adopted by a little dog and I'm guessing he might well keep it if no one comes to claim it.'

'Ah, that's good. He had a dog before didn't he?'

'Yes. Peanut. He adored him, and was so shattered when he died, he couldn't bear the thought of losing another one.'

'Funny isn't it, how different people react? After my last dog died, I wouldn't have had another one if my ex hadn't come along and asked me to look after Titch.' She laughed. 'And once Titch had been with us a few weeks, I decided there was no way I was giving him back. Mind you, I think that was the idea.'

'Yes, whereas you know Jane, down the road? After her dog died, she said she couldn't bear being without one, so she adopted a rescue about a week later. As you say, we're all different.'

'So what's this one like? Did Joe say?'

'He sent a picture.' Suki pulled out her phone. 'Look.'

Tess laughed. 'What a lovely scruff! He's gorgeous. Look at that cheeky expression - but he's ever so thin, poor thing.'

'I'm sure he's well fed now,' Suki said. 'After all, who could resist that little face? I bet Joe's going to the supermarket to fill up on dog food every day.'

Tess gave her deep chuckle. 'And by the end of the week, that dog will have a new collar and a plush bed.'

'And treats and a new lead!'

'He'll be sleeping on the end of Joe's bed by this time next week!'

They walked along in a comfortable silence. I was relieved. They both smelt normal again: like new mown grass, all sweet and fresh.

'So have you heard from Joe since you rang about the shower?'

That uncomfortable smell of black pepper wafted over. 'No.'

Tess looked at Suki. 'No phone calls?'

'No. I mean, he's busy. And I get the feeling he needs time to himself.'

'You can always text him though, can't you?'

Suki nodded. 'Yes, but I don't want to bother him.'

'It's a friendly text, Suki, not a marriage proposal.'

'I'll do it when I get home.'

Tess stared at her. 'Go on, Suki. What's the matter?' No reply. 'You miss him, don't you?'

At our feet I sniffed primroses: optimistic and lemon sweet. Snowdrops peeked their white faces out, sturdy and determined. We waited for Suki to respond.

Slowly she looked up. 'Yes,' she said. 'I've got so used to him being here - I mean, in my life. In my bed, sometimes. On the other end of the phone. You know, we talk. And walk. We run, that kind of thing. I mean, nothing heavy. But he's a good friend.'

'With benefits,' Tess chuckled. 'I bet that's how he feels about you.'

'What if he doesn't reply?'

'Then leave it a while. I bet it's only because he's busy. Just have a go.'

'OK.' Getting out her phone, Suki tapped away and there was a whooshing noise as the message flew away to Wales. I looked up, expecting to see it soar through the air, but there was nothing, so I snuffled Titch's ear instead. We liked doing that.

'Good girl,' said Tess. 'Now shall we have a quick run with Lainy?'

'You're on,' said Suki. She put her phone in her back pocket, gave me a quick cuddle and said, 'Won't be long, you two. Enjoy your catch up!' And she and Tess set off at a leisurely pace, leaving me and Titch time to ourselves.

We were silent for a moment, walking along slowly, taking in the smells and treats that had accumulated since our last visit. A man with big boots that smelt of cowpats. Smaller feet; walking boots; from a woman I would guess, with a lighter tread, that smelt of dust and pavements. A damp tissue that smelt of tears and despair. A dry bit of pasty that smelt of pepper and potato, mixed with not enough meat. I shared that bit with Titch; such is the stuff of true love.

Then we sat down on a dry bit of grass and Titch lay beside me. Nose to nose, whisker to whisker. 'What's happening about Zach?'

'Shh,' I said. A patch of sun lit up our spot and my old bones relaxed into it. 'Not now.'

He chuckled and I felt the heat from his nose which made me quiver all over. I closed my eyes and we snoozed together. Just for a few moments...

It seemed only seconds later that Suki and Tess arrived back, puffing and pink faced, whereas Lainy trotted in front of them looking as if she'd had a short walk, rather than a fast run. She was built for speed, that girl.

Suki smiled. 'We haven't had a run for ages. I'd forgotten how much I enjoy it. I am unfit though. Long walks aren't the same as running, are they?'

'No,' Tess gasped. 'And I'm more unfit than you. Shall we aim to do it once a week again?'

'Sounds good.' Suki took a swig of water. 'Right. Better go home. Got to finish a piece on Top Ten Dog Friendly Cafes by 5pm.'

'And I've got a client in twenty minutes, so I'd better shoot, too. Lovely to see you.' Tess gave Suki a hug. 'And next time we meet, you can tell me what happened with Zach.'

Suki looked as if she'd been stung. 'What do you mean?'

'I bumped into a friend who knows the people he's renting his room from. You know what Falmouth's like. Word gets around.'

Suki looked pinker and I caught a whiff like rancid butter. 'You know I promised Joe I wouldn't get involved? Well, we bumped into Zach and he wanted to go for a coffee. So against my better judgement, we did. And I told him about Man Down.'

'And?'

'He stormed off. My fault.'

'On the contrary,' said Tess. 'You've done as much as you can. But try not to think about him. I know that's difficult, but as Joe rightly said, you can expend a lot of energy on someone who doesn't want to help themselves.' She gave Suki another hug.

'But well done for trying. You and I know that someone has to want to get better in order to accept help, and it sounds like Zach isn't there yet.' She looked at Suki. 'And that is not your problem.'

She then jumped into her car and drove off.

We stood there, the three of us, looking after her. 'I know she's right,' said Suki, opening the car so Lainy and I could jump in. 'But I can't help feeling I could have done more. I still think I'm the one who's messed things up, not him.'

21

Suki went very quiet after that. She was busy at work, which was fortunate, but she started wearing small earrings instead of colourful, dangly ones: a true sign of how uncertain she felt about Joe.

'He's replied to my text,' she told us as she prepared our dinner that night, 'he says, "hope all's well. Bigger job than I'd thought so working long hours. Tinker keeping me company." And a smiley face with two kisses.' She smiled at her phone, as if willing him to ring her, but nothing happened. 'He evidently needs his space,' she muttered. 'I'll leave him alone,' and went back to her computer.

A week or so later, we were at Gylly beach in Falmouth with some friends of Suki's. They decided to walk along the seafront, down to the beach then up around Boscawen Fields, which was very popular for dog walking.

Lainy greeted everyone with joy, as she did once she'd got to know people. It was only strangers she was a bit nervous with, and that was fair enough.

The friends were commenting on how much Lainy had changed since Suki had her. 'She's amazing,' one said. 'She's so affectionate now. Shame she has to wear that muzzle, but I suppose you have to be careful.'

'What's she like with other dogs?' said the other friend.

'A bit wary,' Suki said. 'Like people, once she knows them she's fine. She doesn't like spaniels much because she got flattened by one. And she's nervous of terriers because one had a go at her a few months ago. Apart from that, she seems to be OK. She's doing so well.'

We had coffee on the way at a cafe that was very busy. Lainy's ears were twitching like very busy radars, I noticed, and she was a little edgy. Even so, as they said, she had made incredible progress, and we were proud of her. Walking in busy places wasn't nearly as stressful as it had been, for we weren't wondering what would set her off all the time.

When we got to the beach, Suki unclipped our leads, and Lainy ran ahead, relishing the sand between her paws, while I trotted at a more sedate pace. I loved the smell of seaweed - salty and tangy, though the taste was always a disappointment and upset my stomach.

I was having a good forage at someone's left over sandwich on the sand when I heard high pitched barking, followed by shouts. The barking sounded all too familiar, and I looked up to see Lainy charging at full speed towards a spaniel type. She had a habit of doing this; running full tilt towards a dog, then stopping as she got nearer, and dashing back, as if she was unsure how to say hello.

I wasn't sure about this greeting, though, so I trotted forward to see why she was barking, at the same time as Suki dashed forward, for Lainy hadn't stopped, as she usually did, but charged at the other dog.

'Get off!' Lainy cried. 'Get away from us! Go away!'

The other dog backed off, squeaking, but was still too close to us, so Lainy continued to shout at her, 'I said, get away!' As the dog took no notice, she rushed up to her, growling, 'Get off!'

At this point, Suki reached her, shouting, 'Lainy! Enough!' She grabbed her collar, put her on the lead, while Lainy stood, panting and gasping.

'I'm sorry,' said Suki to the owner, who looked stunned, but didn't say anything. 'I hope your dog's OK.'

Luckily the man just nodded and didn't pass judgement, and I was glad for that. Lainy was shaking all over, and Suki stopped and dropped to her haunches in front of her, stroking her gently. Distress was pouring off Lainy like torrential rain, smelling rancid, which got up my nose.

'Are you OK, Lainy-Lou?' Suki asked gently as she stroked her, till Lainy's eyes stopped rolling and her breathing calmed. 'What happened there, Lainy?' she asked quietly. 'What upset you about that dog?'

Lainy shook her head. 'She smell bad. She very nervy dog. I no like, not near us.'

Suki obviously didn't understand, but she continued talking to her in a sing song voice as if she did. She talked nonsense, really, but she couldn't help it. She was doing her best.

'Naughty Lainy,' cried one of the friends. 'What did she do that for?'

I bristled, and I could see Suki did too. However, I'd learnt that many humans could be a bit slow when it came to understanding dogs. 'Please don't shout at her,' she said firmly. 'She wasn't being naughty or bad, and it wasn't her fault. She was reacting to a situation where she didn't feel safe, and didn't know what else to do.'

'But you can't let her go and attack other dogs like that,' came the reply.

I was ready to bite the woman who'd offered this remark, but I suppose she couldn't help being ignorant. I hoped Suki had learned enough by now to explain things.

'She can't do any harm while she's wearing a muzzle,' Suki said. By the way she spoke, she was forcing herself to stay calm. 'I'm responsible for my dog and while I know it can seem alarming when dogs have a pop at each other, she can't do any damage.'

'Well, I wouldn't like it if it happened to me,' came the reply.

I had a feeling that this so called friend was about to be relegated to Past Friend, and listened closely to Suki's response.

'Interestingly, I was reading a piece about aggressive behaviour the other day written by a dog trainer,' Suki said. 'She explained that most quarrelsome behaviour is a defensive response to a dog feeling under threat. Aggression is how dogs communicate and they only use it when they don't feel that other options are open to them.'

'What on earth do you mean?'

'Well, think of how we react when we feel threatened,' Suki said. 'We can run or stay and fight, or we can ask the other person - or dog in this case - to give us space. If this doesn't happen, we, or the dog, have to try and protect ourselves.'

'But it didn't look like that dog was doing anything wrong,' said the friend.

'No, but we can't read other dogs' body language like dogs can. Also, we might have missed Lainy's early flight/freeze signals. Because of her past experiences, Lainy's learned that there's no time to give off signals that are ignored, so she reacts really quickly to save time and protect herself, and us.'

'Right...'

'This is why dogs bite,' said Suki, warming to the subject. 'If dogs are punished for trying to protect themselves - or their owners - and are continually kept in a situation where they can't cope, they will bite. Lainy's not being bad for showing aggression, she's only trying to tell me something's wrong through her behaviour. She can't speak, remember.'

'Oh...'

'Also, I read that dogs can read people much better than we can, and certainly understand other dogs better than we can. Just now, that other dog or its owner could have been giving off their own anxiety, or been ill; the dog might have been on heat, all kinds of things that we have no idea about. Lainy has her own triggers - we don't necessarily know what they are. She was trying to protect herself and us, and that was the only way she knew how. It's up to me to try and get her out of situations where she feels she can't cope.'

'Hmmm.'

The friend didn't sound too sure, so Suki added, 'You know when we have a bad day, we can put up with so much, but then we might stub our toe and that's IT? And it's not the fact that we've stubbed our toe, it's because of a lot of stressful things that have led up to that point, and suddenly we feel we can't take any more.'

She nodded. 'Absolutely.'

'So that's what Lainy's triggers are about. She may have found it too busy in the cafe, or another dog got too close to her, there could have been several things stacking up. I don't know. I watch her carefully, but I don't always see all the signs. In this case, there was something she wasn't happy with, and she couldn't take any more. So she let off steam.'

'I see...'

'So instead of saying that Lainy was being aggressive, I would say she was worried that dog was getting too close as it was ignoring Lainy's fuck off signals.'

The friend laughed. 'I see what you mean now. Dogs are just like us really, aren't they? It's hard enough trying to understand other humans, and we can talk and dogs can't.' She approached Lainy very slowly and threw a treat on the ground in front of her. Lainy, who'd stopped shaking, and was breathing normally, took it graciously.

Then Lainy looked at me and winked. 'Glad she understands,' she said, though I could still smell the sour stress coming from her. 'I really hate it when other dogs don't understand 'fuck off'.'

And with a swish of her tail, she followed Suki along the beach. I watched her closely; I knew the episode had frightened her as her ears and tail were still down, but she was a brave girl, and I loved that about her.

As we walked along the path to Boscawen Fields, my thoughts turned to Zach. It occurred to me that Lainy's behaviour was very like Zach's the other week. Suki had tried to help, with the best of intentions, but had got too close, and Zach couldn't cope. He may well have had too many things stacking up, so he told her to fuck off, and ran.

It wasn't anyone's fault, it was just how he was. The difference was, Lainy trusted us now. She loved us and was part of our family. She was really trying to overcome her fears. Whereas Zach obviously felt lost and isolated. However, Suki had done all she could. It was up to him to ask for help, if and when he was ready.

22

I knew Suki was brooding over Zach. 'I can't help worrying,' she said one day. 'I know Joe and Tess are right, and I should just stop thinking about him, but I hate seeing someone in trouble like that and not be able to help.' We walked on a little, and she kicked a fir cone that skittered along in front of us.

I ignored it, letting Lainy chase it as she needed to expend more energy than me. I knew it would smell of resin and wet earth and the clean smell of fresh rain. She loved chasing cones with her nose, playing capture with her front paws, and chewing them until she realised they smelt better than they tasted.

Suki strode on, ruminating: I could almost hear her mind turning over. 'I keep thinking about him sitting in that little bedsit with no shower, and not washing in the basin, and you can tell he's not eating enough and feels terribly lonely.' She sighed. 'And what happens when he gets panic attacks, and flashbacks? Does he dive under the bedclothes until they've passed? How does he cope?' She stopped for a moment. 'Does he get up at all?'

I decided that was enough. I barked to Lainy who came running back to us. She gave Suki a nudge with her nose, dropped the pine cone at her feet.

Suki looked down, smiled. 'Sorry girls, I've been ignoring you, haven't I?' She picked up the cone and threw it. 'It's very difficult to ignore people, particularly when they're in distress.'

She reached down and patted me, looking ahead to where Lainy was hunting for the pine cone.

'I bet you think the same as Tess and Joe. That I need to let him do what he's going to do.' Her voice lifted slightly. 'After all, I told him about Man Down. He can find them if he wants to. And I know he needs to sort out his shower himself.' She paused. 'After all, once you start doing things for people, they can start to rely on you.'

We walked on, through the rest of the trees, and then I could smell the sea, salty and fresh, ahead of us. 'What do you think Joe's doing now?' Suki's voice had a more wistful tone to it. She smelt of buttercups: hopeful and bright. 'Too busy to text, anyway.' Her voice dropped. 'I bet he's working really hard, then having a walk with Tinker after work.'

She looked down at us and Lainy gave her a wink. Suki laughed. 'Perhaps they're going for a run, like we do. I bet Tinker would enjoy that. I wonder who he belongs to. And if he'll come back with Joe. I wonder...' her voice fell away and I could almost guess what she was thinking. Did Joe miss her? For it was obvious how much she missed him.

That evening, Suki got a phone call from Grant. 'Sorry to ring so late,' he said. He didn't have a loud voice, but it carried clearly down the phone. 'I've had a text to say your shower's in and I've got a cancellation tomorrow late afternoon, so I could come over then and fit it, if you're in. Otherwise it'll be next week.'

'No, tomorrow's great,' Suki said. 'Thanks so much; what time?'

'About five thirty, depending on how long the previous job takes,' he said. 'I'll text you when I'm leaving, if you like.'

'Perfect,' said Suki. She finished the call and looked down at us. 'What a kind man. Now, I'd better get some more coffee, and chocolate biscuits, do you think? Most men like chocolate. Or perhaps he'd rather have pizza? Or cake? I'd like to feed him, because he's been so kind.' And she went off to the kitchen to add to her shopping list. Suki had many talents, but baking wasn't one of them.

The following afternoon, Grant appeared, with pockets that contained treats. My nose quivered as he walked in the door, and even Lainy looked up hopefully. Grant smiled and threw some treats on the floor.

Suki smiled. 'Thanks so much for coming. I never even made you a drink last time. What would you like? And I've got coffee and walnut cake, or chocolate digestives, or pizza.' She was back to wearing larger, more dangly earrings which was a good sign.

Grant laughed. 'What a welcome! A lot of the time I'm not even offered a drink!' He paused to stroke my ears, something I am very partial to. 'A coffee, white no sugar, and a piece of cake would be wonderful, thank you.'

Suki beamed; she liked feeding people, and bustled around boiling the kettle and cutting cake. We hovered, ever hopeful, while Grant disappeared into the bathroom, whistling and banging. When Suki appeared with his cake and drink, he said, 'I'll have it when I've finished this, if you don't mind. I might spill it or drop cake crumbs in your bath otherwise.'

'Of course.' Suki grinned. 'I'm just finishing off some work in the next room, so shout when you're ready.'

We followed her, sorry that the cake hadn't materialised yet, Lainy in particular. She wasn't allowed cake but the odd crumb did find its way into her mouth.

After a while, Grant called to Suki and explained what he'd done.

'I've taken out the old shower and put in the new one, and I've tested it and there are no leaks, so I've covered the tiles up while it all dries, so you can use the shower, but we just need to replace the tile in the middle there; do you have any spares?'

'I'll go and have a look in the garage, but I rather doubt it,' she said. And with that she disappeared. A short while later she was back, shaking her head. 'Sorry, nothing up there. Should I get some new ones?'

'No, I'll have a spare at home somewhere, I'm sure,' he said cheerfully. 'We just have to let it all dry and I'll call back tomorrow if I manage to find another tile. Then we pop that back in, wait for the grouting to go off and you're all ready to go.'

'Brilliant!' Suki grinned. 'Ready for sustenance now?'

'I certainly am.' Grant came into the kitchen and sat down at the table. 'This looks great. Thanks so much. It's been a long day.' He took a big bite of cake and his voice was muffled as he tried to talk, then gave up. 'Sorry. Shouldn't talk with my mouth full. Mum always said.' His eyes twinkled. I edged closer, just to smell that cake. The almost cloying sweetness, rich, dark coffee like a drug, and butter, flour, eggs and sugar, all wrapped up and topped with big chunks of bitter sweet, crunchy walnuts. What joy! I eyed Grant hopefully, lest any crumbs should fall my way. Unfortunately he was hoovering it up like a very efficient vacuum cleaner.

'Have another piece.' Suki nudged the cake towards him. 'Please.'

'Thanks. I didn't have much to eat today.' Grant helped himself and sat back, sipping his coffee as he looked around. 'Nice kitchen. Very original. You been here long?'

Suki looked around the room. 'Nearly twenty years now. We moved here just before we got married.'

'Oh. I didn't realise you were married.'

She bit her lip. 'I'm not. I mean, my husband died three years ago.'

'I am sorry.' Grant was quiet for a moment. 'You've got happy memories here?'

She looked up. 'Yes. Very.'

He nodded. 'You can tell a lot by walking into a house. It's got nice vibes, this place.'

Suki went pink and fiddled with her coffee mug. 'Thanks. He was responsible for the decor. I'm not very good at that type of thing.'

'But you're good at other things: Joe said you're a writer?'

'Yes.' Suki paused. Joe's name had suddenly changed the atmosphere. It now smelt of bonfire smoke on an autumn day. Strong and rich and blown by the wind. 'I'm a journalist and I also write books on Cornish walks.'

'That's it!' Grant beamed. 'I got your Cornish Writers book for my girlfriend for her birthday. She loved it. We're working our way through it, trying to do a walk every weekend when we can.'

Suki's face lit up and her earrings jingled musically. 'Oh, I'm so glad. If ever you want any more, I'm happy to sign them.'

'Brilliant. I'll get her another one, 'cos she loves exploring. Thanks. Has Joe been on any of the book walks?'

'Yes, we did one for the new book a few weeks ago. Over near Padstow. It's a good time of year to walk over that way; it's too busy in the summer.'

'Of course. Heard from Joe recently?'

'A few days ago.' Her smile faltered. 'Have you?'

Grant shrugged. 'Not much. Keeps himself to himself, does Joe. He did mention a dog, though.'

Suki smiled and the crumbly smell dissipated a little. 'Yes. Tinker. He sounds a sweetie. Did you know his last dog?'

'I certainly did. Peanut was a lovely little thing. Went everywhere with him.'

Suki sipped her coffee and sat back. 'Joe told me about how he died. He was obviously devastated.'

'He was,' Grant said simply. 'I was really worried about him; that dog was his life.'

'How old was he? The dog, I mean.'

'Fifteen, I think, so a good age, and he'd seen Joe through a lot when....' He stopped, as if uncertain whether to continue.

'When?' Suki's voice was hesitant. 'I mean, I don't want to pry...'

'Joe and his girlfriend split up at the beginning of last year.'

'Oh yes, he did mention that.'

Grant looked up, surprised. 'He did? Wow. Joe never usually talks about anything personal. I'm amazed he told you about Peanut. That's usually classified information.'

'Yes, I've noticed he doesn't say much about himself.'

'No. He's very private.' Grant hesitated. 'Did he say anything more about Rachel?'

'That she was an alcoholic.'

'He told you that?' Grant whistled. 'Yes, Rachel kept promising to give up the booze, but she never did for long. Joe did everything he could to help her, but she kept falling off the wagon and she was a real mess. In the end he couldn't take it any longer. It was tearing them both apart.' Grant sighed. 'Very difficult when you care about someone and they won't accept they need help.'

Suki looked as if she'd been punched in the stomach and I knew who she was thinking of. 'Poor Joe. What a terrible position to be in.'

'Eventually they had this huge bust up and she stormed off, went up north somewhere, and Joe was so worried about her. But he was utterly drained. She said she never wanted to see him again, and he decided that he couldn't face getting involved with anyone else.'

Suki's face fell. But she recovered herself. 'So he lost his girlfriend and then Peanut, poor fellow. No wonder he's so wary. He did say when we first met that he wasn't ready for another dog yet, so I'd realised how much Peanut meant to him.'

'Yes, but it sounds like Tinker has made quite an impression.' Grant laughed. 'He's such a sucker, that man. I can just imagine Tinker sitting on the doorstep with his head on one side, and that would be it for Joe!'

'Well, Tinker will be good company for him,' Suki said.

'He will, and this break will do him good. When he's not working, he can go walking, running and enjoy his freedom. Nobody to worry about other than himself. He needs some headspace. When Peanut died, he worked extra hard, and when Rachel left, he never stopped, so he's well overdue a break.'

'Oh, poor Joe. No wonder he wanted the job in Wales.'

Grant looked at her and hesitated. 'I'm amazed he started seeing you.' He stopped. 'Sorry, that sounds bad, all I meant was that after Rachel he was very against any more involvement.' He shrugged. 'So I guess he's overdue some time to himself.'

Suki hesitated. 'Absolutely,' she said slowly.

Grant smiled. 'That's OK then,' he said. 'It'll take him a while to get over Rachel, and I wouldn't want you getting hurt.'

'Oh no, we're more good friends, really,' Suki said.

Silence while the lie hung in the room like a deadly fart.

'I had a text from him earlier about Tinker,' Grant said. 'Apparently he belongs to an old woman who's had to go into a care home, and she's very worried about him; Tinker, I mean, so it looks like Joe will be coming back with another dog!'

'Oh, good. I wonder what age Tinker is?'

'Joe didn't say, but I suppose he'll have to take him to the vet and get him assessed, make sure his inoculations are up to date and so on.' Grant drained his coffee mug and stood up. 'That was excellent, many thanks. I enjoyed your company.' He smiled. 'I can see why Joe does, too, but as I said, he's still got a way to go.'

Suki managed a faint smile.

Grant looked at her. 'I didn't ask about your husband. When did he ... pass?'

'Nearly four years ago. I did have another relationship after he died, but ... Well, it was complicated, so I'm getting over things as well.' The smile she gave was so convincing that Grant returned it.

'Glad to hear it. Well, many thanks for that and I'll let you know what spare tiles I've got hanging around at home to finish off your shower.' He bent down to give me a stroke, and throw a few treats for Lainy.

Suki said goodbye, and after he'd gone, she leant against the front door, as if all her hopes had gone, and she had nothing to keep her upright. 'Poor Joe,' she said faintly, though I suspected she was also thinking, 'poor me' and wanted a big hug. She sighed. 'What an awful thing to happen to such a lovely man. No wonder he needs time to himself.' She spoke wistfully as she walked down to the kitchen, and her footsteps were heavy with disappointment. 'I wonder, given his silence, does that means Joe's changed his mind about us?'

23

One morning Suki was looking on her computer when she looked round to me and Lainy. We were lying at opposite ends of the bed, to better keep an eye on her while she worked.

'I don't believe it,' she said. 'Joe's actually liked one of my posts!'

Lainy and I looked at each other and Lainy winked. 'What she talking about?' Lainy said, 'but it make her happy so why not?'

We watched her looking at photographs she'd put on there over the last few days. Pictures of where we'd walked, for the latest book; Mylor Creek at low tide, a tree against a cloudy sky, and a dinghy making its way out to sea. Usually we were in the fore or background, of course.

'He's liked the last six posts,' she breathed. 'He hasn't left any comments but - well, that's most odd. I didn't know he was even on Facebook.' She fiddled around on the computer, changing the pictures on the screen, until, as I leaned forward, I could see a picture of Joe with a small brown and white dog; that must have been his old dog Peanut. They were sitting on a rock and both were smiling. I snorted. Who had taken that picture? Rachel?

But Suki seemed not to worry about that. She looked at his picture and smiled. 'Well,' she muttered. 'So that's the lovely Peanut. And a nice picture of Joe, don't you think? He does have a lovely smile.' She was sort of talking to us but not really. 'Well, that *is* interesting.' She paused and stared again. 'Mind you, he's very busy so - does it look as if *I'm* busy?' Another pause. 'Oh what the hell, I *am* busy!' She sighed. 'And I don't want to play games. However, it's important to make one's posts look good...'

And for the rest of the morning, she set about her work humming. Which didn't make sense but was a nice change.

Later that week we met Tess and Titch for a walk at our old stomping ground, Roundwood Quay. Titch was in one of his quiet moods, so we trotted along in silence, though he was slower than usual.

'Are you all right, my darling?' I asked.

'Not been feeling too good, to be honest,' he said. 'I don't know what's the matter with me, but I've been really tired, and my nose isn't up to smelling much either. I can hardly smell you, darling Moll.' He paused and his nose quivered. 'I know you're there, though, that's the main thing.'

I moved closer, nuzzled his whiskers. 'Of course I am,' I breathed. 'Anything I can do, just let me know. Would you rather just sit for a while?' Come to think of it, he looked rather grey round the muzzle.

'No, I'm fine. We'll just go along slowly,' he said. 'Now tell me what's been happening.' As I brought him up to date, we noticed a cream retriever coming towards us, feathery tail waving high in the breeze. He smelt very male, and his black nose twitched when he saw Lainy. He wasn't interested in us, I noted; we were too old.

Lainy dashed towards him and I kept a close eye. Normally I would have trotted forward to forestall any problems; this time I needed to stay near my dear one, so I watched Suki closely. She was listening to Tess, but I saw her head jerk up and she froze, watching Lainy carefully. Suki tensed, and I could see she was ready to dash forward if necessary, but as Lainy bounced towards the much larger dog, she stopped, within sniffing distance of his muzzle. She looked round, as if to say, 'What do I do now?' then looked back.

This handsome dog edged closer and tried to sniff her butt. Lainy squeaked, and moved out of his way, turning her beautiful eyes round to see his. His nose quivered, and I could smell that happy smell coming off him. It quite took me back to my only sexual dalliance with a dog called Errol, many years ago. I held my breath, waiting to see what would happen.

Finally Lainy curved round, let him smell her butt, then danced back towards us, the poor besotted retriever following her every paw. I think he would have followed us for the whole of our walk had his owners not called him. He ignored them at first, but a woman rushed forwards and put him on his lead, trying to drag him off in the opposite direction. 'Sorry!' She called as she pulled and tugged; he was a heavy dog, by the look of him.

'That's all right!' said Suki, and she and Tess looked at Lainy, who'd danced back, waving her funny tail and looking very pleased with herself.

'She's turning into a real flirt!' Tess said. 'Go for it, Lainy. Knock 'em dead!'

I wasn't sure what she meant, but Lainy came back to us, sniffing my nose quickly. 'He very handsome, you think?' she winked.

'He is,' I said. 'Just be careful, Lainy. It's fun to flirt, but don't take on more than you can handle.'

Lainy looked at me and her nose quivered. 'Is fine, I handle,' she said. 'Remember, I bite, no?' And with another wink, she darted off to explore an elusive squirrel.

The smell of the squirrel, and the relief that she'd avoided another confrontation, were so great that we surged forward, following the scent, and then one of a rabbit. We crashed through branches, trotted through mud, albeit at a more sedate pace than Lainy, and finally returned to Suki and Tess as they waited for us, still laughing.

'Thank god for that,' Suki said. 'I thought we were going to have an argument on our hands. Instead we had a love struck retriever!'

I knew Titch would have something to say on the matter, but he was curiously silent. 'Titch?' I looked around. A few minutes ago we'd both been chasing a bunny, but now he just wasn't there.

I sniffed, trying to trace his scent. I gave a yip, and Suki and Tess looked around immediately. 'What is it, Moll?'

Tess looked at me. 'Where's Titch, darling?'

I barked again, as Lainy came running back, and told her. 'I go look,' she said, and ran off again, nose to the ground like the hunting dog that she was. I followed slowly, retracing our paw prints, but when I caught a whiff of him, the scent disappeared. I turned around, sniffed the ground once more, then the air. Dogs smell the past on the ground, smell what's coming in the air. Nothing of Titch.

A rumble of panic appeared in my guts, twisting itself into a knot that I tried to shake off. He couldn't just have gone. Lainy came dashing back, panting, nose alert. 'I smell him and then he gone,' she said. 'Is very strange. What happen?'

'I don't know,' I replied. 'It's very odd. But we can't give up.'

Suki and Tess appeared as we continued our search. We all spread out, through the woods, calling and sniffing, examining every inch and every paw print. But no sign of Titch.

Part of me refused to believe that he had gone. I mean, he couldn't just disappear. Could he? And then my mind started playing tricks. He'd not been feeling well. What if he'd fallen down a rabbit hole? Or into the water? I barked instructions to Lainy, and we rushed to the river's edge, scanning the water closely. It was low tide so if he'd fallen, he'd be on the foreshore. But there was no sign of any dog, let alone Titch.

Panic twisted inside me, and I could tell Suki and Tess felt the same, though they struggled to remain calm. But their voices grew higher and the smell of fear was like rotting flesh.

Then we came across a lone woman walking her Labrador. 'You looking for a terrier?' she said. 'We passed one looking a bit lost, near the lay-by where we parked.'

Tess thanked her and we hurried back the way we'd come. It wasn't far to the cars, and we felt a huge sense of relief. Titch would be there, waiting for us! Though a small voice in the back of my head asked why he would have done that? Why not come and find us?

As we grew nearer, hope hastened our paws. We hurried along the path, scarcely stopping to sniff, and even Suki and

Tess were quiet. Reaching the steep slope, they puffed uphill while we ran ahead, arriving at the lay-by.

But no Titch.

Half an hour later, we still hadn't found him and the general mood smelt like rotting leaves.

'I don't have a torch, other than the one on my phone, and I've only got 15% battery left,' said Tess in a voice that reeked of despair. Her ponytail had slithered to the back of her neck.

'Mine's really low, too,' said Suki. 'What shall we do?'

Tess looked around, as if Titch might suddenly appear out of the gloom. 'I suppose we'll have to go home. We can't search for him in the dark. I'll put an appeal out on social media, tell the local radio stations, all that kind of thing. And come back at daylight.'

'I'll come too,' Suki said. 'We can put up posters ...' she stopped, seeing the horror on Tess's face. 'Though I'm sure he'll be home by then,' she added. 'I'll ring all the vets in the area, see if someone might have brought him in.' She looked at Tess. 'Meanwhile, we both need food and rest. Let me know if you hear anything, won't you?'

'Of course.'

The two women hugged, not daring to say any more. Tess got into her car, and we watched her drive off, too aware of the empty space beside her where Titch should have been.

Up until then, I'd managed to blot out the fact that he was missing. I was so sure that any minute, any second, he'd just reappear, muddy and panting, a little worse for wear, but he'd come back. Now it hit me, and I started to shake, from my nose to the tip of my stubby tail. He hadn't been himself today, so was he ill? Why hadn't he answered our calls? Why had his scent gone cold? What on earth had happened to him?

I felt cold and old, and was reminded of the time, not long ago, when I'd been so poorly. When I'd thought my running days were up. But I hadn't just vanished into thin air. Where had he gone? It couldn't be the end for my darling Titch... I felt as if black smoke had filled my nostrils, was getting in my eyes and making me choke. I spluttered and sneezed, to try and get rid of the dark thoughts and darker smells.

Suki bent down to give me an extra special stroke. 'He'll be fine, Moll, I know he will,' she said, though her voice was shaking and I think she was trying to reassure herself as much as me.

All we could do now was wait.

That evening we did our usual routine - tea, Suki put on the TV for us and went back to work but I don't think she could concentrate, for after a while she came and joined us and we all sat on the sofa and stared at a film. I don't think any of us watched it. Every now and then she picked up her phone, as if willing Tess to ring with some good news.

I couldn't bear to think about Titch out there in the cold night, on his own. For all his bluster and bounce, he didn't like the dark, and was frightened by owls and other night predators. He must be so chilly and tired, and if he wasn't well anyway - was he even alive? I dragged my thoughts back from those murky recesses: we had to stay positive, for each other.

Lainy nudged my nose. 'Our thoughts will keep him safe,' she said.

I nuzzled her back. For all her faults, sometimes she could say the sweetest, wisest things. 'Thank you,' I said. 'You're right. We must think the best, and he will come back.'

She didn't say any more, and for that I was grateful. After all, she'd been through so much. I lay there, trying to imagine what it must have been like when she was separated from her mother, then her siblings.

'Were you very frightened when you lost your family?'

'Yes,' she said simply. That's what I liked about Lainy. She was always honest. 'But I think I must keep near other dogs and places where I get food. We have to rely on ourselves on the streets. Always there are peoples around and dogs somewhere.' She sounded very sanguine about it.

'But weren't you cold and scared at night?'

'Yes.' She came closer and lay down beside me. 'So I think of my brother and my sister, and I imagine them close to me. And I think of my mother, and I remember her warm and her smell and the way she say we must be alert all times. And so am I.' She paused. 'But yes, I still scared. But the nights pass and then they are days, and that not so scary.'

I noticed she hadn't mentioned being worried about being captured by the Raptori, so I didn't bring it up. After all, we didn't have people like them here in Cornwall, so that was one thing Titch didn't have to worry about.

Or did he?

Tess rang later that night. 'No news,' she said, in a flattened voice that smelt of fear and worry.

'OK. What time shall we meet at Roundwood in the morning?' Suki sounded brisk and businesslike.

'Paul's coming with me. But if you've got time, that would be great,' Tess said. 'I've rung all the local vets and done social media and local radio.'

'Brilliant,' Suki said. 'I'll meet you both there at eight, OK?'

'Thanks, Suki.'

'My pleasure.' Suki put down the phone and looked at me, gave me a hug. I wouldn't normally allow it as I hated being picked up beyond anything else. But these were exceptional times.

In fact I relaxed, allowing myself to sink into the warmth of Suki's jumper that smelt so reassuringly of her. Of lemon and coffee and a tinge of fresh air from our walk. Of course she knew how I felt. Titch and I had almost grown up together. He was as much a part of my life as Tess was of Suki's. We were bound together by ropes of friendship and trust, loyalty and togetherness.

Suki didn't speak, but stroked me and that gave me strength as I looked back over the past years filled with a young, bouncy Titch. A chasing squirrels Titch. A growing older, grumpy Titch. The wiser, older, listening Titch. The Titch who had been beside me for most of my adult life. Sharing my life in the best possible sense.

My other half; the term that humans used, and yet he really did feel like my other half. When I needed to talk, he would listen. When I was worried he would ease my fears. When I was joyous he shared my happiness. How could I live without my Titch?

24

None of us slept much that night. I lay close to Suki, as I had done all those years ago when we lost Pip, both of us needing the warmth and comfort of the other. She tossed and turned, and I could smell her anxiety, like rancid butter. It was a long, long night, and half way through she turned on the light and got up to warm some milk.

We followed her into the kitchen but for once I wasn't bothered about biscuits, or dropped food. I just needed to be close to her, to feel her reassuring presence.

'You've looked after me for so long, Moll. It's my turn to look after you now,' she said, and gave me the most lovely smile which made everything worthwhile.

We went back to bed where she read for a while, and I snuggled under her arm while Lainy lay watching us from the other end of the bed. A little before dawn, she turned the light off and we all dozed fitfully, and I had terrible dreams of seeing Titch's body at the bottom of a huge quarry, where I knew he was in trouble but I couldn't get to him.

By the time we had to get up, Suki smelt like newspaper that'd been left out in the rain. She sighed. 'I do so wish Joe was here. I don't mean that he could find Titch, just that it would all seem less scary.'

A pause. 'I wonder how he's getting on. Mind you, he'd probably want to know about Titch. After all, he's met him enough times.' She grabbed her phone and tapped away. Then she tutted. 'No.' And she deleted it all. Another sigh and she tapped away again. 'I'll just send it,' she said, and we heard the familiar woosh as the message flew off to Wales.

We set off to meet Tess and Paul, and when we got to Roundwood, it felt bizarre and so wrong to be retracing our footsteps without Titch. Neither Tess nor Suki spoke much, and we sniffed as much as we could but it had rained heavily overnight and yesterday's scents were mostly wiped out, replaced by fresh overnight smells. Both phones were disappointingly silent, and I felt ancient and weary and desperately sad. I so wished I could *do* something, but most of all I longed to be with my darling Titch.

All this made me think about my own mortality, something I had avoided doing, since my health scare. I was happy that Suki was looked after by Lainy. Admittedly she could be a bit of a liability, given her strong views, panic attacks and propensity to get into trouble, but her heart was in the right place, and I knew she would defend Suki to the end.

What I hadn't thought about was how I would cope without Titch. The future loomed ahead, gloomy and tasteless. It smelt of burnt tyres, and was ominously silent. No running and jumping, though we were getting a bit old for that. None of the quiet companionship that we enjoyed so much while the youngsters did their own thing.

I wasn't afraid of getting old. I was just afraid of getting old on my own. And much though I loved Suki and Lainy, they could never replace my Titch.

We had to leave because Suki, Tess and Paul all had to go to work, and it was terrible to leave the area knowing, or hoping desperately, that my beloved Titch was there. Somewhere. Wasn't he? Trouble was, Lainy and I had sniffed all the possible routes and there was still no smell of him. What more could we do? As Lainy said, 'you must rest and look after yourself, Moll. That's what Titch want.'

I knew she was right, so we headed home to recoup.

Joe rang a bit later, and I could smell her relief, just from hearing his voice. Knowing that he cared.

'I'm so sorry to hear about Titch,' he said, and I have to say his voice gave me a lift, too. 'I can't think of anything worse.'

'It's horrible, the uncertainty...' she didn't need to say any more. We all knew.

'How's Moll bearing up?'

'I'm really worried about her,' Suki said. 'She's off her food, which is unheard of, and she's been lying under the bed all morning.'

'Oh bless her,' Joe said. 'She must be devastated.'

'Yes, she's very despondent, poor thing. Well, we all are.' Her voice wobbled.

'You've advertised on all the social media sites, I presume?' Joe said.

'Yup. And vets, radio stations, all that kind of thing.'

'There are several lost dog charities in Cornwall. Might be worth trying those?'

'Oh, good idea,' she said.

'Something like Cornwall Search Dogs and Lost Dogs; if you Google them I'm sure they'll come up,' he said. There was another pause. 'I'm so sorry,' he added, and he sounded like the Joe we knew. Sincere and caring. It made my whiskers tremble.

'Thank you,' Suki said, and her earrings wobbled as much as her voice. I thought, if she starts crying, I'm done for. We're trying to hold it together, girl. But she took a deep breath and said, 'How's the job coming along?'

'It's fine. In fact, they've asked me to do their other cottage,' he said.

'Oh. Well, they must be very pleased with your work,' she said, her voice dipping. I knew she was thinking that he'd be away even longer.

'I suppose so,' he said.

'So how are you and Tinker getting on?' she said.

'We are becoming good mates,' he said gravely. Then he laughed, and straight away, that was our Joe again and the sound was so uplifting that for a minute I forgot about Titch.

186

'I think Grant said you'd found out who he belongs to? Thanks so much for organising that, by the way, he's sorted my shower out, bless him. I'm so grateful.'

'He's a good bloke, Grant. Great business partner, and I'm glad he's fixed your shower.'

'He's coming back with some tiles and going to grout it all, then it's as good as new, which is brilliant.' She paused. 'But you were saying, about Tinker?'

'Oh yes. He belongs to an old lady who's had to go into a care home. She was so worried about him. Her son had been looking after him, but the son is at work all day, so that's no good. So I said I'd have him.'

'I am glad. I bet the old lady is really pleased, and relieved.'

'Yes. I went to visit her and she was delighted. Lovely woman, she'd been a writer all her life and Tinker loved sitting with her while she wrote her books, apparently.'

Suki laughed. 'So you've inherited a literary dog!'

'Yes. I said I'd take Tinker in to see her while I'm here, and she was so pleased, it made me think that he should really go to someone local, so she can still see him.'

'That's very thoughtful. But there's no guarantee that they'd take him to see her.'

Joe sighed. 'No, I guess not.'

'And you could always send her pictures of Tinker.'

'True.' A pause. 'I never thought I'd have another dog.'

'Well, just proves how special Tinker must be,' Suki said. We were both aware that Joe didn't usually talk about personal things like loss. And that he was avoiding talking about Peanut dying...

'Yes, he is,' Joe's voice was quiet and thoughtful.

A silence, while I thought, once more, of losing Titch. A stabbing pain in my guts, as if my entrails were being pulled out. How could I bear it? Surely he wouldn't leave me; not yet?

'Anyway, don't want to keep you,' Suki said. 'I know you're busy and I've got a couple of deadlines and...'

Neither of them added, 'a dog to find,' but we all thought it.

'Yes. Well, good luck,' Joe said. 'Let me know what happens, won't you?'

Her voice cleared, and she said, 'Thanks, Joe, I will.'

'And Suki?'

'Yes?'

'I was wondering if you and the girls would like to come up one weekend?'

Silence. 'To Wales?'

'Yes. I've got to be here a while longer and I thought you might like to come and see Wales.'

Silence.

'But maybe you're too busy...'

'No!' Cried Suki. 'No, that would be lovely.'

Joe gave a laugh that spoke of relief and anticipation. 'Oh good. If you were able to leave earlyish on Friday, you'd miss most of the work and school traffic and get up here in reasonable time.' Pause. 'If that suits you...'

'Yes, that would be...' Suki's voice grew brighter and happier with every word... 'that would be lovely. We'd - we'd love to see you, Joe.' She laughed. 'And meet Tinker.' She paused. 'But obviously we have to wait and see...'

'Of course. Just let me know when you'd like to come and I'll get things organised up here. You can stay in the cottage with me.'

'Thanks, Joe, it obviously depends what happens with Titch. But I'll let you know. Sleep tight.'

'And you, Suki. Love to you all.'

And while I could hear the mix of emotions in their voices - joy and sorrow - it was too hard to think of going away while Titch was missing. So I slunk off, under the bed, where it felt safe and quiet. The world was altogether too painful. And while I had lost touch with Titch, at least I could imagine him beside me. And that gave me the strength to carry on.

We had a quiet, sniffy walk that afternoon with Anne who was perfect company. Quiet but cheerful, sympathetic as well.

'So Tess is getting in touch with the dog charities, is she? That's a good idea.'

'Yes, she contacted them earlier. I don't know how they go about finding dogs, but anything's worth a try.'

'I know one of them has a local Facebook page and they have lots of people keeping an eye out, whereas another one has volunteers and sniffer dogs so perhaps one notifies the other,' Anne said.

'That would make sense.'

'It was Joe's idea, you said? How was he?'

'He was fine - he's asked us up to Wales when ... You know.'

'When you can. That's great.'

'He's going to take Tinker to see his old lady in the care home.'

'What a lovely thing to do,' Anne said. 'Not many people would think of that, yet alone do it.'

'I know.' Suki's voice grew stronger. 'And it's made me think...'

'Think what?'

'Well, poor Moll's really suffering. She and Titch are so close, and I can't begin to think how much she misses him.'

I could feel their kind eyes gently alighting on my back. Just as well they didn't know how I felt. It was like having my insides dragged out, very slowly, by a particularly aggressive predator.

'Poor darling. It must be terrible.' Anne sighed. 'You said that Joe had told you about his ex-girlfriend being an alcoholic?'

'Yes. Poor Joe, it must have been so hard. Then Grant, his business partner, said that Joe never stopped working, after Rachel left him and then Peanut died, so he really needs a break, poor fellow.'

'Poor Joe. Living with any addiction must be terrible. In which case, this is just what he needs. Time to think, a new dog and a visit from you lot!' She smiled. 'It's great news that he's invited you up there, isn't it? I know you can't go till you find out more about Titch, but at least that's something to look forward to.'

'Absolutely, and we all need that.' Suki bent down and stroked my back. 'Come on, Molls. We need to keep each other going, don't we? Let's find Titch first.'

Time crept on, and there was still no sign of Titch. With every minute, every hour and every day that passed, our hopes dwindled. Suki was struggling to keep Tess positive and to cheer me up, but for the first time in my life, I had no appetite and no energy. I couldn't sleep, but spent my time mostly under the bed, trying to think of where Titch might be, and how we might find him.

Suki let me be, though she did try and tempt me with bits of sausage and cheese. Even that was no good. I had to conserve the little energy I had, and the only way to do it was to lie still. Even talking with Lainy was too much of an effort, but once again, this clever dog just said, 'If you need me, I am here, Moll. You just say.'

I nodded, glad that she was so quick to understand.

The second day, she and Suki went out for a walk and a run. They kept going back to the Roundwood area, to see if there was something we might have missed.

This time, Lainy told me later, they met a man in the woods with three big rescues dogs who had all been sniffer dogs.

'They were very big and smell brave and their noses...' Lainy swivelled her nose so that even I had to smile. 'I think I have good nose for finding things, but these dogs have super powers. You know?'

I wasn't in the mood for chat, but from the energy fizzing off her, I guessed there was more to this story. 'Yes,' I said. 'So?'

'So I talk to these dogs and they coming from Spain and very badly treated until they are rescue and go and work in Wales finding peoples!'

I was so tired, I didn't have the energy to work out where this was going. I twitched my whiskers half-heartedly.

'And I tell them about Titch and they say they help us find him!'

Her energy and enthusiasm were touching but I'd come to terms with the fact that I'd lost Titch and I couldn't bear any false hopes. That would be far too hard. I opened my mouth to tell her this but she rushed on.

'I know you think it too late, but we go and find Titch today!'

I stirred as a faint whisper of hope spiralled up inside me. It was faint, like me, and I knew it could be extinguished very quickly, but for the first time in days, I began to think I might actually see Titch again. I opened my mouth to ask more when Suki came running in, clutching her phone.

'Oh, Moll. We met this man just now and he and his dogs used to work for a charity that finds missing people. He's still got lots of contacts, so he said he'll organise a search party for this afternoon. If anyone can find Titch, he and his dogs will!' And she dashed off, ringing Tess as she hurried down the hallway.

We set off that afternoon, armed with trepidation on my part; the others brimming with nervous hope. It spilled out in uncertain-smelling waves which made me feel quite sick, but I had to come, just in case we found him.

When we arrived at the layby near Roundwood, it was full. A big van with three huge dogs was parked nearest the woods, along with several other cars. Out of these came men and women wearing bright jackets and talking in loud, important voices to Suki and Tess.

'I'm Bill,' said a tall man standing near the van with the big dogs. He smelt of outdoors and kindness, and he held out his hand to shake Tess's and said, 'and these are Olly, Ebo and Dave.' He laughed at her puzzled expression. 'Named after Oliver Twist, Ebeneezer Scrooge and ...'

'David Copperfield,' Tess finished. 'Good to meet you, Bill. And this is Suki and Moll, Titch's best friend, and Lainy, another family friend.'

'Glad to meet all of you. Now, Tess, you've brought something with Titch's scent?'

Tess nodded and produced a blanket that I knew well. It came from Titch's bed, and the sight of that poor bedraggled blanket brought tears to my nose. I was so overcome I choked, but Suki was there with a reassuring stroke.

'There, there, Moll,' she whispered.

Tess said to Bill, 'so what's the plan?'

'We give the dogs Titch's scent,' he said, and gave the dogs the blanket which they duly sniffed, noses rotating like I'd never seen before, tails wagging, whiskers shimmering. It was truly impressive.

'Then, when we're all ready, we set off. As soon as the dogs get a scent they alert us, and we may need to get these other guys,' he gestured to the men in bright jackets, 'to dig the little fella out.'

Tess held herself straight, fear and hope radiating off her. 'That's supposing they *find* a scent. What if they don't?' Her voice wobbled alarmingly.

Bill looked down at her and gave a smile. 'They've never let me down yet,' he said. 'If he's here, we will do our best to find him. Now. Are we all good to go?'

He shouted to the others and we all set off down the hill, into the woods. I turned down Suki's offer that she should carry me. I was tired, yes. Exhausted even, but if we were going to find Titch, I wanted to be the first to greet him.

The only thing that bothered me was Bill's reply. He'd said IF Titch was here, they'd do their best to find him. But what if he wasn't?

We followed the sniffer dogs as they crashed through the woods, noses to the ground. Lainy went ahead with them, while I stayed close to Suki and Tess: I didn't have the energy to follow the young ones. The other people in the bright jackets walked ahead with Bill, as they strode along the path towards the wooden bridge.

We followed, but after a while hopes began to flag, smelling of decaying flowers. Even Lainy's tail, that had been flying like a banner, drooped a little, though she winked at me before she shot through the undergrowth.

Bill called a halt at Roundwood Quay. 'OK everyone, I think we can safely say we've covered the western side of the woods. Now we'll try the eastern side. Keep your eyes peeled for any sight of a bit of tan or white. The poor fella will be a bit tired by now, and thirsty and hungry. Bit like us!' He smiled and passed round thermos flasks which the other walkers took gratefully. For us dogs he produced collapsible bowls which he filled with water from a rucksack on his back. This was followed by treats, and another sniff of Titch's blanket.

Dave, the oldest of the dogs smelt worried. 'I'm not sure about this,' he said. 'I don't think we're looking in the right place.'

'He's always right,' explained Olly. 'So where do you think we should search, Dave?'

Dave shook his head so his ears flapped. 'I'm thinking...'

'He thinks with his nose,' said Olly. 'Always listen to Dave.'

We sat in silence while Dave stood with his eyes shut, nose swivelling in different directions. If my spirits hadn't sunk so alarmingly, I would have found it fascinating. We held our breaths while he did his thing, then he opened his eyes. He looked gloomy.

'What you think, Dave?' Lainy said.

He looked down from his great height to me and Lainy. 'Can you tell us again exactly where you were when you noticed he was missing?'

'We were near that bend in the path, where you can go down to that little path to the foreshore. Lainy chased a squirrel, and Titch and I followed her.' I looked at Lainy. 'Can you add anything, Lainy?'

Her nose twitched. 'We chase squirrel, yes, and then I think maybe Titch hurt his foot because I hear him trip and I look round and he falling over tree root. He say something I not hear, and he follow, and we go down to beach and we play on sand and then Suki calling, and when we come back, suddenly Titch is not here.'

Dave nodded. 'OK. And you've looked down that path, I take it?'

I nodded. 'Yes, every stone of it.

'OK. Well, we'll do what Bill suggests, and take the eastern side of the woods.' But he didn't sound convinced, and it was with heavy paws that we set off again, followed by Suki, Tess and the other humans.

We were silent along this stretch of the woods. Even the people were quiet, as if aware that the rescue was doomed. I felt like going back to the car. I couldn't bear it, but Suki looked around and said, 'Lift, Moll?'

It pained me to say yes, but I didn't have the energy or the hope to continue, so she picked me up, tucked me in the front of her rucksack so I could see where we were going. And I decided I rather liked this view, so high up, that humans had. I felt a bit dizzy at first, so far off the ground, but it was interesting, and I could see further ahead.

I could also smell failure. It leaked out of the Spanish dogs' noses, and every paw print contained less and less hope. I thought, well, at least we had a few hours when the world seemed brighter. We can be thankful for that. I tried not to think of my poor darling, lying lost and abandoned somewhere. I tried not to think of the dark times ahead without my love. What was the point of living without him in my old age? Why didn't I just give up now? Suki would be sad, but she had Lainy now, and Tess, and if Lainy stepped in, maybe Joe could be on the scene again. I'd done what I came to do. I could just drift away peacefully.

'Moll?' Lainy said, as if she knew what I was thinking.

I looked down from my lofty perch. 'Yes?' I could hear how weak my voice was.

'We not give up yet,' she said. 'We nearly there.'

But she seemed at odds with everyone else, who carried defeat on their backs.

We continued until we came to the gates that either led back into the woods or up the steep track to the cars.

Dave shook his head again. 'No, he's not here.' He barked. 'Sorry, folks. We've done our best, but he's just...' His head shot up. 'Hang on.' He looked at Lainy. 'You hear that?'

We all stood motionless. Lainy's ears went round like satellite dishes. She froze, nose twitching, whiskers swivelling, and then she said, 'I got it!' And she plunged off down a drive towards the river. The other dogs followed, as did Suki and Tess.

'What's going on?' said Tess.

'No idea, but Lainy knows,' panted Suki as we ran along.

Down the drive the big dogs galloped, ears streaming behind them, with us following. At the bottom was a farm with many barns, and Lainy and Big Dave raced ahead to the far one, where they started barking and scrabbling at the big double doors. Suki and Tess arrived at the same time as Bill.

'What is it, Lainy?' asked Suki.

Bill looked at Dave and gave him a large treat. 'Good *boy*,' he said, and I heard all the love and admiration in his voice, and thanked dog for this good man, for these wonderful dogs. I still didn't dare hope, but by now my nose was quivering, and Suki put me gently on the ground. 'Lainy?' she said, and her voice was so full of longing that tears came to my nose.

'In there,' Lainy said, nosing the door. 'Look in there. Now!'

Bill shoved his shoulder against the barn doors, which buckled but held firm. He tried again, and again, and then some other men joined him and finally, after some muffled swearing, the door creaked open, and Dave and Lainy led us inside. The barn was dark and smelt of straw. Rain had come in through an open window and I smelt mud and rats and pellets for feeding cows.

I could smell a pile of straw against the darkest part of the barn. But not just that ... Lainy dashed forward at the same time as Dave. As our eyes accustomed to the gloom, all four dogs scrabbled in the straw, until I heard a whimper, and my heart literally froze. There was the tiniest, faintest cry, but that was enough. I nosed forwards, past the big dogs, getting straw in my fur and my eyes, but then... I smelt him.

Lying on a patch of muddy straw was my Titch. He smelt so old and so tired. But he was there, and he was alive! I whimpered back, 'I'm here, darling. I'm here, hold on!'

He tried to raise his head, but it was too much effort. I could just hear him mouth the word, 'Moll,' before he slumped back onto the ground.

Tess was next, crying with relief as very carefully she crouched over him, gently feeling every section of his body with skilled fingers. 'Poor Titchy, my darling boy,' she said, tears plopping onto my fur and his as she examined him. 'Poor poppet, never mind, we're here now. You're safe.'

'How is he?' breathed Suki.

'Very weak, I should think he's dehydrated and very hungry, but from a first examination, I can't find anything broken,' she said, wiping her nose on her jacket sleeve. 'Oh, Bill, and you wonderful dogs, Lainy and Moll - you are incredible!'

Bill came up next. 'Shall I have another look? I trained in animal first aid so if we both satisfy ourselves, you can take him to the vet if necessary.'

'She's a vet nurse,' added Suki.

'Ah well, that's grand,' he said, and looking round, gave all of us dogs treats and another bowl of water.

I inched forward, not wanting to let Titch out of my sight a moment longer. I was concerned about him, obviously, when he was so weak, but just to have him here, nearby, was the best possible present I could ever have. Once Bill had finished his examination, I lay down beside Titch, who opened one eye and looked at me.

'Love you,' he whispered, before he slumped onto the straw once more.

25

We went home soon after that. I was loath to leave Titch, but Tess said, very gently, 'sorry, Moll, but I have to take him to the vet. He's very dehydrated, so he probably needs to be on a drip overnight, to help him get better really quickly. But as soon as he's well enough to come home, I'll ring Suki and she'll bring you over, OK?' She glanced at Suki who nodded.

'Of course,' Suki gulped. 'You can stay over if you like, Moll. If you don't mind, Tess. I think it would do them both good; they've been through hell.'

'So have we,' replied Tess. 'But of course Moll can stay over. Anyway, I'll ring when I get the verdict from the vet.' And very gently she lifted Titch into her arms, cuddling him like a pup.

At this point Bill stepped forward. 'I hope you don't mind me saying, but he might get heavy after a while,' he said. 'I've got a special carrier for poorly dogs, and some of these blokes here would be happy to carry him to your car for you, if you like.'

Tess smelt of relief and exhaustion. 'Thanks,' she gulped. 'That's really kind. I'm a bit worn out, to be honest.'

He touched her shoulder briefly. 'Of course you are. Now, let's get this organised and we can get this fella back to your car in no time.' He turned to Suki. 'In fact, his girlfriend looks like she could use a lift, too. Would she like to go with him?'

Suki's face was smothered in tears: I could smell them without looking at her. 'That would be amazing,' she said. 'Poor Moll's been off her food, so she's far too weak. Thanks so much.'

'My pleasure,' said Bill, and in no time I was scooped up alongside Titch in what seemed like a portable cosy box. We snuggled up together, were lifted into the air, and though I couldn't see what was going on, and we swayed a bit as they carried us along, I was content to lie there, hearing Titch's heartbeat against my flank; feel his whiskers against mine, and be incredibly grateful that we had found each other again.

Bill gave me a quick health check before we set off home. 'She seems OK but she needs food and water, doesn't she?' he said. 'You said she's been off her grub?'

Suki nodded. 'Yes. Never known her not eat before. But I think now we've found Titch, she'll be fine. Thanks so much, Bill, for everything. We're so grateful.'

Bill shrugged and smelt a bit embarrassed, an unsure smell like dandelions in the rain. 'It's what I do,' he said gruffly. 'Anyway, might bump into you again if you're ever around this area. My three love the woods round here, and your Lainy's got an amazing nose.'

'She has, hasn't she?' Suki said. 'It might do her good to make friends with your gang; perhaps she could learn some scent work.'

'You're on,' he said. 'I usually come on Tuesdays, so any time you're free, drop me a text.' He handed her a card. 'Be good to meet up again. Now we must go. 'Bye all!'

Turning round, he thanked all the volunteers in their bright jackets, shaking them by the hand, while his three dogs lolled in the back of his van, panting happily.

Job well done.

We were all quiet on the way home; relief and exhaustion mingled to form a contented, tired smell like toast.

'Special tea tonight,' Suki said when we got home. 'Celebration for Lainy being such a clever dog to find Titch.' As she made our tea, her phone rang, and I noticed her spark of joy as she answered it.

'Joe!' She said. 'How are you?'

'I'm OK, but more to the point, how are you all? Any news?'

'We found him!' Suki cried. 'We're not long back, and I've just fed the girls, then I was going to ring you. Oh, I can't tell you the relief!'

'I can imagine. So what happened?'

'This guy called Bill arranged the search, with his search and rescue dogs, so they covered the woods and then we stopped and the top dog, Dave, wasn't happy...'

Joe laughed. 'It sounds like a Disney cartoon!'

'It was, almost!'

'Sorry, do go on.'

'Well, we stopped and Dave the top dog looked at Lainy and it was almost like they were having this conversation, and suddenly Lainy's ears shot up and she ran down a private drive towards the river, and she and Dave took us to this disused barn and Titch was lying inside on the straw.'

'Good for Lainy,' Joe said. 'What a star. And Dave, too.'

'I know. They were all brilliant, but I'm especially proud of Lainy.'

'So you'll all be able to sleep tonight. Poor Tess, and Moll.'

'Yes, poor girl, she's really been pining. I've never known her off her food before,' Suki said. 'She's really weak, and I've been so worried about her. But Bill checked her over and pronounced her fit, so I think she just needs feeding up and plenty of rest.'

'That's good.' Pause. 'So who's Bill?'

'He was this guy I met in Roundwood Woods who used to organise search and rescue work with his rescue dogs in Wales. He's back in Cornwall now, but still has lots of contacts so he does it now on a voluntary basis through a charity.'

'Oh, right.'

'He's got three Spanish rescue dogs; huge great hounds, with the most incredible noses.' Suki laughed, and it was a joyous gurgle. 'Their noses sort of rotate, and I could swear Dave, the biggest one, actually thinks through his nose. It's incredible!'

'Sounds fascinating. How lucky you met him.'

'Yes, we're going to meet up again because I think Lainy would really benefit from learning more about scent work from his dogs. He's a pleasant man. Looks like a lumberjack.' Again she giggled.

'Right,' Joe said. 'Well, I'm glad that's all worked out well.'

'How's Tinker?'

'He's really made himself at home. I've brought his bed into the cottage so he can keep me company in the daytime and we go back to the other place I'm staying in at night and take his bed back with us.' He chuckled. 'As soon as I go to the van to get some tools, he's there. When I go to the loo, he comes with me. This morning he even wanted to come in the shower with me!'

Suki laughed. 'Oh bless him. He must be so happy to have found you.'

'The feeling's mutual. I'd forgotten what unconditional love feels like.'

There was silence while we digested this. Say something, Suki, I willed her. Now's the right moment...

'It's wonderful, isn't it?' she said, rather feebly, and I groaned.

'Anyway, very glad Titch is safe,' Joe said gruffly. 'I must go. Let me know when you'd like to come up.'

'I will, thanks. Probably the weekend after next, if that's OK?'

'Of course. That will give me time to prepare things for you.'

Suki laughed. 'You don't have to get anything ready for us, Joe. It'll just be good to see you.'

'You too.' His voice was deep and caring, just how I knew him to be. 'Love to you all. Speak soon.'

As soon as Tess brought Titch home, we went over there, leaving Lainy at home. Suki had taken her for a run earlier and Lainy needed time on her own. She was tired after all that scenting which is more exhausting than humans realise.

Tess smelt as if she'd been crying when she opened the door, and Suki gave her a huge hug while I sought out Titch. It took me back to the time when, several years ago, Titch and Tess had been absent for a very long time. The parting was terrible, but the anticipation and the joyous reunions made it all bearable. I tried to look on this the same way.

I was still a bit weak, although I'd managed to eat my tea, a portion of cheese, some ham, biscuits and a pigs ear without being sick. Having food in my belly certainly helped, so I felt stronger, and more able to look after my poor darling.

Titch was lying in his bed looking very thin and smelling exhausted, but he raised his head when he saw me and wearily thumped his tail and I caught the sweet smell of his love. I trotted over and lay down beside him, as he whispered croakily, 'Sorry, Moll, bit tired to get up.'

'You stay right there,' I said. 'We'll have a little snooze as I'm tired too.'

I knew I wouldn't sleep, but I just wanted to lie beside him and enjoy being close. So I breathed in his faint scent and listened to what Suki and Tess had to say.

'Is he OK?' Suki said in hushed tones.

'He's a lot better than he was,' Tess replied. 'Paul's been great, but he had to go to work today.' She hadn't even bothered to put her hair in a ponytail: it hung exhaustedly in a limp curtain. 'Titch was really dehydrated, which you'd expect, so they put him on a drip overnight and by this morning he was feeling a bit better, but it turns out he's got heart damage.'

'Oh no. Is it serious?'

'I hope not. But I didn't want to subject him to tests when he's so weak, so I thought I'd bring him home and that's when I rang you, 'cos I just want him to be here, with me and you and Moll.'

Suki gave her a hug. 'Quite right. He needs to get better at home.'

Tess smiled. 'And a huge thank you to Lainy for finding him.'

'I know. I'm so proud of her. She's having a much needed rest at the moment. Have you any idea how Titch came to be in that barn?'

Tess shook her head. 'Nope. Maybe his heart made him go a bit weird. He's quite deaf now so he wouldn't have been able to hear us, and the barn wasn't far from where we were walking, so perhaps he smelt food or something; he'd been eating some of the cattle food I think, and it was warmer there than out in the open. That's my guess, anyway.'

Silence while I sensed them looking over at us.

'They do look sweet, don't they?' Tess said. 'Love's old dream!'

Suki laughed. 'Just like you and Paul.'

'Tess grunted. 'I know, I'm lucky. He's been so wonderful since Titch went missing. He's grand, really. As Pip was. And Ted, in his way.' She paused. 'And Joe - he loves you. Doesn't he?'

'I think so. He's asked us to go up there for the weekend,' Suki said, and I could hear the smile in her voice.

'That's fantastic news, Suki. I'm so glad!'

'Thanks.' Again that grin, in every syllable. 'I've really missed him. I love sharing a bed with Joe.' She blushed. 'Not just the sex. I just love snuggling up to him at night. And he's very good at listening when I'm worried about things. And I love walking with him, cooking together. Having a laugh. Watching telly, that sort of thing.'

'Of course.' Pause. 'And I bet he's missed you too. And it's much better not living together, because you don't have someone hogging the telly all the time, leaving wet towels on the bathroom floor, cooking a meal so the kitchen looks like a bomb's hit it... shall I go on?'

Suki laughed. 'No. I get the picture.'

Silence while I could almost hear Tess's mind ticking over. 'You said his partner told you that Joe needed time on his own. To get over his ex and his dog?'

Suki nodded.

'So he's getting that, right?'

'I presume so.'

I tuned back into Titch, who had gone to sleep. His breathing had turned shallow, and I felt the first prickles of unease creep down my spine. I moved closer, and got a strong waft of a smell I'd encountered only once before. With Pip.

Suddenly all my senses were alert. I took in every precious part of my Titch: his dear snout, his fine eyelashes, his grey whiskers. The smell of him was imprinted on me. As I edged closer, his heart started beating faster, as if he was running a race, and I knew that this was one he wouldn't win. 'Titch?' I whispered. 'Are you OK?' Which was stupid, because of course he wasn't. 'I'm here.'

I pressed myself even closer, determined to keep him with me for as long as possible. Jumbled thoughts swirled round my head. I'd never thought that he really would leave here before me. What was I going to do? What was the point of being here without him?

His scent was much weaker; he didn't have much time left and I started to panic, then realised I must help him be strong and make the most of our last moments here.

He opened one eye. 'I'm not afraid of dying, Moll,' he breathed. 'But I don't want to leave you.'

All I wanted to say was, don't go! I need you! But I had to make it easier for him. I swallowed hard, twitching my whiskers to give me strength. 'We both know that we don't have much say in the matter.' I laid my nose against his, and gave him a butterfly kiss, so he knew how much I loved him. His eyes closed and I waited, drinking him in, every smell and particle of his dear, familiar fur.

After seconds, minutes, I forced myself to speak. 'Are you hurting, darling?'

His eyes fluttered open. 'Not really, but my heart feels very heavy. It's not working properly.'

'I know.' I tried to stop the tears that were looming. What could I say when my heart was breaking?

'This isn't goodbye, Moll.' His voice was very feeble.

'No, I know.' I nuzzled his whiskers; I had to be upbeat. 'Just think, you'll meet Pip and have such fun.' Was I trying too hard? 'And I won't be long and then we'll be together forever.'

'Look forward to that, darling.' His voice was so weak I could hardly hear him. 'Don't hurry. You've not finished with Lainy yet.'

'She's coming along brilliantly. She did so well finding you, I think she's got a bright future ahead of her. And that can only help her confidence. And...'

Then I realised that my Titch had stopped breathing. Ever so quietly, and gently, he just ... wasn't there any more.

Still I clung to him, pressing my warmth to his slowly cooling body. I shut my eyes, in case that might keep him with me a minute longer. As I lay there, I shut out the sound of Suki's voice, of Tess's response, and wished I could just slip away too.

And then it all grew dark.

26

Time blurred. I remember Suki's smell as she hovered over me, her worried lemon scent reassuring, and Lainy's sharp concern, the way her whiskers tickled me gently. 'Take your time, Moll, but don't go just yet,' I think I remember her saying.

When I finally came round, I could hardly raise my head. I could smell Suki's anxiety nearby, then Lainy's outdoor smell: they must have got back from a walk.

'She's awake!' Suki came rushing over. 'Oh Moll, we've been so worried. Do you remember going to the vet? You've been there for several days, on a drip.'

That explained the sour medical smell that came from my left leg. I raised my head as Suki stroked me so gently, as if I might break. I lay back, my head fuzzy, and then the darkness came crashing in as I remembered ... No Titch.

'Moll?' Lainy stood over me, her presence both a challenge and a relief. 'Titch would not want you to starve yourself.'

I looked at her; how did she know?

'I know how much he love you.'

I lay there, trying to connect my thoughts. She was right, but everything was such an effort.

'He want you to carry on,' she said. 'He want you be your normal brave self. And you are so brave, Moll!'

She was clever that dog. She knew just what to say to rouse me. But she was also right. Titch would not want me to give up.

For his sake, and for Suki's and Lainy's, I would have to rally. It wasn't my time yet, and I still had work to do.

I looked at Lainy and she winked. 'I look after you for a change, OK? So you have sleep now and wake up and eat dinner. Titch say.'

I closed my eyes again, relieved that Titch was sending messages to me, even if I couldn't see him. A faint thought occurred to me that Lainy might be making this up, but I let that float away. I'd think about it another time.

It took me a while to regain some strength. Lainy and Suki cajoled me into eating, and although that dark voice kept telling me there was no point in being here, I knew I couldn't give up just yet.

I'd lost my energy though, and for the first time in my life felt really old. My bones creaked, my head felt slow and after another week I could still only just manage a short walk round the block before collapsing, exhausted.

Suki took me to the vet, a trip I normally enjoyed as she had high quality treats, but this time I had no appetite. She seemed to understand though, and stroked me gently and told Suki, 'I can't find anything medically wrong with her, except that she's a bit older and I suspect she's got a broken heart. Dogs grieve just as much as we do.'

I could smell Suki's tears, even if I couldn't see them. 'What can I do?' came a watery voice.

'Just do what you're doing. I think you said you had a younger dog?'

She nodded.

'That's good. That should help. Just make sure Mollie eats when she can, and I hope she'll soon have enough energy to go for walks again. Keep me posted.'

I learned to keep Titch in a separate box in my mind. Thinking about him was too raw, too painful, and made me feel even more ancient. I felt useless, and Suki had to lift me onto her bed at night time, where I lay hoping for some release from the daytime thoughts that crowded my head.

I kept seeing us, like an ongoing film in my head. Titch and me as young dogs, Titch in silent mood, trotting along at Trelissick. Chasing squirrels at Roundwood. Lying still with bloated stomachs after Christmas lunch cooked by Paul. Titch, my Titch, everywhere. And now nowhere. I didn't want him to feel I was letting him down. But he didn't know what it was like to feel so abandoned, so lost. All I wanted to do was drift off and join him.

'Moll?' Lainy stood over me one day, tickling me gently with her whiskers till I woke up. 'I worry of Tess. She so unhappy.'

'So am I,' I thought. But then I felt guilty. What did that say about me? I'd been so wrapped up in my grief, I hadn't even thought how much Tess must be missing Titch too. Sorrow makes selfish bedfellows of us, indeed. I looked at Lainy. 'What's the matter with her?'

'She so sad.' Lainy lay down next to me. 'She cry and she cry and she cry and Suki she try and help but Tess is so very sad. She not eat and she not working even.'

I sat up at that. Tess had her own business, so if she didn't work, she didn't get paid, and she let people down. 'That's not good,' I murmured.

'What you think we do?'

'Do?' My nose twitched for the first time in what seemed like ages. Titch loved it when I did that. He called it my Thinking Nose. And although tears rushed to it, I snorted to blow them out, and tried to concentrate instead on Tess. 'We must go and see her.'

I looked up and heard Suki next door, on the phone. On wobbly legs I got up, followed the sounds of her voice, low and soothing, but with traces of tears. She looked up as I came into the room and said, 'Oh, Tess, Moll's up!' I walked over and sat next to her, leaning on her heavily. She was warm and smelt of honey and lemons and outside and sorrow and all the things I loved, so I gave her a lick, and then licked the phone.

Suki held me tight for a moment. Not too long; she knew I didn't like it. 'You're quite right, Moll,' she said. 'And I'm so glad to see you up again.' She gave a chuckle which reached down to my paws. 'We're coming over, Tess,' she said.

Paul opened the door when we arrived, and showed us in. The house was cold when we went inside, Titch's bed gone from the kitchen.

'I couldn't bear to see it,' Tess said when she saw me looking round. I could smell traces of him, but they were very faint. Tess had shrunk, too, and her hair hung lankly, the ponytail gone. She was sitting in an armchair with what smelt like a mug of cold coffee and despair as companions. Far too like me.

I went over to her and did what I did to Suki. I leaned on her, heavily. She smelt of sorrow, deep and raw like a fresh wound.

'Don't blame you,' said Suki. 'What can I do?'

Tess shook her head. 'I know I've got to pull myself together, but it's just so hard.' She looked up with a blotchy face, her eyes red and sore. 'I've got to get back to work. But I can't even think straight.'

I licked her face, tasting her smooth skin which was full of pain. Licking was supposed to help her, but she cried silently, a rush of salty tears that streamed down her cheeks. I licked again, and again, till I felt a bit sick, and just as I was about to give up, she gave me a hug, which I tolerated because her need was greater than mine.

'Thank you, darling Moll,' she croaked. She let go and stroked me, then blew her nose and looked at me with watery eyes that smelt of Titch and so much sadness and loss that it was like smelling myself. But underneath that, I smelt the first flicker of hope, like the first snowdrops in winter, and I think she did too, for she whispered, 'We'll get through this together.'

And though I wasn't sure how, I felt that we would. And suddenly I could almost feel Titch's snout against mine and his whiskers tickling my cheek. 'Well done, darling,' he said.

Losing Titch was like trying to wade through thick mud wearing a heavy sorrow blanket. Everything was so much harder. I would have given up if it wasn't for Suki and Lainy, who watched me every step of the way. And Tess, too. She came round a lot, though not so much for walks as I was still not up to speed, and it felt wrong walking without Titch.

Suki and Lainy went out together, for runs and to meet other friends and I was glad to have some time alone for a little while, just to think about Titch in peace. My feelings were private, and I needed time to deal with them.

It made me think back to when Pip died. I'd missed him terribly, but I was so busy looking after Suki that I didn't have much time to notice my own grief. All my energies were spent in trying to stop her from drowning in her own tears.

Now the roles were reversed, and it was wrong. I had promised Pip I would look after Suki, and make sure she was happy, but how could I do that when half of me had been ripped apart? I knew, now, how Suki had felt in those endless, dark days, and it made me feel humble and useless at the same time.

But gradually, and thanks to Suki's gentle kindness and Lainy's bouncy persistence, I started to feel a little better. Loss was in my every breath, but when I finally went on a walk, I realised how much I had missed. Spring was all about me with its emerald bounce; anemones sprouted forth in Suki's garden, and the tulips waved their bright, optimistic heads.

Spring always had a special smell of promise for me, and one morning I felt as if a great weight had been lifted from me. When we had our round the block morning walk, we met a woman called Laura, who Suki had met before, with a dog called Pedro. A large, gentle fellow who sniffed but didn't say much.

'Is Pedro a new addition?' Suki said. 'I was so sorry to hear about Eddie.'

I could smell the remnants of Laura's sadness on her coat. Like us, she knew loss, I could tell.

'He's staying with us while his owner is in hospital,' Laura said. She smiled at Pedro with such love that I was glad that they had found each other, for however long.

'That's great,' said Suki. 'How lucky for you all.'

'How are things with you?' Said Laura.

'We're fine, but we lost a very dear four legged friend recently.' Suki's eyes filled with tears and I could feel that familiar wave of sadness wash over us all.

'I'm so sorry,' said Laura. 'I remember you were so kind to me when Eddie died. It's just terrible, isn't it?'

Suki nodded. 'He and Moll were especially close. They'd almost grown up together. So it's hardest for her, poor girl.'

I could feel Laura's and Pedro's eyes on me. 'Poor Moll,' said Laura. 'It's so hard to know how to help dogs, isn't it? But at least she's got you and Lainy.'

'Yes, I only wish I could wave a magic wand and make it better for her.'

'I'm sure you do that just by being there for her,' said Laura. 'I've got to go now, but shall we have a walk sometime?'

Suki beamed. 'I'd really like that, yes, let's.'

They exchanged numbers and just before they left, Pedro gave me a gentle sniff. 'It will get better,' he said in his deep voice. 'Don't give up.'

I looked up, into his black eyes that were tinged with quiet understanding. 'Thank you,' I said. It was wonderful to be surrounded by such support and love, from almost-strangers. And from that moment, I knew I would keep going, and was glad I hadn't given up. I couldn't let Pip and Titch down.

When I finally started taking more notice of what was going on around me, I realised Lainy had a little smile around her mouth. She hummed in her sleep. I waited, thinking she'd tell me what was going on, but after a while I could bear it no longer.

'What's up, Lainy?'

Her huge dark eyes fixed on mine. 'Up?'

'You seem very contented.' Though that wasn't an adequate description. It was something more subtle than that. Joy tinged with excitement. I'd forgotten what that was like.

'Contented? What is that?'

'Happy. Looking forward to life.'

'Ah yes.' Lainy fluttered her eyelashes. 'I look forward to see Dave next week.'

'Dave? Who's he?' But then I realised, 'Oh! You mean, big Dave the rescue dog?'

Lainy looked smug. 'Yes he arrange with his Bill and he talk to Suki and we meet up once a week so I learn more skills.' She tossed her head so that her ears flapped. 'And yet I found Titch, so I think maybe I teach them scent skills, no?'

'Yes, maybe,' I said. 'And you like Dave?'

She smiled and that smile spoke of many things, but mostly how I remembered feeling when I first met Titch. 'Yes, I like,' she said, 'but I think he like me more.'

From any other mouth it might have sounded arrogant, but from Lainy it was just what she thought. And she was generally good at reading situations. 'Well, that's good,' I said. Though I'm ashamed to say, I felt a twinge of jealousy. Titch, why did you have to go?

I tried to concentrate on Lainy, or rather, Dave. 'So did you find out much about him?' It was always important to learn about those we may love. Or in Lainy's case, flirt with. I wasn't sure how seriously she was taking this.

'Ah yes,' she said cheerfully. 'The other dogs are brothers, and Dave is older, and they all rescue from house in Spain where they tie up outside and it very hot and little water and not enough food, and they suffer very much.'

'Poor things.'

'But peoples rescue them and travel in van very far, like me, and take them to new peoples in Wales and they do job of searching for peoples who are lost. And they are very good at this and it mean all brothers can stay together, but then the man get very ill and they have to find new home, like me, and Bill hear about them because they are so good rescuing dogs and he bring them to Cornwall where he live and they carry on rescuing peoples. And dogs,' she added.

'Well,' I said, for she spoke very fast and I could hardly keep up. 'That's... interesting. So you like Dave?'

'I do,' she said. 'We like each other very much, and he says I am best sniffer he met who not been trained. But you not need learning to be sniffer. We use noses all the time!'

'Of course. But some dogs have better noses than others,' I said. 'For example, your nose is better than mine.'

'Oh yes,' she said. 'I like finding peoples. And dogs. It like having a ... what you say, a puzzle, and I have to find all the pieces to make sense.' She winked. 'You like my joke? Scents?'

My whiskers twitched involuntarily and I almost smiled. 'Very funny. You're obviously very gifted at finding. Perhaps you should join Dave and his team.'

Lainy looked scandalised and her whiskers swivelled alarmingly. 'But I don't want leave you and Suki. You mean, you no want me?'

'No I didn't mean that,' I said. 'I mean that, maybe you could work with Dave because you're so good at it.'

'Ah yes, that is what Dave say. But I am thinking...' she tailed off and looked out of the window, but I had a feeling she wasn't seeing anything out there.

'You're thinking?' I prompted.

'Yes, I watching the news and I thinking that life is not fair. And I seek justice for peoples and dogs like me. We immigrants.'

I had a nasty feeling she was veering into political waters and I would be lost. 'Yes?'

'And I thinking it very difficult doing justice because I get into troubles. Stupid peoples they no understanding that when I attack it is to defend peoples who need me. Why are they so ignorant?'

'I don't know,' I said. I had a feeling we'd got off topic though I wasn't sure what the topic was any more.

'Well, I can't help if peoples are stupid but what else can I do to help peoples like me?'

'Helping find people is very important,' I said.

Lainy's eyes glinted. 'Ah yes, maybe I work with the peoples coming over to England on lorries. Or boats. I could earn money for Suki!'

'I think if you do that, you'd have to work ... where people come into England,' I said. Though I wasn't sure where that was.

'Dover!' She said. 'That near here?'

'I think it's a long way. But I'm not sure.'

She was quiet, brooding. 'Then Dover no good. I want stay with you and Suki.'

'Good,' I said. 'I'm glad you're not dashing off somewhere with Dave so we'd never see you again.'

'Of course not,' she said. 'But working with Dave is good work, no?'

'Very good work. Why?'

'I think maybe I can help peoples other way.'

'That's... very inspiring.' The speed at which Lainy's mind worked was impressive. 'How?'

She looked at me, smelling very earnest, like freshly cut pine wood. 'I thinking maybe I show peoples who have the panic that we can still work and be ... be benefit to society.'

'That's very good Lainy.' I stared at her in awe. I wasn't sure what she meant, but I did know that she was passionate about helping herself and others. 'You mean like a therapy dog?'

'What is this?'

'I think you have to train to be very calm around people,' I said, for once again I wasn't sure. 'No flashbacks and no biting.' But I smiled to lessen the blow.

'OK, well maybe not therapy dogs then, but I think of something.'

As I settled down for a snooze, I thought that while Lainy did want to help people, was something else going on in that head of hers?

Was I being overly wary, or was she plotting something on the quiet? How I missed Titch's quiet reassurance, his steady understanding. He would have dismissed my fears with a quick bark, and a brush of my whiskers.

My thoughts were interrupted by Suki's phone ringing. 'Joe!'

'Hi Suki. How are you?'

'Fine, thanks.' She laughed. 'So you're officially going to adopt Tinker?'

'Yes.' He gave a short laugh. 'I realise how much I miss having a dog. He's so special.'

'And he needs a good home, poor thing.'

'He does.'

'I can't wait to see him,' Suki said. 'He looks a real sweetie.' She reached for her mug of tea and drank. 'I do hope he gets on OK with my two. It'll be good for Lainy to get to know other dogs. Might give her more confidence.'

Silence from Joe.

'Are you OK?'

Joe cleared his throat. 'I've got a bit of a problem with this weekend.'

'Oh.' Suki's voice dropped. 'Well, never mind. I mean, it's a shame, but we can come the next weekend.' She hesitated. 'Can't we?'

An uncomfortable silence. Then Joe said, 'Rachel rang me earlier.'

'Rachel?' She paused. 'Your ex-girlfriend?'

'Yes.'

Suki sat very still. I could smell fear racing through her veins.

'Her mum's got cancer and hasn't got long to live.'

'Oh, poor thing,' Suki said automatically.

Joe cleared his throat. 'Rachel asked if I'd go and visit her mum with her. And I feel I should.'

'Of course...'

'So I said I'd meet her in London this weekend.'

'Oh. OK.' I could hear the thoughts swirling round Suki's head.

'I'm really sorry it's going to mess up our weekend, but I need to deal with this.'

'Yes,' she said. Which sort of meant, no.

'And she said she's been dry for eight months.'

There was a horrible silence. I could smell the hope leaking out of Suki, and it smelt vile. 'Right,' she said. 'Well, I... good luck.'

'I'm really sorry,' he said. 'I was so looking forward to seeing you all. This has come as a bit of a bombshell, but I do need to try and sort things out. One way or the other. Goodbye, Suki. Love to you all.' And he put the phone down.

27

Suki went very quiet after that. Her eyes were red and wet looking but she blew her nose and said, 'Well, onwards and upwards, eh, girls?' And she went back to her computer and tapped away busily.

'What can we do?' Lainy said wrinkling her nose. 'She not happy.'

While I had to keep positive for Suki, it was a real struggle. 'Sometimes we can't do anything,' I said at last. What would Titch say?

'Nothing?' Lainy said, head on one side.

'Usually it's best to wait and see.'

Lainy wrinkled her nose which was always a sign that she was thinking. This troubled me, so to forestall any possible problems, I added, 'please don't do anything foolish, Lainy.'

'Me? Foolish?' She winked.

'I know you have the best possible motives, Lainy, but please tell me if you have one of your ideas. I don't want ...'

'I know, you want no problem,' Lainy said cheerfully. 'I promise if I think of idea, I tell you first. But Suki not happy and she deserve be happy, and she deserve be with Joe. You think?'

'I do think,' I replied. 'But I also think we need to see what happens with this Rachel woman. It might just blow over.'

'Blow over?' Lainy looked at the door, as if something might blow in.

'I mean, Joe and Rachel need to see her mum, and they need to talk, by the sound of things. But I'm sure it'll be perfectly all right,' I said hopefully.

'OK,' said Lainy. 'But I have idea already!'

I felt that wriggle of unease. 'What is it?'

'Dave and brothers work in Wales before they come to Cornwall. Maybe he have friend there so if Rachel go back to see Joe in Wales, he can warn him? Maybe give Rachel little bite to warn her off?'

My whiskers twitched at the thought of Rachel faced with one of Dave's mates, taking a chunk out of her leg. 'It's a good thought, Lainy, but as I said, let's see how things go, OK?'

'Okey dokey,' she said with a cheerful swish of her tail that did little to reassure me. I knew she was meeting Dave the next day and had a feeling they might cook something up between them.

The next day, however, my thoughts were diverted from darling Titch and wretched Rachel by a trip into town. This time, as we came out of the library, we crossed the road towards the old Methodist church, where a group of homeless people usually set up camp. Today we could smell unrest, and heard angry voices, which was unlike them; they were friendly and Suki usually stopped for a chat.

Now she stopped for a moment, then advanced slowly. 'Zach?' she said as we grew nearer. I could smell her wariness, and knew she was thinking of her promise to Joe.

There was no reply, but a tall fellow, smelling sour and frightened, shouted at one of the other men, and ran off. He smelt like Zach, though his scent was so full of chemicals it was difficult to tell.

'What's going on?' Suki said as we grew nearer the other men. We couldn't get too close because Lainy was frightened of them. I think they probably smelled too like the Rapitori people.

'That Zach, he's in trouble again,' said one of them. 'Ever since he's been back on the smack.'

'Smack?' Suki's voice shook.

I looked at Lainy. 'Who's he smacking?'

'Not smacking, it is drug,' said Lainy. 'Bad drug. No wonder he loopy.'

I sneezed. Smacking? Drugs? I couldn't make sense of it all. I tuned back to the man to see if I could find out more.

'Yeah. Sold bloody everything, stupid man. Told him not to.'

Suki stared at him. 'So that would explain the shakes, runny nose, insomnia...' She shook her head. 'I didn't realise.'

'Why should you? He's been stealing food which is bad enough, but then he wants to sit with us, and it gives us a bad name. Cops think we've been nicking stuff, and none of us would do that.'

'Of course not,' Suki said. 'How long's he been doing this?'

'Last week or so,' one of them said. 'He just turned up, in a right old state. Kept going on about the pain, and shakes, how he couldn't get hold of his painkillers. That's why he got on the smack, I think. Easier and cheaper to get hold of than prescription painkillers.'

Suki was almost white now, and turned to the speaker. 'I thought he had somewhere to live?'

'Don't know if he does now. Think he fell out with the landlord. He's always falling out with people. Drugs do that.'

Suki bit her lip. I could smell the rush of frustration, anger and sadness coming from her. 'That's such a shame. What about his music?'

'What music?'

'He's got an accordion.'

'Not now he hasn't. Sold it along with everything else.'

Suki went very quiet.

'You been trying to help him, Suki?' One of them said.

She nodded.

'Don't take it personally,' he said. 'He's very messed up. Doesn't know what he's doing.'

'I know,' she said. 'Nothing I've tried has worked.'

'Not your fault, love,' said another. 'We've all messed up at some time or other. He'll work it out. But that's up to him, not you.'

Suki smiled. 'I know,' she said, bid them goodbye and we turned right up the hill towards a park that we both liked, where we could meet all kinds of other dogs. There was a caravan cafe there, so Suki bought a coffee and drank it at one of the outside tables while we sat beside her, munching treats, listening to what was going on around us.

Children shrieked in the adventure play area on the far side of the park. Robins and blackbirds chirped, trying to outdo each other with the loudest song. Traffic rumbled in the distance, and from a house nearby came the heavy beat of a drum.

Near the cafe was a huge tree with dark red flowers that heralded spring: the flowers were magnificent, and led the way for all the other flowers in the park, and the trees coming into bud.

The smells were varied; rich dark coffee from the cafe. Sickly sticky cake sitting on the counter. A waft of drains from the public toilets not far away. Sweet, fresh grass cuttings. And another smell that I vaguely recognised. Looking at Lainy, she did too.

Suki drained her cup, put it in the bin and as soon as she unclipped our leads, I tried to follow Lainy, who dived in and out of the tables at high speed, scattering children and ice creams, women and men with their coffee cups.

'Oi!' shouted a man who Lainy dodged at high speed.

'What are you doing?' A young mum grabbed her child's ice cream.

'Control those dogs!'

We weaved in and out of the chairs, Lainy more nimble on her feet, so it was largely my clumsiness that knocked over tables and chairs, but I couldn't help it for I too had got the scent and we just had to follow it. I could hear Titch whispering, 'Go, Moll, Go!' So I went.

I could just hear Suki's voice behind us calling, 'Moll! What are you doing? Lainy, COME BACK!'

But it was too late. We were off, panting as we tore round the corner, Lainy dodging a large black Labrador (not her favourite), growling at a boxer for being in the way, weaving round a corner... and then I lost her.

I stopped, panting and heaving, and rather worried about my heart which was thudding like a generator.

'Steady, darling,' said Titch, and it occurred to me that I was still a bit weak, so I waited till I heard Suki's footsteps pounding the pavement towards me.

'Thank god you're here, Moll,' she panted, smelling hot and panicky. 'Where on earth is Lainy?'

We looked around but I'd lost the scent now.

'I thought she was doing so well, but when something like this happens, I worry what she's up to.'

I felt the same and remembered, with a fear that made my spine twitch, how she'd been going on about Doing Good Things with Dave. Oh no. What had she got up to now?

As my heart calmed down, I took a deep breath, had a good shake (excellent for stress relief) and barked quickly to Suki. I had a whiff of that scent again, and it was time to find Lainy.

Up the hill we went, towards the children's play area, but having got there, I sensed that was wrong. That smell wouldn't be near children, and there were plenty of them, giggling, shouting and playing. I stopped, uncertain, then got another whiff, so off we set, along the top perimeter of the path. This led eventually to some gardeners' huts and I thought this might be the source of the smell.

But no. Faltering slightly, I breathed separately through each nostril. Apparently humans can't do this, but we can smell different things from different directions. From the right came a smell of chips. Yum. I was about to track them down, when from the left I got a faint waft of that other smell, which was more important. We had to find Lainy. Dog knows what trouble she'd got herself into by now.

Barking to Suki, I set off down the path knowing that she'd follow me. We arrived at the gardening huts, where I dashed in to investigate, but all I could smell were musty old boots, rusty forks and shears, and the pervading aroma of mud and composting leaves. That was no good, so I nipped out again and joined Suki on the path.

Raising my nose to the air, I sniffed, deeply. There - another faint scent, so I trotted off, with Suki behind me. Heading down the hill, the scent grew stronger, and I could also smell Lainy: she wasn't the only scent dog in Falmouth. The smell grew stronger as we got to the bottom of the hill, to a wooded area behind the public toilets. She was in there, I was sure of it, with the smell.

I yipped, sharply, and sure enough, came her answering yip, 'I'm here! Hurry!'

Crashing through the undergrowth, I fought my way through, Suki behind me, getting snagged on the brambles judging by her cursing. There, hidden in the trees I could smell unwashed, frightened men. Three of them. Lainy stood guard, tail wagging, growling gently to prevent any of them from running off.

'Lainy!' Judging by Suki's voice, I don't think she'd realised the men were there. 'What are you...oh!' She stopped, and took in their faces. Thin and smelling of mud and hunger and fear. And then I realised the other smell. Zach was lying at the back of the clearing, on a piece of sacking, asleep. When she realised it was him she did a double take. I could hear her thoughts, wondering if she should get involved. But she couldn't just leave him there...

'Zach. What's going on? Are these your friends?'

Silence. Zach didn't wake up, but the other men stared at her, wide-eyed, smelling terrified.

'Are you OK?' Suki said, though I could smell a tremor of fear. After all, it was one woman against three men. Mind you, she had me and Lainy so there was no need to worry. Not with Lainy's teeth.

One of the men glanced at the others, shaking his head. Suki bit her lip, said slowly, 'Can you speak English?'

One shook their head, and I saw Lainy go towards Zach. The other men shrank back, and Lainy nudged Zach gently with her nose. Nothing. She sniffed, then turned around and barked to Suki. 'Come here! He not well.'

Luckily Suki got the message and stepped forward, knelt beside Zach. She shook him gently, but there was no response, so she reached for his wrist. 'Just checking there's a pulse,' she muttered. Silence while we all waited. 'Yes, there is, but it's very slow and he's so pale,' she said. 'I'm going to ring for an ambulance. Stay there, Lainy.'

Lainy wagged her tail and looked delighted. I have to say, she was good at this finding people business. And she didn't seem scared of the men. She was alert and wary, but in control and it was good to see her confidence growing.

The men shrank back as Suki ran out to the path, then spoke into her phone. She came back and sat by Zach, checking his arms and his face. 'He seems OK. I wonder what's the matter?' She turned to the other men. 'Are you sleeping here?' She spoke slowly and clearly.

They nodded.

'Do you need somewhere safe to stay?' she continued.

The men glanced at each other, and anxiety rose off them in sour smelling waves.

Suki got up and glanced at me and Lainy. 'They're going to be discovered by the paramedics in a minute,' she muttered. 'Damn, what have I done? Do they have to report them to the police? I don't want these poor guys to get into trouble. But they really need help. They can't stay here.'

At that moment we heard the loud whine of a siren, saw blue flashing lights along the nearby road. Was this the ambulance? The noise grew louder as it turned into the park and Suki stepped out into the path, waving it down. I saw her go and talk to the people driving it, a man and a woman. There was much nodding, then they ran towards us and Lainy started her Beware Bark.

Suki put Lainy on her lead and led her outside, tied her to a bench. I could smell Lainy's frustration, but she was making a lot of noise, so I hissed at her. 'We need to be able to hear what they're saying,' I said. 'Quiet, please!'

Lainy obliged and the people in uniform went straight to Zach, talking softly and gently to the other frightened men. They rolled Zach over onto his side, gave him an injection, then the man went and got a stretcher and they carried him to the ambulance, talking quietly to him all the time. Once they'd got him inside, the woman turned to Suki.

'Well done for alerting us. He's taken an overdose but you caught him just in time and hopefully he'll be OK. Do you know of any relatives? Next of kin?'

Suki shook her head. 'No. I only know he's got PTSD and he's been having panic attacks, he's really depressed and in a bad way. I think he's on heroin. I did tell him about Man Down, but he didn't want to know.' All this came blurting out in a rush.

'He's very lucky to have you. Sorry, you can't come with us. Mind you,' she smiled and looked at us. 'I don't think your two would be happy. If you want further information, ring the hospital but give it a few hours.'

'Thanks.' Suki hesitated. 'What about the other guys? They don't speak English and they're homeless. I'm worried about them.'

'Hang on,' the woman dived into the front of the ambulance and came out with a few leaflets. 'This is the procedure for reporting people sleeping rough. This charity should be able to help. There are hostels nearby if they need somewhere to stay.'

'Thanks.' Suki took the leaflet and put it in her jacket pocket.

'Right, we've got to go now. Good luck!' The woman got into the driver's seat and the ambulance sped off, leaving just the sweet sound of a blackbird and a chirpy robin, the distant rumble of passing traffic.

Suki looked down at us. 'I do hope he'll be OK. Tell you what, we'll go to the supermarket, get these guys some food and I'll ring this number, see if we can get them a roof over their heads.'

So back we went, to buy pasties and sausage rolls. The smell was tantalising. Suki spoke to the homeless guys opposite, told them about Zach and the men in the park.

Finally we headed back to the park where she distributed food like Mother Christmas, and at last we could have a run while Suki disentangled herself from the homeless people and we headed back for tea.

As we arrived home, she looked down at us and grinned. 'Don't know about you two, but I'm knackered. Enough good deeds for one day. You were brilliant, you two, especially you, Lainy, finding them. Clever girls!'

We got extra for tea that night and Lainy looked at me and winked. 'See?' She said. 'I *can* help people.'

28

After that surge of adrenaline, I was exhausted. 'Take it easy, darling,' I could imagine Titch muttering. So I did. It wasn't getting easier, but I was getting more used to his absence, and I gained comfort from his occasional communications. I wasn't sure if it was actually him, or part of my brain *wanting* it to be him, but it made me feel better.

The next day, Tess and Suki took Lainy for a run and when they returned, they took us all for a walk round the block. As we trotted along, I heard Tess shriek. 'Wow, look at this,' she cried. 'You're famous!'

'What?' Suki leaned over, started reading from Tess's phone. 'Blimey. "Riot in local park led to overdose victim taken to hospital. Homeless persons identified".' She looked at Tess. 'They haven't exactly got their facts right.' She frowned. 'I wonder who reported that?'

'People are always taking pictures with their phones. And you know how word gets round Falmouth.'

'That's true.'

Tess laughed and her ponytail swung. I was glad to see that ponytail. 'You didn't say you'd caused a riot!'

'We didn't really. If Lainy hadn't found Zach, he would have died. She obviously smelt him, and ran off in rather a hurry. Quite a few people got in the way, as did their tables and chairs. To say nothing of coffee, ice cream and cake.'

'Not exactly a riot, then?'

'No. I mean, a few people were a bit upset at having their snacks interrupted, and there was some shouting, but it wasn't a riot.'

'And what news of Zach?'

'The hospital said he's recovering but he fell out with his landlords so they don't want him back. He's got a social worker now, and he needs to go into rehab, so he's trying to organise that.' They stopped as Lainy and I had a good sniff at a particularly interesting bit of wall.

'That's good,' said Tess. 'Have you been to see him?'

We moved on and Suki shook her head. 'No. I was going to, but I decided not to.' She smiled. 'I could hear you and Joe saying NO!'

'Quite right. You saved his life, Suki. And he's got a social worker now. You've done enough.'

'I know. He's got to want to help himself.'

'Exactly. This might be the final shove he needs to accept that he needs help.' We walked on in silence for a moment, then she said, 'Aren't you going to Wales this weekend?'

'Ah, no.' Suki sighed. 'Apparently Joe's ex-girlfriend, Rachel, got in touch. Her mum's dying of cancer and she asked Joe if he'd go to London with her to see her mum.'

'Really?'

'Yes. And Joe said she's been sober for eight months and they have some sorting out to do.'

'So no trip to Wales this weekend?'

Suki shook her head.

Tess wrinkled her nose which meant she was thinking. We turned right, along past the Greenbank hotel. It was bin day, which meant lots of tasty food had dropped on the pavement, scattered by the gulls.

'What if he decides he wants to get back with her?' Suki's voice wobbled slightly.

'Why should he?'

'He said they've got unfinished business.'

'I expect they have. No relationship finishes tidily, does it? And if she stormed off in a drunken tirade, which she might well have done, they must have a lot they need to say to each other.'

'I guess,' Suki said sadly. 'It doesn't make me feel any better, somehow.'

'Look, Suki. Joe loves you. It's not like you to be so wobbly. What's up?'

'I don't know... I've been very wary since splitting up with Ted, so it's taken me a long time to trust someone. I really love Joe. He's kind and patient and generous and he loves dogs and makes me laugh. And I thought we were solid. And now this happens.'

'If he said they're going to sort things out, then that's what they'll do. And how nice of Joe to go and see her mum.'

Suki kicked a pine cone which skittered along the ground. I almost felt sorry for it, but I was more sorry for her.

'I wonder if she likes dogs?' Tess said.

The spoils from the spilt bins were very good this week; good work, seagulls. Lainy and I shared a very tasty bit of pork pie.

'I presume so; she must have been around when Joe had Peanut.'

'Doesn't mean she actually *likes* dogs,' Tess said. 'And now he's got Tinker.' She gave a wicked smile. 'I wonder whether Tinker bites?'

Suki gave a half hearted smile in return. 'We can but hope.'

'When's she going to meet him?'

'Today, I think. He should be there now.' Suki smelt like an old blanket that had been left outside.

'In that case, why not ring him? Nothing like putting a spoke in the wheel.'

'Ring while she's there?' Suki sounded bemused, but I could see part of her liked the idea.

'He might welcome the interruption. Anyway, I was thinking that it wouldn't do her any harm to realise there's another woman in his life.'

'No...' Suki said. 'Although it might make her more determined. Mind you, I can be determined too.'

'Exactly. You've got to fight your corner, Suki. Wasn't that what Pip used to say?'

She grinned, a proper smile this time. 'He did, you're quite right.' She took a deep breath. 'And yes, I'll ring tonight. After all, I've got nothing to lose.'

It was hard, going for a walk without Titch, but I could sense that Tess was still hurting just as much as me, so I made a fuss of her, trying to show solidarity. And she appreciated it, I could smell, as she bent down to stroke me. 'Thanks, Moll,' she whispered, closing her eyes, and I knew she was trying to conjure Titch up, just as I was.

'Will you get another dog?' Suki said tentatively, proving how much we all felt that huge Titch Hole in our hearts.

'Not right now,' Tess said. 'I'm too sore. But I will, at some point.'

'Good,' said Suki. 'I'm quite sure Titch wouldn't want you to be dog-less for long.'

I agreed. It was bad enough me facing a bleak old age on my own, but I was a One Man Dog; I wasn't interested in anyone else, whereas Tess definitely needed another dog, and soon.

A flicker of an idea came into my head, and I tucked it away so I could think about it later; I could start planning to find Tess another dog! I could almost hear Titch saying, 'Good idea, Moll!'

So we parted, but I tucked into my tea that evening with a feeling of purpose that had been lacking for so long. However, I could sense Suki getting more nervous by the second about ringing Joe. She kept watching the clock and muttering. 'I wonder what time he'll get to London?' She paced back and forth in the kitchen. 'He's probably got there and they're having a cuppa. Or maybe a cosy dinner for two?' As she turned, she bashed her knee on the kitchen table. 'Shit, shit, shit!'

I wished she would hurry up; this twitchiness was catching. Then she said, 'sod it, I'm going to ring now.' And we breathed a sigh of relief. Whatever the outcome, it was better than this tense waiting.

She put the phone on loud so we could hear, and the ringing tones echoed round the kitchen. It rang and rang... and no reply. Then suddenly a female voice said, 'Hello?'

Suki froze. 'Is that - is Joe there?'

'Yes, but he's having a shower right now.' There was a laugh, but not a pleasant one. 'So you're Suki, judging by the contact on Joe's phone.'

'Yes...'

'This is Rachel.'

'Hello,' said Suki, sounding a bit stunned. 'I'm glad Joe got there OK. Could you ask him to ring me back?'

'He's busy right now,' she said. 'And we have a lot to catch up on, so I don't think he'll have time to talk to you. So just leave him alone. Right?' Then she finished the call.

Suki stood and stared at the phone as if it contained a bomb. 'So that was Rachel,' she muttered. 'Bloody hell. How dare she answer Joe's phone? What a cheek. And saying he wouldn't talk to me.' She paused. 'What have they been talking about? Oh god...' She sat down hurriedly, swaying slightly. 'Feeling really dizzy. Better eat something.'

She walked over to the fridge, opened it and inspected the contents. 'What shall I eat? Beans on toast tonight. Can't be bothered with anything else.'

She shut the fridge, put a slice of bread in the toaster and searched for the beans. As the toast popped up, she pulled down a saucepan, and then her phone rang. She jumped as if she'd been scalded and grabbed it. 'Hello? Joe!'

'Sorry I missed your call,' he said. 'I was having a shower and ...' his voice dropped. 'I'm really sorry, Rachel shouldn't have answered my phone.' Judging by his tone of voice, he hadn't heard what Rachel had said.

'How's Tinker?' Suki was struggling to keep her voice steady.

'Tinker seems fine, despite the fact that we're staying in a strange flat.' His voice softened as he mentioned the dog's name and Lainy and I looked at each other.

'They staying with Rachel?' She said, her eyes growing dark and huge.

'I suppose so,' I said, a very unpleasant sensation growing in my stomach.

'Tinker must feel very safe with you,' Suki said. 'I can't wait to meet him.' She cleared her throat.

'And how's Moll? And Lainy?'

'Moll's recovering a little, bless her. But I wanted to tell you about Lainy's new career as a rescue dog.'

'Really? What happened?'

Suki gave a feeble laugh. 'We were outside Tesco's talking to the guys who live outside the Methodist Church; you know?'

'Oh yes, the big guy with the pierced ear seems to be in charge.'

'That's right. He's Jim. We were crossing the road when Zach came along with some food he'd nicked from Tesco and wanted to sit with the other guys. They don't like that because it can get them into trouble with the cops, so there was a bit of a fracas and Zach ran off.'

'I see.' Joe's voice had grown chillier at the mention of Zach, I thought.

'And I know I promised I wouldn't see Zach, but this was a different scenario.' Suki paused. 'Apparently Zach couldn't get his prescription painkillers for his burns, and was desperate so he got hold of some heroin. Can you believe it's cheaper and easier to get than prescription drugs?'

Joe sighed. 'Sadly, I can.'

'Anyway, we went up to Kimberley Park, and suddenly, Lainy and Moll ran off like dogs possessed. Tables and chairs scattered, food flying, children yelling; it was quite dramatic.'

'Sounds like it.' He gave a half hearted chuckle. 'What then?'

'Lainy obviously had the scent of something, and ran off, but Moll and I can't run that fast. Finally Moll tracked her down and she was standing guard over Zach and three other guys hiding behind the sheds in the park. They'd been sleeping there.'

'Oh.'

'I thought Zach was asleep but I couldn't wake him so I rang for an ambulance and it turned out he'd taken an overdose so they took him off to hospital.'

'My god, was he OK? And what about the others? Who were they?'

'Zach was OK, just. If Lainy hadn't found him, he would have died. As for the others, I don't know; they didn't speak English but they looked Eastern European. The paramedic gave me a leaflet about how to help them, so I rang the charity and they said they'd send some people down there and get them food and shelter.'

'My god. Well done.'

'I also spoke to Jim outside Tesco and asked him to keep an eye on them, and I got the men some food from Tesco and then I had to bring Moll and Lainy back here. But the woman from the charity said she'd keep me informed. They're trying to get them into a hostel outside Falmouth, she said.'

'Wow,' Joe said. 'Well done, Suki. Those men must be so grateful.'

'Well, you just want to help, don't you?'

'Not everyone does,' Joe said. 'Makes me wonder what I've been missing. It sounds like an episode of some Scandi thriller!'

Suki laughed: a joyous sound. 'I know. I just hope they're all OK. Apparently Zach has a social worker now who'll keep an eye on him. So I'm going to keep well clear.'

Silence from Joe.

'But I do worry about the other guys. Who knows where they're from and how they got here? And imagine, sleeping in the park, and they can't have eaten for ages: they were starving when I took them some food. They looked so cold and frightened and desperate.'

'I expect they were. Well, good for you and well done Lainy. I bet she had an extra special dinner that night?'

'She certainly did; well, they both did,' she added, as I glared at her. 'Moll did her bit too; she found Lainy, so it was a team effort.'

'It always is,' he said, and he sounded relaxed again, like he did when we were out on our walks.

'We're very much looking forward to meeting Tinker.'

'Yes, it will be good for him to have some doggy friends in Cornwall.'

'So you'll be back next week sometime?' An element of hope had crept into her voice. Hope and excitement.

'Well, I hope so. I told you I've got to sort a few things out here first. Oh hang on,' there was a pause while we heard Rachel shouting in the background. 'Sorry,' he said, 'I'm going to have to go. Speak soon. Well done girls!' And with that he finished the call.

Suki's smile slid off her face like rain. Cold, wet drops. 'Fuck it!' she said, and threw the piece of toast into the bin.

29

Suki was so quiet the next morning, even Lainy was worried.

'What can we do?' she asked. 'That Rachel is bad, bad woman.'

'We don't know that, but she sounds determined.'

'I want go there and bite her very bad,' Lainy said. Then she smelt my unease. 'No worry, I not do that. I just want protect Suki. I promise be very good.' She wrinkled her nose. 'It hard when you want to help and you can't, no?'

'It is hard,' I said. 'But Joe and Rachel have to sort this out between themselves. If the relationship is over, then he will tell her to go away. He's the only person who can do that.'

Lainy gave a big sigh and rested her nose on her paws. 'Humans,' she said as her whiskers twitched. 'Why they not smell more and think less?'

She had a point. But at least she had an assignation with Bill and Dave to look forward to that afternoon.

I was in two minds whether to go, but I was feeling stronger, and knew Titch would want me to resume normal activities as soon as possible. It was hard, going back to Roundwood which had such unpleasant memories for all of us. Still, I told myself, best to overlay difficult memories with good ones, and that's what today was all about.

'Hi, Suki!' Bill said. 'Good to see you. And Lainy and Moll. Now, what I've done is lay a scent trail for Lainy and Dave and the boys. That will take them a few extra miles, but the actual walk isn't too far, so it might be all right for your Moll.'

'Thanks, that's very thoughtful,' Suki said. 'In that case, let's go and I can tell you about Lainy's recent exploits.' As we walked down the steep path into the woods, she told Bill about Lainy finding Zach and the other men.

'Wow, that's incredible,' Bill said. 'What a clever girl. Think what she could do with some training!' He grinned.

'What's involved?' Suki said. 'It sounds a great idea, but I've got quite a lot of work on at the moment.'

'Training does take up a lot of time so it might not be right for you just now.'

'What would we have to do?'

Bill dodged a greyhound running towards us, far too fast. 'Whoa boy!' He turned back to Suki. 'It takes about 2-3 years to qualify you and your dog and be on the Call Out list, and you have to be assessed along the way. And once you qualify you still have to undergo training every month. But from what I've seen, Lainy would love it.' He grinned. 'I think you would too, and it'd give you plenty more to write about. I've been looking up your articles, and I really like your books.'

Suki blushed; I could feel the heat coming from her cheeks. 'Thanks.' She strode on and I could smell that she was trying to collect herself. 'The training does sound quite a commitment,' Suki said. 'But you're right, I think Lainy would love it. It's just finding the time.'

'Well, there's no point in getting stressed if you don't have the time. You could always apply in the future.'

'Yes, maybe.'

'Meantime, there are several scent work classes that I'm sure she'd enjoy,' Bill continued. 'There's a lady in Devoran who does evening classes, and you can go on to compete. That would take up less time but still give her scent training.'

Suki grinned. 'That sounds more manageable. We'll give that a try. Thanks, Bill. I really appreciate it.'

I trotted along in front of them, pausing to sniff at a rabbit hole. No bunnies recently, but it was worth checking. Plenty of rabbit poo, like crunchy bits of kibble. Delicious. Titch's favourite. I gulped and looked back, where Bill was talking about a rescue he'd done in Wales with Dave and his brothers.

Lainy and Dave and the others had scooted far ahead, noses to the ground, tails wagging. I could smell Lainy's delight from here, lying in excited bursts along the ground. I was pleased for her. She definitely had a talent, and this might take her mind off her politically motivated ideas.

'After this, would you like a coffee at the Punchbowl?' Bill was saying as I tuned back into their conversation.

'Thanks, that sounds good,' said Suki.

The Punchbowl and Ladle was a pub nearby and had lots of tiny rooms, but there were always rich pickings on the floor that people couldn't see because it was so dark. But as I listened to Bill chatting to Suki, heard the rise and fall of their voices, I wondered if Bill was more interested in her than I'd realised?

I looked at them closely, to check body language. They were walking side by side, in step. Good sign. He was gesturing as he spoke; she was looking at him and laughing. Another good sign. Suki appeared to have no idea that Bill was interested in her, if he really was. Her posture was open and relaxed. If she had realised, she'd be nervous, and I couldn't smell any anxiety.

But it made me think. It seemed years since Ted had been in our lives, though it wasn't that long. I looked over at Bill again. He and Suki both loved dogs, and he smelt good and kind. His voice was deep and gentle. He was tall, with broad shoulders, wore jeans and a checked shirt, big clumpy walking boots. He had a beard but only a small one. I was sure I could get rid of it if necessary. Compared to Joe, he was much bigger and broader. But did that make him any better?

Twitching my nose, I part listened to their conversation. We didn't know Joe that well, but he'd been in our lives for a while now, and he made Suki happy when everything was going to plan. But things had suddenly gone off piste in the last few days. It had all become rather complicated, and out of our control.

I decided I would listen to Bill, see what I could ascertain about his life. 'Good idea, Moll,' whispered Titch. After all, he might have an ex-wife, or children living with him. A cat, even. He could have all kinds of problems.

At this point, Lainy and Dave and the boys came bounding back, all lolling tongues, flapping ears and delight pouring off their hot fur.

'Having a good time?'

'Marvellous!' She panted, which was a new word - from Dave? 'Are you OK?'

I waited while she cooled off, trotting round in circles before the next scent trail. Then I told her, 'Bill's asked Suki to the pub after this.'

'Really?' Lainy stopped and looked at me. Gave a slow wink. Then she looked over at them, then back at me. 'You like Bill?'

'From what I've smelt of him, he seems OK. But we need to find out more. Can you do that?'

'Of course,' she said, flapping her ears vigorously. 'Dave know Bill long time. He tell us if he good for Suki.' She nuzzled me gently. 'See you later!' And she bounced off, after Dave.

All the other dogs were hot and exhausted but happy by the time they got back to the cars, but as they were muddy, Bill and Suki decided to leave us all in the car while they went into the pub for a coffee. I restrained my impatience till Lainy got her breath back.

'So what did you find out?'

Lainy fluttered her eyelashes. She had obviously worked this trick on Dave and he was hooked, poor boy. It didn't, however, work with me. 'Well?'

'He had a wife but they ... how you say? Split.'

'Divorced?'

'That's it! They divorce in Wales. They have a girl but she grown up now and live in London.'

'Do you know why they split up?'

'No. It happen before Dave go to Bill. But he hear Bill talk about his wife, she call Sandra.'

'OK.' This wasn't of any help. After all, a lot of people were divorced. 'Anything else?'

'He have other girlfriend when he come to Cornwall. She call Taggy.'

'Any bad habits?'

'He drink in pub most night,' Lainy said. 'And he not like cooking much.'

I thought back to when Pip was alive. He liked to go the pub every night. But he did the cooking as well. 'I think a lot of men are like that. Anything else?'

'And he cry a lot when wife go.'

'Well, presumably he missed her.' Just as I missed Titch. 'Does he still cry?'

'Sometime he play music very loud and drink the whisky and cry, Dave say.'

I lay down, head on my paws. Missing people, or dogs, was what happened when you loved someone and they went. Bill smelt quite cheerful now, so perhaps all that was in the past? I'd have to sniff him out more carefully when they came back to their cars.

On cue, we heard footsteps, and Suki and Bill laughing. As they got nearer, I could hear them arranging to meet next week for another scent trail.

'Thanks, that would be great,' Suki said as she opened the car door. 'Lainy had such fun today.'

I could smell a faint whiff of that musky smell coming from Bill. 'So did I.' But he said it in a very casual way. 'Look forward to seeing you next week then. Bye for now.'

He gave each of his dogs a treat and a cuddle then swung into the cab of his van, waved a long arm out of the window and drove off.

Suki stood watching him for a moment, then got in the car. We waited for her to speak but she turned the radio on and sang along to the songs. Lainy and I looked at each other, our whiskers twitched and we smiled.

Sadly, Suki's good mood didn't last long. That evening she received a text, and after a certain amount of huffing, she rang Petroc.

'I'd like your advice, please,' she said.

'Of course, my dear. About what? Or whom?'

'About Joe. I told you his ex-girlfriend got in touch and asked him to go and see her mum with her in London?'

'Yes. What's the latest news?'

'I've just had a text saying, "Things taking longer than anticipated. Not sure when I'll be back. Joe Xx"

'I see,' said Petroc slowly. 'So we can safely assume who the difficulty is.'

'Yes. And she answered his phone when I rang a few days ago and told me that he would never have time to talk to me.'

'But he did?'

'Yes. He rang me straight back.'

'Well then.' There was a silence, then Petroc said. 'Is there something else?' He paused. 'Or someone else?'

Silence.

'Ah. Weren't you seeing Bill today?'

'You've got a good memory.'

'What happened?'

'It was great. Lainy did really well.'

'I'm sure she did. Are you going to tell me what happened?'

'He asked me for a coffee afterwards, so we went to the Punchbowl.'

'That sounds encouraging.'

'And we're meeting for a walk next week.'

Pause. 'So you like him?'

'Yes, he's interesting.'

He paused. 'But you're still very fond of Joe, I think?'

'Yes,' said Suki. 'Though Bill is a very nice distraction. And balm to my injured soul.'

Petroc laughed. 'You sound like Anne of Green Gables! We all need balms to our injured souls. What do you know about Bill?'

'He's divorced, got a grown up daughter who works in television in London, his ex-wife left him for another woman and it took him a long time to get over it.'

Petroc whistled. 'I should think so. Poor man.'

'And he enjoys a pint, plays in the darts team and likes classical music.' She paused. 'Actually, I think he likes most music, but he says he plays it very loudly if he's feeling down.'

'I see.' Petroc thought for a moment. 'I'm sorry Joe has these Rachel problems.'

'Me too,' Suki said. 'But he's got to sort himself out. I can't help him with that.'

'Yes. It sounds difficult for him.' He paused. 'If Bill invites you out, I hope you will take full advantage of it. Or him, should the occasion arise.'

'I will.' Suki laughed, but it was rather a feeble one.

'And talking of that, is there any news on those poor homeless fellows?'

'The charity I got in touch with said they'd found a hostel for the guys and they were being assessed. Difficult when they don't speak English and I wonder if they've got passports? But the woman said she'd let me know how they get on.'

'Excellent. So you don't have to worry about them.'

No. And I rang the hospital and they said Zach had been discharged but they couldn't tell me more.' She sighed. 'I know I said I wouldn't get involved, but I do worry about him.'

'Of course you do, but his social worker will have found him somewhere to stay.'

'I hope so,' said Suki in a small voice. 'It's so hard when you really want to help someone and they won't let you.'

'I know.' Petroc's voice was soft. 'But if you keep on trying, it's like hitting your head against a brick wall. It'll destroy you.' He chuckled. 'Or at the very least give you a terrible headache, and for what?'

Suki gave a weak smile. 'I know you're right, but knowing it doesn't make it any easier. Does it?'

'Of course not. Just try and put him out of your mind and enjoy your next walk with Bill.'

'I will.' But underneath her bravery, I could smell disappointment and the beginnings of a bruised heart. Lainy and I would have to get our noses together to stop Suki getting hurt again.

Suki's disappointment wasn't easily identifiable, but it hung in the air like a bad smell. Unwanted and difficult to get rid of. I should know: Titch had terrible wind after he'd eaten Cheddar.

We had a few quiet days at home as Suki had several deadlines for work, and was writing her next walks book. So we had a much needed respite.

There was no more news from Joe, though I noticed that several times in the evening she glanced at her phone, and looking over, she was reading old messages from him. It didn't seem to make her any happier, though.

One day the next week, we'd been out for our morning walk and Suki had settled down to work on the latest book. I liked seeing the pictures she'd taken when we did the walks; it was like looking at a diary. This one was down at Zennor, where we'd had a very nice drink in the pub afterwards. The Tinners Arms, if my memory served me correctly. They had a proper fire and roast potatoes on the bar. Excellent.

She was sorting the photographs into files on her computer when the front door bell rang continuously. Lainy dashed to the door, barking loudly; she always did this but I had a feeling that this time she knew who it was. My ailing nose couldn't pick up on those things any more.

Suki opened the door cautiously to reveal Zach standing on the doorstep. He smelt of sweat and fear and anger and hopelessness, overlaid with that chemical smell. It was a horrible mixture, much worse than farts. His hair was standing on end and he smelt as if he hadn't slept for ages: a tired, musty odour.

'Hello,' Suki said, her voice faltering. 'How are you?'

Don't ask and don't let him in, I thought, for I sensed that Zach was in a strange mood. Lainy was busy barking and telling him to back off, but I don't think he understood.

'I've had a shit time and it's all your fault,' said Zach, his voice slurring.

The chemical scent was really strong, and I noticed he was swaying. This was not good news. 'Good girl, keep him away,' I barked to Lainy, though she was doing her best.

Suki smelt as if he'd slapped her. 'I'm sorry, I was only trying to help.'

'Well you made things worse,' he said, and I saw that his eyes were swivelling and he looked as if he was about to fall over. 'Poking your fucking nose in. Why can't you just leave people alone? You bloody do-gooders, all you do is fuck things up even more.'

Suki trembled and I growled, loudly. Lainy bared her teeth and would have gone for Zach's leg but Suki noticed and dragged her away just in time. 'Lainy, go next door,' she said hurriedly, put her in the living room and shut the door, so Lainy barked even louder in outrage.

Returning (I made sure Zach didn't put a foot over the doorstep), Suki said, 'I'm sorry that's how you feel,' very formally, but I could hear the tremors in her voice. 'But it's not actually my fault.'

'Oh yeah, so you think it's mine? You don't know what it's like when everyone's against you.'

Suki took a deep breath. 'I know what it's like when you *think* everyone's against you, but it isn't usually true.'

He laughed, a bitter sound that smelt of scorched wood. 'How would you know?'

'Because several years ago, I felt just like you do now. It's a horrible, lonely place to be because you think no one cares. But people do.'

'That's such crap. You have no idea.'

Suki drew herself up and, against the volley of Lainy's furious barking next door, I could tell she was summoning strength. 'I have plenty of idea, because I've felt sorry for myself too. And while we all do it, it's not good to indulge for too long. Stop, have a look around and you'll realise that people do care about you.'

'Fuck off,' he growled, leaning against the wall for support.

'I do for one, though you don't seem to appreciate that. I'm sure your family cares, if you bothered to contact them.'

'You know nothing about my family,' he spat.

Suki took a deep breath. 'And your social worker cares.'

'He's an arsehole.'

'He might be, but he can help you if you give him a chance. And he's one of the few chances you've got,' she said, and I could smell her anger, sharp and strong and hot.

'Make me feel better, won't you? Rub my nose in it, how useless I am.'

'Has he found you somewhere to live?'

'I've got to go to rehab,' he cried.

'That's great. You'll be able to talk to counsellors and get help, Zach. You need it.' She waited, but he said nothing. 'Where are you living now?'

Zach added. 'In a horrible hostel. Full of these old men who stink.'

'You don't smell so fresh yourself. And it's a roof over your head, which is better than living in the park.'

Zach looked down. 'The shower doesn't work.'

'I seem to remember the shower wasn't working in the last place.' She paused. 'What about your music, Zach? Why have you stopped playing?'

Zach shrugged and tears trickled down his grubby face. 'Can I come in?' He smelt utterly defeated.

Suki took a deep breath. 'No. Sorry, I'm working and I've got deadlines,' she said, and I felt like cheering. There was another long silence, then Suki said, 'You should contact your family, Zach. They love you and I'm sure you love them, too. They're really important.'

'They don't want to see me,' he spat. 'My father hates me. You have no fucking idea what he's like.'

Suki opened her mouth and shut it. She stood firm, arms folded, and finally said, 'I've got to go back to work now, Zach.'

He looked up and I smelt the hot tears stinging his eyes. 'So much for you caring.'

Suki paused and I sensed she was trying to keep her words in check. 'Talk to your social worker about your panic attacks; he'll understand. And don't be frightened of rehab. It will really help you.' Her voice was softer now, gentle.

Zach looked doubtful, and was about to open his mouth when she continued, 'And you must get back to your music. You're so talented.'

Lainy's barks had risen to a crescendo, so Zach had to speak up. 'I hate you,' he shouted. And to our great relief, he turned round, swayed down the steps and wobbled along the pavement. I noticed a piece of shoe had come off the bottom of one and it made a slapping noise as he walked. At the corner of the road he turned and yelled, 'You have no fucking idea!' Then he gave a V sign with his fingers and disappeared round the corner.

Suki was shaking as she exhaled, then shut the front door firmly and let Lainy out. She danced round us, still barking, till I said, 'Quiet, Lainy!'

She stopped, instantly, and said, 'He no good, that Zach. He still taking drug, you smell?'

'Yes,' I said, for I had; I just wasn't sure what it was. 'How do you know about drugs?'

'Lot of drugs in Romania,' she said, as if it was obvious. 'Horrible smell, and he move on his feet, you know?'

I nodded. 'Yes he was swaying.'

'And his eyes they go all weird,' and she rolled her eyes in such a dramatic fashion that I snorted. She winked, evidently pleased that she'd cheered me up. 'And he smell terrible. The drug, they make peoples do strange things, dangerous things.'

'I think he's strange enough without taking any drugs,' I said. 'I just hope he leaves her alone now. We don't want him here again.'

'I could bite?' Lainy said hopefully.

'NO.'

'OK. Just idea,' she said. Then she looked over at Suki. 'What she do now?'

Suki was looking down at her phone, which was pinging madly. She smelt of disbelief, then of sour fear, and I trotted over to be beside her, Lainy on the other side.

I nudged her with my nose till she looked at me. 'He's gone bonkers,' she said, in a gravelly voice. 'He's sending me all these crazy texts. They don't make sense, but he won't stop.' Another ping, ping, ping came from her phone and she held it out with a shaking hand, as if it were contaminated. 'Shit, what do I do?'

We sat there, feeling helpless. What on earth *should* she do with a dangerous man on the other end of her phone?

Suddenly she shook her head. 'Of course, I'm being stupid. I can block him.' Her fingers whizzed over the screen, and suddenly the pings stopped. I twitched my whiskers as the silence settled, true and clear, enveloping us in a safe cocoon.

'There,' she said, throwing her phone to the other side of the room. 'He's blocked now. He can't do anything.' Though there was a slight tremor in her voice as I'm sure she was hoping that he wouldn't come back here. Mind you, Lainy's teeth would come in very handy, and there was no way Zach would report her to the police.

Suki looked down at us and gave a watery smile. 'I feel a bit shaky after that. Thank god I've got you two.' She let out a deep breath and sat down on the sofa, and we jumped up, one either side of her. 'I see now what Joe means. Zach's his own worst enemy. I've done all I can. I'm not doing any more. And I really mean that.' She sighed. 'He acted very like Rachel did with me on the phone, didn't he? Both really hurt, both trying to wreck other people's lives rather than take responsibility for their own.'

She stroked us both, up and down our spines, which we both loved, and she turned to Lainy. 'It can't be easy trusting people when you've been so let down in the past, but *you* have, Lainy, haven't you? You've trusted everyone who's tried to help you with your worries and your panic attacks, and you're so much better now.' She smiled proudly at her. 'I need to learn a few lessons from you, Lainy.'

30

'I can't believe it!' Tess cried. We were walking along the narrow path down to Grebe beach which smelt of pine cones and salt. 'You actually said no to someone? And not just anyone, but Zach! This is progress indeed.'

Suki grinned. 'Well, it was a long journey getting there, but yes I did.' Her voice dropped. 'It was really frightening, actually. He said he was taking painkillers, but I didn't know he was on heroin. He was on a different planet, that's for sure.'

'Heroin's lethal, that's awful. Did he threaten you?'

'No, but he was shouting and swaying and giving me the finger. I don't think he really knew what he was doing, which was worrying.'

'Bloody hell,' Tess said, giving Suki a hug. 'You poor thing. What did you do?'

'I tried to talk some sense into him, but given that he was off his head, I don't suppose he took anything in.'

'Well done for trying. You were very brave.'

'I didn't really have an option,' she said. 'I kept thinking of Pip saying, "fight your own corner," so I took a deep breath and I did.'

'Well done,' Tess said. 'And blocking Zach from your phone is essential.' She looked at her, pony tail swinging. 'I don't think you need worry about him coming back. I bet once he sobers up, he'll be mortified at what he did. If he can remember.'

'I just hope he learns something from it. Though that's probably a lot to ask, given his circumstances. It's just so sad that he's given up his music.'

'Sometimes people need to hit rock bottom before they climb up again. This might be the nudge that he needs.'

We stopped by the litter bins where there were always a lot of messages to exchange, so Lainy and I had a good sniff while Suki said, 'Maybe. I'd like to think so. He's so talented, and his music really does keep him sane.'

'I know. Any news of those other blokes that Lainy rescued?'

Suki smiled. 'Yes, I talked to Jim the other day. He said that one of the men is in hospital with pneumonia, poor fellow, but the others are in a hostel in Truro, so at least they're fed and have somewhere to sleep.'

Lainy looked round at this. 'My successful rescue!' She winked. 'So who I rescue now?'

'Keep sniffing,' I said, rather shortly. I was reading a particularly interesting message from a dog I hadn't seen in years. 'There's lots to learn from Dave and the others, I'm sure.'

She looked at me as if not sure if I was joking. 'I teach *them* too,' she said. And gave a swish of her tail.

I couldn't think of a reply so I finished my message before tuning back into what Tess was saying.

'That's great news; poor fellows. Do you know where they came from? Just think of the journey they must have had to get here, and then having to sleep under a bush in a park. Hardly a step up, is it?'

'If they're from Ukraine or Syria or somewhere at war I suppose it's better than living in the middle of a battle zone where you might be blown up or shot at,' Suki said. 'But it's far from ideal. I just hope they'll be OK and are able to find somewhere to live and work.' She looked at Tess. 'But I did hand the case over to that charity, so I'm not going to worry any more.'

Tess laughed. 'Of course you will!'

'Well maybe a bit,' Suki smiled, 'And Jim said he'd keep an eye out for Zach.'

'Hah! He's got you sussed then!'

Suki grinned. 'Well, he knows I care,' she said. 'But after that recent incident, I'm more than happy to keep well away from Zach.'

'Good. And your conscience is clear.'

'As clear as it's ever going to be.'

We had walked down the steep path to the beach by now and reached the sand, where both Lainy and I liked to dig, scattering the sand with our claws. It was very satisfying, though I lost interest after a few moments.

'A client contacted me this morning about fostering a dog,' Tess said, and my ears pricked up. Had Titch already done my job for me?

Suki swung round. 'Really? How come?'

'My client's been evicted and the only place she can find is a short term rental that won't accept dogs. So she's asked if I'd foster hers till she finds somewhere else.'

'Would that be OK?' I could tell Suki was almost holding her breath.

'I think it would,' Tess said. 'Paul likes the idea, too. She's a sweet whippet, very bouncy but cuddly. Bit reactive but that's fine. I'd rather do this and see how I feel about having another dog.' She carefully avoided mentioning Titch's name and for that I was grateful. It was too raw for me, as well.

'That's a good idea.'

'She's coming over tomorrow to talk about it, but I'd like to help her out, anyway.'

'Good for you, Tess.'

There was silence for a moment as we walked along, digesting the news. I was part relieved that I didn't have to find another dog for her, and partly disappointed, as I needed another challenge. Or did I? Wasn't Lainy challenge enough? And Tess was only fostering the whippet, not adopting her, so I could still keep an eye out for the perfect dog for Tess. I thought of this dog, who we would doubtless meet. Whippets always looked half starved, but they could run fast. I snickered. That would give Lainy a run for her money.

'What about Joe?'

'The last text just said it was taking him longer to sort stuff out and he didn't know when he'd be back,' said Suki. 'I know it must be difficult for him, but I do feel really disappointed.'

Tess threw a stone over the water, where it skipped and danced before disappearing into the sea. 'I bet you do. But bear in mind that none of this is your fault, or has anything to do with how he feels about you.'

'No, I know, but it's hard not to take it personally. And I suppose I won't know until he gets back. Whenever that is.' At that point her phone pinged and she took it out of her pocket. 'Talk of the devil. It's Joe. He... oh.' Her voice dropped.

'He what?'

Suki couldn't take her eyes off her phone. 'He says he's really sorry but things are complicated. But he's enjoyed our walks and thanks for being a really good friend.' She looked up. 'Oh God. That sounds like a polite brush off.'

Tess abandoned her stones and gave Suki a big hug. 'Let's have a look?' She read it and handed the phone back. 'I'm sorry, Sukes. I really am. But it's just as well you hadn't known each other long. I mean, if you'd been heavily involved, that would have been far worse.'

Suki nodded miserably, as tears trickled down her cheeks. 'I guess so. I just...I just really liked him. I thought we had something *there*. Something to build on.'

Tess held her even tighter. 'I know,' she whispered into her hair. And as she pulled away, I heard her mutter, 'bastard.'

I barked to Lainy, who was exploring seaweed on the shoreline. She came running back and I jerked my nose in Suki's direction as she sat down on the beach with a thump. Tess joined her and we sat on either side of her, breathing warm air from our nostrils in order to comfort her.

I couldn't begin to think of how to put this right. And I was fairly sure Lainy couldn't either. Worst of all, as I'd promised Pip, I'd spent so long trying so hard to keep Suki safe and happy. I thought Joe was really the right one. But now it had all gone horribly wrong.

At least we'd arranged to meet Bill and Dave in a few days time. That gave Suki time to come to terms with her disappointment. Until then we had several quiet walks; Mabe quarry and Little Palestine, where she could talk to us about her feelings, which was important. We were there for her as we always were.

'Maybe I got the wrong end of the stick but I do feel really hurt,' said a little voice. 'I mean, obviously I don't know him well, but even so...I mean, I'm quite happy on my own, and I've got my work, which I love, and brilliant friends, and of course I've got you two.' She looked at us and I could sense her smile. 'So I've got a lot more than most people.'

I could sense a 'but' coming.

'But I really miss what I had with Pip. And Ted. You know, cuddling in bed. Someone to go on holiday with. Cooking together. Walking, chatting, watching a film. The togetherness of it all.' She gave a sigh and stopped as we'd reached the crest of the hill. She looked out over the fields.

'After all that heartache with Ted, I decided to be really careful. I didn't want to get hurt again. Joe seemed a quieter man, less intense. Though sometimes he could be too quiet. It was difficult to talk to him then. He sort of shut himself away. And shut me out. And that's not good. But he'd finally started talking to me - about Peanut, and Rachel. I thought he trusted me. I thought he was my friend!'

We walked on, round the brow of the hill, where there were horse droppings. A bit rich for me, but Lainy liked them.

'But now it looks like he's decided to get back with Rachel. So that means letting go of our relationship.' Her voice wobbled slightly. 'And I'll really miss that.'

We'd reached the quarry by this time which was always a good place for quiet reflection. We looked at the towering walls of rock, at the branches trailing in the water.

'But I'm independent, earning a living and content,' said Suki, her voice cracking. 'So what am I complaining about?' She blew her nose. 'Anyway, tomorrow we're seeing Bill and Dave, so that'll keep you happy, Lainy,' she said, and her voice sounded determinedly lighter. 'Perhaps I'll just concentrate on making sure my dogs' love life is happy. Much easier than mine.' She looked down at us and gave a lop sided smile. 'I must learn from you, Lainy, and not get knocked down by setbacks.'

As we stood by the quarry, there was a quiet plop as something dripped into the pool. Say something, Titch, I thought. Give me a sign. What on earth do I do now? She's so unhappy and I've failed her. And failed Pip. And you...

There was nothing.

31

The atmosphere at home was horrible. It wasn't the same as when Pip died, of course, or when she said goodbye to Ted, but this was an all pervading, dragging sense of disappointment that threatened to smother us all if we weren't careful. Humans should realise how much of their emotions spilt over onto us. I was sure they'd be more careful if they knew.

At least Lainy was cheerful. She kept mentioning Dave, till I said, 'you're really looking forward to seeing him, aren't you?'

'Ah yes,' she said. 'I very much enjoy him.' She looked down. 'But I feel bad for Suki, that she not happy.'

'Don't let that spoil your enjoyment,' I said. 'Something usually comes along to cheer her up.' I only hoped I was right.

Lainy looked up and grinned. 'That's me!' she said. 'You and me both. We cheer her up!' And she was so vivacious that I had to laugh.

We met Bill and Dave at a different location. Down on the Lizard (I had never managed to see an actual lizard, despite looking hard, which made me doubt the sanity of some humans). This time we visited a place called Windy Ridge, which Bill said was one of his favourite places.

'It says Predannack Wollas on the map,' said Suki, when we got out of the car. 'Why do you call it Windy Ridge?'

Bill pointed at the farm behind him. 'That's the name of the farm.' He stroked both me and Lainy, very gently in Lainy's case, and smiled up at Suki. 'We stayed down here last night with a friend who lives nearby, so we came up here this morning and laid a scent trail. That'll be good for the dogs, and it shouldn't be too far for Moll.'

Suki smiled. 'Thanks, that's really thoughtful. I'm thinking of investing in a dog rucksack so I can carry Moll when she needs it.'

'Good idea.'

This was news to me, but given that I had been feeling so tired recently, it was a welcome idea. Plus I'd rather enjoyed being carried in that sling thing when we rescued Titch.

'I've got a spare one in the van if you'd like to borrow one today.' Bill rummaged around in his car boot.

'That's really kind, thanks,' Suki said.

Bill produced a battered looking old rucksack and handed it over. 'I don't know if you've tried carrying Moll for long? After a short while even a dog her size feels incredibly heavy.'

'Oh. That's a good point.' Suki sounded crestfallen.

'I'm happy to do the carrying.'

Suki blushed: she always did when people were kind to her. 'That's really generous,' she said. 'Thanks so much, Bill. We'll see how we go but I might take you up on that offer.'

We set off, down past the farm, with wonderful smells of several types of dung, free roaming chicken (my mouth watered) and a faint whiff of fox, but given that the chickens were all clucking around, the fox evidently hadn't had any hen dinner.

Lainy looked round at me but I wrinkled my nose. 'You go ahead with Dave and the others,' I said, for I could see she was longing to. 'Go and do your scent work and I can listen to Suki and Bill. I need to know what's going on.'

'OK, I go,' she said, and plunged into the undergrowth with the other dogs, tails wagging and noses to the ground. They ran ahead of us and it was quite peaceful once they'd gone, trotting along the lane past the farm, onto a wider path with smells of the sea coming in from the right. We passed a little bridge over a stream and turned right, onto the cliff top, where the smells of the sea grew stronger and I could hear seagulls crying above me, waves crashing far below and smell the cattle in a neighbouring field.

'Look!' Said Bill, pointing out to a far part of the clifftop. He was looking through some funny glasses. 'Choughs! Have a look.' He passed the glasses to Suki who raised them to her eyes.

'Oh, yes,' she breathed. 'Several of them; babies as well!' There was silence while they looked at these creatures; birds I presumed, though I couldn't understand what the fuss was about till she said, 'amazing to think they'd all but died out, isn't it?'

'It certainly is,' he said. 'A friend of mine is one of the volunteers who looks after them. They've had Chough watchers for years; I think the birds are deemed safer now they've bred so many more of them.'

'That's great,' Suki said handing back the glasses. 'I like to hear that kind of thing.' There was a pause.

'Are you OK, Suki?'

'Yes, fine,' she said, her voice unnaturally high.'You?'

Bill nodded and they walked along in silence but it wasn't a comfortable one. I could smell the undertones of Suki's distress and the rush of approaching tears. I could also smell Bill's confusion and desire to help. Why were humans so slow? Why did they prevaricate so much?

Just as I was about to take matters into my own paws, Bill said, 'You're clearly not all right. And if you'd like to talk about it, I'm here. But if you don't, that's fine too.'

Suki glanced at him and I could sense she wanted to talk, but I could smell her reticence.

'I know we don't know each other well, but I think you'll find I'm a good listener,' he added, as if he could read her thoughts.

Suki smiled, a little wanly. 'Well, the thing is...' she said, then stopped. Her confusion smelt of black pepper and musty dried herbs.

'Thing is?'

She took a deep breath. 'It's nothing really, but ...'

Bill waited a moment then said, 'It's obviously not nothing or you wouldn't be so upset.'

He sounded so calm and gentle that Suki turned to him with a lopsided smile. 'You're very kind,' she said. 'You see, it's about a friend...'

I nudged her leg with my nose and she looked down, gave a nervous laugh. 'Sorry, I'm making a mess of this.'

'Start at the beginning,' said Bill quietly. 'That's usually the best place.'

Suki took such a deep breath I thought she was preparing to dive underwater, but then she said, 'You see, after my husband died I had a very intense relationship with someone for several years. It was very... very special.'

'It sounds like he was very important,' Bill observed, striding down a steep part of the footpath. 'Mind that bit; it's slippy there.'

'Thanks.' Suki negotiated the tricky part and then said, 'I finished it because of his circumstances. It meant we couldn't ever really be happy together.'

A slight pause. 'That's a shame.'

'I had to end it and I was very upset, but it was the right thing to do,' Suki continued. 'And so I thought, I've got a lot of friends, but I don't want another relationship. And then I met someone else. He got in touch because he wanted to buy some of my books for his mum.'

Bill nodded, leading the way as we went downhill. It was steep and he was right, the ground was slippery from recent rain.

'And we got chatting by email, you know. And then we decided to meet up for walks. His dog had died and he really missed him, and we became good friends.' She paused. 'At least, I thought we were.'

'More than good friends?' Bill queried.

Suki blushed: I could smell the fiery blood racing round her cheeks and neck. 'Yes.'

'Sounds good.' Bill jumped over a stream. 'Do I sense a 'but'?'

'Yes.' Suki navigated the stream too, and they both waited while I had a drink. 'I thought things were going well but then he had to do a job in Wales. It turns out his girlfriend left him last year and his dog had died, and he'd carried on working through it all, so it was sort of catch up time.'

'So he needed time to himself. Fair enough.'

'Absolutely,' said Suki. 'But then his ex-girlfriend rang up, out of the blue. She asked him to go and see her dying mother with her, so he did. And then I had a text saying thanks for being such a good friend but he still had to sort things out with Rachel.'

The silence was thick and indigestible. Her words sank, the name Rachel sending shock waves through the air.

'Well, that doesn't mean that it's over,' said Bill cautiously.

'I thought we really had something there,' Suki said, and I could hear that tears were about to spring forth. I wasn't sure if she'd heard what Bill said. 'Or at least...'

'You would have, had it not been for Rachel,' he finished. 'But you know what they say. It's not over till the fat lady sings.'

There was another silence, but it was a kinder one. Then I noticed Suki's shoulders shaking. 'Sorry, I'm just being over sensitive,' she said. 'I haven't been sleeping well and it's catching up with me.'

I could tell that what she really needed was a big hug, and Bill turned to her. 'I'm so sorry,' he said simply, and took her in his arms. He held her, not like Pip or Ted used to hold her, but like I imagine a father would, very tenderly, and he stroked her hair. He didn't speak, but waited while Suki's tears of disappointment leaked out. He patted her back and I could tell that he was kind and gentle and wouldn't hurt her. I wasn't sure that he wanted the sex thing; he didn't smell like that, and that made him safer, which was a good thing.

When she stopped, she pulled back and he handed her a tissue. She blew her nose and laughed jerkily. 'I'm so sorry,' she said. 'I'm not usually so oversensitive. What was I thinking? Blubbing all over you. I don't even really know you.'

Bill smiled. 'Be my guest.' And he started walking up the other side of the valley, giving Suki time to collect herself. She blew her nose again and they walked up to the top of the next cliff and looked down at the sea, plunging and crashing far below us.

That was a contented silence, then Suki said, 'Thanks. I really needed that.'

'A good cry?'

'And a good hug,' she said.

He looked at her and for once I couldn't smell how he felt. 'You know, I'm always here for you,' he said. 'It's horrible being where you are now, and I know how vulnerable it makes you feel. But if ever you're upset, or want a chat, or just to walk and not talk, you've got my number. Just give me a ring.'

The sun made a brief appearance just as Suki looked at him and the light shone in her eyes. 'Thanks,' she gulped, and I could tell she was overwhelmed again. 'That's so kind.'

'Right then,' he said and looked round to where Dave and Lainy and the others were tiny dots on the cliff path. He whistled, a high shriek that was for dogs rather than for humans, but at once Dave and Lainy looked up, exchanged glances and started running back towards us, the others close on their paws.

As we waited for them to return, I reflected on how much had happened in the short time since they'd been away. And at the same time, nothing had.

The rest of the walk passed amicably. Bill talked of his time in Spain, of how he went to Wales, of his daughter who worked in television in London. How she loved dogs too, and took hers to work which caused problems when they were filming.

I realised he was diffusing the tension, letting Suki think of other things. But he did so unobtrusively and I was grateful for his quiet thoughtfulness. The more I smelt him, the better he seemed.

Once we got back to the cars, at the end of the walk, Bill smiled and said, 'Lainy's done so well today. Do you feel ready to enter her into a competition?'

'Really?' Suki sounded surprised. 'So soon?'

'I wouldn't suggest it if I didn't think she was ready. There's one at the end of this month that I'm going to in North Cornwall.

I'd only suggest entering her for one event to see how she gets on. But I think she'd really enjoy it.'

Suki frowned. 'Are you sure? She's still very nervous around strange people and places. I'd hate to set her back.'

'I know. But I've been watching her closely. I think if you and Dave were there, she'd be fine. He's given her a lot of confidence.'

We all looked at Lainy who, it was true, looked glowing. Her coat shone and her eyes sparkled; there was no doubt that this was a content, confident dog. Beside her, Dave nodded happily, tongue hanging out, his eyes never leaving Lainy.

Suki smiled, somewhat enviously, I couldn't help thinking. 'You're right. She looks great, and Dave's obviously very good for her. Let's give it a try and see how it goes. But she's easily upset, and I don't want to risk any setbacks.'

'I promise you, I won't let that happen,' Bill said. 'The slightest problem and we'll go straight home.'

Suki took a deep breath. 'OK.' Still she hesitated. 'You probably think I'm being overcautious, but...'

'I don't,' he said firmly. 'I've got rescues myself, remember? I know what it's like, and how easily they can go backwards. We won't let that happen to Lainy. I promise.'

Suki nodded and I bet she liked the 'we' part of that sentence. It made me feel that he was looking after us, in the best possible way. And who could argue with that?

That evening, after our tea, Lainy couldn't stop talking, about Dave and his brothers, about scent work competitions, and it was lovely to see this nervous dog looking so happy and at home.

The same couldn't be said for Suki, who smelt like rotten fish and looked pale and drawn. She wasn't sleeping well, and I worried how much this business with Joe was dragging her down. Why had I encouraged her, approved of him, when it seemed he wasn't who we thought he was?

'You OK, Moll?'

Lainy came nearer, gave me a nose nuzzle. Now she was happy, she wanted to lick everyone all the time, which I found difficult to live with. However, her happiness was infectious, if mildly irritating.

'I'm fine,' I said. 'Just thinking.'

Lainy calmed down instantly. 'I know you worry because Suki not happy. You think you not done your best for her, and your promise for Pip?'

I'd thought she was just besotted with Dave, but in fact she didn't miss a trick. 'You're right,' I said. 'I do worry about her. I just want her to be happy.'

Lainy was quiet for a moment. 'You think she be happy with Bill?'

I wrinkled my nose. 'Maybe.'

'He seem good man. He caring and gentle and kind.'

'He is. And I'm very glad that they've met. But ...'

'But he not Joe. And we like Joe,' she said simply.

I nodded. 'Yes. And I think ...well, I thought Joe would be good for her. And I'm not usually wrong,' I added.

'You not wrong,' Lainy said hotly. 'But maybe it not over with Suki, but Joe just need time to sort things out with Rachel.'

'Maybe.'

'And maybe he come back when he work things out?'

'I'd like to think so. But it seems unlikely right now.'

Lainy lay down, nose on her front paws. 'Things often not work out how you think,' she said slowly. 'Sometime for good and sometime for bad.'

I nodded, not really in the mood for more introspection. It was making me gloomy.

'I never think, when I in kill shelter, or with horrible peoples at my first home, that I ever be happy again. And now I am!' She grinned, and her dark eyes shone.

'That's good, Lainy, and I'm very glad you're living with us,' I said. 'But Suki is my responsibility. And I can't be happy if she isn't happy.'

Lainy shrugged. 'I know,' she said. 'But maybe something happen with Joe in another month. And in meantime, she have Bill! He like her and she like him and it good to have friend, no?'

'It is, Lainy.'

'And if they just friends, Suki won't get hurt! No complication!'

I smiled; she really was trying her best. 'No, Lainy, you're quite right. And no complications is a very good thing.'

Though as we lay down for a snooze, I reflected that it was impossible to have a life without *any* complications. And even if there was, wouldn't it be boring?

That weekend, we went over to Petroc's for early supper and Scrabble. Suki liked going there because, I think, she felt safe and protected. He made her laugh and gave good advice. Lainy and I liked it because the kitchen was always littered with toast and biscuit crumbs, bits of cheese, ham - the choice was endless and varied. Plus, he had digestive biscuits which were my favourite.

This evening, I noticed him eyeing Suki closely. He took her coat and gave her a kiss on the cheek.

'Sit down my dear. Glass of wine?'

'A small one would be lovely. Thank you.'

'Good.' He poured her a glass of red wine. 'We're having pot luck stew, so I can't guarantee what it'll taste like.'

Suki smiled and sat back in a chair. 'It smells delicious. Anything is if I haven't cooked it.'

Petroc stirred the pot on the cooker and talked about an art exhibition he and his partner had been to. Of the Cornish language classes that he was taking; the teacher was very good. Idle chatter, I sensed, to relax Suki and put her at her ease.

There was a comfortable silence while he ladled the meal into bowls and put them on the table. 'There's some grated cheese to go on top, and that's yogurt because it might be a bit spicy,' he said.

'Looks fabulous,' said Suki, tucking in. I could smell paprika and fried bacon, onions and black pepper, coriander and cinnamon; a lovely mix of unlikely tastes. My mouth was watering as Lainy and I sat on either side of them, scrutinising every mouthful.

'It's very good,' she continued. 'Chick peas and bacon go really well, don't they? And sweet potato. Very tasty.'

'And some garlic bread,' he said, putting a plate on the table. The smell of that bread was acidic and pungent and so beckoning that my nose twitched violently. 'Now what's your news?'

Suki took a sip of wine. 'I'm about to become a TV star,' she said, smiling.

'Really? Tell me.'

'This morning I got a phone call out of the blue from a production company who are making a programme for Channel 5 about Cornwall, and they asked if I'd be willing to discuss literary influences in Cornwall with Fern Britton.'

'My goodness,' said Petroc. 'That is wonderful. When are they filming?'

'In a few months, they said, but I don't have an exact date.'

'Well,' said Petroc. 'I am so very happy for you, my dear.'

'Thank you. I'm delighted, and it's done a lot for my confidence.' Suki took a piece of garlic bread and a few choice crumbs drifted to the floor where I snaffled them before Lainy did. Suki said, 'can I ask you a question?'

'I was hoping you would.'

Silence.

'Is it about Joe, by any chance?'

'Yes. I told you his ex-girlfriend had turned up?'

Petroc nodded. 'And he went to London to see her dying mother.'

'Yes. Well, a few days ago he sent me a text saying I'd been a really good friend but he had to sort things out with Rachel. And he wasn't sure when he'd be back.'

'And that was the last you heard from him?'

'Yes.' She put her spoon down and took a sip of wine. 'And I'd thought that he was... fond of me, but now I think I was wrong. Or he's changed his mind.'

'You don't know that.' Petroc's voice was kind. Gentle. He took a swallow of wine and looked at her. Smiled. 'Just because you think that doesn't mean it's right.'

Suki made a face. 'No. I realise that. But I feel ... rejected.'

Petroc got up and refilled his glass of wine. 'We can speculate all we like, but it does seem that Joe has unresolved issues with Rachel which he wants to try and resolve.' He sat down again. 'That's perfectly reasonable.'

'Yes...'

'And he was thanking you for being a good friend. Telling you what he was doing.'

'Yes...'

'Which again, is entirely reasonable.'

A glimmer of a smile crept across Suki's face. 'Why are you so ... reasonable?'

Petroc smiled. 'As you know, I am often very *un*reasonable. But in this instance, I would try and think about *his* needs. I know they may not coincide with yours, but that's a sad fact of life; other people's needs very often don't. But he will be back, sooner or later, and then you will find out whether there is any future for you two.'

'You make it sound so simple.'

'It is and it isn't, as we both know. But either way, he is the one with issues to sort out, not you.'

Suki absent-mindedly stroked both of us: we were sitting right beside her. 'Right,' she said. 'And it does take time, doesn't it?'

Petroc nodded.

'I promised Joe I wouldn't get involved with Zach, but it took quite a while to actually cut off all contact. It's not that easy. You're battling with their needs, and trying to help, and finally realising that you can't. That's really hard.'

'Exactly,' said Petroc with a smile. 'And in the meantime, you said you were seeing Bill again. He sounds like a decent man. Another good friend?'

Suki nodded. 'Yes. He's interesting; he's done a lot.'

'Sounds good.'

Suki laughed. 'I'm not looking for anything other than friendship.'

'You mean you don't find him attractive?'

'I mean, I don't think of him that way.'

Petroc raised an eyebrow but said nothing.

'I told him about Joe and he was very understanding. Poor man, I cried all over him, and he mopped me up, said he'd always be there for me.' She smiled. 'Isn't that lovely?'

'It is. He sounds worth hanging onto.'

'Oh, he is. He's very good, easy company.'

'Just what you need at the moment.'

'Yes.' Suki smiled, and it was a contented smile. 'I think he is.'

On that note they finished their meal, cleared the table and set down to play a few games of Scrabble, which was the sign for me and Lainy to retire by the fire for a snooze. I must have dropped off, as the next thing I knew, Suki was gathering her belongings and saying thank you to Petroc.

'Any time, my dear. Always welcome.'

'My turn to cook next time. And thank you for a lovely evening. I always feel better after I've spent time with you.'

Petroc laughed. 'What a compliment. You do look better, even if I did beat you at Scrabble.'

'Only because I was off colour.' She grinned, and kissed him on the cheek.

'Goodbye, Suki. Maybe concentrate on the very good friends you have, rather than the possible relationship that you may not have.'

'Excellent advice, as ever.' Suki called us and we went out into the dark, jumped into her car and headed home.

I liked the evening ritual; a walk, followed by biscuits and settle down for the night. But as we walked round the block, her phone pinged, and there was something about it that made my fur stand on end. Suki seemed oblivious, and it wasn't till we got home that she read it.

'Oh!' She cried. 'Oh, it's Joe.' She read the message slowly. 'He says, "So sorry for lack of communication. Rachel and I had a lot to sort out so it took much longer than I'd anticipated. Well done for passing on responsibility for Zach; I can appreciate just how hard that was, particularly after my time in London. Just got home, introducing Tinker to his new lodgings. Be lovely to see you soon." She looked down at us and I could smell the relief ballooning out of her. Then another ping. 'Oh, he's asked if we'd like to walk tomorrow!' She laughed and it was a clear, joyous sound, like pure spring water.

She started to type something back, and then her phone rang. She looked at the caller, then I heard her intake of breath. 'Joe?'

'Sorry to ring so late,' he said. 'It took an age to get home, and I'm sorry I've been so bad at communicating, but I had to sort out a lot of stuff.' He paused. 'With Rachel. But it's done now, and she's gone back to Devon and I wanted to say hello, and ... how are you?'

'I'm fine.' She gave a noise that was half a laugh and half a smile and a few other things in between. 'It's good to hear from you.' She paused. 'From your last message I thought things might be over.'

'What? Oh god, no. Far from it.' He sighed. 'Bloody texts. It's so easy to misread them. I am so sorry, Suki. Damn, I should have rung. I...'

'It's OK,' Suki said. 'Well, it is now. You're right, texts can be very confusing. But it's good to hear from you.'

'Next time I'll ring,' he said. 'I mean, not next time, but...'

She laughed and sounded freer and lighter. 'It's fine, Joe.' She sighed contentedly. 'How's Tinker?'

'He's doing really well,' he laughed, 'He looks a bit confused in this strange house, but I'm sure he'll be OK when he's settled in.' He paused. 'I was wondering, are you free for a walk tomorrow? Late afternoon?'

'I've got an interview at 3, so I'll be free about 4.30,' Suki said.

'Great! I was thinking, would you like to go over to the North Coast for a walk? If it's nice I could get together a picnic. If not, perhaps you'd like something to eat in that pub near Polly Joke afterwards.'

Suki caught her breath and I could smell joy blossoming from her. 'That would be lovely, Joe,' she said. 'I'd really enjoy that.'

'Fantastic,' he said, and we could hear the relief and happiness in his voice. 'Well, shall I meet you in the car park at Devoran at 4.30 and I'll drive us from there?'

Suki nodded, even though he couldn't see her. 'That would be great,' she said, and I could tell by her choked voice that she was so overwhelmed she could hardly speak.

'Fabulous. And Suki?'

'Yes?'

'I'm really looking forward to seeing you again.'

She grinned and her happiness wrapped around us like a warm duvet. 'Me too, Joe. We've missed you.'

He laughed then, a joyous sound that said everything that he wasn't saying. That he'd missed us, that it had been a long time, that he'd done a lot of sorting in his head. That his head was clear now, and more to the point, so was his heart. All that and more. 'I've missed you too. See you tomorrow, Suki. Sleep tight.'

'And you.' Reluctantly she finished the call and looked down at us. 'Well,' she said. 'Off with Joe and Tinker tomorrow, you two. What do you think?'

Lainy and I exchanged a grin, and after several extra biscuits (Suki *was* in a good mood), we trotted off to bed where, I knew, she would toss and turn for a few hours.

'We see,' Lainy said. 'If he hurt Suki, I bite him. OK?'

'OK.' I said. 'He deserves a bite if he hurts Suki again.'

So the next afternoon we set off for Devoran, and the air smelt full of spring flowers; sweet and full of promise and sunshine. In fact it was overcast, with a few spots of rain on the windscreen, but that didn't deter our feelings of hope and excitement.

On the way there, I had a quick chat to Titch. I wasn't sure whether he replied, or if it was my imagination, but I liked to tell him things anyway.

'I'm looking forward to seeing Joe again. I do hope he really has sorted things out. Perhaps I'm worrying unnecessarily. Bill seems a kind and thoughtful man, but we don't know him well...'

'Stop worrying, Moll,' it seemed that I could hear Titch's voice clearly, and I closed my eyes, imagining him beside me. 'I think you'll be pleasantly surprised, but maybe not in the way you think.'

I opened my eyes. He sounded so close, his voice was almost in my ear. 'What do you mean?' I squeaked. 'What's he going to do?'

But Titch was silent.

So it was with even more agitation that we arrived in the designated car park and looked for Joe's van. Sure enough, there it was, looking a little more battered than the last time we'd seen it. He got out when he saw our car, and watched us approach with the biggest smile which lit up his face, then spread over his whole body.

I could smell Suki's nerves and hesitation and wanted to tell her not to worry. Not with a smile like that. Just then she turned off the engine and looked at him, and her whole being flooded with warm happiness, like autumn sunshine.

She got out of the car, and he came towards her and gave her a big hug which went on for ages, till Lainy gave a yip, and they broke apart and laughed, still looking in each other's eyes.

'Better get the dogs,' Suki said, and let us out. We ran up to Joe, who bent down and gave us each a treat and a cuddle. He smelt good, and happy, and I could tell that the unhappiness had gone from him and was very glad. But I could also smell another dog on him...

'And here's Tinker,' Joe said, and opened the back doors of his van. A scruffy black dog, a bit bigger than me, jumped out and I smelt curiosity mixed with hesitation. He didn't know us, after all. 'I've been telling him all about Moll and Lainy,' Joe said, with a smile in his voice.

Lainy and I waited to see if Tinker would approach us; it was only good manners, after all. He was obviously unsure, so I yipped a quick 'hello' and he looked up.

Oh, I thought, looking into his coal black eyes, which flashed with recognition and a spark of amusement. He was older than I'd thought. Not quite as old as me, but definitely a mature dog. He trotted forward, at a polite 90 degree angle, and we sniffed each other's butts, and then our noses.

We introduced ourselves, then he said, 'I've heard so much about you both. But it's wonderful to meet you at last.' And as he looked into my eyes, my nose went squiffy.

'Delighted to meet you too,' I think I said, though I could hear my heart pounding. In a good way.

I heard a snort, and looked at Lainy who gave me one of her famous winks.'You like?' she said.

I was about to tell her off, but I looked at Tinker, then back at her. 'I do,' I said, but what I really meant was, He's intriguing. I want to get to know him!

Lainy nodded, as if she knew. 'Pleased to meet you, Tinker. We are looking forward to walking together.' She turned back to me. 'Oh, Moll, I forget to say. On the news, there is rally in

Newquay. Lots of peoples protesting for and against refugees. What you think, Moll? You come along?' She looked at Tinker. 'You too?'

I stared at her, astonished. I'd never done anything like that before. But it was too late; you couldn't teach an old dog new tricks. Then I looked at Tinker and detected a spark of interest in those dark eyes. I felt a rush of adventure, breathing life into my old limbs. 'Well, why not? Would you like to join us, Tinker?'

His black eyes twinkled at me. 'Sounds an excellent idea. However, I've been on rallies before, and they can get quite dangerous sometimes. We could always head for the van if it gets too rowdy.'

'Good thinking,' I replied, delighted by such a practical approach and I snuffled a little, excited by the idea of an adventure with such interesting company.

Lainy trotted on ahead, tactfully giving me and Tinker some time on our own. I was looking forward to finding out more about him, and start planning our next walks together. Suddenly, life was opening up, it seemed.

Suki and Joe walked in front of us, very close together. He reached out for her hand, and it seemed to fit, just right. Their voices mingled and happiness shone from them, sliding into the earth so we walked in a path of sweet smelling joy.

We trotted behind while Tinker told me about his previous lady owner in Wales, and how he met Joe, then he asked me about Suki. I told him how special she was, and how good she and Joe were together. About her books, and that Suki was on the way to becoming a television star. And my promise to Pip, and how there was no way I was going to let her be hurt again. And Tinker looked at me with those dark eyes and though he didn't reply, I knew that he understood.

But I had a strong feeling that Suki and Joe would be all right. They'd have their ups and downs, like everyone, but it really seemed that he'd resolved his issues with Rachel and he could start loving Suki properly now.

Of course she had me and Lainy, but she also had a good friend in Bill. Lainy was more settled, and had her Dave. And right now, with Tinker beside me, I had a feeling I would be happy too.

Thank you, Titch, I thought, for sending me a second lease of life.

Acknowledgements

A special tribute to Donna Christensen who emailed me having read *The Rescue* to say that she and her Border Terrier, Tinker, were reading it every night in bed and how much they were enjoying it. I loved the name Tinker so much, and it really suited the dog who adopts Joe, so I asked if I could use it. Thankfully she said yes.

Bright Dog Training for superb advice on Dog Aggression and how to handle it.

Many thanks to my editor, Kerry Barrett, for her editorial skills, brilliant ideas and her belief in my writing.

Also to my wonderful readers; Ali Churchley (and ace proofreader), Christina Lake, and my dear sister-in-law Shelagh Smith in Vermont.

To Tammy Barrett for another terrific cover, website and all the amazing design work.

To Alexa Whitten for typesetting and doing all that clever and vital book stuff.

To Lainy, of course, for being her (but no more bites, please?) wink.

To Jenna Steadman-Bailey for social media magic and some of the few photographs of me and Lainy I've ever really liked.

To everyone who has helped me on the Lainy journey, particularly Ruth Collett, Jac Morris, Corinne Elleboudt, Pauline Causey (who was there for the original bite), Bridget Woodman, Hannah Crook and Lynn Stonehouse.

And of course to Malc and Twig. For being you...Both of you.

About the author

In real life, when Moll died Sue was utterly distraught, but a week later a friend saw Lainy being walked in nearby woods and rang Sue saying, "I've found your next dog!" Many of Lainy's struggles in this book are true - she does have PTSD and panic attacks, and she is reactive and highly nervous of strangers, four legged and two, but the rest is fiction.

Writing about such dark topics could have been depressing, but as soon as Lainy padded onto the page she showed her quirky sense of humour, her intelligence, and her desire to do anything for those she loved. She made Sue laugh and cry as she wrote, so I hope you enjoy her as much as Sue does.

Sue lives in Cornwall where she writes, trains Lainy, walks and gives talks about her life and her books. She also sings with the Suitcase Singers, most recently at Falmouth Tall Ships. Sue spends most weekends with her partner and his rescue dog, Twig, where they explore, swim, grow vegetables and go camping in his motorhome. When forced indoors he's addicted to shouting at politicians on the news, the perfect excuse for Sue to write.

Sue is also the author of five Cornish literary themed walking books - *Discover Cornwall, Walks in the Footsteps of Cornish Writers, Walks in the Footsteps of Poldark Walks in the Footsteps of Daphne du Maurier* and *Walks in the Footsteps of Rosamunde Pilcher*, all available from the 'Books' section of her website www.suekittow.com

Sue Kittow Author – Facebook @suekittow2016

Instagram @walks_cornish_author

Twitter – @floweringpot

Other books in the series

The prequel to *Lainy's Tale* is *The Rescue*, Before Suki's husband dies, he makes Moll promise to look after Suki and make sure she's happy. But how does she do that? A quirky tale of second - and third - chances, narrated by woman's best friend. Moll. Signed copies available from www.suekittow.com and Amazon https://amzn.to/3Wshi9k

If you have read any of Sue's books and enjoyed them, please leave a review on Amazon - reviews really matter!

You can sign up to Sue's newsletter to receive news on upcoming books, launches and other events on her website.

Dog Training

Bright Dog Training for superb advice on Dog Aggression and how to handle it. www.brightdogtraininguk.com

For dog advice in Cornwall, and for any animal behaviour problems, contact Ruth Collett at www.info@ruthspetbehaviourservices.co.uk

Peer Support

Man Down is a Cornwall based non-profit Community Interest Company that provides informal peer-support talking groups all over Cornwall for men with mental health concerns. Together we can end the stigma and reduce the number of male suicides in Cornwall. www.mandown-cornwall.co.uk

Printed in Great Britain
by Amazon

45912072R10152